BOSS

ALSO BY TRACY BROWN

Criminal Minded

White Lines

Twisted

Snapped

Aftermath

White Lines II: Sunny

White Lines III: All Falls Down

ANTHOLOGIES

Flirt

BOSS

TRACY BROWN

ST. MARTIN'S GRIFFIN

NEW YORK

BOSS. Copyright © 2017 by Tracy Brown. All rights reserved. Printed in the United States of America. For information, address St. Martin's Press, 175 Fifth Avenue, New York, N.Y. 10010.

www.stmartins.com

Designed by Omar Chapa

The Library of Congress Cataloging-in-Publication Data is available upon request.

ISBN 978-1-250-04300-9 (trade paperback)
ISBN 978-1-4668-4099-7 (e-book)

Our books may be purchased in bulk for promotional, educational, or business use. Please contact your local bookseller or the Macmillan Corporate and Premium Sales Department at 1-800-221-7945, extension 5442, or by e-mail at MacmillanSpecialMarkets@macmillan.com.

First Edition: April 2017

10 9 8 7 6 5 4 3 2 1

For Madison, the light of my life.
Dream BIG!

ACKNOWLEDGMENTS

Sara Camilli, I thank God for the opportunity to work with you. You are a literary lioness! I believe the best is yet to come for us as a team. Thank you from the bottom of my heart for all that you do.

Monique Patterson, I owe you far more than I can repay. You are an extraordinary woman who inspires me to go further, to push harder, and to dream even bigger. Just when I think I've reached my limit as a writer, you go and pull even more out of me, challenging me to dig even deeper. You are one of my greatest teachers. On top of that you are my friend. You rock! THANK YOU!

Vanessa Karen De Luca, thank you so much for taking the time to offer your insight and knowledge for this book. Despite your incredibly busy schedule, you took the time to answer my questions and to offer me guidance and encouragement to help me bring this story to life. Watching you reign with such grace, class, and humility is an inspiration to many women. Keep making us proud!

My son, Justin Carruthers, I'm so grateful to you for the

countless times you helped me revamp the plot for this book. You helped me brainstorm, offered alternatives, and never complained when I peppered you with questions and constantly asked for your opinion. I appreciate you so much and I love you lots.

BOSS

GAME CHANGER

November 2016

She glided her lipstick smoothly across her full lips, rubbed them together, and stared at her reflection, admiring the results. Mahogany skin, ebony eyes, and her grandmother's high cheekbones complemented those lips. She was feeling extra badass today. Her work in the gym was paying off, her hair was acting right, and her pearly white teeth seemed to sparkle with brilliance as she smiled at her reflection in her compact mirror. She knew she was bad. A woman full of confidence, intelligence, and class. She had summoned all of those things in order to rise to the heights she had in her career and in her life in general. She sat now in her office preparing for one of the most significant meetings of her life. She had maneuvered, plotted, and sacrificed a great deal to get here. Sleepless nights and impossible odds were the norm. But now her face shone with a broad grin as she contemplated this moment. She was on top of the world.

Crystal Scott was the editor in chief of a magazine that was taking the fashion world by storm. *Hipster* was a creative, bold, and cutting-edge magazine that targeted a fashion-forward and socially conscious reader. She had accomplished a great deal in her career so far. She had already traveled to places she never thought she'd go. It was a source of great pride for her that she had achieved so much all on her own. It hadn't been easy. She had fought her way here with a mixture of intelligence, charisma, and guts.

Years ago, when she was fresh out of college, she worked odd jobs before she finally snagged a dream job as a staff writer for *Sable* magazine. *Sable* was a monthly publication geared toward an upscale, professional demographic, and had an enviable reputation as the top fashion and beauty magazine for women of color. She worked her way up to editorial duties quickly. In those days, she worked for Angela Richmond. Angela was the editor in chief at *Sable,* and had a well-deserved reputation as a bitch. She had been in the top position at the reputable magazine for close to twenty years, building solid relationships with black America's elite. Still, she never seemed to be enjoying herself, even during the most profitable sales years. She appreciated Crystal's work ethic, though, and promoted her to executive editor. Always stony, never smiling, Angela Richmond was notoriously rigid in the way she worked. She didn't welcome suggestions, or encourage new perspectives. Instead, she preferred to stick to her same old tried-and-true formula, leaving little room for her writers and contributors to spread their wings. It wasn't long before Crystal grew tired of that.

She had quit that job three years ago, against the chorus of protests from her family and friends. They all thought she was crazy to leave her position at one of the top magazines in the world for women of color. Many believed that Angela's best years were behind her and Crystal was positioned to take over. But there was an opportunity of a lifetime at a new publication that was being assembled by the renowned urban media giant Stuart Mitchell Enterprises.

Stuart Mitchell was a black-owned publishing, advertising, and marketing company started in the nineties by William "Fox" Mitchell. Known as the "silver fox" around Harlem because of his prematurely gray hair, he had risen to prominence as a community leader and philanthropist. His wife, Lorraine Stuart Mitchell, had been his partner in the business until her death from breast cancer in 2002. In the years since then, Fox had taken the company global, distributing several major urban publications. *Hipster* was started in 2010, targeting celebrity gossip driven readers. The early years were tough, as sales suffered in a floundering industry. Readers hadn't been eager to embrace new magazines in lieu of the older, reliable ones like *Sable*. Several staff members came and went in those years, and for the first time, Fox was facing the failure of one of his magazines. That was when Crystal took a chance, and requested a meeting with the man. It was a shot in the dark as she strolled into Stuart Mitchell headquarters, and met with the man himself. She presented her success at *Sable* and her ability to gain the trust and respect of the notorious Angela Richmond. She touted the success of her work with *Sable*'s creative director, Oscar Beane, and alluded to the fact that she could persuade him to follow her wherever she went. And, she offered herself to *Hipster* as its interim editor in chief. Fox had been wowed.

"Give me a year," she had said. "Let me step in and completely change the look and feel of the magazine. There's a generation out there that is not being served by the old-school magazines we see on the shelves. Their formulas are set in stone. *Hipster* needs to be a living, breathing expression of the urban landscape. I have the team to make that vision come alive, Mr. Mitchell."

He had smiled at her, admiring her confidence. "Call me Fox," he said.

The gamble had paid off and the magazine was thriving. She had successfully persuaded Oscar to come on board. Angela's rigidity had begun to suffocate him also. Oscar wanted to appeal to a younger, more current audience than the one Angela was interested in. He cashed in his retirement fund and followed Crystal out the door. He used the connections he had from his days at *Sable,* and landed fashion spreads with coveted subjects. Crystal kept the articles engaging and provocative. Now *Hipster* boasted competitive sales and an imposing online presence. For Crystal, it had been a daring move, leaving such a lofty position at a publication as renowned as *Sable.* But she was confident in Oscar's vision as well as her own abilities as an editor. Fox's faith in her had begun to pay off majorly. Having started out as an online magazine, they were at an advantage. Digital was outperforming print tremendously, and that was where *Hipster* had its strongest presence. With an aggressive social media presence, powerful articles by up-and-coming writers, and bold print fashion spreads featuring the "It Girls" of the moment, *Hipster* was giving old-school publications like *Sable* a run for their money. Ad sales were way up, and Crystal and Oscar were enjoying unprecedented success just shy of their thirties. The magazine was a hit.

Fox was older now and ready to step down as CEO of Stuart Mitchell Enterprises. He was considering a run for city council in Harlem, where he was from. He had established himself as a prominent member of the community there, and was hoping to enjoy a coveted position in his golden years. His late wife Lorraine would have been proud to have her husband serve in political office. As he pondered the idea, he decided to hand over the reins of the company to his youngest son, Troy. Troy Mitchell would head the day-to-day operations of the company, in effect making him Crystal's new boss. Crystal and Oscar would be meeting him for the first time today.

Aware that her heart was racing just a little bit, she sat back in her chair and took a deep breath. There was really no telling how this would all play out. She reminded herself that she had come this far, and there was no turning back now. She stood up, and shook off some of the nervous energy, smoothing her black Chanel dress in the process. She smoothed her hair and tightened the clasp on her pearl-and-diamond earrings.

A familiar knock on her door signaled Oscar's presence now. She smiled as he stepped into the room. Oscar was always a welcome distraction. A large man with an imposing presence, he stood six feet, two inches tall and weighed a solid two hundred and eighty pounds. At first glance, he seemed better suited as a football player because of his size. But the moment he opened his mouth, it became clear that one should never judge a book by its cover. Fashion, luxury, and flamboyance were all he ever spoke of. Oscar's tailored and sophisticated flair was unmatched. He took fashion a step ahead without going too far. He had styled some of the most prominent women in entertainment and politics over the years. It made him the most sought-after black fashion insider, and he loved the spotlight.

He stepped inside her office, shutting the door behind him. Oscar looked and smelled like money. Crystal drank him in as he entered. Dressed in a navy blue bespoke tailored blazer and pants, he looked like he could be the owner of Stuart Mitchell himself.

He took one long, sweeping look at Crystal and smirked.

"I see you're trying to make the man drool before breakfast," he said. He winked at her approvingly, noting that her cleavage was just perfect and her waistline was cinched. "You look incredible, love."

He sat down in one of the chairs facing Crystal's desk and whipped out a handkerchief from the inside pocket of his blazer.

Glancing at her, he handed it to her with a smile. "Lipstick on your teeth, though."

Crystal took it gratefully, sat back down in her chair, and reached for her compact again. She loved how Oscar always managed to bring her back down to earth whenever she got too lofty or started to believe her own hype.

"How'd the visit go with your dad?" Oscar asked.

Crystal sighed, ever so slightly. Then she smiled. "He's coming home in two months. Well . . . not home, exactly. But I got him an apartment a few blocks from me."

Oscar's eyes widened. "You got the place already?"

She nodded. "As soon as I saw it, I knew it was perfect. And at the price, it wouldn't be on the market long. So I snatched it up."

Oscar nodded, impressed. "You do so much to make sure that your family is okay. They must love you for it." Over the years, Oscar had seen how hard Crystal worked. Once, during a particularly lonely holiday season, he had found himself without a place to go. Crystal had invited him to visit her mother's house in Maryland that year. He had traveled with her on what was now one of their most memorable road trips. Crystal's family had welcomed him with open arms, and he had been amazed by the opulent and lavish lifestyle her mother enjoyed. He could only imagine how nicely she intended to set her dad up once he came home.

"I know he'll like it," she said. "But it's going to take some getting used to for him. It's definitely not the Brooklyn he remembers."

Crystal lived a few blocks away from Brooklyn's new Barclays Center. The neighborhood had undergone quite a transformation in recent years. But Crystal's father, Quincy, had even more of a reason to be amazed by Brooklyn's transformation. He had spent the past twenty-five years locked up in New York's notorious prison system. He had paid dearly in blood, sweat, and tears for a crime he still maintained that he didn't commit.

Oscar glanced at her sympathetically. "I'm sure he'll get himself together. Don't try to shoulder it all yourself. You can't be Superwoman all the time, you know?"

Crystal nodded. "I know." She tucked Oscar's handkerchief into her purse, and made a mental note to launder it and return it later. "He looks good. He's been working out, reading, getting his head together. He seems ready." She smiled proudly at the thought of her dad. He planned on wasting no time getting back on his feet after soldiering through a long prison stint. Crystal had no recollection of her father as a free man. She had been just three years old when he was sent away to prison to serve a sentence of twenty-five to life. Over the years, she had gotten to know him mostly through phone calls and letters. Though his correspondence was frequent, there was nothing like the real thing. Having him close by, in the flesh, would be far more fulfilling than the occasional visits she had with him now.

Quincy went to jail in 1991, when Crystal was a toddler, and her brother, Malik, had been eight years old. Crystal was too young to remember the circumstances surrounding her father's arrest and incarceration. But she later learned the truth of what had taken place. The circumstances were sketchy and complicated. The topic had always seemed a sore spot for her mother Georgi to discuss. But Crystal had learned a lot more about all of that in the time since her brother was killed.

Oscar nodded, smiling. It was clear that visiting her dad had done her well.

"I know I don't have to remind you. But, please never mention anything about my personal life to this new guy or any of his cronies. Not even Fox knows about my family history. The only one I trust is you."

Oscar smiled, honored by what she said. His smile faded quickly. "I would never tell anybody your business. You should know that by now. We know things about each other we oughta take to the grave."

Crystal laughed. It was true. Still, it felt good to have his reassurance that her secrets were safe with him.

Now that they were on the subject, he went ahead and asked, "Are you nervous about meeting this guy—our new boss?"

Crystal looked at him and shrugged. "Curious, more than anything. You know?"

Oscar nodded. He waved his hand as if it didn't matter anyway. "So, are you personally interviewing Alicia from Black Lives Matter later on today, or are you sending Dana?" he asked. Dana was the executive editor at *Hipster* and Crystal's right-hand girl.

"I'm taking the lead on the interview. But I'm bringing her with me," Crystal said. "I want to make sure this is one of our boldest issues yet."

Oscar nodded. His idea for the accompanying fashion spread was fabulous. He had styled Taraji, Kerry, Viola, and Uzo as iconic black women in the struggle for civil rights. Coretta, Betty, Angela, and Assata came to life amid Oscar's elaborate backdrops and flawless styling. Crystal wanted to make sure that the black history month issue wasn't all flash and little substance. Personally conducting these interviews was her way of ensuring that. Although Thanksgiving was just a few days away, they were already preparing their February issue. Like most other publications, each issue was finalized months in advance, making it even more difficult to keep their fingers on the pulse of pop culture. But Crystal and Oscar managed to do just that.

"Great," Oscar said. "I'm going to send Tonya with you to take some candid pictures." Tonya was his assistant and *Hipster*'s social media manager. Her position at Oscar Beane's side was a coveted one and she knew it. Tonya was the type to arrive early and work late in order to ensure that her boss had everything he needed before he even asked for it. Crystal often referred to Tonya as Oscar's "work wife."

Crystal realized that she was much calmer than she had been before Oscar's arrival. She marveled at how easily he could set her mind at ease. He was a great friend, the two of them having grown in their careers together over the years they'd spent working together. Their work camaraderie had blossomed into a close friendship.

Tonya, Oscar's young assistant, knocked on the office door and then peeked her head inside.

"Oscar, you told me to come and get you when the new boss arrives." She stepped inside quickly and shut the door behind her. "Well, he's here. Him and his entourage." Tonya smiled brightly. "Fox is giving him a tour of the building and then he'll bring him down to the conference room for the meeting."

Oscar didn't budge. "Tonya, what's he like?" he asked, one eyebrow raised curiously.

Tonya smiled, a bit sheepishly. "He's *handsome*! Oh my God . . ." She was blushing. She seemed flustered by her brief encounter with Mr. Mitchell's son. "He's tall, nice skin, a solid build. He looks *good* in his suit. Like it was custom-made just for him. His complexion is like . . . he looks like a Hershey's Kiss. Nice teeth, clean fingernails—"

"Well, *damn*!" Oscar mumbled. "I didn't ask for a forensic profile. What was he *like*? Was he friendly? Rude?"

Crystal stared at her wordlessly, pondering her description. Tonya was embarrassed now. She hadn't meant to go on and on like that. But in the brief moments she had spent in his presence, Tonya had become intoxicated by him. She had not expected to meet the muscled stallion dripping with sex appeal who walked through the doors of the magazine, *rightfully,* as if he owned the place. Tonya was already smitten. In fact, he had all the women in the office struggling to keep their professional masks on.

She cleared her throat. "He seemed very professional. Like he was trying to memorize everyone's name. He doesn't smile much, though."

"Okay. Thanks," Crystal said. "We'll head to the conference room in a minute."

Tonya nodded and left, shutting the door behind her.

Oscar looked at Crystal, his eyes narrowed. "I bet you he's *arrogant!*"

Crystal laughed. "She didn't say that." She was thinking about the look she'd seen on Tonya's face. She had never seen the young marketing assistant so dazzled.

Oscar counted off his points on his long fingers. "Handsome, wealthy, doesn't smile much."

Crystal nodded in agreement. "Arrogant."

Oscar gave her an arched eyebrow in agreement.

"Well . . . I'm ready for him." Crystal sounded rather unconvincing. She pushed her nervousness down deep and checked her reflection in her mirror one last time. She winked at Oscar.

A broad smile crept across his face in response. "You better let him know." He stood, and together they headed to the conference room.

On the way, they noticed that the atmosphere in the typically upbeat office was much calmer. It was certainly quieter than usual. Workstations where radios usually played were now silent. Crystal noticed that the general staff was on their best behavior, dressed fashionably as usual. But with an added polish today that could only be attributed to the arrival of the new boss. The office staff would not be attending this meeting. It was a closed-door conference for executives only. Crystal noticed the staff clustered together in groups having whispered conversations. She saw Tonya giggling with one of the girls from accounting.

She busied herself with the papers she had brought with her. Her résumé, the magazine's sales statistics, and their plans for the upcoming issue. She watched as Oscar went over his presentation with Marlo Stanton from the marketing department one last time. Crystal's hands trembled ever so slightly now. She clenched them into fists as the doors of the conference room swung open.

Fox walked in along with three other people. One of them was instantly recognizable as his son Troy. They had an unquestionable resemblance, and Troy walked in with the air of a man accustomed to running the show.

Crystal's eyes swept over him from head to toe. God, he was beautiful. His body looked toned and powerful in his custom-made suit. His lips were so intoxicating that she found it hard not to stare. Suddenly, her mouth felt cottony dry, and the palms of her hands were clammy. Tonya's description hadn't done him justice. Troy was *incredibly* handsome. Clearly aware of his allure, he stood at the head of the conference-room table with a strong and self-assured presence. He wore a perfectly tailored black Tom Ford suit and matching tie. Crystal recognized the look from a shoot *Hipster* had done with Morris Chestnut. The dark suit accented Troy's chocolate skin beautifully. It hugged him in all the right places. Monogrammed cuff links completed the look in perfect simplicity as he gazed around the room at the staff of his company's top performing acquired magazine with confidence. Crystal forced herself to look away, feeling suddenly underdressed.

She focused her attention on Fox, who greeted her with a bright smile. "This is the woman who saved the magazine," he began. "Crystal Scott." He looked at his son. "We all call her Crys. She's the EIC here, and she runs the show."

Crystal smiled and finally made eye contact with Troy. He extended his hand to her and she took it. She locked eyes with him, and saw the glint of vague recognition in his eyes. She could see him trying to connect the dots.

Crystal shook his hand firmly and smiled.

He nodded, staring at Crystal, a slight frown on his face. "Where do I know you from?" he asked.

Crystal's eyes danced as she spoke. "I met you briefly last year, I believe. At one of your father's functions."

He smiled, though not as broadly as his father. "I would have remembered meeting you." His tone was suggestive and Crystal took note. "It's nice to meet you, Crys."

"Same here, Mr. Mitchell."

He held on to her hand as she moved to retrieve it. "Call me Troy."

She exhaled and smiled, instantly relieved. Just as she expected, he didn't remember her. "Okay, Troy," she said. "Welcome aboard. Oscar and I are looking forward to working with you."

She turned and gestured toward Oscar, who stepped forward to meet their new boss. As she swiveled, Troy took the opportunity to get a good look at Crystal's well-toned ass. He was already looking forward to working with this lovely brown beauty.

Oscar shook his hand and introduced himself.

Fox introduced the other people who were with him. She watched as he gestured to the Shemar Moore look-alike on his right.

"This is Eric Donovan, the new chief revenue officer of Stuart Mitchell. Eric oversees our corporate sales, marketing, and digital sales for all of the company's magazines and Web sites."

Eric smiled, revealing a Hollywood-worthy set of veneers. "Hello, everyone," he said simply. She noticed Tonya checking him out. Marlo Stanton sized him up, too, from where she sat at the conference-room table. As marketing and sales director, Marlo would no doubt be working closely with Eric to increase *Hipster*'s sales and advertising income. Eric was younger than what she had expected. In fact, every member of the new executive team was young—all of them under fifty years old. That was unusual in their field, with most professionals who reached this peak of success doing so in their golden years. Marlo was intrigued.

Fox continued. "Dru Beckford is our new CFO. Obviously, he presides over all of the accounting, finance, and treasury facets of the company. But he also oversees the strategic sourcing, real estate, and editorial rights and permissions departments."

Dru, a middle-aged brother with a caramel complexion and precise goatee, smiled at them warmly.

Fox gestured toward the table. "Let's sit down and talk about the transition from one generation of Stuart Mitchell to the next."

Everyone took a seat, and Crystal noticed that Troy immediately moved toward the seat at the head of the conference-room table. That seat had always belonged to Fox. And to Crystal, in his absence. But it was clear that Troy was enjoying his new position of power. She, Oscar, and Marlo took seats to Troy's left, while Fox and his team sat on the opposite side of the table.

Fox spoke first. "Everyone here knows that I'll be stepping down as head of Stuart Mitchell, and that my son Troy here will be taking over. Over the past few weeks, my team and I have been transitioning the work over to Troy, and it's all been going smoothly. I expect the same will be the case now that the two of you will start working together to keep *Hipster* on top." He glanced at his son, and then at Crystal. He smiled at her softly. "Crys, why don't you tell Troy and the rest of the new team about your background?"

She nodded and launched into her verbal résumé. "I earned my bachelor's degree in English from the University of Maryland. Then I took a job at *Sable* magazine, where I worked my way up to editorial duties. I worked as an editor there for three years. But the work became unchallenging. So I left and came to work here at *Hipster*." She smiled then and glanced at her peers. "We have a great team and we work well together."

Troy nodded while Fox beamed proudly. He often spoke about Crystal, and Troy could see why his dad was so smitten. She was charming and lovely. Troy was intrigued.

"Crys is being modest," Fox said. "When she came on board here, the magazine was struggling. Big publications like *Essence* were outselling us in every region. She came in, brought Oscar and Marlo and their whole team. It's made all the difference. Sales have been on a steady incline. Our covers and content are competitive. She's got a formula that works."

She smiled in appreciation. "There's no real formula," she confessed. "Our team just ebbs and flows with the tide of pop culture, politics, and entertainment. That's what our readers are interested in. As long as our staff remains current and we give them the freedom to push the envelope, the readers will continue to respond."

Oscar agreed. "Crys is the type of editor in chief who believes in giving her staff room to stretch themselves. We both came from a climate at *Sable* magazine that felt rigid and inflexible. Angela Richmond is a legend in this industry. But she's too tied to her own vision. It's her way or the highway. Crys isn't like that. The editorial and creative staff all rise higher with her direction."

Crystal made a mental note to thank Oscar later. At the moment, Fox was explaining his plan to introduce Troy to the general staff that afternoon. Everyone listened, including Troy. But each chance he got, he stole a glance at Crystal as she sat beside him at the conference-room table. She had an unmistakable allure, and it took some effort to avert his gaze.

Oscar gave a presentation with Marlo's assistance. Troy listened, though he continued watching Crystal discreetly. Or so he thought. She caught him staring while Oscar gave a PowerPoint presentation on the black history month theme of the issue. Their eyes locked, and she held his gaze for a long, intense moment before coyly looking away. His eyes swept over her again before he gave Oscar his attention once more. He applauded along with everyone else when the presentation concluded.

Next Dru spoke about Stuart Mitchell's goals for the upcoming quarter. Now Troy was all ears as the topic turned to dollars and cents. Troy was impressed by the magazine's success in comparison to similar ones in recent years. Print was a floundering industry in a digital age. But *Hipster* was doing well in both markets. As he listened to Dru's assessment of the magazine's sales potential over the next few months, Troy decided that *Hipster* would be his pet project among Stuart Mitchell's holdings. He would give Crystal a better budget, and watch her work her magic. He looked at her now and was confident that she could take the magazine even higher with his support. Even though he'd just met her, he could sense a real spark in her. He grinned, more excited than ever to move into *this* sector of the family business.

For years, Troy had worked behind the scenes, often straddling the fence between two different worlds. One was corporate and legal, the other one was quite the opposite. Now that his father was retiring, it was apparent that he was the chosen one to take over. His brother Wes was older than him by five years, but far less personable. There was no way that he could take over with a trail of legal woes and a penchant for violence. The business of Stuart Mitchell was the real deal. Not the cutthroat game with unwritten rules that their uncle had introduced them to. Troy was ready to embrace a new normal. Running Stuart Mitchell was just the beginning.

Fox wrapped up the meeting and looked on like the proud father that he was as Crystal and Troy exchanged business cards. She gathered her things quickly afterward, and apologized for having to leave so abruptly.

"I'm interviewing the subject of my next piece this afternoon," she explained. "I've got to run."

"Of course!" Fox nodded.

He and all of the men present watched, rapt, as Crystal sauntered out of the conference room in her curve-hugging dress.

Fox turned to his son. "You're gonna love her."

DÉJÀ VU

Crystal returned to her office, and shut the door. She needed a minute to catch her breath. She was proud of herself for keeping her cool. But on the inside she felt several things at once. Relief, angst, and adrenaline primary among them. She hadn't expected to feel that way after one simple meeting. She wondered how long she could keep her professional integrity and avoid ending up spread-eagle beneath her new boss.

She buzzed her assistant, Monica, and asked her to call for a Town Car to take her uptown for the rally. Assured that her driver would meet her curbside in ten minutes, she gathered her belongings while mentally preparing herself for the interviews she was about to conduct.

A young man named Arnold Jackson had been shot by police during a traffic stop in the Bronx. Jackson was unarmed at the time and had his hands raised, according to several witnesses at the scene. But the young man had been vilified in the press, his criminal background mentioned as frequently as his shooting. He was clinging to life now at Bronx Lebanon Hospital. His

parents had held several press conferences alongside Reverend Al
and other community organizers who had become prominent
members of the Black Lives Matter movement. Crystal would be
interviewing the organizers of the rally that afternoon. But she
was really hoping to score an interview with one of the victim's
family members. Unlike so many of the other journalists vy-
ing for the same opportunity, Crystal didn't seek to exploit
the family's turmoil. Instead, she sympathized with them more
than any other reporter might. She had watched her mother pray
and cry for Malik as he fought for his life. It was a heartbreaking,
gut-wrenching experience to watch a mother grieve for her child.
She hoped to capture the humanity of the Jackson family more
than their anger.

Her desk phone buzzed. It was Monica. "Crys, your car is
downstairs."

"Thank you." She glanced at her watch and tucked some papers into her bag. They were articles she would review on her
way to the rally. Even her downtime was work time. But she
wouldn't change a thing.

She grabbed her jacket, her cell phone, and headed downstairs to meet her driver.

Her cell phone buzzed just as she reached the lobby of the
office building on the Upper West Side that *Hipster* operated out
of. With a flourish that was natural for her, she whipped it out of
her pocket, glanced at the screen, and answered the call, her
sunglasses perched on the tip of her nose.

"Hello?" She strolled through the lobby, pretending not to
notice the security personnel admiring the sway of her hips.

"Hey, baby." Her mother's voice sounded more upbeat than
usual. Crystal felt a twinge of hope that she might be having a
good day.

"Hi, Ma. What's up?" She walked through the revolving doors and merged into the crowds on the street below.

"Baby girl, I know you're busy. But we need to talk about this situation with your father. I can't even sleep. I'm so worried about it."

"Calm down, Ma." Crystal located her car and sighed as she climbed inside.

Her mother persisted. "I can't calm down. I can hardly sleep, I'm so worried. The last thing he needs to do is go back to Brooklyn. You know what can happen." Her words sounded rushed, anxious.

The driver headed for Fourteenth Street, and Crystal sighed. "Ma, it's all gonna be fine." She unbuttoned her coat. "Where's Aunt Pat? Are you guys okay?"

"Yeah, yeah," her mother assured her. "Pat went out to the supermarket. We're fine. I just . . . I just want you and your father to be alright out there."

Crystal could hear the concern in her mother's voice. The woman was always worried about something. Crystal could picture her now, probably sitting at her dining-room table in her pajamas. Surely with all of the doors locked and the windows tightly secured. Her mother existed in a virtual prison that was entirely self-inflicted.

"You don't have to worry. I keep telling you that," Crystal assured her. "I have to go, okay? I'll call you tonight. I love you." She hung up and changed out of her heels into a pair of designer flats. Her feet seemed to breathe a sigh of relief.

She rubbed her neck, feeling the tension there. Her mother's fear and anxiety seemed contagious at times. Crystal loved her mother, there was no doubt. But she wanted her to stop being afraid of the boogeyman. The added burden of trying to help their dad get sorted out was beginning to take its toll on her. Lately she found herself missing her brother more than ever. If Malik were alive, she knew that things would be much different. He wouldn't have allowed her to shoulder the pressures alone.

Their parents had met in 1982, back when the two of them were guests at a party in Harlem. Georgina "Georgi" Scott was from Brooklyn, but she loved to take the train uptown with her girls to see what the Harlem boys were wearing, saying, and what they were selling. It was a time of high stakes and big profits in New York, and money flowed through Harlem like hooch in the Prohibition days. There seemed to be an underground railroad of crack and money flowing through the streets of the city. And Georgi and her friends enjoyed incredible evenings on the arms of the dudes who were simultaneously brave and foolish enough to gamble on the drug game. Quincy Taylor was one of the young warriors hugging the block back then.

He'd followed her sauntering hips down a hallway at a house party one of Georgi's friends was hosting one night. He hardly let her take a step without him, mesmerized as he was by the way her booty jiggled in her Lees. To him, she was *fine*. He knew he was being a bit aggressive, but couldn't help it. She seemed to like him, too, though. She was looking at him with the same intensity and hunger in her eyes as he felt. She seemed turned on by his bold approach, and she let him buy her drinks all night. Georgi's very air had made it clear from the start it was a *privilege* to do so. Many men sought her time. So she learned early to capitalize on that. She knew what her face and body were worth. She thought she did anyway. Eventually she would learn the hard way how wrong she was.

Quincy was aware of the way heads turned when Georgi walked in a room. From that night on, he hardly left her side. The money flowed in, and she grew distant from her mother and

sister. The trips and shopping sprees monopolized her time. But she had fallen in love with Quincy. A cocky hustler from uptown, getting money enough to spoil her rotten. Malik was born a year later. Quincy convinced Georgi to marry him and their baby girl was born soon after. The couple had been madly in love.

No one could have predicted the turn their lives would take years later. How a tragic series of events would lead to an encounter between two long-standing rivals and culminate in Malik's death. And in the wake of that fateful day, the family existed under the weight of a dark cloud.

The years after the incident that left her brother slain were filled with angst. Her mother was a shadow of her former self, no longer as preoccupied with her own desires. Suddenly, Georgi Scott had been humbled completely. There was no safety net to catch her and for the first time she was expected to figure it out alone. All while their father, Quincy, sat in prison feeling powerless and frustrated. Their entire family dynamic had been shattered.

She pushed those thoughts aside now, and busied herself sending text messages to Dana and Tonya to let them know that she was on her way. Then she went over the questions she wanted to ask during the interviews she had lined up. The wounded boy was not without his troubles. But he wasn't the hardened criminal that the press seemed determined to depict. Crystal intended to humanize the boy and his family, and to try to do so without painting every police officer in the country as a villain.

The driver dropped her off on the corner and she tipped him generously as she always did. She melted into the sea of people moving toward the center of Union Square. A large crowd had already gathered, full of people from all walks of life. The sight of such a diverse crowd of people united under the common cause of human rights made her feel reassured. The march itself wasn't

scheduled to start for another hour at least. Crystal hoped that would give her enough time to get a good interview in with all her subjects. The weather was unusually warm for New York at this time of year. Crowds of people milled about in T-shirts, hoodies, and carried signs, all emblazoned with the face and name of Arnold Jackson. She spotted Tonya heading toward her in the crowd and smiled as she approached.

"What's up?" Tonya smiled back, her eyes shielded by dark Chanel sunglasses. "I got here early so I could get some pictures of the crowd, get a feel for the energy." She glanced around now, nodding. "The people are fired up. The organizers are keeping them on message, though. They want this to be a nonviolent, peaceful protest against police corruption and the murder of unarmed black men." Tonya snapped some pictures of a father and his two sons standing nearby. As the magazine's social media manager, she kept *Hipster* on the scene at every epic event in arts, culture, and entertainment. It was a job she was well suited for, as a young black woman living single in the city she loved.

Crystal glanced at her cell phone. "Dana just texted me. She's trying to find parking."

Tonya laughed. Dana was a transplant from L.A., still accustomed to driving everywhere. It made her late all the time, which was at times irritating to Crystal. When she had worked for Angela Richmond at *Sable,* it would have been unthinkable for any member of the staff to arrive at any event after her. Angela perceived lateness as disregard for the value of her time. Her insistence on punctuality had forced Crystal to form a habit of arriving early to everything. As she watched Dana scrambling through the crowd now, juggling her purse, her phone, and her tablet, Crystal shook her head in pity. She wondered how long it would be before her patience ran out and she had to tell Dana to get it together.

"Sorry I'm late," Dana said, as if on cue. "I should have just hopped on the train . . ."

Tonya nodded. "Exactly. I'm buying you a MetroCard."

Crystal laughed, though Dana seemed mildly annoyed by the dig. Tonya seized every opportunity to chide her about the fact that she wasn't a true New Yorker. Crystal changed the subject.

"I want to meet with Alicia and, hopefully, with Arnold Jackson's family. Let's get in here and see if we can make this as powerful a story as possible."

The ladies fanned out, and meshed into the crowd, their press credentials prominently on display. Heading past the police barricade toward the tent where the organizers had set up a headquarters of sorts, the two ladies followed Crystal's lead. She greeted Alicia Oliver, one of the movement's founders, and the two of them caught up like old friends. Crystal had first interviewed Alicia for a feature piece on prominent women in the fields of entertainment and politics. The women had hit it off instantly then, as evidenced by the broad smiles, hugs, and hand-holding they exhibited now as they reconnected.

"Let's sit back in the corner, away from all the preparations going on," Alicia suggested, leading the trio in that direction. They passed throngs of people setting up sound equipment, passing out bullhorns, toting signs. Finally they arrived at a small section in the back of the tent, where a few milk crates were available for them to perch on during the interview. They made do with the makeshift venue, and Dana began snapping photos while Crystal peppered Alicia with questions. Dana took feverish notes amid the bustle of the swelling crowd.

"The Jacksons are a good family," Alicia was saying. "Arnold's sister is joining us today. But the rest of the family is holding vigil at his bedside, praying desperately for a miracle."

Crystal nodded. "Of course."

Alicia nodded. "Arnold's father is from Harlem. He runs a bunch of businesses, and mentors a group of young men from the neighborhood. Seven of them went to HBCUs last year, and ten more are on target to do the same this school year." Alicia smiled like a proud mom. "He was trying to make a difference with children in the neighborhood, and his own son was a victim of violence. And, at the hands of the police at that." She shook her head in dismay. "I'll go get his sister now so that you can speak with her for a few minutes." She left, and returned a few minutes later with an older man and a beautiful brown girl who Crystal estimated to be around sixteen years old. She looked sad, angry, and terribly afraid all at the same time. Crystal had to resist the urge to hug the young lady.

Alicia introduced them. "This is Craig Bradley. He's the attorney for the Jackson family. And this is Lisa Jackson. She's Arnold Jackson's younger sister."

Crystal greeted the girl and introduced Tonya and Dana.

"I have some more details to tend to, so I'll leave you ladies for a little while." Alicia scampered off to prepare for the march. Everyone else got comfortable as the interview began.

Crystal looked at Lisa warmly. "How is your brother doing?"

Lisa shrugged. "He's still alive. The doctors said it's a miracle that he survived. They said now it's up to God. So we're all just praying." Her voice cracked and Mr. Bradley handed her a tissue in anticipation of the tears to come. Lisa took it and continued, "We've been at the hospital all day and night, praying, talking to him, and playing the music he likes." She shook her head. "It's hard."

Crystal felt the tears threatening to plunge forth. But she fought them back. It was moments like this that made it hard to keep her professional poker face on. This subject in particular hit a raw nerve within her. She knew the pain that this girl was experiencing firsthand.

"How old is your brother?" she asked.

"Twenty."

"And how old are you?"

"Seventeen."

Crystal nodded. She turned on her recorder.

Mr. Bradley spoke up immediately. "Lisa is not here to speak on behalf of the family. She's here to speak about her own thoughts and opinions. And, she's not going to comment on any plans for future litigation against the police or the city."

Crystal nodded. "That's fine." She looked at Lisa. "I'm not here to get in your business, or to try and create more tension between your family and the police. I want to hear your story as a young woman of color dealing with a situation that is way too horrific for anyone your age to have to face. This interview is about you, about your relationship with your brother. I want you to tell your story in your words. That's it."

Lisa seemed to relax a little. She nodded and Crystal began.

"Tell me what kind of guy your brother is. Describe your relationship with him."

Lisa thought about it. She opened her mouth to speak, but got choked up and began to cry softly. Dana rubbed her back comfortingly. Lisa took a deep breath and finally spoke.

"He's hilarious." She laughed through her tears as she said it. "He likes to joke around and make everybody smile. We're close. He's always looking out for me. Making sure none of the guys in the neighborhood try to holla at me." She shook her head, and wiped the tears that trailed down her cheek. "He's a good person. He doesn't bother nobody."

Crystal thought about Malik's laugh and how it filled an entire room. She missed that laugh and imagined that Lisa would give anything to hear one of her brother's jokes now.

Lisa went on. "Since the shooting, the media keeps highlighting his arrest record, his Facebook posts, and all the things that make the shooting justifiable to them. But that's not who my brother is. None of those things justifies shooting an unarmed boy so many times."

Dana's pen moved across her notepad rapidly, even though her recorder was capturing the entire interview. She was the type of writer who liked to capture the nuances not found in words. She noted Lisa's passionate and angry delivery, her animated body language, and the intensity in her eyes.

Tonya snapped several pictures of Lisa as she spoke. She caught a few of Mr. Bradley, too, for good measure.

"What do you know about the night of Arnold's traffic stop?" Crystal asked.

Lisa shook her head, glancing at her attorney for confirmation. "I wasn't there. So, I can't say what happened. All I know is that they brought my brother into the hospital with two gunshots in his chest. One in his leg. He's not responding to anybody. He's just laying there, hooked up to them machines. He's not laughing no more. He's just laying there." She dissolved into tears, and Dana hugged her as she cried. Mr. Bradley pulled out more tissues, and everyone took one this time.

Crystal pulled herself together. She remembered the condition she had found her brother in when she arrived at the hospital that fateful night. Malik had been beaten so badly that the doctors had given him only a fifty-fifty chance of survival. She looked at Lisa, her eyes full of empathy and compassion.

"One last question, Lisa. I know this is hard for you."

Lisa nodded, and dabbed at her eyes.

"What do you want to say to other young women who are

reading this article? Women like you, who have seen a loved one victimized by gun violence?"

Lisa thought for several moments about that one. She sighed before she answered. "We have to do something. We can't just keep marching and making hashtags. I see so many black men dying around me. My uncle got shot by some gang member and died. Now my brother is laying up in the hospital shot by the cops. I'm tired of it." She shrugged her shoulders. "I don't know what to say to your readers, honestly. They probably want to hear me say something positive and kumbaya or some shit. But I'm fucking mad. My brother doesn't deserve to be laid up in the hospital right now. He doesn't deserve to have machines breathing for him and tubes down his throat. My mother has cried so much that her voice is gone. This is crazy. And, I'm ready to fight somebody. I want to hurt something the same way my family is hurting right now."

Lisa's voice boomed, and people around them stopped and stared. Crystal nodded her head, and held the young woman's gaze. "I feel you," she said sincerely. "I really do."

Alicia arrived at the perfect time to ask them to wrap things up.

"We have everything we need," Crystal said. "Thank you, Lisa, Mr. Bradley." She shook both of their hands. Alicia hugged Crystal good-bye before shuttling Lisa Jackson and her attorney off to lead the march.

Crystal let out a deep sigh.

"That was intense," Tonya said.

Dana nodded. "Definitely."

Crystal slid her sunglasses on, and prayed that the women hadn't noticed the tears in her eyes. It had taken every ounce of her willpower not to cry. She was barely holding it together now.

"I've got an appointment uptown," she said abruptly. "I have to go." She hurried off without another word.

Dana and Tonya exchanged glances and shrugged. They parted ways, heading off in opposite directions as the march got under way. Crystal found a secluded spot on the side of a wall near the perimeter of the square. She leaned against it and closed her eyes, willing herself to relax. Memories of that fateful day flashed in her mind. Malik in that hospital bed dying, her mother distraught, their family in ruins. She could still feel the shame and the hurt and the feeling that it was all her fault. She hadn't expected that interviewing Arnold Jackson's family members would bring up so much raw emotion. Those old familiar feelings of anger, helplessness, and betrayal resurfaced with as much intensity as they had back in 2006.

"Crys. You okay?"

Her eyes flew open at the sound of her name uttered by that familiar voice. A chill ran down her spine. She shivered at the feeling, adjusted her sunglasses, and turned around to face him.

"My goodness! Troy." She stammered a little and forced a smile. "Yeah, I'm fine."

He was frowning, and didn't seem to believe her. "You sure? I saw you leaning on the wall like you might faint or something."

She shook her head, still smiling. "Please. I'm fine. My feet were just hurting, honestly. I thought I could rest for a second while nobody was looking." She looked at him questioningly. "What are you doing down here?"

He tucked his hands inside his coat pocket. "It's ironic, right? When you mentioned having an interview earlier, I had no idea that it was here. Otherwise, I would have offered you a ride," he said. "Craig Bradley is a family friend. He invited me to the rally today and I came to offer my support."

"I see." Crystal looked around at the march that was already under way. "I think you might've missed him."

Troy looked at her oddly, guilt written all over his face. Finally, he came clean.

"Truthfully, my friend Craig told me about this rally days ago. I didn't plan on coming. But when my father mentioned that you were interviewing the Jackson family today, I changed my mind. I came down here, hoping that I would see you and convince you to have a cup of coffee with me." He smiled at her shyly. "I figured since we'll be working together so closely, we could get to know each other a little better. You know?" He shrugged.

Crystal smiled. "Okay."

UNFINISHED BUSINESS

They found a Starbucks nearby, grabbed some coffee, and sat together in the back of the café, facing the door. Troy was talking about his plans for Stuart Mitchell Enterprises and how excited he was about stepping into his father's footprints. Crystal watched him, listening intently as she sipped her coffee. His eyes twinkled with a boyish charm that made her smile. He was so passionate about what he was saying that it disarmed her.

But it was hard for her to focus on what he was saying. She found herself distracted by his appearance. She watched his lips as he spoke. The way he moved his hands, and gestured. His expensive coat, his watch, his resemblance to his father. The man had impeccable style. Every piece in his current wardrobe was impressive. But that was no surprise. The Mitchell family had amassed a fortune over the years. In publishing alone, they had several top urban magazines in their portfolio. *Hipster* was the most successful one. But all of them were performing well. They also had their hands in a number of lucrative marketing and advertising campaigns. Troy had certainly been born with a silver spoon in his mouth. And with a very high self-esteem, evidenced by the soliloquy he launched into now about his success so far.

"My father's vision for Stuart Mitchell was narrow," Troy was saying. "When he started the company, it was the early nineties and he was thinking print media. Everything is digital now. So my plan is to make sure each of our publications has a highly visible online profile, like *Hipster* does." He smiled at her then. "I applaud you for having the foresight to make that happen."

Crystal raised her coffee cup in a mock toast. "If you're not digital you don't exist in this day and age."

Troy agreed. "That's what gives *Hipster* such an advantage. Unlike its competitors, *Hipster*'s average reader is between the ages of eighteen to forty. That's a young, progressive audience and they expect their favorite magazines to keep up. You've been successful at doing that."

Crystal nodded. "Sounds like you did your homework, Troy."

"Of course." He sat back in his seat and looked at her. "My father can't stop singing your praises. Over the past couple of months, I've been hanging out with him a lot while he shows me the ropes. And he talks about *Hipster* like it's a miracle. His investors were urging him to cut his losses and pull the plug on the whole thing. He was considering that. But he said that when you walked into his office and told him your vision, he knew right away that it was a perfect fit. He has great respect and admiration for you." Troy smirked playfully. "I can see why."

Crystal frowned a little. "What does that mean?" she asked. "You just met me. You couldn't have seen much."

He shook his head. "Not true," he said. "I've seen plenty. For one thing, you met me and my team this morning. Then you excused yourself to go and personally conduct an interview that you could have easily handed off to one of your writers. That tells me you're serious about your job, and about the magazine overall."

Crystal grinned as she listened.

"As if that wasn't enough, I got here and found you nearly in tears after an interview."

She shifted uneasily in her seat. She hadn't thought he noticed the tears in her eyes. And, truthfully, she didn't appreciate him bringing it up.

He held his hand over his heart. "That type of compassion for someone you just met is incredible. Especially in media. You hear so many different stories from day to day that you kind of become desensitized to it. *Numb*. You know what I mean?" He shook his head. "But not you. I could tell that you were emotional about it, even though you tried to play it off. I understand you wanting to keep your professional mask on. But, truthfully, I liked seeing you vulnerable like that. It speaks volumes that you can feel that type of compassion for someone whose life is so different from yours."

Crystal stared back at him and smiled. Of course he had no idea how wrong he was. Lisa Jackson's life paralleled hers in more ways than Troy knew.

"Tell me about yourself, Crystal," Troy said. "I'm curious about you."

She smiled broadly now. "Is that right?"

"Yes."

"Well, I'm sure you've heard all there is to hear from Fox."

"Nah," Troy said, waving his hand. "I want to hear from you. Not all the professional shit you talked about earlier. I want to know who Crys Scott really is." He smirked. "What's your story? Where do you live? What kind of car you drive? What type of music you like?"

Her eyes narrowed instinctively. She wondered where this was going. She noticed that he had slipped out of his professional speech. She let out a soft sigh. "I live in Brooklyn. I drive an Audi."

Troy's eyes widened, impressed. "A five?"

"A six."

His eyes widened even more. "Whoa. Okay." He sat back and flexed a little on her behalf.

She laughed.

"Okay." He nodded, impressed. "I imagined you in something more subtle."

Crystal was distracted for a moment by an angry customer arguing with the cashier. Her grande latte wasn't whipped to her standards or something. She gave Troy her attention again.

"I like speed. And power." She took another sip of her coffee.

He stared at her. "I don't know what it is about you," he said. "I can't put my finger on it. But I like you. You seem like the kind of woman I will enjoy working with."

She grinned. "What kind of woman is that?"

"Smart, driven, focused. With a passion for power and speed." He chuckled a bit. "Sounds like I'm describing myself."

Crystal chuckled, too. But at his arrogance.

"Tell me more." He took a bite of his pastry.

She shrugged. "There's really not much to tell."

He looked skeptical. "Come on," he coaxed. "Tell me about your family. What do you do for fun?"

She smiled. "I don't have much family."

"No siblings?" he asked between bites.

She thought about Malik, but decided not to dredge up that old history right now. "No," she said simply. "But my cousin is like a sister to me. I hang out with her a lot. My parents. I have a few close friends, but I'm not much for crowds. Not unless it pertains to my work."

"Are you married?" he asked.

Crystal let the question linger between them for a moment before answering. It felt inappropriate on some level, him asking her that. But she decided to answer him anyway.

"I'm not."

He nodded, a grin tickling the corner of his mouth. "Neither am I."

Her eyes narrowed again. "But that's about to change soon, right? Aren't you engaged to Vanessa Nolan?"

She could tell that he hadn't expected her to know that. After all, the engagement was only a couple of days old. There had been no big announcement. In fact, Troy had kept an extremely low profile for the most part. Until now. Fox spoke about his sons from time to time, though. He had mentioned the engagement to Crystal after a weekend away in Vegas. Vanessa Nolan had some very prominent parents. Her mother was Roxy Nolan, a former Miss USA. Roxy was gorgeous, exotic, and had a body that put women half her age to shame. Vanessa's father was Harvey Nolan, one of the top civil rights attorneys in the country. He had been a partner at the firm of Wakefield Crawford since its inception in the eighties, and was one of the power movers in the political arena. He rubbed elbows with the likes of Obama and Clinton, and many urged him to pursue political aspirations of his own. Instead, he was content to continue mostly pro bono work at the firm, while maintaining strong ties to D.C. and reaping the rewards of both.

Harvey was one of Fox's old friends, which made their children's relationship a sweet twist of fate. Troy had proposed to Vanessa at her parents' anniversary party in Las Vegas, surrounded by their family and closest friends. According to Fox, it had been a beautiful and romantic display.

Troy laughed. "I see my father talks a lot."

She nodded. "He's very proud of you. He mentioned you have a brother. His name is Wes, isn't it?"

Troy appeared to tense a little at the mention of his brother's name. He looked at Crystal oddly. "That's right." He seemed uncomfortable. She wondered what that was about.

"Your dad is a pleasure to work with," she said. "He's laid-back and calm. But he's a lion in the boardroom and he expects results. I respect his business sense and he respects my vision. We've done well together. From time to time, we chat about our family life. He mentioned your engagement the other day and he could barely contain his joy." She smiled at him.

Troy returned the gesture and seemed to relax a little. "He's happy."

"Are *you* happy?"

He stared at her blankly. For a moment, she regretted asking the question. Just as she opened her mouth to apologize, he spoke.

"You know what I'm happy about?" He smiled and his eyes sparkled. "Taking over Stuart Mitchell and working with movers and shakers like you." He drank the last of his coffee and winked at her as he set the cup down.

Crystal smiled and decided that was a nice way to end this. She felt they had crossed enough professional boundaries for one day. She rose to leave.

"I'm looking forward to working with you, too, Troy." She extended her hand to him across the table.

Troy looked up at her. "You have to leave so soon?" Disappointment was evident in his face and tone.

She nodded. "I do. But thank you for the coffee."

Reluctantly, he rose and shook her extended hand. As he had done earlier during their first meeting, he held her hand longer than necessary.

"Take care," he said.

Her grip tightened involuntarily, and she pulled her hand away hoping that he hadn't noticed. Grabbing her purse off the table, she forced a smile, and waved as she rushed out the door.

He watched her go, wondering what it was about her that piqued his curiosity so. Being around beautiful women was nothing new. He was engaged to one of the most gorgeous creatures he had ever laid eyes on. Crystal, though, had appealed to him in ways that weren't purely physical. Her intelligence and drive made her more attractive somehow and Troy found himself wanting more.

He thought about the question she had asked him about his engagement. Whether he was happy. He cared about Vanessa, there was no question. But happiness was something that had eluded him all his life. He found it interesting that Crystal had asked him that. As a journalist, he guessed she had developed a knack for asking the right things. It was something he hadn't considered for some time. And now, the question haunted him like a ghost in his mind.

Are you happy?

He gathered the trash from the table, and deposited it in a garbage can on his way out the door. The cool autumn air smacked him in the face as he emerged and melded into the crowd on the streets of New York City.

Crystal greeted her cousin Destiny as she entered her apartment. She took off her coat, and flung it across the sofa. Destiny had given her a spare key a year ago after injuring her ankle in a fall. Crystal lived a few blocks away, and had come by often in those days with groceries and toiletries for her cousin. Now that Destiny was healed, she wondered how long Crystal would continue the practice of letting herself into her apartment unannounced.

She shook her head jokingly at Crystal now. "Girl, give me back my keys."

Crystal pouted, and hid them behind her back. "I'll call next time. I promise." She held up the bag of Cuban food she brought with her. "I come bearing gifts."

Destiny laughed and led the way into the kitchen. Crystal followed, set the bag of food down on the long oak wood table, and poured herself a glass of wine. This was the type of indulging she tried hard to avoid, knowing what it did to her petite frame. She told herself that today was an exception. Comfort food and alcohol were just what the doctor ordered.

Destiny grabbed plates and utensils and joined her. "How did your interview go today with the Jackson family?"

"I'll tell you all about it," Crystal promised, "but first we gotta eat. I'm starving and this food is smelling good."

Destiny agreed. "I hardly ate all day. Too stressed."

Crystal frowned and glanced at her while she prepared her plate. "Stressed? About what?"

Destiny sighed. "I just got off the phone venting to Mommy. I broke up with that nigga Dwayne."

Crystal shook her head, grinning. "I thought you stopped saying the 'n' word after you saw *Twelve Years a Slave*."

Destiny sucked her teeth. "Yeah," she admitted. "It's hard to stay woke, though, when you're dealing with a nigga like Dwayne." She surveyed the food Crystal had brought over. She put a couple of empanadas on her plate, and told herself to be satisfied with that. Destiny had always been a hefty girl, but now that she was nearing the age of thirty, she was determined to get her weight under control, once and for all. She doubted that she'd ever transition the way that Jennifer Hudson had. But she thought she could at least get her Jill Scott on.

Crystal laughed. "What happened?" she asked, though she truthfully couldn't care less. It seemed like Destiny and Dwayne broke up every two weeks. She was sick of hearing about it, but loved her cousin too much to say so.

Thankfully, Destiny had vented to her mother enough already. She looked at Crystal and rolled her eyes dramatically. "He's a fool, like Mommy said, and ain't never gonna change," Destiny said simply. She started fixing her plate. "Now tell me about the interview."

"Girl!" Crystal took a long sip of her wine. She sat back, her eyes dancing as she spoke. "I had the craziest day! Arnold Jackson's sister was the only family member at the rally today. So I interviewed her and the family lawyer. It was a lot harder than I expected it to be."

Destiny glanced at her cousin sympathetically. She had witnessed firsthand how devastating Malik's death had been for Crystal.

"I knew going into it that the subject was a sensitive one for me," Crystal said. "Had I known I was going to be interviewing his *sister*, I probably would have let Dana take the lead. It was like looking at myself in a mirror ten years ago and seeing how scared and broken I was then." She shook her head. "I was pretty shaken up." She shoveled some rice into her mouth and chewed.

Destiny nodded. She stared at her cousin oddly. Something was off. "Sounds traumatic," she said. "So why are you so upbeat when you talk about it?"

Crystal glanced at her cousin. Her face melted into a grin and her eyes were more alive than ever. "I got to meet the Boy Wonder today."

Destiny's eyes widened. She stopped chewing and sat back in her seat. She glared at Crystal, a smirk now appearing on her own face as she let her words sink in. Finally, she nodded. "Tell me everything and don't leave out a single detail."

Crystal chuckled so loudly that it sounded a little maniacal. She gleefully launched into a recap of her workday and Destiny was all ears.

ORIENTATION

Crystal arrived for work the next morning with nervous excitement bubbling beneath the surface. She expected that Troy would stop in at some point. Although his main office was at Stuart Mitchell headquarters up in Harlem, she knew it wouldn't be long before he found some excuse to make the trip downtown to *Hipster*. She wasn't a bit surprised when she arrived that morning to find Troy smiling back at her from behind the desk in his father's office.

She chuckled.

"Good morning, Troy."

He bounced a little in his father's oversized leather chair. Despite his size, to Crystal he looked like a little kid role-playing at Daddy's job.

"How did my dad sit here?" Troy asked rhetorically. "This thing is uncomfortable. I'm gonna have to order a new one."

Crystal raised an eyebrow. "You're planning on spending a lot of time here?"

He smiled at that. "Yes, I think so. You know, just until I get familiar with the way things are done around here."

Crystal nodded. She suspected that Troy wasn't only inter-ested in familiarizing himself with the office mechanics. She was well aware of the way his gaze lingered a little too long on her curves.

"Well, I'll see you around then." She held up her coffee cup in a mock toast, spun on her heels, and stepped down the hall toward Oscar's office. She found him standing near the window, a glorious view of Midtown just beyond him, while he stared in-tently at some pictures spread on the ledge.

Oscar glanced up at her for just a moment before turning his attention back to the photos.

"Come look at this," he beckoned. He stood with his arms folded, one hand resting on his chin.

She stepped closer to see that he was studying four pictures of an aging former model.

"What's wrong?" she asked.

He looked at her, eyes wide. "What's right?" he shot back. "She's not working."

Crystal shook her head. The pictures looked fine to her. But she had worked with Oscar long enough to trust his instincts. She looked at him.

"Let's use Roxy Nolan instead. Make it part of our Mother's Day issue. Roxy Nolan and her daughter, Vanessa." She waited for Oscar's reaction.

He gave it some thought. Then he looked at her sidelong. "You sly fox."

She smirked. Oscar saw right through her.

"This will go over well with the boss."

She shook her head. "*I'm* the boss," she reminded him. "But you're right. Fox and Troy will love the idea. If we're lucky, we'll get Vanessa to agree to a bridal-themed shoot. Kill two birds with one stone."

Oscar looked at Crystal closely, his eyes narrowed. "Funny," he sneered. "I think Troy has his eyes on you."

She scoffed, although she knew it was true.

"He was looking for you this morning. And when he saw that you weren't here, he started asking about you."

Crystal's heart sank for a moment. "Asking what?"

"About your schedule and your work habits." He glanced at her suggestively then.

"What's that supposed to mean?"

Oscar shrugged. "I wonder if he's this interested in all of the other magazines his family owns. It might not be just the work that has him excited."

"He's engaged to Vanessa Nolan," she reminded him. "What else did he ask?"

"Nothing really, darling. It wasn't *what* he asked, to tell you the truth. It was the way he went about it. He seemed like a boy with a crush in school. It's obvious that he likes you." Oscar winked at her coyly. "I think he's showing up here so *early* in the morning for more than just the free coffee."

Crystal laughed. "Save the melodrama for this morning's cover meeting. I'm on my way in now, so you should join me." She gestured toward the photos he had been staring at. "I'll set up the Roxy Nolan thing. We'll figure out a way to use these somehow. Don't worry."

"Worry makes wrinkles," Oscar said, waving his hand as if something smelled bad. "I don't do that."

He followed her to the conference room down the hall, where they found the executive team already assembled. Troy had taken the seat at the head of the table. The same one his father always occupied during his rare visits to *Hipster*'s headquarters. She felt his gaze all over her as she moved to a seat near Marlo and her marketing team.

"Crys," Troy called out.

The buzz of conversation in the room died down at the sound of his voice. Crystal glanced at him, a bit embarrassed by all the attention. At the moment, it felt like every pair of eyes in the room were on them.

"Sit closer. I might have some questions during the meeting."

Crystal changed seats, aware that with every step he watched her like a hawk. She sat beside him and called the meeting to order.

She gave a brief overview of the direction she wanted the issue to go in. While she spoke, she was aware that Troy was watching her closely. She pretended not to notice and spoke confidently. Crystal took her job seriously. Her career had been the one constant in a life that had seen its share of peaks and valleys. Despite whatever chemistry there might be between the two of them, she was determined to focus on the task at hand. She laid out her plans for the March issue in exquisite detail.

After her presentation, she handed the floor over to Oscar, sat back, and listened.

Troy paid attention to Oscar because it was impossible not to. Oscar had a flair for the dramatic that made it impossible to look away. It was the juxtaposition of his large, imposing frame against his fluttery words and the flick of his wrist. The entire room was riveted.

Troy still managed to steal a glance at Crystal every now and then. She sat with her spine straight, chin up, and with her breasts struggling against her skintight dress. She was a lovely sight. He forced himself to focus on Marlo Stanton, who had now taken the floor. Marlo shared her ideas for improving sales and subscriptions during the next quarter. Crystal noticed that Eric Donovan was listening intently, as now Marlo was speaking his language—dollars and cents. She stole a glance at Troy and was startled to find him watching her.

He leaned in and whispered, "Have dinner with me tonight."

She shifted in her seat uncomfortably, then looked around to see if anyone else had noticed. Everyone was giving Marlo their rapt attention as she outlined potential revenue streams. Everyone that is, except for Troy. Crystal glanced at him again. This time, he appeared visibly amused by her discomfort. He stifled a laugh as she self-consciously tucked her hair behind her ear. She averted her gaze and focused on Marlo, who was speaking now about consumer research and growth opportunities that might help them surpass the magazine's performance in the last quarter.

This time when Crystal looked at him, she held his gaze flirtatiously. Her lips stretched into a slow and sexy smile and finally she nodded. She looked away, feeling his energy from inches away. He was hungry for her and he *expected* to have her. She knew all about men like him. Used to having their way with everything and everyone in their path. She was simultaneously amused and aroused by him. He was, after all, sexy and wealthy. Two very tantalizing qualities in a man. But his assumption that having her would be as easy as whatever he had planned for the night made her giggle. For the rest of the meeting, she refused to look his way. Like a spoiled brat, he tried everything to get her attention. He asked her to repeat what Marlo was saying, although she knew that he could hear the woman clearly. She was grateful when Marlo heard him and spoke louder so that even the people outside the conference room could hear her. Crystal had to stifle a laugh.

He settled back into his seat, and watched her. He wondered why his father hadn't introduced them sooner. Or had he? Crystal had mentioned something earlier about meeting him at some party. His eyes lingered on her slim, tight waist and the seductive curve of her back as she sat forward in her chair. Surely, he wouldn't have been so blind as to let a woman like this pass him by. Not that he wasn't juggling enough women already. But there was something about Crystal that had him intrigued. He wanted to know more about this coy fox who was running his father's top magazine.

Once all of the key players had their say, Crystal adjourned the meeting. A buzz spread across the room as everyone engaged in their own follow-up conversations. Troy leaned over and whispered in her ear, "Meet me in my office at six o'clock."

He gathered up his things and exited the conference room with Eric not far behind. Crystal smiled to herself, aware that she had just become a willing participant in a very mature game of cat and mouse. She doubted Troy was aware that this time he was not the cat.

It was twenty minutes past six and Crystal was running late and rushing back to the office to meet Troy. She had gone out and enjoyed a working lunch with Dana that afternoon. Afterward, she had done an interview with the NY1 television network about the election. Next she filmed a segment at BET about diversity and inclusion in media. The segment had gone on longer than expected. Now she was trotting up Sixth Avenue, aware that her new boss was being kept waiting. She was so focused on getting back upstairs as quickly as possible that she rushed past Troy standing in the lobby.

He called out her name as she hurried by.

She stopped in her tracks and faced him, immediately apologetic. "I'm sorry. I hate to keep people waiting. I was stuck over at BET and I couldn't get away in time."

"Don't worry about it." He gestured toward the elevators. "Do you need some time? Want to go upstairs?"

"No," she assured him. "I'm ready. We can go now." She

frowned a bit, realizing that he still hadn't disclosed his plans for the night. "Where are we going?"

He smiled. "I made reservations at Beauty and Essex. Afterwards, I want you to come with me to a party Dru's hosting for one of our primary investors."

They exited through the lobby's revolving doors, and Troy led her toward a black Benz parked at the curb. A well-dressed older black man stepped out of the driver's seat as they approached. He opened the back door and held it ajar as Troy and Crystal approached. She slid her sunglasses on and ducked her head down as they climbed inside the car.

The driver shut the door behind them and then climbed back behind the wheel. He was a very handsome, older black man with salt-and-pepper hair and a neat appearance. He peered at them through the rearview.

Troy leaned forward and smiled. "This is my driver, Butch. And this is Crystal Scott. She's the woman I've been telling you about."

Crystal whipped her head in Troy's direction, surprised. "Telling him what?" she asked. She avoided eye contact with Butch, but was aware that he was smiling at her from the front seat.

"Troy's been telling me how excited he is to work with you. He said you're the reason his father's company has been doing so well."

She chuckled, embarrassed. "That's not entirely true," she said modestly. "I'm just doing my job." From behind her shades, she eyed Troy. She wasn't sure if she liked the idea that he was talking about her to his driver; questioning Oscar about her work habits. His invitation to have coffee, even his plans for tonight, were more than she'd expected in such a short period of time.

Butch had apparently been made aware of their destination in advance. He headed downtown and turned the music up in the car. Some smooth jazz and rhythm-and-blues station that made the trip feel mellow despite the crazy Manhattan traffic. It was obvious that Butch had been doing his job for a long time. He drove so calmly and quietly that it was easy to forget that he was there. Crystal peered at him from behind her sunglasses and noticed that he kept his attention focused on the road and not on their conversation in the backseat.

Troy was regaling her with a story about his meeting with Oscar that afternoon.

"Why do you still have your sunglasses on?" he asked. He gestured out the window at the sun setting low in the distance. "What are you hiding from?"

She shook her head and smiled. "I'm not hiding." She slid them off and turned to face him. "Is that better?"

He smiled back at her. "You're beautiful. Pardon me for saying so. I know that's not professional."

She stared back at him. "Thank you," she said, "you're not so bad yourself. Vanessa is a lucky woman."

He sighed. "Don't be so sure about that. Things ain't always what they seem."

Crystal wondered what he meant by that. He changed the subject before she could ask for clarity.

"My father wants me to step into his shoes and keep the same momentum he has right now. I'm not really used to doing business the way my father does it. My methods can be a little more unorthodox."

Crystal sat back, all ears. "What do you mean?"

He grabbed a bottled water from the console in the backseat and opened it. He took a swig and twisted the cap back on before answering.

"I earned my bachelor's in finance and my MBA at Columbia. After I graduated, I wanted to start my own company. But my father was already established in certain circles and he was just starting to expand into publishing. He wanted me to come on board right away and learn the business from the ground up." Troy glanced out the window a bit wistfully. He shrugged. "Instead, I wound up doing some work with my uncle's nonprofit. That's where my energy was focused for the past few years."

Crystal watched him, aware that he didn't seem very enthusiastic about it. "Sounds like rewarding work," she said archly.

He nodded and turned to face her again. "It was in some ways. But I'm glad to be shifting gears now. This is much different from what I was doing before. In a way, it's more challenging. I'm learning about consumer research and how to stay ahead of the game. At all the meetings I've sat in on, I hear you talking about anticipating which stories are gonna be hot ten weeks from now. I see you making the decision on whether to launch a story online or to put it in one of the print issues. You're out there building relationships and working as a brand ambassador for the magazine and for Stuart Mitchell as a whole. It's impressive, Crystal." He shook his head, his gaze sweeping over her seductively. "And you manage to look good while you're doing it. I need to know your secret."

She laughed as Butch pulled up in front of the restaurant. "Okay, I'll tell you," she said. She lowered her voice as if she were really about to tell him some ancient well-kept secret. "I love what I do."

He smiled. "It's that simple, huh?"

She nodded. "I love the social circles I'm invited into. Working with new writers, serving on panels, building celebrity relationships. None of that feels like work. To be honest with you,

I wake up every morning and have to pinch myself to make sure it's not all some incredible dream."

Butch stepped out of the car and opened the door for Troy and Crystal to emerge. As she stepped out, Butch offered Crystal his hand, smiling. He tried to get a good look at her, but her face was slightly obscured by her long bangs. He did get a good look at her body and he was impressed. Ms. Crystal Scott was built like a brick house. She graciously accepted his hand and thanked him as she and Troy headed inside the restaurant.

"He's sweet," she said. "Has he worked for you long?"

Troy nodded. "Butch has been part of my family for a long time. He's the best."

They followed the waiter to their table and settled in. Crystal didn't bother to really look at the menu. This was one of her favorite restaurants. Clearly, Troy was familiar with the tapas-style fare, as well. He ordered a couple of dishes and one of the restaurant's signature drinks. Crystal did the same and the waiter left them alone at last.

"So, tell me what you think sets *Hipster* apart from the competition." He sipped his water.

"There is no competition as far as I'm concerned. *Hipster* is young and vibrant. Our writers and contributors are bolder and more audacious. We employ more women of color than any of our competitors. And women's voices are crucial in our current climate. We need to hear more of them. Our readers are successful, ambitious people who enjoy pop culture and politics with a twist. That's what we deliver." She shook her head. "I really can't take all of the credit. Oscar is a big reason for the magazine's success. He gets an idea in his head and he runs with it. He's not afraid to go there." She beamed with pride as she spoke of him. "Oscar and I have a chemistry that doesn't come along every day. I trust his vision and he trusts my instincts. It just works."

The waiter brought their drinks and was gone as quickly as he came.

"How do you balance your professional life and your private life?" He sipped his gin.

She noted that he was asking about her personal life again. He had disguised it more cleverly this time, so she gave him points for that.

"Every quarter I take a week off. I visit my family, catch up on my reading, travel."

He nodded. "Where do you travel?" He was picturing that body in a bathing suit.

Her eyes lit up as she spoke of her trips to Europe, South Africa, and most recently to Egypt.

"I traveled alone. It was the most powerful thing I've ever witnessed." She took out her cell phone and showed him pictures she had taken at historic sites during her trip. In each one, her smile shined as bright as the sun. She tucked her phone away and sipped her drink. "Those are the times when all the hard work pays off. When I can travel and see things bigger than I ever dreamed I'd see."

He nodded. He enjoyed hearing her speak so passionately about the things that made her happy.

"The hardest part is remaining impartial," she said. "Trying not to lean too heavily toward the left or the right. Like the Arnold Jackson story. Collectively, we're all angry that this young man and his family have to go through this. But, as a journalist, it's important for us not to condemn law enforcement as a whole. It's not always easy to toe the line."

"I think you're doing a good job," he said. "The magazine is doing well. And that's no easy feat from what I'm told. According to Dru and Eric, print publishing is on life support."

She hated hearing that. But she had to admit it wasn't the first time. "Print isn't dead yet. The Internet and social media have changed the game. No question. But we've changed right along with it, giving the brand more depth by keeping our online profile provocative and competitive. Without a social media presence in this day and age, you're asking to be ignored."

Their food arrived and they both dug in. Crystal filled him in about the meetings she had scheduled later that week with the entertainment director, her senior editors, and the director of operations. He marveled at how she kept it all organized in her mind. She rattled off meeting dates and times like a robot.

She took a bite of a lobster taco and looked at him. "Typically, I met with your father about once a week. He liked to go over everything with all the top people, discuss the editorial calendar, that type of thing." She took a sip of her water. "Do you anticipate keeping that same schedule?"

Troy grinned. In a nutshell, she was wondering how often he would be around. He nodded. "Eventually, I'll be keeping that schedule. But in these early days, I think I'll be there much more often. Just learning the ropes. You know?"

She smirked. "Okay," she said. "That's cool." She watched him as he ate. So well mannered. Her curiosity was piqued.

"Mind if I ask you a personal question?" she asked. She suspected it wouldn't be a problem, considering that he had spent the past hour digging into her private life.

He looked up at her. "Not at all."

She dabbed at her mouth with her napkin. "What was it like growing up as a *Mitchell*?"

Troy laughed. "You make it sound like we're the Jacksons."

She laughed, too. "Well, in publishing and marketing, you kind of are." She sipped her drink. "Your father is a very powerful man."

He nodded. "I've always idolized my dad," he shared. "When I was a kid, I wanted to be just like him when I grew up. I imitated him. Tried to walk like him, talk like him, and all that."

Crystal smiled. "Was your brother the same way?"

Troy's jaw tensed at the mention of Wes. Crystal noticed and hoped that he would reveal the reason for it. He took a long swig of his drink.

"No," he said at last. "My brother never really got over our mother dying. She passed when I was a freshman in high school."

"How did she die?" she asked gently.

"Breast cancer," he said. "It happened so fast. She was diagnosed and then four months later, she was gone." Troy sighed deeply. "Ever since then, my brother's never been the same. My dog died three weeks after my mother. The vet called it 'separation distress.' I think we all had it, honestly. My father threw himself into work even more than he did before. And that's saying a lot, since he was hardly ever home to begin with. My brother started getting in more trouble than ever. It felt like we were watching him self-destruct." He shook his head. "Wes is six years older than me, but he might as well be ten years younger. His mind is . . . he's more like my uncle, Don. I'm more like my dad."

Crystal glanced at him questioningly. "What's the difference?"

Troy shrugged. "My father is rational. Calm. Keeps his hands clean. Uncle Don is . . . I don't know." He seemed to catch himself saying too much. "He's the opposite." He looked at Crystal oddly, aware that he had already said far more than he had intended to. She was so easy to talk to that he had momentarily let down his guard.

Troy's cell phone vibrated and he apologized as he took the call.

"What's up, Dru?"

Crystal listened to his half of the conversation while she finished the last of the tacos.

"Okay," Troy was saying. "I'm on my way."

He summoned the waiter and requested the check. Crystal watched as he slipped a black card into the leather pocket and downed the rest of his drink.

"Dru's party is rocking and he wants me to meet a couple of people. He's at the Boom Boom Room. You heard of it?"

Crystal laughed. "Yes. Of course. Very nice!" She had attended an event at the rooftop lounge at the Standard Hotel before, and easily added it to her list of favorite New York City haunts. All the sexy people hung out at the "Boom Boom Room," as it was known around town. The crowd was sexy, cool, and at times a little spicy. It was the scene of the infamous elevator ride the king and queen of music took after the Met Gala. Tonight Crystal was hoping for a much more peaceful outcome than that. But she was prepared for whatever.

He signed the check, left a generous tip, and confirmed via text that Butch was outside. "You ready?"

She nodded. "Let's go."

FAMILY TIES

Butch was waiting curbside with the same smile on his face. They climbed inside the car and Troy told him they were going to the Standard Hotel. Butch nodded and headed for the Meatpacking District.

Before long, they arrived at the venue and walked inside together. Troy summoned the elevator and stood back while she stepped inside. She couldn't help noting that this was the infamous elevator where Solange had kicked Jay Z's ass. Again Troy admired her hourglass figure in the curve-hugging Chanel.

"I love this place," Crystal said.

He followed her in and eyed her as the elevator doors closed. He felt an indescribable attraction to her that had him standing there doing his best to resist the urge to pin her to the wall and stick his tongue in her mouth.

He cleared his throat. "Thanks for joining me tonight," he said.

She looked at him at last. "I'm glad I came."

Troy watched her hungrily. She fidgeted a bit, unnerved a bit by his clear attraction toward her. She tingled under his gaze.

There was so much unspoken passion and intensity bubbling between them.

The elevator finished its ascent to the top of the eighteen-story building, and they stepped out into the bustling activity of the Boom Boom Room. Crystal looked around and was visibly fascinated by what she saw. The invitation-only event was packed with fabulous, seemingly wealthy people. As she looked around, she caught sight of a few celebrities. Singer Andra Day, stylist and fashion maven June Ambrose, and all around Mr. Entertainment himself, Nick Cannon. The whole venue felt sexy and it pulsated with the presence of important people. It was clear that Dru had pulled out all the stops for this party. The band was going hard and Crystal began to dance without realizing it. She was shocked to see that the Roots were playing, one of her favorite bands. They had the crowd on their feet, dancing, laughing, and enjoying themselves. It was hard not to stop and stare as they entered. But Troy made a beeline for Dru, who was standing at the far end of the room. Impressed, Crystal followed.

The crowd cheered as the legendary Roots crew went *in*, playing their hearts out. The event was littered with famous names in the fields of publishing, music, sports, and politics. Everywhere their gazes fell, a cluster of established household names mingled with more obscure media professionals. It was an exclusive gathering of their counterparts in the magazine and news fields as well as well-known celebrities and their handlers. She and Troy greeted Dru and he introduced Crystal to his wife, Lisa. He also introduced them to two other men nearby who turned out to be the investors he was trying to impress.

"I've been telling Mike and Alan here about the plans we have to take Stuart Mitchell even higher. We have a lot of growth opportunities on the table. If we take advantage of the right ones, the results could be staggering."

Troy nodded. "I like to think of myself as a numbers guy, but Dru makes me look like an amateur. Since he came on board, Stuart Mitchell has already profited. He delivers." He shook his head. "But I'm sure he don't need me to sing his praises. Dru does a good enough job of that all by himself."

The men all laughed, aware that there was some truth in Troy's joke. Dru smiled at his friend.

"Troy's dad is about to run for city council. I think Troy should follow in his footsteps. He could make it all the way to the White House." Dru chuckled.

Troy laughed hard at that. "Too many skeletons in my closet. I'm not a Boy Scout like Barack."

Crystal raised an eyebrow.

Dru laughed. He looked at Crystal. "I'm sorry. How rude of me, Crystal. We should introduce you to these guys."

Troy agreed. "*This* is the person you all need to get familiar with. Crystal Scott is editor in chief at *Hipster* magazine. She's spent the past couple of days showing me why the magazine is leading the competition in newsstand sales, subscriptions, and in ad sales. If anybody is responsible for the profits investors like you have been enjoying, it's Crys."

She smiled, flattered. "Thank you, Troy." Looking at the investors, she turned on the charm. "The best is yet to come. My team and I have some great ideas for how we can advance the brand. I think you'll be pleased."

The investors peppered her with questions about her experience as editor in chief. She answered them and asked a few questions of her own about their investment portfolios and their level of risk. She confessed that she was an amateur investor herself and was interested in learning more. Mike and Alan ate that up and their conversation was effortless.

Crystal was in her element. In her role at the magazine, she attended parties like this on the regular. She caught herself enjoying herself more than usual this time, though. As she chatted with the company's investors and her new bosses, she felt more confident and comfortable in her own skin than she ever had before. She wasn't sure if it was the music, the drinks she'd enjoyed earlier, or Troy's company that had her feeling this way. At the moment, it didn't matter. She felt alive.

Troy stared at her as she spoke. The moment there was a lull in the conversation, he pounced. "I'm gonna steal her away." He took her by the hand. "Dance with me." He smiled, his eyes sparkling in the light.

She followed him to the dance floor and two-stepped with him. He was playful and light on his feet. The Roots were on fire and the dance floor was crowded. His hands encircled her waist as he spun her around. She thought she felt his palm sweep across her ass as she turned, but she wasn't sure. Then he was facing her and she was pressed close against him, their faces merely inches apart. He grinned.

"I like you."

She could feel his hand tightly gripping the small of her back. She could also feel the girth of his woody. "I can tell."

He smiled, encouraged by the fact that she wasn't pulling away.

"Let's get out of here," he suggested. His voice was a husky baritone as his eyes bore into hers. He had a room key in his pocket that he was praying she would want to use.

She smiled at him. The offer was tempting. Troy was handsome, his body was right, and he had charm and power. Crystal found everything about him attractive. But he was her boss. And, even bigger than that, he was the type of guy who expected her to fall into his arms the way that all the other women had. She wasn't about to play into his hands.

"No," she whispered softly. "That wouldn't be a good idea."

He stared at her for several silent moments before his lips spread into a playful grin.

"But you *want* to. Right?"

She watched the way his eyes danced as he spoke. This was a game to him. A game that he was accustomed to winning. She smiled back at him.

"I want a lot of things," she answered.

"Troy," a voice called. Even with the party in full swing around them, the voice cut through the noise. There was a hint of alarm in its tone.

They both turned in the direction of the voice, and Troy's eyes widened at the sight of his fiancée. Vanessa Nolan stepped toward them in a curve-hugging electric blue dress that revealed a flawless figure. She was gorgeous.

Despite her beauty, Vanessa's expression was unnerving. She looked at Crystal icily, then turned her attention to Troy.

"Who is this?" she asked, nodding in Crystal's direction.

Troy let go of Crystal then and instinctively took a step back. Crystal smiled at Vanessa, despite the fact that she looked pissed.

"Vanessa, this is Crystal Scott. She's the editor in chief at *Hipster* magazine." He cleared his throat. "We're working together now. So I brought her here to meet some of our investors."

Vanessa's eyes narrowed suspiciously, but she said nothing.

Crystal extended her hand and waited for the woman to take it. Reluctantly, Vanessa shook it.

"Troy has told me a lot about you," Crystal lied. "Congratulations on your engagement."

Vanessa seemed to relax then. "Thank you."

"Dru didn't tell me you were coming." Troy seemed genuinely confused by her presence there.

"He didn't invite me." Vanessa gestured toward the bar. "I

came with my mother. Your dad told her there was a party here tonight. And you know she loves a party."

Troy and Crystal looked in the direction of the bar and had no problem locating her. Roxy Nolan stood with a drink in one hand and some man's tie in the other. She seemed to be telling a story, demonstratively, evidenced by the small crowd gathered around her. Roxy appeared to be reveling in the attention, laughing giddily at her own tale. She spotted her daughter with Troy and a mystery woman and headed in their direction. Her audience seemed disappointed as they watched her go.

Troy smiled at his future mother-in-law as she headed in their direction. "I thought your parents were flying to L.A. tomorrow."

"They are," Vanessa said. "But not until the afternoon. Daddy is meeting with your uncle in the morning. Then I'm taking them to Teterboro."

Roxy was at their side in moments. Crystal thought she looked even more beautiful than she did in all the magazines she had seen her in while growing up. She had thought Roxy Nolan was the most gorgeous woman alive. Seeing her now, well into her sixties, not much had changed.

"Troy! We were wondering where you were." Roxy planted a big kiss on Troy's cheek and linked her arm through his. She turned her attention to Crystal, flashing her beauty queen smile. "Hello," she sang.

Troy chuckled a bit. "Crys, this is the infamous Roxy Nolan, Vanessa's mother." He looked a bit embarrassed at the moment. "Roxy, this is Crystal Scott, editor in chief at *Hipster*."

Roxy looked impressed. "Wow. Pretty and smart, huh?"

Crystal smiled. "Mrs. Nolan, it's a pleasure to meet you. I've followed your career for years."

Roxy beamed. "How sweet. You can call me Roxy, darling. Everybody does."

Crystal was smiling so hard her cheeks hurt. "Actually, Roxy, I was just speaking to my creative director, Oscar Beane, about featuring you in *Hipster* next year. We prepare our issues months in advance. So we would need to get started soon. But we'd love to have you come in and do an interview and a fashion spread." She noticed the questioning look on Troy's face and hoped that he had no objection to the idea. She couldn't see why he would.

Roxy waved her hand modestly. But Crystal could see the delight she was trying her best to cover up. "Oh, please. I'm just an old lady now, out here trying to hold on to my husband. You should feature Vanessa by herself," she said, nudging her daughter forward subtly. "She's got a new swimwear line."

Crystal feigned interest. "That's great. Maybe a mother-daughter spread then."

Roxy smiled. She loved that idea. "Yes! Vanessa and I can model her swimwear."

Crystal smiled graciously. But the last thing she wanted to see was Roxy Nolan's old ass in swimwear.

Vanessa was practically leaping with joy. "Mom, this is gonna be so much fun!" Vanessa looked at Crystal. "Thank you. We've been trying to convince Fox to let us do a feature in one of his magazines. But he said he doesn't have . . ." Her eyes wandered skyward as if she expected to find the words floating there. She looked at her mother for help. "What did he call it?"

"Creative control." Roxy adjusted the strap on her dress.

Vanessa nodded. "Yeah. So, thank you." She smiled, her gorgeous dimples on display.

Roxy looked Crystal over from head to toe, silently sizing her up. She made a mental note to look into the background of this Crystal Scott. "How soon can we get started?"

Crystal shrugged. "I leave that sort of thing to Oscar. I know he'll be excited to work with both of you. I want you to meet him." She fished around in her bag and produced a business card. She handed it to Roxy. She reached back inside her bag and retrieved one for Vanessa, too.

Troy stepped forward as Vanessa reached for the business card. It seemed like he wanted to intercept it, but Vanessa was too fast. She snapped it up before he could reach for it.

"Wow," he said, watching Vanessa tuck the card into her bag. "Yeah, Crys has a lot of good ideas."

Crystal looked at him and smirked. His tone of voice said that he didn't like the idea one bit. She decided that it was probably time to go.

"Listen, Troy," she said. "Thank you for inviting me tonight. It was great to meet the investors and to talk about the magazine's future. I'm going to head home and get ready for a full day tomorrow." She smiled at both ladies. "It was wonderful to meet you both. I look forward to featuring you in *Hipster*!"

Roxy showered Crystal with air-kisses. She closed her eyes behind the older woman's back.

"Lovely meeting you, dear! Let's do lunch soon!" Roxy sang.

Vanessa was far less dramatic. "Nice to meet you, Crystal," she said simply.

Crystal nodded. She looked at Troy and saw the look of disappointment on his face. She wondered again what was really going on in his personal life. It was clear that his pretty fiancée didn't have his full attention. Crystal told herself that it wasn't her business. She plastered on a smile, bid them all good night, and headed toward the infamous elevator. She had a lot to ponder on the way back to Brooklyn.

CHANGING FACES

Crystal stepped off the curb at the corner of Forty-ninth Street and hailed a taxi to take her the few blocks downtown to *Hipster*'s offices. She had just finished an interview with Tamron Hall on *Today,* where she talked about the Obama legacy and how the votes of black women were more important than ever. She was feeling full of black girl magic as a cab pulled up to the curb beside her and she climbed inside.

"Forty-second and Sixth," she instructed the driver. Normally, she would have walked those few city blocks. But today her towering Charlotte Olympia heels made that impossible. She was smart enough to know that not all shoes are made for walking. Some are meant for sitting pretty on a morning talk show and hopping into a taxi afterward.

On the way, she scrolled through her iPhone and reviewed text messages and e-mails she had gotten while she was working. Her eyes widened at one in particular.

HI, CRYSTAL. THIS IS VANESSA NOLAN.

IT WAS NICE MEETING YOU YESTERDAY.

I'M LOOKING FORWARD TO BEING FEATURED
IN THE MAGAZINE.

Crystal smiled. She saved Vanessa's number in her phone and then dialed her back. She answered quickly.

"Hi, Crystal."

"Vanessa, hey. I got your text message. Thanks for following up so soon."

"No problem," Vanessa said. She sounded much friendlier than she had been the night before. "I'm really excited about doing the shoot."

Crystal pulled a twenty out of her purse and handed it to the driver. "Keep the change," she told him as she climbed out and rushed inside the building. "Vanessa, why don't you come up to the office today? Oscar is here and we can discuss the ideas we have."

Vanessa jumped at the chance. "Okay. What time should I come?"

Crystal used her security keycard to access the bank of elevators. She glanced at her watch. It was just after 10:30 A.M. "How's noon? We can talk to Oscar about the idea, and then go grab a quick lunch."

"Wow," Vanessa said. She couldn't believe how down-to-earth this Crystal Scott was. Initially, she suspected that Crystal might want her man. After watching the two of them interact at the Boom Boom Room last night, she thought they were too close for comfort. Before Vanessa had made her presence known, she had watched Troy dancing with Crystal and looking at her like she was the only woman in the whole room. But now she wondered if she had misinterpreted what she saw. The woman on the other end of this phone sounded harmless. "Okay. I'll see you at noon."

"Great." Crystal hung up and boarded the elevator, grinning from ear to ear.

Troy handed his uncle Don an envelope full of cash. "That's the last of the money Dad owes you." He sat back and loosened his tie. Troy had just come from a trip to the bank with his father. All of the Stuart Mitchell accounts—what was left of them, anyway—had been updated to reflect Troy as CEO, removing Fox from his position at the top of the family food chain. Today marked a changing of the guard in the Mitchell clan and this payment made it official.

Don glanced at the envelope his nephew had passed to him and chuckled a bit. "Is that right?" He picked it up, opened it, and thumbed through the stack of large bills inside. "Why didn't he deliver it himself?"

Troy grinned, though he wasn't really amused by his uncle's facetiousness. The bad blood between Don and Fox ran deep. Much like Troy's relationship with his own brother, Wes. Some pathologies were generational, he realized.

"He has a busy schedule today," Troy lied. "Getting all his ducks in a row for his upcoming campaign."

Don nodded. "Sounds exciting." His tone was flat and emotionless. He smiled at his nephew. "So, now you're the man in charge, huh? How's it feel?"

Troy couldn't suppress his smile. It spread across his face like the Kool-Aid man.

"It feels like this is how it should have been all along. You know, if things had played out the way they should have back in the day." He sipped his water.

Don stared him down. "Sometimes things don't work out like we plan. But in the end everything turns out like it's supposed to. That's how life works."

Troy thought about that. "Maybe you're right." He prepared to leave.

"Wait," Don said. "When's the last time you spoke to your brother?"

Troy laughed, and shifted closer to the edge of his seat. "Probably the last time you spoke to yours." He shook his head. "Why? He do something crazy again? Is he on the run?"

Don sucked his teeth. "You always assume the worst about him."

"You think that's by accident? Or could it be because of all the shit he's got himself into over the years. And you bail him out every time. It's like you're encouraging him."

Don waved his hand at Troy and laughed. "Wes does half the shit he does to get your father's attention. But Fox is too fuckin' worried about you to see that."

Troy stood up. He was ready to go now. "Somebody had to worry about me, right?"

Don didn't respond. Troy's words lingered between them.

"Who else was gonna do it, Uncle Don? Huh? *You?*" He laughed at the absurdity of that. "You take care." Troy walked out, grateful that the business between his father and Uncle Don was concluded. Now he could try to salvage what was left of his freedom and live his life. And his father could do the same. He left his uncle's house and determined in his heart that it would be the last time he set foot in there.

Don, meanwhile, dialed his nephew's cell phone almost as soon as Troy hit the door. Wes answered on the third ring.

"What's up, Uncle Don?"

"Your brother was just here. Looks like Fox put him in charge of everything." Don picked up the envelope and spread the money out on the table to count it. "I don't know if they told you."

Wes was silent for a moment as the gravity of it all sank in.

His father had officially passed him over. Countless times over the years, he had been led to believe that their father loved Troy more. Troy had been given the best education, the biggest parties, the better gifts. And now he had been given the keys to their father's kingdom. A company their parents had built together. Not always by the noblest means, either. Despite the public's perception of their father, Fox had his own skeletons. That was hard to tell now, though. He walked around like his shit didn't stink. So did Troy, as far as Wes was concerned. Finally, he replied, "Thanks for letting me know."

Wes hung up the phone, got off the couch, and put on his Timbs. Grabbing the keys to his truck, he headed out the door. Game on.

Troy walked down the hall toward Crystal's office, and spotted Oscar coming toward him. They greeted each other with a masculine handshake, which Troy appreciated considering Oscar's flair, for lack of a better word.

"How's everything going?" Troy asked. He rationalized his visit today as part of his routine duties as CEO. He had stopped by the offices of *Champion,* the male magazine his family operated as a health and fitness alternative to *Hipster*'s fashion and entertainment vibe. Stopping by here was just par for the course, he told himself. The possibility of running into Crystal was just a nice added bonus.

"I just finished taking a few test shots of your future bride. She is truly beautiful. You're a lucky man, Mr. Mitchell." Oscar smiled, still dazzled by the lovely Vanessa Nolan.

Troy frowned. "She was here?" he asked. "Today?"

Oscar nodded. "She's still here. In Crystal's office."

Troy had a sinking feeling in the pit of his stomach. He forced a smile and headed in that direction.

Crystal sat behind her desk, smiling as she gave Vanessa her full attention. The women had enjoyed lunch at Aureole. Crystal had hoped to get to know the woman a little better and ask some of the burning questions she had. But Oscar had insisted on joining them, hogging the conversation with talk of fashion and entertainment gossip. Now Oscar was gone and Vanessa was telling Crystal the story of her first date with Troy.

"We knew each other growing up. But we didn't really get to know each other until he came home from Howard. Our fathers are friends. So we would be at a lot of the same parties. My father liked him. And, that's saying a lot because Daddy is very protective. Troy had transferred to Columbia. It took him like a year to get up the courage to ask me out." She giggled. "We went to a Lil Wayne concert on our first date."

"What was he like back then?" Crystal asked.

"He was an asshole," Vanessa deadpanned.

Crystal laughed. "Really?"

Vanessa chuckled, too. "He still is sometimes. But that night I could definitely tell that he didn't want to be there."

Crystal's smile faded. She waited for Vanessa to elaborate.

"He was always—"

There was a heavy knock on the door. "Come in," Crystal called out, annoyed by the interruption. To her surprise, Troy walked into the office.

He stood in the doorway and greeted them. His eyes locked on Vanessa, his jaw clenched a bit tightly as Crystal watched.

"What's this?" He plastered a fake smile on his face. But Crystal wasn't fooled by it. Neither was Vanessa apparently. She sat forward in her seat, seemingly alarmed.

"I came to have lunch with Crys," she explained.

Troy frowned. *Crys* now? he thought.

Crystal cleared her throat. "Oscar and I wanted to discuss

the possibility of that photo spread we talked about last night. He has some great concepts."

Troy nodded. He turned back to Vanessa. "Can I talk to you for a minute, please?"

She nodded. "Actually, you can walk me out. I have to rush across town for my nail appointment." She flashed a smile at Crystal. "Thank you for lunch today. I had fun." She reached across the desk and squeezed Crystal's hand gently. "You're easy to talk to!"

Crystal smiled back warmly. "It was my pleasure! We have to do it again soon."

The look on Troy's face was priceless. It was clear, despite the phony grin, that he wasn't comfortable with this. He held the door open for Vanessa, his eyes on Crystal. "I'll be right back," he said.

Crystal nodded, hoping he didn't take too long. Her curiosity was piqued and she had questions.

Troy walked Vanessa down the hall toward the elevator. "What did I tell you?" he asked through clenched teeth. "I don't want you and your mother getting involved in my business here."

Vanessa glared at him. "Nobody's in your business, Troy! It's a damn photo shoot. You're acting like I'm in here going over the bank accounts." She sucked her teeth.

He gripped her arm a little tighter. "I'm serious. Photo shoots lead to interviews, and the next thing you know—all eyes on us. I didn't sign up for that. Your mother likes the spotlight. I don't."

Vanessa stared at him, still confused about why he was making this such a big deal. Ever since Crystal had suggested the idea last night, Troy had voiced his disapproval.

"You like her?" she asked him flat-out. "That's why you don't want me coming up here? You're scared I'm gonna get in the way?"

He laughed. "You're crazy." The elevator doors opened and he gestured toward them. "Go home."

She looked hurt. "Watch how you talk to me." She boarded the elevator and turned back toward him. "You might make me upset."

He laughed and shook his head as the elevator doors closed. He walked back to Crystal's office. He knocked and she beckoned him in.

He stepped inside and looked at her seriously. "We need to talk. Come have a drink with me."

She stood up, grabbed her purse, and followed him out the door. Her instincts told her that now she would begin to finally connect all the dots.

SWEETEST TABOO

They went to a bar two blocks away, found a quiet spot, and ordered drinks. Troy ordered some appetizers that they both picked at while they talked.

"So, was I crazy, or did I detect some tension a little while ago in my office?" Crystal asked. "I didn't mean to start any trouble by having Vanessa in the magazine. I get the sense that you don't approve."

Troy sighed. He looked at Crystal for a few moments, pondering whether or not he should be completely honest. He wanted her to understand a few things. But there was also a lot he didn't want her to know.

"It's like this," he began. "Everything in my family is about image. I'm learning a lot about how my dad represents my family to the people he works with. I speak to the staff and they all have this idealistic view of who we are. Like . . . yesterday, I talked to Marlo Stanton. She told me that my father always brags about my degrees and the fact that I went to an HBCU." Troy laughed. "I went to Howard for *one* semester. Then I transferred to Columbia, where I earned my degrees. But, if you didn't know better, you would think I was the poster boy for historically black colleges." He shook his head. "My father is the king of urban marketing and promotion for a reason. His conversations are like mini–press conferences, full of . . ."

"Shit?" she offered.

He laughed. "I'm not saying that. But my relationship with Vanessa isn't . . . what you might think."

Crystal set her drink down, wondering where this was going.

He shrugged a little. "I guess . . . look." He sighed. "I know I don't have to go into the details of my private life."

Crystal nodded.

"But I'm not like my father. I like to tell it like it is."

Crystal nodded. He had her full attention. She felt like she was getting a coveted peek behind the curtain of the closely guarded Mitchell clan. She was mesmerized. She sipped her drink. She had always known that Fox's carefully crafted façade of a family wasn't as perfect as it seemed. In all the time they had worked together, Fox had spoken of his family only in the most positive light. He regaled Crystal and her staff with news of family gatherings, holiday dinners, and special occasions. She realized now, listening to Troy, that there was much more to the story. She was surprised by his candor.

He continued. "I find it a little harder to play that game. I guess I'll need to learn if I'm gonna take over the company now. I'll have to work on it." He shrugged and looked Crystal in the eye. "But, behind the scenes, I think you'll find that I'm a little more honest than my father."

She nodded. "I like that."

"Good. So Vanessa is someone I care about. But our relationship is more of a merger than a romance." He took a swig of his cognac and watched for Crystal's reaction.

She stared back at him, unsure how to respond.

"Look," Troy said, "Vanessa's dad and mine are good friends. My dad is running for political office. Harvey Nolan has a lot of great connections."

Crystal nodded. She understood it now. "Got it. So you're really just with her to help your father further his political aspirations." She sipped her drink.

He smiled. "In a nutshell. Yes."

"Does Vanessa know that?"

He looked at her strangely. That was a question he hadn't expected. "She's a smart woman." He ate a French fry.

"Okay. I get it."

He shook his head. That was just the least of it. But it was all that Crystal needed to know for now.

"I hope you don't think I'm a dick," Troy said. "I'm not trying to break anybody's heart. Like I said, Vanessa is a smart woman. We're all adults. I'm not proud to admit that I'm not completely in love with the woman I'm engaged to. But, suffice it to say, my family is the most important thing to me."

Crystal nodded. She believed him on that.

"This thing with Vanessa is more for them than it is for me. Most of the things in my life are like that." He shrugged.

She thought of her conversation with Vanessa earlier in her office. Even during lunch, she had seemed more excited about the dresses that were being designed for her than she was about the man she was marrying.

Troy looked seriously at Crystal. "I just don't want her at *Hipster*. You seem like you have your heart set on doing this spread with her and Roxy." He shook his head. "I'd rather you didn't."

Crystal stared at him. "Okay," she said. "I think Oscar might be disappointed. But I'll deal with that." She sipped her drink again, a dozen thoughts in her head. To her, he sounded sad. His tough and confident exterior had cracked. She watched as he downed the rest of his drink and ordered another. She ordered another one, too.

"When I come to work, it's my own world. *My* space." He winked at her. "I don't want those two worlds to collide."

Crystal nodded. "I got it. And I apologize. Now that I know, you don't have to worry about me crossing that line."

"You don't have to apologize," he said. His second drink arrived and he thanked the waitress.

"She's a really nice person, though," Crystal said. "I enjoyed my time with her this afternoon. She seems excited about the wedding." Crystal was replaying their lunch conversation in her mind.

Troy chuckled. "Of course," he said. "Roxy and Vanessa love a reason to get dressed up and shine for the cameras." He swigged his drink. "That's the type of shit they live for."

Crystal rested her elbow on the table, her chin in her hand. "I'm not trying to rub salt in the wound," she said. "But it just sounds . . . kinda sad." She twirled her straw around in her drink. "Have you *ever* been in love?" she asked.

Troy thought about it. He stared down at his drink for a long time. Finally, he nodded. "Yeah. Once I loved a girl. It was a long time ago." He nodded again, slower this time.

"What was her name?"

He locked eyes with her. She gripped her glass, feeling exposed under the weight of his gaze.

"Sydney." He said it without blinking. His tone was flat, unemotional. But his eyes told so much more than that. In them, Crystal saw hurt, regret, and sadness.

Her eyes narrowed. Like a journalist who smelled a good story, she gave him her full attention. She wanted him to keep talking.

"Tell me about that."

He smirked slightly. "My family fucked that up for me, too."

Crystal felt a lump in her throat and swallowed past it.

He seemed lost in thought. She had hit a nerve.

"Why did you let them?" she pressed gently.

He looked up at her. "Family first." He chuckled, tossed back the rest of his drink, and shrugged. "I'm sitting here sounding like a sucker. Complaining, when I have a lot to be grateful for. You can't have it all, right?" He smiled at her.

Crystal didn't smile back. She felt consumed by a sadness so complete that it momentarily paralyzed her. She hated the thought that she might never have it all. She planned to get everything she was owed and then some.

"You good?" he asked.

She snapped out of it and her face slowly softened. She smiled. "Yeah. I just hate to hear a sad love story."

He laughed. "Don't think of it like that. Like I said, life goes on."

He motioned the waitress for the check. When it arrived, he took out his wallet, tossed a bunch of bills on the table, and gestured toward the door. "Butch is outside. Why don't you let me give you a ride home?"

Crystal hesitated. She lived all the way in Brooklyn. Surely, it was out of his way. She thought about it. She was a little tipsy, she reasoned. A ride with Troy would be safe and convenient. Plus, he knew where she lived and he had offered anyway. She nodded. "Thank you. That would be nice."

He smiled, glad that she accepted his offer. They headed outside, and crossed the street to the spot where Troy's Benz was parked.

Butch greeted her with the same smile he had yesterday.

"Crystal! Good to see you again."

She thanked him as he held the car door open for her. Troy climbed in behind her.

"I could get used to this," she said, gesturing toward Butch. "Being chauffeured around the city in style like this is addicting."

Troy smiled. "You should get used to it," he said. "You work hard. You deserve it."

She nodded. "You're right. I do." She opened a bottled water that Butch kept on hand in the backseat and took a sip.

Troy watched her throat as she swallowed. He felt his dick throb at the sight of her throat muscles contracting.

She turned toward him. "I appreciate you filling me in. I don't like to walk into situations blindly, so I'm glad to know where things stand," she said.

He shrugged. "I figured if we're gonna be working together, you need to know the deal. I get the feeling you and I are going to be seeing a lot of each other. I like your energy and I'm impressed by what I see you and Oscar doing. The company needs to take a more aggressive approach in the next few months. And I think you and your team are gonna be the ones to lead the charge."

Butch drove across the Brooklyn Bridge, and the passing streetlights illuminated their faces intermittently. Troy watched the lights dancing on Crystal's face and thought about what Vanessa had said earlier. It was true. He did want to fuck Crystal. It was hard to deny it, considering the involuntary bulge that formed in his pants whenever they were together for long. But as he listened to her speaking now about the respect and admiration she had for his father and for the Stuart Mitchell brand, he suspected that his attraction for her went beyond the physical. Vanessa was beautiful, but she had never stimulated his mind. Not that she was dumb. She wasn't. But she had no depth, no purpose other than to look good and turn heads. Crystal, on the other hand, turned him on not just physically, but mentally as well. She was smart. He had to hand it to his dad. He had chosen wisely with this one.

"Fox gave me the chance to show what I was made of. I'll always be grateful to him for that," she was saying.

Butch pulled up in front of her place and she smiled as he put the car in park.

"Thank you," she said, leaning forward. "You're a great driver. Not like the yellow cab drivers I usually have to deal with."

Butch laughed.

She turned to Troy. He stared out the window at her brownstone.

"Nice place," he said.

She smiled proudly. "Thanks! I love it here." The big apartment was far more than she needed as a single woman. But having the extra space allowed her the freedom to spread out. When she moved there years before, she had fallen in love instantly with the neighborhood. Brooklyn had undergone an incredible facelift, and parts of downtown were really fresh and new. But her Fort Greene block had preserved so much of its Huxtable charm that it was impossible to resist living there.

Troy leaned toward her and grinned, his voice a husky whisper. "You gonna invite me up?"

She giggled and shook her head. "For what?"

He shrugged. "I mean . . . it's the polite thing to do."

She knew where this was heading. She had known it the moment they met. As inappropriate as they both knew it was, the chemistry between them was impossible to deny. She thought about everything he had told her tonight about his complicated relationship with Vanessa. She glanced at Butch to see if he was listening. Troy's driver had mastered the art of rendering himself nearly invisible. If he was listening to their exchange, his face betrayed no signs of it. He stared straight ahead and fiddled with the radio.

"Okay." She said it before she knew it, the effects of the alcohol taking hold. "Come in."

He smiled, thrilled, and followed her out. As she headed up the stairs, he turned to Butch and flashed a grin.

"I'll call you tomorrow."

Butch nodded and gave him a knowing smile. He pulled off and Troy followed Crystal inside.

His eyes scanned the place as he stepped inside. Her living room was dimly lit, but he managed to feel the coziness of the space.

She turned on a lamp nearby. "Can I get you something to drink?"

He shook his head, his eyes canvassing the room. "No. Thank you." He looked around at the art on the walls, at the plush furniture, the candles, exotic sculptures, and all of the books on her shelves. "I love your place."

She smiled modestly. "Thanks. I love it, too."

An awkward silence fell between them. Crystal wondered whether she should offer to show him the rest of the house. But, something felt odd about that, too. He was her boss. The very fact that he was in her home past 10 P.M. was in itself inappropriate. She cleared her throat.

"I'm gonna get a glass of wine. I'll be right back."

He nodded and watched her walk into her kitchen. He stood there for a brief moment before following her.

Troy entered the kitchen and saw her opening a bottle of red wine. A wineglass rested on the counter beside her. Hearing him enter, she gripped the corkscrew in her hand and faced him. He closed the distance between them quickly, catching her a little by surprise. She backed up.

He cornered her, hovering over her as she stood with her back pressed flat against the wall. He leaned in to kiss her and she bit his lip, drawing blood.

He drew back and looked at her, his eyes wide. She stared back at him in silence, aware now that she still held the corkscrew in her hand. She had been squeezing it so tightly that her hand now bore the imprint of it. Troy looked at her, unsure. She stood like she was ready to fight. But she had the slightest smirk on her face. Her eyes were playful. He wasn't sure whether to be mad or aroused. Tentatively, he stepped toward her again and pulled her into his arms.

She could practically hear her own heart beating fast in her chest. His hand gripped hers and he pried the corkscrew from it, placing it on the counter beside him. He took her face in his hand gently, his eyes locked with hers.

"Don't bite."

Lightly, his lips brushed hers. He kissed her softly and she let him. Slowly, he released the grip he had on her face and his hands roamed her body. It felt like every molecule she possessed responded to his touch. She pushed him away, but he didn't budge. She tried to turn her face away and he kissed her again, deeper this time. She held on to his arms, torn between battle and surrender.

She couldn't deny how badly she wanted him. Pressed against the wall, under the weight of his body and his desire for her, she gave in.

"Come with me," she whispered breathlessly in his ear. She led him by the hand up the stairs to her bedroom.

She opened the door and he stepped inside and scanned the room. She was neat. All of her accessories were piled on top of a glass table. Her perfume and makeup rested on a dainty vanity against the wall. He walked through her room, seeing her in all of the details. There were more books in here, and he smiled at her orderliness, her attention to detail.

She stepped toward him. This time, she was the one who initiated the kiss. She clung to him. Her kiss intensified and he could feel her nipples pressing against his hands. She bit him again, even harder this time, and he drew back in pain.

Crystal laughed. He tried to remember what she was drinking tonight. Whatever it was, it was making her wild. The metallic taste of blood was sobering him up quickly.

She stepped toward him and he fought the urge to retreat. He felt like a punk for even considering it.

She stood inches from him, grinning like she could read his mind.

"Let's play," she whispered. Even in the darkness of the room, he could see the smile in her eyes. She walked over to the bed, lying down on top of it.

He followed her, aware that his lip was starting to swell up. Oddly, it turned him on. It was clear that she liked it rough. He climbed on top of her and nudged her legs wide. He peeled himself out of his shirt, peering down at her mercilessly.

"You want to play?"

Crystal nodded, her lips puckered playfully. She slapped him so hard across his face that the sound resonated in the room.

He recoiled, then grabbed her by the throat and stuck his tongue in her mouth. She tried to bite him, but he was too fast. He pulled away and slapped her back, though not as hard. She held her face, momentarily dazed. He was the one laughing now. But it only encouraged her. She clawed at him, digging her nails into him so deeply that he backed off of the bed. When he was no longer on top of her, she lunged at him, scratching wildly.

Troy swatted her hands away, then grabbed a good handful of her dress and tore the fabric roughly from her body. She felt a twang of regret at the sight of the shredded designer frock at her feet. That was one of her favorite DVF dresses.

In her hesitation, he pulled her toward him and gripped her in a bear hug. Her La Perla bra and panties were the only barrier between her skin and his. She gasped a bit at the sensation of flesh against flesh.

"Stop fighting me!" His voice was stern and he tightened his grip on her.

She chuckled again, amused by his frustration. She knew a man like Troy was used to having things his way. As badly as she wanted him, she was determined to make him work for it.

He scooped her up and carried her back to the bed. Loosening his grip, he spun her around, kissing her neck, sucking on it. She moaned and he spanked her hard on her ass, eliciting a yelp of delight. She turned around and faced him again, grabbed his face roughly, and kissed him. Troy was so hard he could barely contain himself.

"Damn," he whispered, his lips tickling her ear. His hands gripped her ass, squeezing it tightly, kneading it with increasing desperation. Despite the effects of the alcohol and the bliss Troy was making her feel, she was aware in that moment that they were crossing a very dangerous line. She no longer cared. In reality, she reasoned, that line had been crossed a long time ago.

Troy tried his best not to rush. He wanted her so badly that it surprised him. He stripped down to his boxers, the sparse moonlight shining on his chiseled physique through her venetian blinds. She discarded her bra, but kept her panties on. His hands roamed her body, caressing her shoulders, her arms, her waist. With painstaking patience, his touch wandered up to her breasts, stroking them until a moan escaped her parted lips.

His hand stroked the outside of her panties. She swallowed, her mouth suddenly dry. Up and down, he brushed her lips through the thin material. Back and forth, like a guitarist expertly pulling her strings. The sensation sent shivers through her body and she grinded her hips upward into his hand.

Troy watched her, smirking. She had her eyes closed and passion soaked her as he toyed with her. She spread her legs wider, welcoming his touch, beckoning him further.

He slid one hand inside her panties, cupping her hot wetness in the palm of his hand. Her heart galloped so fast she worried that she might self-destruct. She felt feverish with longing for him. He gripped her tighter there, palming her pussy in his hand, his thumb brushing hard against her clit.

"Yeah . . ." Crystal purred. Her face looked so rapturous and sexy. Her hands roamed her own body, as she thrust against him. She spread her legs wider. Her moans got louder.

Troy watched her, aware of every subtle change in her body, and it excited him. He squeezed and touched, rubbing her clit, and pressing against it so expertly that she felt herself rising toward her peak. He slid her panties off and worked his finger inside of her, pushing her thighs apart even wider. Crystal's walls felt so tight and she was audibly wet. Her slickness sounded like waves crashing against the shore as he slid his fingers in and out of her. The sound of it, mingled with her soft sweet moans, drove him crazy.

"Damn," he whispered breathlessly. With his free hand, he teased her nipples, which stood hard against the darkness of the room, begging for attention. He kissed her and she gripped his face tightly between her hands, pulling him closer.

The feeling of her clawing at him anxiously caused a low growl to escape from somewhere deep inside of Troy. He bit her lip, then sucked it softly. Crystal could feel his hardness between her legs leaping in response to their desire for each other, filled to the tip with desire.

Troy reached down, and unleashed his warrior. Her eyes widened at the sight of it. She took a breath. He was *blessed*. She took him into her hands, stroking all of him firmly. She wanted to memorize its structure and mass. Surely, this could only happen this one night. She had to make the most of it, searing the feeling of him into her memory. She spread her legs apart and grabbed the length of his dick with one hand, squeezing the head with the other.

He growled deeply and pinned her hands above her head. Looking deep into her eyes, he licked his lips, then planted a trail of kisses from her chin downward, stopping just below her belly button.

Troy positioned himself between her legs with his face hovering erotically above her kitten. He blew on her pussy softly. Her legs quaked in anticipation. He scooped one hand firmly beneath her, gripping her ass in his palm. With the other, he spread her pussy lips apart, exposing her clit, and dove in.

Crystal moaned deeply at the sensation of his mouth on her. Troy's tongue flickered as she fought the urge to pass out from pure ecstasy.

"Oh . . . *shit!*"

His mouth completely, unrelentingly devoured her sex. She grabbed his head between her delicate hands. The power of him was evident then. The passion. It rendered Crystal helpless. She watched him, his hands spreading her wider, his lips covering her clit, his head moving erotically between her legs. Troy inserted two fingers, stroking her inner walls while sucking her pussy like a champion.

She felt herself building toward her climax. Troy knew it, too. Her hips rocked against his face as he ate her. She tasted sweet, her body so tender and soft. His fingers worked magic inside of her and she grinded her hips back at him, intensifying the pleasure. He feasted on her, grunting encouragingly as she came, shuddering and spent, while Troy lapped away at her without ceasing.

Her legs trembled and she held the sheets tightly between her fisted hands as he slowed down, sucking gently until she could no longer stand it. She cried out in anguish until finally, he eased up, releasing her from his mouth, and kissed the insides of her thighs gently. Crystal wanted him inside of her. She pulled him closer, longing to feel the fullness of him within her walls. She breathlessly crawled over and reached into the top drawer at her bedside. She produced a condom and slid it on him, kissing him hungrily. He gripped Crystal around her waist and flipped her over on all fours.

She felt her excitement soar. She lowered her face and shoulders until they were flat against the mattress, tooting her ass in the air toward him bravely. He slapped it, sending a sharp sound reverberating throughout the room, and she cried out in response. He did it again. This time she pushed herself back against him, causing his manhood to leap in anticipation. He eased her lips apart and nudged himself toward her opening, still slick from the orgasm she'd already experienced.

Troy entered her slowly, gently pushing himself deeper inside her, filling every inch of Crystal until she was overflowing with pleasure. His hands caressed her body while he stroked her, toying with her while he plunged deeper with each stroke. His rhythm quickened and the sound of their bodies clapping together in such raw and forbidden passion aroused her even further.

"Yeah," he breathed.

With her back arched like a cat and her ass high in the air,

Crystal groaned with each thrust. He filled parts of her she had never before discovered, forcing her to cry out in ecstasy. Again she climaxed, this time the sensation of her orgasm throbbing against him. Troy did his best to restrain himself, aware that the full power of his size was more than she could accommodate. But Crystal's body, her moans, the way she held on to the sheets for dear life—it overpowered him. He sank himself deeper inside of her and held on tightly as her body tensed beneath him.

She groaned, feeling the most intense mixture of pleasure and pain. Troy was filling her body to its capacity.

"Wait," she pleaded breathlessly. "Please."

Troy steadied his breathing, forcing himself to relax. The last thing he wanted to do was hurt her. He pulled himself out of her and turned her over. Despite the physical desire he felt for her, this moment was more than just a physical thing. He connected with Crystal on a whole new level. He hadn't been this excited about anything in a very long time. As he lowered himself on top of her, kissing her deeply, he reentered her at a slower pace. To her amazement, she had yet another orgasm. Troy joined her soon afterward.

They lay together in bed with their legs intertwined. She lay her head on his chest, rising and falling as the pace of his breath slowly steadied. He held on to her tightly, his fingers in her hair. He wasn't sure what he was feeling. He had no words for it. Only the swell of emotions he felt as he lay there holding her in his arms.

Crystal's breath came fast, then slowly steadied. He pulled her closer toward him, seemingly determined to soak up every inch of her.

"You're aggressive," he said.

She laughed.

He touched his lip. "I'm gonna look crazy in my meetings for the next few days."

She made a sad face. "I'm sorry. I get a little freaky sometimes when I drink tequila." She leaned back against the pillows. The truth was she had been fighting her desire for him. Her bites, scratches, and kicks were all in retaliation against herself, against the incredible way he had her feeling long before he even touched her.

"Crystal." He breathed her name so eagerly. She didn't protest when he kissed her. Didn't fight back this time. They made tender, sweet love all night, the sounds of their passion echoing off the walls of her brownstone.

She lay awake, watching him sleep at 4:15 A.M. the next morning. She dreaded the impending sunrise. She watched for signs of it through the parted curtains that morning, wishing it would be miraculously delayed somehow. She needed time to process everything. Her mind was still reeling from what they'd done. Troy had fucked her in every possible way. She felt the welcome soreness of extraordinary sex between her legs and watched his chest rise and fall as he breathed.

Finally, she drifted off to sleep, but woke soon after and watched him some more. Even as it lay limp against his thigh, his dick was impressive in size. She chided herself, aware that she was capturing snapshots of him that she might conjure up later when he wasn't around. She checked herself. There would be no staring out the window days from now, reflecting on this moment. She could not allow herself to catch feelings of any kind for this man.

She rose before the sun that morning. She climbed out of bed while the sky was still dark, careful not to wake him, and headed for the bathroom. Staring at her reflection in the mirror, she shook her head. Last night had been a mistake. Closing her eyes, she reminisced about the feeling of his hands on her, inside of her, his mouth in both places, too. For better or worse, there was no turning back now.

She had sobered up watching him sleep. She couldn't imagine how they might move forward, how some normalcy might emerge from all of this messiness. She relieved herself on her fancy toilet, aware that her pussy was swollen and tender to the touch. Troy had consumed her wholly, owning her inside and out. And she had loved every erotic second of it.

She turned the shower on and stepped into the stream of water, lathering up with flashbacks teasing her each time she shut her eyes.

She forced the guilty thoughts to the furthest corners of her mind, denying herself the agony of beating herself up over thoughts of his fiancée. A woman she had broken bread with. Instead, she focused on tenderly washing the places he had sullied her. She smiled as she slowly lathered her lady parts, Troy's mark evident in every crevice.

She gasped a bit when he slid the shower door open and stepped inside with her.

"Good morning," he said, his voice still husky with sleep. He kissed her on her forehead and used his hands to soap up her body.

She exhaled, relishing the feeling of his hands against her skin once more. She returned the favor, washing his toned physique as the water cascaded around them.

"You're up early," he said.

"Yeah. I always am."

He rinsed off, the water dousing his face and clinging to his skin.

She watched him. His body was mouthwatering. She saw the scratches she had left on his body and wondered for a second how he would explain them.

He kissed her gently on the lips. "What are you doing today?"

She marveled at the fact that he wasn't in a rush to get home and make excuses for spending the night out. He wasn't acting like a man who was about to get married. She decided there must be some truth to the things he had told her last night.

"I have plans today," she said simply.

He nodded, disappointed. She stepped out of the shower and he followed her. She passed him a towel.

She wrapped one around herself and walked over to her sink. She grabbed her toothbrush, and set about rinsing the taste of him into the stream of cool water pouring forth from the faucet. Standing upright again, she met her reflection in the mirror. He was standing behind her now. He wasn't touching her, and yet she felt him all over her. They studied their reflections in silence together. Though neither of them spoke, so much was said in those moments. Things were so complicated between them, and yet there they were.

His hands circled her waist at last. She leaned back into him and closed her eyes. Strangely, this was the safest she had felt in a very long time.

"I want to see you tonight. After you do all the things you need to do today."

She shook her head. "I'm leaving for Maryland this afternoon. Thanksgiving is tomorrow, remember?"

"Damn." He inhaled the scent of her. Thanksgiving had been the furthest thing from his mind. "Forgot about that."

She turned to face him. "We can't keep this up anyway," she said softly. "We both know that."

He stared down at her and wasn't sure how it was possible

that she looked even more beautiful than she had last night. Her hair was tousled and her face was void of any makeup, but she looked more radiant than ever.

He didn't respond. The silence between them lingered as he dressed and gathered his things. He called Butch to come and get him, his voice full of sadness that their time together had to end. Crystal wrapped a bathrobe around her nakedness and she didn't protest when he snatched her up by the door, showering her with kisses, nibbling at her ear, neck, and her lips.

When Butch arrived, she walked Troy downstairs, their fingers intertwined until they reached her front door.

He leaned in and kissed her lightly. Their eyes locked afterward and he dreaded the thought of leaving her. Again he marveled at what she was making him feel.

"This ain't over," he whispered, his lips tickling her ear. He kissed her cheek, then forced himself to let go of her. He walked out to his car, greeted Butch, and climbed inside. Crystal stood behind her door and watched them drive away. She wasn't sure how to explain the tears that pooled in her eyes or the lump that formed in her throat. She didn't know whether she was happy or sad. For the first time in a long time, she didn't have the answers.

HOME SWEET HOME

The drive down to Maryland felt longer than usual. And not just because of the holiday traffic. Crystal had so much on her mind. She had taken another shower after Troy left, and cleaned her apartment from top to bottom. It was her way of erasing any trace of him. Any remnant of what they had done. She had changed the linens on her bed, washed her hair, gotten a fresh mani-pedi. And still, as she gripped the wheel of her car driving blindly through the bumper-to-bumper traffic on I-95, she couldn't forget the way he had made her feel.

Despite her attempts to focus on the beautiful fall foliage and the scenery as she drove, her mind continuously wandered back to Troy. He had texted her when he got home, letting her know that she was still on his mind. She didn't reply. Instead, she turned off her phone and put it on the charger while she finished packing the last of her things. She had to prepare mentally and emotionally for returning home to her family for the holidays. Not that she didn't love them. She certainly did. But the memories that always surfaced were tough to deal with.

As she pulled into the driveway of her mother's beautiful

home in Germantown, Maryland, she breathed a deep sigh. This was the home where she had transformed into a self-assured and self-made woman. This was where she had come to know a life without her brother and a void so deep that it ached.

She used her key and let herself in. The moment the door swung open, she was greeted by Destiny.

"Hey, cuzzo. What's up?" Destiny stood beaming at her, wearing an apron and holding a large spoon. She had taken the train down ahead of Crystal two days ago. She hugged her, getting a little flour on her from the cakes she had been baking. "You look good! What you been doing?" Every time Destiny saw Crystal she looked better and better. After college, she had gotten a nose job and lost a bunch of weight. She started wearing makeup, getting her hair done, and going to the gym. Before long, Destiny could barely recognize her cousin.

Crystal laughed. "Nothing. Just working hard. That's all."

Destiny wiped her sweat with a towel, and glanced toward the kitchen. "Girl, Mama got me going hard in the kitchen. You know how she gets down."

Crystal laughed. She did know. Aunt Pat *loved* to cook. It was a trait she had inherited from Crystal's grandmother. Creating delicious meals with no regard for caloric content was what the women of the family were known for. Unfortunately for Crystal and Malik, *their* mother, Georgi, hadn't been as blessed in the culinary department. She had no desire to slave over a hot stove unless it was absolutely necessary. Typically, she cooked on Thanksgiving and Christmas. Every other night of the year while they were growing up, Crystal and Malik survived on fast food, their own culinary concoctions, or they ate at Aunt Pat's house.

"What's she making?" Crystal asked.

"Everything! Every time I go to the supermarket, she sends

me back for more shit. She's the reason I'm still fat." Destiny giggled, only half-kidding.

Crystal was well aware of her cousin's struggles with weight. Now that Destiny was turning thirty in a few days, she was trying to get a handle on her food issues before they resulted in diabetes or hypertension. Those were the things that ended their grandmother's life so early.

Destiny looked her cousin over from head to toe. She narrowed her eyes at her, leaned in, and whispered, "When these heifers go to bed, you better tell me what's been going on with you and Wonder Boy. I've been waiting for you to call me with the tea, bitch!"

Crystal giggled. "Okay. Later on."

Crystal set her bags near the stairs and looked around. She remembered moving into this house with her mother after the robbery. Buying new furniture, painting, starting over. It had been a sad time for Crystal. Not just because Malik was gone. It was the realization that she would have to leave Howard University, now that her parents could no longer afford the tuition. She had been tempted to drop out of college altogether. She felt tired of trying. But, after a few weeks of feeling sorry for herself, she had enrolled at the University of Maryland. She had dreams to chase, after all. She became obsessed with the notion of finishing school, despite the expense of it. She had accomplished that earning scholarships, and taking out loans until she graduated. She earned her degree, moved to New York, and rented a studio apartment on the Lower East Side. She paid off her student debt using half of her salary at *Sable,* and maintained excellent credit. The first major purchase she made was paying off her mother's house.

Destiny always felt like her cousin felt guilty for what happened to Malik. Everything she did seemed to be an attempt to repay a debt she somehow believed she owed to her family. Soon, her father was coming home, and she would be repeating the pattern. Crystal was the one making sure he got back on his feet, and she wouldn't have it any other way. As far as she saw it, she owed a debt to him, too.

Crystal followed Destiny into the kitchen where she saw her mother sitting at the table. Georgi wore a black V-neck sweater and jeans. Her hair was longer now, hanging just past her shoulders. It had taken years to grow back after the robbery left her with bald spots and breakage. The damage done to her confidence had been much worse, though. Gone was the Georgi who had taken the eighties by storm on the arm of Quincy. Now, she was more inclined to spend a weekend at home with her alarm system activated and her gun at her bedside. She went out from time to time. But these days she spent most of her time in seclusion, emerging every now and then to slay at an event one of her friends or family invited her to.

Georgi smiled at the sight of her daughter. She saw less and less of her these days, busy as she was with her duties at the magazine.

"Hey, sweetie." Georgi's smile only made her look lovelier.

Crys greeted her mother with a long hug and a kiss on the cheek. "Hey, Mommy. You look nice."

Georgi thanked her and returned the compliment.

Aunt Pat stood by the stove, preparing her famous peach cobbler. She beamed when she saw her niece. Crystal looked incredible. She wore jeans that hugged her toned curves so tightly they seemed painted on. Her little cream-colored turtleneck and leather motorcycle jacket clung to her frame like they were custom-made. Crystal smiled at her aunt brightly.

Pat looked down and checked out Crystal's footwear. She always wore the most beautiful shoes, and today she didn't disappoint. She rocked a pair of black suede stiletto boots that made her appear six feet tall.

"Damn, you look good, girl!" Pat smiled proudly and hugged her tightly. She had been sipping some cognac while she cooked, and Crystal caught a whiff as Pat stood back in her apron and head scarf. "I love this new hair! Turn around, let me get a good look at you."

Crystal did as she was told, and Aunt Pat gushed about her new look before turning to shut off the butter she had melting on the stove.

"It smells so good in here!" Crystal looked around for something she could nibble on.

Aunt Pat shook her head, and shut those hopes down immediately.

"You know I don't play that. Go take your jacket off, wash your hands, and come in here correct before you start nibbling. Always running in here smelling like outside looking for something to eat. Been doing that since you was a kid!" Pat chastised her, smiling at the memory of her niece as a sweet wide-eyed little girl. These days, she was a tough-as-nails executive up in New York City. It was too much as far as Pat was concerned and she was worried about her niece. They all were, in fact.

Crystal laughed and apologized. Even though this was her mother's kitchen and not her aunt's, she knew better than to talk back. Aunt Pat was one of the few people in the world she could accept a scolding from. Aunt Pat's house had been like a second home to her. In some ways, she had mothered Crystal more than Georgi had. Not that she didn't love her mother. Georgi had raised Crystal and her brother well. But it had been Aunt Pat who nurtured and nourished Crystal's soul, often serving as her motivator and pep talker. She had driven the message home clearly that Destiny and Crystal never needed to compete with anyone else.

Aunt Pat was confident, laid-back, and down to earth. The complete opposite of Crystal's mother, Georgi. As little girls, Pat and Georgi hadn't really been close. Georgi was the beauty of the pair. Or at least the superficial definition of beauty that men seemed to gravitate toward. Crystal's mom had the winning combination of a big ass, long hair, and a tiny waist. Her face was also lovely. But with a closer look, and a little conversation, most people quickly surmised that she was shallow, self-absorbed, and utterly neurotic about her looks. Already beautiful, she still spent a small fortune getting her hair and nails done every week. At least, that had been the case in her heyday.

Aunt Pat, on the other hand, couldn't care less about what anyone thought. Of the sisters, Pat had been closer to their mother, Bonnie. While Georgi was out painting the town on the arm of Crystal's father, Pat was at home, gleaning wisdom from their mother. Learning that the silent one is usually the most powerful one. It took Georgi a little longer to figure that out.

Crystal returned to the living room now and retrieved her bag. She kicked off her shoes and carried them to her room. She stepped inside and looked around. Everything was so neat and in its place. Exactly the way she liked it. As a child, she had always been orderly, even painstaking in her placement of things. It was a trait she had carried into adulthood. Always having her ducks in a row. She set her bag and shoes down and went to the bathroom and freshened up before going back downstairs.

She shoved her cousin playfully in the arm when she came back in the kitchen.

"Happy birthday!" She hugged her and handed her the large bag in her hand. "I hope they fit, but if not there's a gift receipt inside."

Destiny squealed, and wasted no time opening her gift. While she did so, Crystal pulled up a seat at the long oak wood table and set two smaller bags on top of it.

"Who are those for?" Georgi asked.

"You and Aunt Pat," Crystal said. "I saw them on sale, and thought you both would like them."

Pat frowned. "Why are you giving us gifts now when Christmas is right around the corner?" She set some fried chicken on the table. "It's Destiny's birthday, not ours."

Crystal marveled at the fact that Aunt Pat was frying a full feast although Thanksgiving was the next day. This was the type of eating Crystal tried hard to avoid, knowing what it did to her petite frame. She told herself that the holidays were an exception. She dug in. Comfort food was just what the doctor ordered.

She poured herself a glass from the bottle of wine on the table and shrugged.

"Like I said, they were on sale and I thought you would like it. It's no big deal." Truth was, she was feeling guilty as hell for the things she had done with Troy the night before.

Georgi opened a pair of diamond stud earrings. Aunt Pat's were pearl. Destiny got a pair of Jimmy Choo boots. Everyone gushed over their gifts and thanked her.

Pat set a platter of mashed potatoes on the table and paused to say grace.

"God, thank you for Destiny, and for bringing us all together to celebrate her thirtieth birthday. Thank you for bringing our prodigal daughter home safely down the highways and byways, and help us to talk some sense into her while she's here. Bless this food that we are about to enjoy. Amen."

In unison, the women said, "Amen."

Crystal eyed her aunt, her face twisted into a grimace. "The *prodigal daughter*? Really?" She piled her plate moderately, doing her best not to overdo it. She wanted to save some of her naughty calories for her aunt's cornbread stuffing and desserts tomorrow. She glanced at her mother, hoping Georgi might come to her defense. Instead, Georgi kept her eyes downcast, and sipped her wine.

"Just messing with you, baby. You know I'm just glad you're home." Pat winked at her. She set a box down in front of her daughter, and sat back, waiting to see her open it. Destiny set her fork down, and grabbed the blue box, pulling the ribbon off. She unwrapped it to reveal a long narrow black box. Inside she found a topaz bracelet and matching earrings. She gasped.

"It's my birthstone!" she gushed.

Pat laughed, thrilled that she clearly loved her gift.

Georgi pulled out her niece's gift. It was a beautiful coat. Destiny thanked them all for their presents, and gushed about all the delicious food she had helped herself to. The four of them passed the spread around, enjoying Pat's good cooking.

"So, how was the drive?" Georgi asked. She sucked on a piece of perfectly seasoned chicken.

"There was a little traffic," Crystal said. "But it forced me to sit still for the first time in weeks. I've been on the go lately." That was putting it mildly.

"How's everything going at work?" Destiny asked.

Crystal looked at her mother and her aunt, waiting for them to pounce. Neither of them made eye contact with her, though, focusing instead on their meal.

"Fine," Crystal answered flatly. "There's a lot going on right now. But I have it all under control."

Georgi's eyes darted toward her then. "Do you?"

Crystal nodded, though she didn't meet her gaze. "Yes, I do." She sipped her wine.

Georgi was far from done. "What about your father? Have

you thought about what I said? How crazy it is for him to parole to the very place he got locked up?"

Crystal sighed. "Do we have to do this now?"

Georgi slammed her hand on the table. "You're so damn stubborn!"

Silence reverberated through the kitchen. Aunt Pat and Destiny froze. Crystal stared at her mother.

"Why are you blaming me?" Her voice was small, almost childlike. "Daddy has a mind of his own. He had the choice of coming here or going to Brooklyn. *He* made the choice. I'm just doing my part."

"What you're doing is handing him a gun and pointing—"

"Now you're just being ridiculous!" Crystal stood up and prepared to leave. This was the last thing she needed right now.

Aunt Pat intervened. "Georgi, you gotta calm the fuck down in here!" She frowned at her sister. "You have things you need to say to your daughter. Fine! But why you gotta ambush her before she can even finish her food?" She gestured toward Destiny. "It's her birthday. Can't we just eat, and let the child rest after doing all that driving today?"

Georgi shrugged and turned her attention back to her food. Fuck it. She was done talking for now.

Pat looked at Crystal. "Sit down, baby. Come on." Pat lived in a gated community not far from the one her sister lived in. She and Destiny had decided to spend the night at Georgi's to help her get things ready for their holiday meal the next day. Now, seeing the tension between Georgi and her only surviving child, Pat was glad she was there to referee.

Crystal returned to her seat and avoided looking in her mother's direction. She could tell how the next couple of days would go. Ever since her father had defied his wife's wishes, things in the family had been tense. Georgi was scared to death of what might happen. Echoes of the robbery in Staten Island all those years ago came flooding back each time she thought about it.

She looked at her daughter now. "I'm just scared. You have to understand that."

Crystal continued chewing her food, but nodded slowly.

"We all lost so much already. Your father has been in jail for twenty-five years. They would love to send him back there to do twenty-five more. All it'll take is one little mistake. One wrong move." Georgi's eyes bore into her daughter.

Crystal finally looked up and locked eyes with her. "He won't make any mistakes. I'll be right there to make sure that he doesn't."

Georgi stared at her and sighed. Her baby sounded so sure. "And what about you? Who's watching after you?"

"Do I need to remind you that I've been doing pretty well all by myself these past few years? I don't need anybody to have my back. God's got my back."

"Amen." Destiny winked at her cousin and attempted to sway the conversation elsewhere.

"Aunt Georgi, are you really upset because you won't be able to see Uncle Quincy when he comes home all toned and fit after working out all these years?" Destiny pretended not to notice the look her mother shot her way. She knew the question was provocative. But it was her birthday celebration and she knew that tonight she could get away with asking the question that had been burning in her mind for weeks.

Georgi sucked her teeth and tossed an ice cube at Destiny. "Shut up!" She laughed. "I don't want to be with Quincy."

Destiny and Aunt Pat both twisted their faces in disbelief.

"Tell the truth. You still love him, Aunt Georgi?"

Georgi cleared her throat. "I guess . . . part of me is always gonna love him. He was my husband and we had a family. But some of the decisions he made . . . some of the people he chose to be around . . ." Georgi's voice trailed off, and she shook her head. "That cost us a lot." She had often imagined what life might have been like if Quincy had never gotten caught up the way that he did. If he hadn't been the one to ride shotgun on that robbery in the Diamond District, their story might have turned out quite differently. They might have settled into a life of simplicity and normalcy, raising their kids together without all the scars they all bore now.

Crystal stared down at her plate, her appetite suddenly waning.

Georgi chuckled about it, as she strolled down memory lane a little. She looked at Crystal and Destiny. "Your grandmother hated him."

Pat chuckled, too. "She sure did. She wanted both of us to marry doctors, lawyers. Like we didn't grow up in the hood." Pat didn't mean to make it sound impossible, but the odds were slim. "Georgi and I liked bad boys, but Mama did all she could to change our minds."

"Eventually, even Mama had to admit that Quincy really loved me. He made that very clear over the years. He took care of business and kept us all afloat by any means." Georgi sipped her wine again. "I loved him, too. I really did. If he hadn't gone away, we'd probably still be together."

Silence enfolded them again. Finally, Georgi's laughter broke the ice.

"Pat, remember that time Mama set you up with the guy from the choir?" Georgi could barely contain herself.

Pat gave her a side-eye. "That wasn't funny. That guy was corny as hell."

Georgi kept laughing and Crystal and Destiny joined in. They couldn't imagine Pat with a man who wouldn't approve of her cussing and occasional weed-smoking.

Georgi took a sip of her drink and exhaled at that long-ago memory. "Quincy was always a good man, though. He loved his family. Now that he's coming home, I really just want the best for him. I just want him to be safe."

Destiny swigged the last of her wine and refilled her glass. "I believe in real love. Maybe he'll wind up moving down here after all. I bet you he never stopped loving you. You two can be together again and get it right this time."

Pat smiled. "That would be nice. I would love to see the story end that way."

Georgi shrugged and took another bite of her chicken.

"Did you know Mama has a new boyfriend?" Destiny nodded in her mother's direction. "Mmm-hmm. Aunt Georgi told me."

Aunt Pat stared at her, openmouthed. "If you don't shut your mouth—"

"Met him at the grocery store in the produce aisle," Georgi chimed in.

Crystal laughed while her aunt hurled curse words at all of them.

"Y'all stay out my damn business."

Everyone finished their meal, and sang happy birthday to Destiny. She made a wish, cut the cake, and the conversation focused on the demise of her recent relationship. She was optimistic that she would find love again. As long as her next man had a real job.

When they were finished, Crystal carried her plate to the sink. Aunt Pat met her there.

"You know your mama worries about you. That's all it is."

Crystal nodded. "I know."

"She lost so much already. All of us did. But she couldn't stand it happening again." Pat didn't flinch as she spoke. "She couldn't stand it."

Crystal got the message. Her aunt took the plate out of her hand and shooed her away.

She cleared her throat. "I'm a little tired after that long trip," she said. She yawned for good measure. "I'm gonna call it a night so that I can wake up early and help you all cook."

Destiny and Aunt Pat laughed loudly.

"Please, boo. Don't nobody need you burning the house down. Just bartend like you do every year."

Crystal rolled her eyes at Destiny and laughed.

Destiny tossed her napkin in the trash. "Let me holla at you for a minute."

She walked upstairs with Crystal to her room and shut the door. Crystal sat on the bed and prepared for the interrogation.

"Have you slept with him?" She asked the question more bluntly than she had intended.

Crystal sucked her teeth and looked away.

Destiny watched her, looking for an answer.

Crystal forced herself to tell the truth. She could trust Destiny not to judge her.

"I did. Just last night."

Destiny didn't respond. She wasn't sure what to say. Surely, that complicated things.

Finally, she asked, "How do you feel?"

Crystal shook her head. "I don't know."

Destiny sat down on the bench at the foot of the bed. "Was that part of the plan?"

Crystal laughed. She closed her eyes, shaking her head in exasperation. Opening them, she looked at her cousin. "What plan? I'm starting to wonder if I even have one anymore."

Destiny scoffed at that. "This is me. I know you better than anybody. And you always have a plan."

Crys rolled her eyes, though she knew it was true. She had often been described as deliberate, calculating, and strategic. Once she set her mind on a goal—from putting herself through college to snagging the top job at *Hipster*—she accomplished it intentionally.

"I have it all under control," she said, sounding more certain than she really felt.

Destiny looked doubtful. "Your dad is coming home soon. What happens then?"

Crystal yawned again, hoping her cousin would take the hint and go away. She was asking the tough questions now. Ones that she already knew there were no answers to.

"Let's talk about it in the morning. One day at a time. Today has already been a lot for me."

Destiny nodded. She stood up and offered a weak smile. "Okay. Sweet dreams, cousin."

She walked out, shutting the door behind her.

Crystal stared at the door long after she was gone.

"Sweet dreams."

She dreamed of Troy that night. In her dream, he was watching her while she did chores around the house. While she mopped, vacuumed, and dusted, he sat watching her in that way that was all his own. Music played and she sang along. In her dream he watched her, smiling but saying nothing. He didn't have to. His presence was speaking to her. Telling her that he loved her, that he was sincere. In her dream, she was so content, so at peace. She woke up reaching for him and was sad to find that he wasn't there.

THE MITCHELL MEN

Troy unraveled his tie and unbuttoned the collar of his shirt. He removed his cuff links, while Vanessa poured him a glass of Rémy on the rocks. They had just returned to his apartment after yet another dinner party. It was one of her father's many political fund-raisers. Events that he insisted Troy attend. Night after night, he was subjected to superficial conversations with shallow people. It was all beginning to bore Troy. Each event was a huge production and tonight had been no exception. Vanessa and her mother had insisted on being photographed with every notable person in the room. Troy had sat back, watching it all with a mixture of disgust and indifference. Roxy, especially, was shamelessly unapologetic in her self-promotion. She had single-handedly orchestrated her own rise and her daughter's impending ascension to the ranks of the nation's black elite. Nothing Roxy did was unintentional.

Troy was well aware of her résumé. After all, whispers within the intimate ranks of the entertainment industry were hard to avoid. Roxy had dated several A-list celebrities before marrying

Harvey Nolan and was known for her extravagant and expensive tastes. Troy knew the apple didn't fall too far from the tree.

Vanessa handed him the glass of cognac, then kneeled in front of him. Silently, she undid his pants, freeing his monstrous dick from the confines of his underwear. Troy glanced down at her, kneeling before him clad in nothing but a pair of emerald earrings and some stilettos.

He cupped her pretty face in his large hands. "I meant what I said earlier," he told her.

After the party wrapped up, Troy had laid into Vanessa about her coming to *Hipster*. He told her that he felt ambushed and stressed the fact that he didn't want his personal life in the spotlight.

"Okay," she said softly. She looked up at him, her eyes wide and innocent.

She went to work. As irresistible as she was, he wasn't aroused as she stroked him. She began lapping at him, licking it like a fruity Popsicle on a hot summer day. She wrapped her lips around the head of it, sucking, and slowly taking more and more of him into her mouth. Troy pushed himself a little further into her mouth, causing her to gag a little. She regained her composure and continued sucking him, doing her best to accommodate more of his girth down her throat. Still, he dangled there limply.

She sat back on her heels, annoyed.

"I'm tired," he said.

She nodded. "Let's go to bed."

He shook his head. "I'm gonna take a shower." He stroked her cheek again. Despite her many flaws, she was beautiful. "You go get some sleep."

He walked away, leaving her there on the floor. Even without looking at her, he knew that she was pissed. Still, his mind was preoccupied with other things. Chief among them, Crystal Scott.

He hadn't stopped thinking about her. It occurred to him that Vanessa hadn't even questioned him about being out all night. He wondered if she even cared. While watching her and her mother angling for camera time, his mind had drifted to Crystal. By contrast, she worked a room effortlessly, attracting attention without clamoring for it. He imagined himself with a woman like her on his arm. One who could stimulate more than just the pendulum swinging between his legs.

His conscience tugged at him while he showered, knowing that Vanessa was probably mad about being left on her knees that way. He didn't mean to hurt her. In fact, in some strange way, he had to admire her family's hustle. Vanessa had emerged from a very chaotic childhood with an unmistakable edge, and an unquestionable agenda. He had always been aware that she was in it for her personal gain. Like him, this was more about family than it was about love. Troy was the man. And Vanessa wanted to be the woman on the arm of that man. He believed that she was in love. But with his power, wealth, and status. The Mitchell name was a reputable one. As early as their teen years, Roxy had been prancing her pretty daughter around Fox's sons.

Unlike his brother, Wes, Troy had managed to keep himself out of trouble, making him more acceptable in the circles Roxy and her daughter liked. It helped that Harvey was an old friend of Fox and Uncle Don.

Through it all, Troy and Vanessa had forged an electrifying physical relationship. She was fun, full of energy, and a freak in every sense of the word. She had her own goals, self-serving as they were, and had mastered the art of marketing and publicity in an age where anyone could become a star with the right looks and the right team behind them. He didn't necessarily agree with her blind ambition, but he respected her dogged determination to succeed.

He emerged from the bathroom after his shower to find her already sleeping. He kissed her tenderly on the cheek as she snored softly. He told himself that was enough of an apology for his rejection of her earlier. He glanced at his cell phone, tempted to call Crystal. But he decided against it. After all, it was late. Instead, he climbed into bed beside her, and drifted to sleep within minutes.

When they awoke the next morning, Troy gave Vanessa what she wanted. They had sex before breakfast. What she lacked in intelligence or legitimate talent, she more than made up for in looks and sexual prowess. She lay naked across his bed afterward. Her expertly polished toes seemed to sparkle in the sunlight pouring in through the parted curtains.

"Mom thinks we should film the wedding." Her voice was hoarse after multiple loud orgasms.

He glared at her.

"You know my parents are filming the pilot for a reality show. Production thinks they should get some of the footage for—"

"No!"

She jumped, startled as he yelled.

He shook his head. "I already told you. I'm not into all of that. I like to keep my private life private. No cameras. None of that. I'm not gonna say it again."

Vanessa pouted. "Well, it's my wedding, too, Troy. The producers want to see it," she said. Her mother was the show's executive producer and the loudest proponent of the idea.

"Your mother is the one pushing for all of this. The TV show, the photo shoots, all of that shit. Your father doesn't even want to do it. He just can't say no to her." Troy shook his head, disgusted by how Harvey had long ago given his wife custody of his manhood. "I'm saying no. Don't ask me again."

Vanessa was furious.

"You can be on the show if you want. Do it. Fuck it. But I don't want anybody filming here. You have your mother, your friends, your swim line. You don't need me to make your plot more interesting."

She frowned. "You're a fucking hypocrite."

"What?"

Vanessa sucked her teeth. "Why are you with me, Troy?"

He rolled his eyes. Lately, he had been asking himself that question more often than ever.

"What's wrong with me? Really?" She shook her head. "What am I doing wrong? I've tried everything I can think of lately to get your attention. And you're just not interested. Not for long. It's like you're distracted."

"Vanessa, I'm not in the mood for this right now."

"You're not in the mood for anything." Vanessa looked dejected.

Troy sighed. "I have a lot on my mind. Taking control of Stuart Mitchell is a lot of work. Plus all your dad's fund-raisers. Your mother's parties. It's a lot. I'm tired."

"I'm getting bored," she said. "I hate being bored."

Troy sneered at her without responding. This was all just a game. But there was far more at stake here than Vanessa could even begin to understand. She thought she was so smart. She was aware that Troy's interest in her was motivated by his father's political gain. She used that to her advantage. Whenever she felt like he was drifting too far from shore, she dared him to cross her. Not blatantly, she had never issued him an ultimatum. But she would say things like this to let him know that he was dangerously close to sending her running to her powerful daddy.

He winked at her, then stepped into his closet and began choosing his look for the day. His father was on vacation in Hawaii with one of his pretty young campaign staffers. Troy and Wes were on their own to celebrate this Thanksgiving. It didn't matter much to him. Since the death of his mother, the holidays had lost much of its emotional value. All he really wanted was to eat a good meal and watch some football. This year he would settle for doing that at the home of his future in-laws.

Vanessa pouted, though he wasn't in the room to notice.

"Butch will be here to get us in twenty minutes," Troy called out to her. "You should get ready."

She heard his muffled voice coming from his large closet. She snatched her panties off the bed as she headed for the shower.

He decided on a casual look for the day, blissfully unconcerned about the anger Vanessa felt during her shower. She felt dismissed, like a child. As usual, Troy's focus was on his own gratification. He had no patience for wounded pride.

She dialed her mother's number the moment she turned the shower on.

After dinner that night, Roxy was on Troy's nerves extra-heavy.

"I was talking to Fox the other night. I've never seen him look better by the way. He looks happy and relaxed now that he's retired. Anyway, he told me that you were thinking about having a small wedding." She rolled her eyes dramatically. "That's unacceptable. Your mother would beat your behind if she heard you say that."

Troy doubted that.

"Your mother was a close friend of mine," Roxy went on. "I know that if she were here, she would feel the same way I do." She looked at her handsome future son-in-law. "Your mother and I polished off so many bottles of wine together during those days when our husbands were away on business." Roxy laughed at the memory. "Your mother . . ." Her eyes were wet with tears, and she looked away. "Oh, boy. There I go bringing the mood down."

Troy was the one who rolled his eyes this time.

Roxy smiled, her light brown eyes still misty. "We always used to joke that the two of you would grow up and fall in love someday."

Vanessa blushed a little. "Ma, seriously?" She shook her head, and glanced sheepishly at Troy. "How embarrassing."

He laughed.

Roxy dabbed at her eyes again. "We hosted so many fund-raisers together. She could always convince the donors to cut the biggest checks. Lorraine Stuart Mitchell was a lioness." Her smile sparkled in the light of the chandelier as she recalled his mother. "She loved her boys so much." She winked at Troy. "I miss her."

He smiled weakly. "Me, too."

The doorbell rang and Roxy rose to get it. Troy was grateful for the break in her rambling, until she returned with his brother and his uncle in tow.

Don walked in the room, all smiles.

"How's everybody doing tonight?"

Harvey rose from where he had been dozing off in a corner. Suddenly, he looked wide-awake. He greeted Don and Wes warmly. Though this visit was unexpected, Don was welcome here.

Troy looked at Vanessa, confused. She shrugged.

He stood up reluctantly and greeted them. Both his uncle and his brother gave him a lukewarm reception, adding to the tension. Troy wondered what this was about.

Wes stared his brother down. His expression was filled with disapproval. He looked Troy over. All sharp and pressed like their father, even on a relaxing family holiday. By contrast, Wes wore jeans, a hoodie, and construction boots. His typical uniform for visits like this.

Don and Wes took a seat at Harvey's invitation and wasted no time getting to the point.

Don looked at his nephew. "It's Thanksgiving."

Troy waited for him to say more. When he didn't, he held up his hands, confused.

"Everybody spends Thanksgiving with their family." Don said it like it was obvious.

Troy nodded. "My father is out of town."

Don didn't blink. "We're your family, too, Troy. We're right here. In town."

Troy stared back at his uncle. He was aware that Vanessa and her family were present, so he held his tongue.

Don didn't hold his. "Speaking of family. I just want to say that I didn't like the way you came into my office the other day. I bailed y'all out of debt when Fox gambled away all his money."

Troy swallowed hard. Uncle Don was embarrassing his father on purpose, destroying his own brother's reputation in front of Harvey.

"All of his properties were in foreclosure. Half a million dollars in debt. And I bailed him out."

Harvey looked appalled.

Don wasn't done.

"Put you through Columbia University, and made sure you set yourself up nice. Still, you come in my house and drop off the final payment like I'm some common loan shark on the street, shaking you down."

Troy glanced at his brother and saw the amused expression on his face. Wes didn't care that Uncle Don was belittling their father. He had always hated Fox anyway. Hated Troy, too. Both of them were cowards in his eyes. Too scared to put it all on the line and be gangsters. Growing up, Wes had idolized their uncle, with his foul language and ruthless ways. In his eyes, his own father was a weak substitute. And, Troy was his punk-ass minion.

Troy looked at Vanessa and her family, embarrassed. "I wasn't trying to make you feel like a stranger, Uncle Don. We're family." Troy noticed Roxy shifting nervously in her seat. "But you could have called me and we could have talked about it. No problem. You didn't have to come here."

Wes leaned forward. "He don't have to do shit," he deadpanned. He glared at Troy.

Troy looked at Vanessa. "You and your mother should step out for a minute. Let me wrap this up here."

Vanessa didn't appreciate being dismissed. Still, even she could recognize that things had taken a major turn. She and her mother headed for the kitchen, where they could listen at a safe distance.

Troy sat forward in his seat, his focus on his brother. He looked incredulous. "Why the *fuck* would you come in here like this? You come in this man's house and disrespect his family gathering with this bullshit?" His fury was evident as he nearly spat his words at Wes.

Harvey gestured with his hands in surrender. "It's okay, Troy. It's fine." Harvey knew Don well enough to know that the man was a powder keg waiting to go off. He didn't want this to turn into the real possibility of bloodshed here. Not in his home. Definitely not on Roxy's expensive Persian rug.

Troy kept staring at his brother. Wes had been envious of him for a long time. At every turn, he looked for ways to undermine Troy's success and foil his plans. It was a pattern that began when they were kids and escalated in the years after their mother's death. In the end it had forced their father into a contentious relationship with his own brother. Wes was a tyrant whom Troy was growing sicker of by the minute.

"You're trying to make me hurt you, Wes. That's what it is. You're trying to see how far you can push me before I kill you."

"Fuck you," Wes said. "You sitting up here with Harvey Nolan now thinking shit is sweet. So what, now you think you got a clean slate and you and Dad are gonna cut me off? I don't get no parts of the company now? Like I didn't put in work all these years and help him keep it all going."

Troy scoffed. "Yeah. You helped." His expression said otherwise.

It stung Wes, hearing his brother belittle his contribution to the family. He stared daggers at him. "You ain't better than me, Troy. With your fucking degrees, your fake-ass girlfriend, and all this bullshit. You ain't better than me."

Troy shook his head. "I'm not," he said. "Never said I was. You were the one that always felt that way. Always projecting your shit onto other people." He sat back in his seat. "We got the same parents, came up in the same house. Same blood in our veins. The only difference between us are the choices we made."

Wes sucked his teeth. That wasn't at all the way he saw it.

"I chose to go to school. Tried to do the right thing, even though I didn't always succeed. You chose to run around like a fuckin' ghetto bastard with a point to prove." Troy looked at his uncle then. He believed with all of his heart that Uncle Don was the man Wes was trying to emulate. Troy was angry with his uncle for not seeing what a poison he had been to Wes over the years.

"You love to play the victim. You fuckin' bitch! Crying like a little girl in your room. Laying all across the altar at the church and all that shit. You always been a punk." Wes laughed. "Talking 'bout killing somebody. Nigga, do it."

Wes stood up. Don did, too. He could see that it was time to go.

Wes pointed in his brother's face. "Watch. You're gonna come crawling to me for help just like your father did."

Troy laughed. Wes was terrified that Troy was going to take the reins of the family business and succeed. Proving everyone right. That Troy was the chosen one and Wes was the fuckup.

"He's your father, too. And, you don't ever have to worry about me coming to you for anything. I've been getting money for years without your help."

Harvey watched it all unfold. He had learned a lot here tonight.

He looked at Don. He had known the man for years. Harlem was a small world and Don had a name that rang bells. Fox walked a straighter line. Or so Harvey had believed before this exchange. Still, despite the fact that they operated in different worlds, Harvey respected Don and the power he held in the streets. But they were old men now. Harvey's thoughts were turning toward the prospect of retirement and grandchildren. Fox's success at Stuart Mitchell mirrored Harvey's own. Their children getting married symbolized the prospect of a real legacy. Not some street notoriety that Don was still determined to hold on to after all these years. Harvey and Fox had realized that it was time to pass the torch. Don was deeply in denial.

"When you gonna retire?" Harvey asked.

Don didn't crack a smile. "I'm not ready for retirement," he said. "I'll retire when I'm dead."

"Not me," Harvey insisted. "My wife and I are gonna watch Vanessa get married and have some babies. And we're gonna do our best to make them famous." He laughed. "We've been blessed over the years, Don. Couple of boys from Harlem that made a fortune. I want to stop and enjoy what I worked hard all these years to build. We're too old to hold grudges."

"With all due respect," Wes said, "this is family business. You should keep your mouth shut."

Harvey glared at the young man. He had always liked Fox's sons. Obviously, he had more of an affinity for Troy seeing as how he was dating his daughter. But Wes had always been pleasant, although he was a bit of a hothead. Often over the years, Harvey had wondered why Fox didn't talk about his other son more. Now he was getting his answer in living color.

Troy spoke up. "Y'all should go."

Uncle Don nodded, and took a step toward the door.

Wes stood there. "Dad wants to run for office. Imagine that. Shame if something happened to fuck that up. Embarrass our poor father after all the time he spent keeping his precious name clean. You know what I'm saying?"

Troy did know. He glanced at Harvey and saw his expression change. The last thing the Nolans wanted was a scandal. Like Fox, their carefully crafted public image was precious to them. Harvey looked truly nervous for the first time since the men had walked in.

"Happy Thanksgiving," Don said.

Don and Wes walked out, leaving Troy alone to pick up the pieces of his family's bullshit yet again. Vanessa and Roxy returned from the kitchen.

"What was that about?" Vanessa asked.

"Pride," Troy answered honestly. "That was all about pride."

BLACK FRIDAY

Thanksgiving dinner was over, and Crystal and her family had feasted on far too much food and a little too much wine. Aunt Pat had come clean at last about the man she was seeing. His name was Curtis and he had been taking her out to dinner and to cozy cafés where they listened to live bands play. The glow on her face had shined brighter than the candles on the dining-room table.

"I feel a little silly," she admitted. "Every time I get a minute to myself, I catch myself thinking about him and smiling. I'm a grown-ass woman. I shouldn't still get like that over some man."

Destiny and Georgi had shouted her down, insisting that it was fine to feel the way that she did.

"Have fun!" they said.

But Crystal knew exactly how her aunt was feeling. She, too, felt silly every time her thoughts wandered back to Troy. Each time it happened, she snapped herself out of it and focused on her family, the food, anything but him. Still, she found it hard to keep her mind from drifting. He texted her a few times, but otherwise kept his distance. She was grateful for that. Despite the pleasure she found in his arms and in his presence, it was time to get back to reality. She even managed to get some work done, reviewing copy for an upcoming issue while her family busied themselves in the kitchen. Her dad had called collect from prison. And no matter what Georgi had said about only wanting the best for Quincy, her facial expression and body language told another story. She came alive while she talked to him and Crystal smiled at the idea of her parents still holding on to what remained of their love after all these years.

But, at the end of the conversation, Georgi had returned to the same narrative as before.

"Quincy, in just a few more days, you're walking out of there for good. All these years you've been away are gonna be behind you. Why would you go right back to the same place it all started?"

Quincy had echoed their daughter's sentiments, though. He assured his wife that everything was going to be all right.

"I know what I'm doing, Georgi. I told you this is just a stop along the way. I'm coming to get you, baby. Don't you worry."

Georgi had accepted that at last, resigning herself to the fact that her husband's mind was made up. For the time being, at least, he was returning to New York. A place Georgi had vowed to never set foot in again.

Now the dishes had been washed, the food had been put away. It was Friday morning and Crystal was returning to New York, too. She packed her suitcase and got ready to make the drive back to the city. Destiny knocked on her bedroom door.

"Hey." She entered and sat at the foot of Crystal's bed. "So, check this out."

Crystal laughed, already certain that Destiny had a trick up her sleeve.

"I tried on the boots you gave me for my birthday. And they're cute." She nodded. "Real cute! But I'm not hitting the red carpet on a day-to-day basis." She flipped her long weave over her shoulder and struck a pose in the mirror. "Even though I should be. I think I need something a little less fancy."

"Okay. You want something different?" Crystal stuck the last of her sweaters into her suitcase and zipped it.

Destiny nodded. "Yes. If you don't mind."

Crystal shrugged. "I don't mind at all. You should get what you want."

"Good!" Destiny said. "Let's stop by Lord and Taylor when we get back and do a little shopping."

Crystal's face lit up. She could use some retail therapy. In fact, that was exactly what she needed to help her stay busy and keep her mind from wandering back to Troy.

"Let's do it. I want to be out of here in thirty minutes. I'm trying to beat the traffic."

"I know. I'm already packed." Destiny winked. She stood up, and headed for the door. "I'll meet you downstairs."

Crystal grabbed her bags, took another long look around her old bedroom, then left. She hoisted her luggage down the long black spiral staircase. When she reached the landing, she looked around for Destiny. Her mother was waiting for her instead.

Crystal smiled. "I'm about to get on the road."

Georgi pulled her into a long hug. She smelled her daughter's fancy perfume and smoothed her hair as they embraced.

Crystal sighed, relaxing in the comfort of her mother's arms. She resisted the urge to cry, full to the brim with a cocktail of emotions. So much weight was on her shoulders and she didn't realize until then how badly she had needed a hug from her mother.

Georgi seemed to sense that as she stepped back. "Come and sit down with me for a minute before you leave."

Crystal followed her into the living room. The décor in here was as dramatic as Georgi was. The walls, furniture, and accents were all white. A large television was mounted on the far wall and two tall green ficus plants offered the only splashes of color in the room. To Crystal, it had always felt like the design was a subliminal expression of her mother's motives here in Maryland, in this house. Particularly in the aftermath of Malik's death. The white seemed to represent Georgi's desire to purify everything. To cleanse the stain of what had transpired and the trauma of what her family had endured. Crystal saw it as a reminder of her brother's hospital room. Cold, sterile, and void of life.

She sat on the sofa beside her mother. Georgi looked relaxed and at peace with things for once. It put Crystal at ease as she listened.

"When you were a little girl, you and Destiny used to play together all the time. You would sit for hours doing your dolls' hair, dressing them up, making up stories. Pat and I used to watch you two and laugh. That was back when we lived in Brooklyn and we used to have card games with Quincy and all his friends." Georgi got a faraway look in her eyes, remembering the life of the party she had once been. She and Quincy had been on top of the world.

"One time, you and Destiny were playing together and Malik got jealous. He kept coming in with his wrestling figure and interrupting the story y'all were telling. He would make his toy push Destiny's toy out of the dollhouse window and things like that."

They both laughed at that.

"After a while, Destiny got sick of it. So she took Malik's toy and threw it across the room. It hit the wall and the doll's leg came off. She actually threw it so hard that it was truly broken. One of the pieces broke off and there was no fixing it. Well, Malik was pissed! He threw a fit and it took me a while to get him to calm down. Hours passed. Pat and I thought everything was over. Then when she got ready to take Destiny home and she went looking for her doll, one of its arms were missing. Somebody had chopped that doll's arm off! Now Destiny was the one crying her eyes out. But Malik swore he didn't do it. We looked at you. I asked if you cut your cousin's doll up. You nodded. I asked you why you did it. And you looked me dead in my face." Georgi chuckled now as she recounted the memory. "You said, 'She didn't have to break his toy. So I broke hers. An arm for a leg.' Pat told me that Destiny cried all the way home. After that, she never challenged Malik again. Everybody knew that you and him stuck together no matter what."

Crystal smiled. That hadn't changed, even though he was gone. They were still a team.

"But what I learned is that you have a vengeful spirit."

Crystal's smile faded. That wasn't what she wanted to hear from her mother.

"You're my baby. No matter how old you get. And I love you. So, I can tell you the truth about yourself." Georgi sighed. "Ever since Malik died, part of you left, too. You created this . . . whole different life for yourself. To the point that I see you in the press and I don't even recognize you anymore. You're my daughter, my last living child, and I don't even *recognize* you anymore." She shook her head in amazement at that.

Crystal's gaze settled on the urn sitting on top of a stone pillar in the corner of the room. Malik. Or what remained of him after they were done with him. It was hard to imagine him in there, literally reduced to ashes. The brother she'd known was alive, athletic, tall, and lanky. Not the object full of dust she saw there. She blinked away the tears that pooled in her eyes. The irony was that all of them had been disfigured that night, having to change form and adapt to a new normal.

"You smile, but it's not always genuine. You laugh, but, if I look closely, I can see the sadness in your eyes. It's always there. It's like you feel guilty for enjoying life too much without him here."

Crystal couldn't look at her mother, afraid of what she might be seeing now.

"I recognize it because I feel it, too. He was my son. My first-born child. I was there. I watched them do what they did to him. And part of me died with him, too."

Crystal remembered the way her mother was when she was younger. Sassy, exuberant, fun. She still had those elements. Only they had been quieted now. She had been brought into submission. That was the worst part of it for Crystal. Seeing her entire family crippled at the hands of another, more powerful one.

"Malik would want us both to live. It's been ten years since he passed. Twenty-five years since your father went to jail. It's time for all of us to move on," Georgi concluded.

Crystal looked at her and prayed that she was done.

"Mommy, you want to know something? You're right. I have changed since he died. We all have. But, it's not my own pain that drives me to stay up there in New York and work as hard as I do. It's coming home and seeing you jump in fear every time you hear gunshots on the TV. It's hearing you on the phone turning down invitations to parties because you're afraid to come home at night when the house has been empty for long periods of time."

Georgi looked away, convicted.

"Honestly, I think about it all the time. What Malik might think of me if he was alive. If he would approve. I'm not sure that he would. I think he was more like you. He would want me to let it go. Sometimes, I'm tempted to do exactly that."

She thought about the past few days. She had felt more alive than she had in years. Several times she had lost focus.

"And then I talk to Daddy. Locked up for most of his adult life in a cage full of angry and hopeless men. How he had to sit in a cell, helpless and frustrated while his family was destroyed. While his son was killed and his wife was beaten and violated." She wiped the tears that fell freely now. "He's coming home now. And he has every right to decide where he wants to go, and what he wants to do after so many years of being ordered around." She took a breath. "I'm going back to New York, Ma. I'm not there by myself. Destiny lives close by. And Tyson is just a phone call away if I need him. It's where I belong. It's where Malik died. It's where Daddy put his life on the line for us. And it's where I need to be right now to take back everything the devil stole from our family."

She stood up. This conversation was over. "I love you. I really have to get going now."

Georgi rose, too. She followed her to the door, where Destiny had been eavesdropping discreetly.

Crystal looked around. "Where's Aunt Pat?"

Destiny rolled her eyes. "She's out having breakfast with her new boo. I already said good-bye to her before she left."

Crystal giggled and gave her mother a hug. "Please give Aunt Pat my love."

Georgi nodded. She looked at Destiny. "You two be careful."

She walked them out, and stood waving at them curbside as they drove away. Every time her daughter left, she wondered if it was the last time she would see her. In a lot of ways it already felt like she hadn't really seen her in years.

Crystal and Destiny made it to Lord and Taylor on Fifth Avenue by four o'clock that afternoon. They exchanged the boots Crystal had given her for a new pair, then decided to grab a quick bite to eat at Sarabeth's Café. They were just about to take their seats when Crystal spotted Vanessa Nolan sitting alone at a table close by. Instinctively, she turned to leave, grabbing Destiny by the arm and pulling her along. But it was too late. Vanessa had already spotted her.

"Crystal! Come sit with me." She smiled brightly as she waved them over. She wore a safari green jumpsuit, nude pumps, and a simple ponytail.

"Who's that?" Destiny asked between clenched teeth.

"Wonder Boy's fiancée." Crystal said it with a fake smile plastered on her face. Her heart was racing.

"Uh-uh!" Destiny froze. "This is too much!"

"Shut up and come on. Just play along." Crystal looked at her cousin seriously. "Matter of fact, just don't say anything. Pretend you're shy and let me do all the talking." The last thing she needed was for Destiny to blurt out the wrong thing.

They made their way over to Vanessa's table and sat down. Crystal introduced the women and peeled out of her jacket.

"I've been shopping all day," Vanessa said. "I'm starving."

Despite those words, she only ordered the Waldorf chicken salad. Destiny rolled her eyes and ordered the pumpkin waffle with a side order of applewood-smoked bacon. Crystal ordered a turkey club sandwich and a ginger ale. Suddenly, her stomach was feeling a bit unsettled.

She decided to address the elephant in the room. "Listen,

I'm sorry that Oscar and I had to cancel the spread with you and your mother. The creative team decided to go in a different direction."

Vanessa nodded. "I was disappointed when Troy told me. But it's okay." He had made it clear to her that it wasn't going to happen. She appreciated Crystal making it sound like it was a decision the creative team had made. But Vanessa was already well aware that Troy himself had shut it down.

"He doesn't want me coming around the magazine anymore." She shrugged her shoulders. "Probably scared that me and my mother will try to take over." She laughed, but it was clear that she was annoyed. She looked at Crystal. "But I like you. I had fun with you at lunch the other day. We can't hang out at the magazine, but we should still get together from time to time."

Crystal nodded and flashed a smile. "Definitely."

"I need friends," Vanessa confessed. "I'm always with my mom or with Troy. That's my problem." She gave that uneasy laugh again. "I need an identity of my own." She looked at Crystal, thinking she was exactly the type of friend she needed. A woman with intelligence, class, and style.

"How was your Thanksgiving?" Crystal asked, anxious to get off the subject.

Destiny cleared her throat. Crystal shot a glance in her direction, and Destiny took a sip of water. She remembered that she was supposed to be shy.

Vanessa shook her head. "Dinner was good. My parents brought in one of their favorite chefs. It was perfect." She chewed her salad daintily. "This year we had quail." She squealed with delight.

Crystal caught Destiny glaring at Vanessa. Already, she didn't like this superficial bitch.

"But then Troy's family came over and it was all downhill from there." Vanessa sat back as the waiter arrived with their food.

Crystal and Destiny exchanged glances again. The moment the waiter had cleared out, Crystal dove back in.

"I thought Fox was traveling to celebrate his retirement."

Vanessa nodded. "He is. He's in Hawaii." She smiled. "I love Fox. He's been a friend of our family since I can remember." Her smile disappeared. "The rest of the family? Not so much." She looked at Crystal. "Have you met his brother, Wes?"

Crystal shook her head.

Vanessa seemed to consider it for a moment. Whether or not to tell Crystal what was on her mind. Troy had warned her to stay away from the magazine. But that didn't mean that she and Crystal couldn't be friends. Besides, she was still pissed about his refusal to let cameras film their wedding for her parents' show. She had charged a bunch of shit on his black card today and she still didn't feel any better. She needed to vent and Crystal was easy to talk to.

"Good," she said. "You don't want to meet him. Trust me. He's a hoodlum." She took a bite of her salad.

Crystal peeked at Destiny, eating her food in silence, her eyes focused on her plate.

"That's a strong word." Crystal laughed uneasily.

"No, I mean like a real-life thug. He's been to jail before, spent time on the run. That type of thing." She shook her head. "He and Troy aren't close. They hardly ever speak. But that didn't stop him from coming over to my parents' house unannounced. I mean, nobody minds a little extra company on a holiday, but at least call first." She ate some more salad.

"I hate that," Crystal said.

"Right?" Vanessa finished chewing. "Anyway, thankfully they didn't stay long."

Crystal frowned. "They? I thought you said Fox was out of town."

Vanessa nodded. "Wes came with Troy's Uncle Don. He's another character."

Destiny choked on a piece of bacon and began to cough. Crystal patted her on her back and gave her some water to drink. Destiny pulled it together.

"You good?" Crystal asked.

Destiny nodded. She sipped her water and apologized.

Vanessa looked concerned. "That happens to me when I eat popcorn."

Crystal kicked her cousin under the table.

"She's okay," she said, resuming their conversation. "So, you were saying his uncle is a character?"

Vanessa nodded. "Yeah. *Uncle Don*." She giggled as she said it. "He's Fox's brother. But Fox is the nice one. Don is the bully."

"They're brothers. They're probably more alike than you think." Destiny shoved food in her mouth as soon as she said it.

Vanessa shook her head. "No. I'm not saying Fox is a saint. But he's nothing like his brother."

Crystal nodded. "How about Troy and his brother. Are they alike?"

Vanessa thought about it. "Well, Troy is a good man. But he's no joke." She sat back in her seat. "He's very serious about his family, and their business. Sometimes, I think he overdoes it. Overall, he's a decent person." She looked at Crystal. "Wes is just a pig."

Crystal sipped her water. "Sounds like you're marrying into a complicated family."

Vanessa sighed. "I don't know about that."

Crystal frowned. Destiny set her fork down.

"I think the stress of everything is starting to get to him.

Daddy thinks we might want to wait awhile before we get married." Vanessa sounded sad about it.

Crystal listened sympathetically. Clearly "Daddy's" opinion held a lot of weight.

"Relationships always go through ups and downs," she said. "That's normal."

Vanessa shrugged. Lately, she was beginning to worry that the spark between them had gone out for good. She thought about the way he had stopped getting aroused for her.

"Love conquers all." Destiny's mouth was slightly full. She caught the side-eye Crystal shot in her direction.

"That's true," Vanessa said. "I've grown to love him over time."

Crystal looked away, her conscience eating her alive.

"Over time? It wasn't love at first sight?" Destiny's eyes were wide. This was good tea.

Crystal tried to kick her again, but Destiny had moved her leg.

Vanessa shook her head. "He was a real asshole at first. I could tell he only took me out because our parents set us up." She laughed about it in retrospect. "We didn't hit it off right away. But sometimes love takes time to grow. It was like that with us."

Crystal smiled.

"After last night, though, my parents are worried." Vanessa glanced at Crystal. "Wes threatened my father. In his own house!"

Crystal frowned. "What happened?" she asked. "I don't understand."

Vanessa sighed. She had so much on her mind. She wished she knew Crystal well enough to tell her the whole twisted story. For some reason, she trusted her. But then she glanced at Destiny, who she was meeting for the first time. She had to watch what she said. She had probably already said too much. She summed it all up like the press releases her parents were known for.

"Family drama. That's all. But those types of things can get messy. You know?"

Crystal and Destiny exchanged knowing glances.

Crystal nodded. "That's an understatement."

CRASH

Crystal arrived at work the following week ready for war. Her weekend with Destiny had been fun and therapeutic. The cousins had laughed, cried, and reminisced while going through old family pictures in Destiny's apartment. By the time Crystal returned to her brownstone on Sunday morning, Destiny had given her a good old-fashioned dose of tough love. She told Crystal that she had already made her family—particularly Malik—proud. Even if she never went any further. She had already done enough. It had given Crystal permission to take it a little easier on herself. She was human, after all.

She stepped into her office at around 10:30 A.M. on Monday morning to find the usual pile of mail on her desk. On top of it sat a black envelope embossed with the initials WM. She sat down, and tore open the fancy paper. Inside was an invitation to Fox's retirement party at his home in Harlem. It was happening the following week. She smiled. This was going to be epic.

"You're so beautiful when you smile," Troy said as he stepped through the cracked door.

Crystal looked at him and swooned a little. He was dressed casually in a pair of blue jeans, a black T-shirt, a Yankees fitted cap, and Timbs. He looked like an ad for New York City.

"Thank you," she said.

"You haven't been answering my calls." He checked her out, too, admiring her cleavage in the tight red dress she was wearing. "I came in here early today, hoping to steal you away for breakfast." Truthfully, he had been hoping for more than that. But breakfast sounded more noble.

"I'm sorry. I was busy catching up with my cousin."

He nodded. "I understand."

"How was your holiday?" she asked facetiously.

He shrugged. "Glad it's over. I couldn't stop thinking about you."

She wasn't sure what to say.

He gestured at the envelope in her hand. "Are you coming?"

She nodded. "Absolutely. I wouldn't miss it. I owe my career to your father."

He shook his head. "I think you give him too much credit." He turned to leave. "I'm on my way to L.A. to handle some business. I'll be back in a few days. I'd like to see you."

She was tempted to take him up on that offer, but she knew better. "My schedule is packed," she said, only half-lying. "But I'll see you at the party."

He stared at her a moment longer than necessary. "Okay," he said. "I'm looking forward to it."

She nodded. "Me, too."

When he was gone, she glanced at her cell phone. She had a text from Vanessa, thanking her for the cupcake assortment from Magnolia Bakery that Crystal had sent to her. The text was full of exclamation marks, hearts, and smiley-faced emojis. She tossed her cell phone aside, picked up the office phone, and summoned

Oscar into her office. He sauntered in minutes later and got comfortable.

Crystal slid the envelope across the desk toward him. He opened it and looked at her, confused.

"What's the problem?"

"What am I going to wear?" she asked. "It's black tie. And you know I want to stop the show."

Oscar reached for her desk phone and called in his assistant, Tonya. Once she arrived, he gave her his instructions. "Remember the shoot we did with Brandy Norwood back in February?"

Tonya nodded. The Brandy shoot had been one of her favorites. It had been all about shedding her girl-next-door image for that of a temptress, a vixen. Oscar had personally styled that shoot, and had been the recipient of much acclaim as a result.

"Pull that black backless Tom Ford dress . . ."

"Backless?" Crystal repeated. "Seriously?"

Oscar narrowed his eyes at her. "Seriously. Troy is running around here every day like a dog in heat. Y'all don't fool me, honey. I see this little flirtatious game you're playing. It's *scandalous* if you ask me. But I'm here for it." He winked at her while Tonya stifled her giggles. "So yes. You're going to serve it."

"Serve what, exactly?"

Oscar smiled. "Classy sex appeal with a touch of whimsy, darling."

Crystal rolled her eyes.

Tonya jumped up and down excitedly. "I wish I could go, too!"

Oscar shook his head. "It's not your turn yet," he said. "For now, go and get that dress!"

Oscar snapped his fingers and Tonya scurried off.

He looked at Crystal with a twinkle in his eye. "Ready for the ball, Cinderella?"

Crystal beamed. It seemed like Oscar was reading her mind. "Yes, Fairy Godmother!"

Oscar tossed his head back and cackled with delight. "I love it!"

The next few days flew by in a typical flurry of events. Meetings, press events, panels, interviews. It had all become par for the course to Crystal. She handled her duties with her usual grace under pressure. Troy called her each day, under the guise of business. And at the end of each conversation, he spoke of desperately wanting to see her. Crystal resisted, though. Until, finally, the night of Fox's retirement party had arrived.

Oscar had seen to it that she was looking better than ever tonight. She stood now, admiring herself in the large oval mahogany mirror, and could scarcely believe her eyes. The floor-length black gown hugged her curves perfectly. The modest neckline graced her collarbone where she'd splashed just a hint of perfume. The dress's long sleeves nestled her wrist at just the right point and an emerald cocktail ring shone against the gloss of her manicure. Her ebony legs played peekaboo through a slight split in the front. Black Brian Atwood heels and a tiny gold clutch complemented the look.

She spun around and peeked over her shoulder at the back. She couldn't get enough of it. The backless gown featured a zipper that could be adjusted for modesty. She had zipped it to the middle of her back, giving her just enough bareness to leave them panting in her wake. Crystal worked out regularly and the result was a toned and sexy back and a very good ass. As Oscar had predicted, tonight she was serving sexy sophistication in a big way.

She had booked a suite at the Surrey hotel on the Upper East Side for the night. Being in Manhattan made it easier to travel to and from the party, instead of making the long trek back to Brooklyn.

Satisfied that she looked perfect, she set out for the party. She arrived at the same time Oscar did. She caught him in the foyer of Fox's opulent Harlem home, straightening his bow tie and the cuffs of his tuxedo. He froze when he laid eyes on Crystal.

"Honey!" he shouted. "I mean, seriously!"

Crystal laughed and thanked him as he continued gushing.

"I outdid myself this time!" Oscar could scarcely take his eyes off of her.

Marlo arrived soon afterward. Crystal and Oscar greeted her.

"Where's David?" Oscar asked.

Marlo's husband, David, was a popular hip-hop producer who had amassed a fortune over the years.

"He's out of town. I had him home for three days. But my baby had to get back to work." As a busy man, David left his wife flying solo at most of the media events she frequented. Marlo was an independent and self-assured woman who had recently celebrated her sixtieth birthday. She was fierce, fit, and a bit flamboyant, and had no problem stepping into a room and own-ing it.

She raved about Crystal's look also. Marlo's look tonight was classic—a black Chanel cocktail dress with Stuart Weitzman pumps. Together, the trio entered the party.

A couple dozen people mingled, danced, and sipped drinks in fancy glasses. A DJ was set up in the far corner of what was indeed a *great* room. The cathedral ceilings were painted in a vibrant gilded gold. The floor-to-ceiling windows were framed in deep mahogany wood that looked as opulent as the house itself. Large white sofas dotted the room. A bold move, Crystal thought. Entertaining this many people with such delicate furnishings in such an expensive-looking home.

"Hello, *Hipster.*"

His voice made the hairs on the nape of Crystal's neck stand up. She tried her best not to show it. She turned to find Troy standing behind her, and nearly fainted from pure desire at the sight of him. Resplendent in a black on black tuxedo, Troy looked impeccable. His facial hair had been lined up expertly, accentuating his lips. They were so kissable that she had to remind herself not to stare.

"Hello," she said, along with the rest of her colleagues.

He looked at her, grinning slightly. Approaching the group from behind, Troy had gotten a fantastic view of Crystal's ass. But as she faced him now, he was even more pleased. To Troy, she had never looked more beautiful than she did tonight.

"What a great party!" Marlo complimented him. "Fox is going out with a bang."

The room reeked of sophistication, class, and, most of all, money. Men in tailored suits and women in fabulous looks and flawless makeup enjoyed themselves. Conversation and laughter filled the room.

Fox entered wearing a white tuxedo and a Hollywood smile. He was greeted by cheers and whistles as the DJ played "Celebration" by Kool and the Gang. Oscar and Marlo rushed over along with most of the other partygoers to form a circle around the guest of honor on the dance floor. Troy was grateful for a moment alone with Crystal.

"You look gorgeous," he whispered. "I want to tear this dress off you like I did that night at your house."

She smiled naughtily. "Watch it. Here comes your fiancée."

Vanessa entered the room with her mother not far behind. Both women looked as beautiful as always. Roxy's look was especially jaw-dropping. The neckline plunged all the way down to her navel. As if that weren't enough, the winter white gown had a sky-high split in the front. Fox and all the other men present did their best to keep their gaze focused above her shoulders.

Vanessa walked toward them wearing a black halter dress. She smiled as she approached the pair.

"Crystal, good to see you again. You look so pretty." Vanessa gave Crystal a hug, then stood beside Troy and took his hand in hers.

"So do you." Crystal returned the compliment.

Vanessa did a little curtsy. "I probably gained ten pounds eating those cupcakes!"

Crystal pretended not to hear her. "I love your hair."

Troy looked uncomfortable. Vanessa squeezed his hand affectionately and he forced a smile.

"Did you bring your cousin with you?" she asked, looking around the party.

Troy glanced at Crystal questioningly.

Crystal shook her head. "No." She looked at Troy. "My cousin and I ran into Vanessa while we were out shopping."

He nodded, still frowning. "Small world." He wondered why neither of them had mentioned it to him before. He didn't like the thought of them having secret meetings and conversations.

Fox made his way over to them, beaming from all the love he was receiving.

"There's my girl!" He threw his arms around Crystal. "I've been asking about you. How's my son been treating you?"

"Not bad," Crystal said. "So far, the apple doesn't fall too far from the tree."

Fox nodded. "Good."

"How was Hawaii?" Crystal asked.

Fox launched right into a story about parasailing in Maui

with his pretty young girlfriend. Everyone listened, laughing along. Then Crystal found herself distracted by a man approaching the group. The man was tall like Troy and appeared to be in his thirties with an unmistakable swagger. A deep ebony complexion and jet-black hair; sideburns thick and perfectly lined, his goatee full. His eyes were deep-set, piercing, and thick eyebrows hooded them. He wore a dark suit, with a charcoal gray shirt unbuttoned at the collar and no tie.

Crystal felt an icy chill travel the length of her spine. The man approached Fox from behind, so he never saw him coming. But Crystal saw him. She watched each step he took in their direction.

"Congratulations, Dad." His voice was as deep as the ocean.

Fox looked unpleasantly surprised as he turned around. "Wes."

Wes smiled at his father. "Congratulations on your retirement."

Fox's smile was forced. "I appreciate that. Good to see you, son." He greeted a couple of his guests as they walked by. He hoped that Wes would take the hint and get lost.

Wes continued looming there. "What's up, Troy?"

He had a menacing presence. Crystal could sense it now. Vanessa nudged her. Crystal saw her mouth "Watch."

Troy didn't respond to his brother. Instead, he eyed him coldly.

"Oh. It's like that, huh?" Wes's smile was maniacal. "Okay." He looked at Crystal, then did a double take. His eyes traveled the length of her body, admiring the curve of her figure in the dress. He licked his lips dramatically. "Hello. I'm Wes Mitchell. Nice to meet you." He extended his hand.

Troy pushed it away. Wes took an aggressive step toward him, but Fox stepped between his sons, keeping them apart.

A couple of nearby guests glanced in their direction. Crystal and Vanessa stepped a few inches away.

Troy had a look in his eyes that Crystal hadn't seen before. Wes looked amused. Crystal had worked closely enough with Fox to tell that he was angry. Although he was smiling and his body language wasn't confrontational, his brow was set in such a way that she knew he was livid.

"Let's go in my office and talk." He touched each of his sons gingerly. "Come on."

Crystal and Vanessa watched as the three men walked toward the corridor. A man stood near the entrance. He was tall with broad shoulders, velvety brown skin, and a salt-and-pepper goatee. He wore all black and stood near the doorway, unsmiling. As the men approached, he exchanged brief words with Fox, then followed them down the hall.

Vanessa turned to Crystal, wide-eyed. "That's Uncle Don!" She looked like a spectator at a movie. It was clear that she was fascinated by this side of Troy's life. As taboo as it was for her family, she was obviously entertained.

"What do you think they're talking about?" Crystal asked.

Vanessa glanced toward the doorway. "I don't know. I'm just glad my parents aren't here yet. They've already seen enough."

Crystal glanced around. "I'm gonna use the bathroom."

Vanessa nodded. "I'll come with you."

Crystal groaned. "I have to make a phone call first. I'll catch up with you in a minute." She hustled off before Vanessa could protest.

She lost her in the crowd, fuller now that more people had begun to arrive. It took her a couple of minutes to make it to the corridor where Troy and his family had gone. She edged past a few people lingering there and she found a narrow hallway leading to a set of doors. She glanced around to see if anyone was looking. Satisfied that she was undetected, she slipped down the hallway, walking on her tiptoes so that her heels didn't make a sound. She heard voices behind the door furthest away. She inched closer and pressed her ear against it, positioning herself so that she could see if anyone was coming.

"Troy stopped by to see me not too long ago," a voice said. "I was expecting you to come and make that delivery personally. I did you a favor when you needed it. The least you could do is show me some respect."

Someone laughed. Crystal recognized it as Fox. "Come on. You did me a favor? Please! Let's not talk about all the money I cleaned for you over the years. All the favors I called in to get you out of trouble."

"I didn't forget. You did a lot for me."

"Yes, I did. And *you* got out of hand. You started doing too much. Running around like you're invincible. I'm out here trying to build a legacy for my kids. How could I do that with you making headlines for all the wrong reasons?"

"So you acted like you didn't know me. Stopped doing me favors. Gave me your ass to kiss."

"And you took it out on me by turning my son against me."

Fox's words lingered. Crystal pressed her ear closer to the door, afraid that she was missing something.

"Ain't nobody turn your son against you, Fox." Don's response was less boisterous this time.

"What do you call this? Harvey told me about your little visit to his house on Thanksgiving. Me and you, Don . . . that's one thing. I can live with the fact that my brother hates my guts. But now you got my son walking in here. In front of all my friends—"

"Nigga, fuck your friends! This is family right here!"

Crystal had no problem hearing that. Don's voice echoed in the narrow hallway where she stood.

"Family." Crystal recognized that voice as Troy's.

"I'm listening to you using that word like it gives you a license to do what you want. I used to believe it, too. That there was something noble about family. But I see now there's no reward in this shit. It's just more and more bullshit. Fuck this family."

Silence. Crystal waited. She prepared to sprint off if the door opened suddenly. She peered down the hall and saw Vanessa heading in her direction.

"There you are!" Vanessa called loudly. "I was looking for you in the bathroom, but you weren't there." Her voice echoed off the walls.

Crystal began walking toward her quickly.

"What are you doing all the way over here?" Vanessa looked a little tipsy.

"I was trying to find the bathroom. I must be lost. Do you know where it is?" Crystal glanced over her shoulder as they reached the edge of the hallway. She saw the door open.

Vanessa giggled. "Yes, silly. It's all the way at the other end of the hall. I'll show you."

Crystal saw Troy come out of the room followed by Fox. Wes and Don came out moments afterward.

Vanessa noticed them at last and she froze in place. Crystal stood back and watched them.

Fox stood and waited for his brother to catch up. He extended his hand. Don didn't take it.

Troy was looking at his uncle so venomously that Crystal was riveted.

"Uncle Don, we'll talk later on. You cool?" Troy's words were gentle, but his stance was puffed up. It looked like he might lay hands on his uncle.

Don shrugged. "I'm always cool." He moved toward the exit.

Wes followed him, a sinister grin on his face. He winked at Vanessa on his way out the door.

Crystal looked for their reactions. Fox flashed a phony grin. "Sorry about that, folks. Can't pick your family."

Fox walked away, clearly embarrassed.

Troy walked over to them. He appeared to be on edge. "I apologize for that."

She shook her head. "No need to apologize. I'm not even really sure what that was."

He laughed, shaking his head. "I told you. My family is complicated."

Vanessa spotted her parents, said "I'll be back," then dashed off in their direction.

Troy seemed relieved to see her go. "I want to taste you again." He whispered it in her ear in a seductive tone. She instantly recalled the feeling of his mouth on her body, pleasure and pain in a perfect marriage.

She smiled. "I told you, we're not doing that again. Once was enough."

He laughed. "That's not what your pussy said."

Roxy appeared out of nowhere, loudly praising Crystal's dress.

"Gorgeous!"

"Thank you." Crystal smiled graciously.

Vanessa stood nearby with her arm linked through her father's while he chatted with Tavis Smiley.

"Crystal, are you going to make a speech tonight? Everyone is fighting for time at the podium before Fox makes his speech."

Crystal's eyes widened. In a room full of so many political types, the last thing she was in the mood for was long-winded speeches. "Oh, no! Actually, I was just leaving."

Troy's head snapped in her direction. "Leaving? Why?"

Roxy, too, looked shocked. "Is everything alright?"

Crystal nodded. "I just have the worst headache. I've taken aspirin and everything. But really I think I just need to rest. I've been keeping a crazy schedule lately. Sadly, it's finally catching up to me."

"Tsk-tsk." Roxy pouted. Crystal could see the resemblance to her daughter then.

Troy took Crystal by the hand. "I'll walk you out."

She bid Roxy good night and Troy walked her toward the front door.

"What's the real reason you're leaving?" he asked.

She shook her head. "I really just need to lay down."

He looked at her. "Can I come and lay with you?"

She laughed. "Your father would be disappointed if you did."

"He's already going to be disappointed when he finds out that you left early. *Hipster* is one of his biggest accomplishments. You know he's going to want to give the credit to you."

"Please give him my apologies. I really loved working with him and I'm so happy for him." She looked around. "He worked hard for all of this."

Troy shrugged. He walked to the edge of the curb and motioned at Butch, who was parked across the street. Immediately, the car's headlights came on and Butch pulled up in front of the house. He got out and greeted Troy and Crystal.

"Butch, can you bring Crystal home, please?"

Crystal shook her head. "I'm not going home tonight."

Troy looked crushed for a minute. He had been hoping that she wasn't leaving early for a date with someone else.

"I'm staying at the Surrey tonight. I got a room for the night so I wouldn't have to drag myself back to Brooklyn."

Troy nodded. "Nice."

Butch held the door open for her. She thanked him and climbed inside. She noticed that Troy remained outside, watching as Butch pulled away from the curb.

Butch played some mellow jazz and engaged her in light conversation on their way to her hotel. Crystal learned that he was a widower and had worked for Troy for close to ten years.

"How did your wife die?" Crystal asked the question gently. She could tell by how he spoke about her that he had loved her very much.

Butch glanced at her through the rearview. "She had cancer. Died suddenly."

Crystal could feel his sadness as he uttered the words. She glanced out the window, watching the city go by. Pulling up in front of the hotel, he waited until she was safely inside before leaving.

She peeled out of her dress and took a long, hot shower. She ordered room service and fell asleep watching a movie on the hotel television. Her cell phone rang at 1:15 A.M., startling her. The vibration coupled with her ringtone pierced the peace and serenity she had been enjoying while she slept. She picked it up and saw Troy's name and number on the screen. She answered it, unsure why her hands were suddenly unsteady.

"Hello?"

"Are you alone?" Troy's voice was low and deep.

"Yes," she said. "Why?"

"Because I'm in the lobby," he said. "What room are you in? I'm coming up."

She paused. "What if I wasn't alone?" she asked.

"I would drive back home," he said. "But I prayed the whole way over here that you would be by yourself."

"Why?" she asked.

"I want to talk to you." He gripped the phone tightly. He wanted to do a lot more than talk.

She hesitated before finally giving him her room number. She hung up, tied her bathrobe around her waist, and waited by the door. He knocked moments later.

She opened the door to find him standing with a bouquet of flowers in his hand. She laughed.

"Where did you find those at this time of night?"

He hid behind them. "I snatched them from one of the centerpieces at my dad's party."

Crystal laughed. "Come in." She took the flowers and set them on the table.

Troy plopped down in a chair.

"Party's over?" Crystal asked. She sat on the edge of the bed.

He nodded. "For me at least. My dad and his friends can go all night. But I'm worn out."

"What about Vanessa? She seems like she can go all night, too."

His eyes narrowed. "Okay. A little play on words, huh?"

She smirked.

"Vanessa went home with her parents." He sighed. "I think she's starting to see that my family might not be all it's cracked up to be." He shrugged. "Her parents love publicity. But not the kind my brother brings."

Crystal's ears perked up. "Tell me about your brother," she said. She curled her feet beneath her.

He sighed. "Wes . . . I'm gonna be honest with you," he said. "He rolls with a different crowd. Hustlers, movers, and shakers."

Crystal raised an eyebrow. "So do you," she noted, "just because they call themselves businessmen doesn't make it any different."

He nodded. There was certainly some truth in that. "True. But the ones I deal with day to day pretend to be legitimate, at least. The people my brother deals with are cut from a different cloth. There's no shame in their game."

"I thought that Wes works for your uncle's charity organization."

Troy stared at her without answering.

She looked at him. "That wasn't true?"

He shook his head. "No. That's what he does. On paper, at least." His eyes told her all she needed to know. Wes was a crook. Always had been and always would be.

She wanted to know more, but Troy was on his feet, walking toward her now.

He stopped and hovered over her.

"I couldn't wait to get out of there tonight. I kept thinking about you in that dress." He stroked her face, her neck, and wrapped his fingers around her throat. He kissed her and slowly peeled her bathrobe off.

She climbed higher on the bed, wearing nothing but a pair of black lace boy shorts. She lay across it, aware that his eyes were fixed on her. She watched his eyes move across her body slowly, settling on the mounds of her breasts. She reveled in him watching her this way, his hunger for her obvious.

Troy licked his lips, his dick harder than a boulder. His eyes roamed her body lustfully.

She stared at him, no longer smiling. Then she tugged at her panties, pulling them slowly down the length of her thighs, her knees, and left them pooling around her ankles.

He took a step forward, so excited at the sight of her there naked before him. He restrained himself from ravaging her, opting instead to explore her with his eyes, inch by inch. He admired her confidence. She parted her legs, giving him an even better view of what he was so anxious to see. She ran her hands along her inner thighs. Tickling her skin with touches as light as a whisper, Crystal pleasured herself, putting on a show for Troy.

He stepped closer and watched her part the lips of her sex, fingering herself. She let out a moan that stirred the beast inside of him.

Troy crawled onto the edge of the bed, his head and torso hovering just above her pussy.

He grabbed her thighs, pulling her closer, causing Crystal to gasp. Pinning her hands down at her side, he held her in position. He buried his face between her thighs, sending her on an erotic thrill ride that left her trembling, breathless across the bed. He held her tightly, her arms pinned at her sides, while he devoured her.

Crystal spread her legs wider, lifting her head to watch him work. He sucked harder, her swollen clit so tender in his mouth. She bucked at him, tossing her head back against the mattress.

"Oh!" she sang out, his tongue driving her insane with desire.

Aware that she was about to cum, he finally released her arms, freeing her to grab at him in desperation. She gripped his head, pulling him closer, deeper. She erupted, her body wracked by spasms as the powerful orgasm coursed through her.

He stood up, pulling his clothes off frantically. He pulled a condom out of his wallet and tore it open. Scooping her up in his arms, he placed her legs on either side of him, rubbing the head of his dick against her pussy, dripping wet from his oral assault.

Crystal spread her legs wider, ready to feel him inside of her. She shifted excitedly, desperate for him now.

Troy thrust himself inside of her. He lifted her up and down, sliding her along the length of his dick as deep as she would allow him to go. Crystal cried out, filled to capacity with Troy. He pounded her, at times hard and rough, and then slower, grinding himself inside her with his hips. Crystal clung to his back, winding herself on him, moaning from the depth of her gut. Pleasure and pain met in exquisite synchronicity as he lost himself, fucking Crystal against the wall, pushing into her while his hands dug into her thighs.

"Oh . . . my . . ." She never finished the sentiment. Her voice trailed off, her teeth sank into his shoulder, and her eyes squeezed shut in ecstasy as she erupted again.

Troy carried her to the bed and placed her on top of it. He spread her legs wide, and stroked her swollen folds. Tender to the touch, Crystal jumped at the sensation he caused. Mercifully, he stroked her gently with his fingers, sliding them in and out of her slowly, erotically, massaging her. She relaxed, her legs parted. He rolled over, and pulled her on top of him.

Crystal urged him back against the bed, straddling him. He grew even harder with the weight of her on top, doing her best to accommodate as much of his massive dick as she could. He patiently held her hips and stroked her back as she took more of him in with each stroke.

"Damn," he breathed. She clung to him, inside and out. He fought the urge to explode inside her. He wanted to see how far she could go.

Crystal's breath quickened as she writhed on top of him. Leaning back on the palms of her hands, fingers splayed behind her in a pose that would have made her yoga instructor proud, she rode him. Pushing her hips against Troy, her legs quivered each time she thrust forward. She wanted more of him than her body was willing to stand.

She could see that he was loving it. Troy's grunts and growls urged her on. Finally, spent, she pulled herself off of him, the soreness he left behind throbbing as an unnecessary reminder of his power.

She knelt forward on all fours, her ass in the air, and took him into her mouth. Tilting her head to the side, she sucked him, determined to take more of him into her mouth than she had managed to get inside of her.

Troy's head fell back against the mountain of pillows on his bed. Her mouth felt so warm, wet, and juicy. Her hands roamed his body, her touch erotically soft and delicate. With one firm hand, she stroked him up and down with the rhythm of her mouth. He watched her, the sight of his manhood sliding down her throat too much for him to stand for long. He broke forth in her mouth, spilling over down her chin, dripping onto her lovely neck.

FREE-FALLING

Troy knew that he was in too deep with Crystal. She consumed his thoughts when they weren't together. And at moments like this when they were, he wished he could stop the clock and make time stand still. He was falling for her, hard and fast. And he knew it. Something about it felt right. He wasn't sure what it was, but there was something different and oddly intoxicating about her. Hers had been a slow seduction that he never saw coming. He felt safe with her. Like he could let down his guard. That was what he was doing now as he answered her question about his uncle.

Troy sighed. "The organization my uncle runs is basically a halfway house for newly released inmates. He really does find them housing and employment. That much is true." He looked at Crystal. "But, really, it's just a way for him to account for the money he gets illegally."

"Where does the money really come from? Guns, drugs?"

Troy shook his head. "That's a question I never bothered to ask. At the end of the day, to be honest I don't really care."

"It sounds like your brother thinks your father is a hypocrite."

Troy nodded.

"In a way he is, though." Crystal stroked his arm.

He frowned.

"You both are, really." She saw the confused look on his face. "Your brother makes money in the streets and you don't. So you think that makes you innocent?"

Something in Troy's expression shifted, but she kept going.

"You want to know what I think?" she asked.

Troy hesitated before finally nodding.

"You speak about your uncle and your brother as if they're the only ones whose hands are dirty. But you're not as squeaky-clean as you think. You reap the rewards of having a thug for a big brother. Having an uncle who runs Harlem. A father whose name opens certain doors in certain circles . . . all of that works in your favor. And, then you get to grandstand and poke your chest out because you're the 'good son.' The one who gets all the benefits without incurring all the risk."

Troy stared back at her in silence. Her words stung.

"I know guys like Wes," she said, rubbing her hand across Troy's bare chest. "I grew up around them. Guys who use their size and their power to intimidate other people." She cupped his face in her hands. Staring down at him, she inhaled his scent. "I know men like your father, too. The ones who think the rules should apply to everybody except them. And men like you," she said, "who look so unblemished in the public eye. But behind closed doors, they're the most dangerous of them all."

She smiled widely, her eyes twinkling.

He laughed at that assessment. "Dangerous?" he repeated. "Is that what you think I am?" He pulled her closer, his hands cupping her ass beneath the sheets.

She squealed.

"There's nothing dangerous about me," he said. "I wouldn't hurt you."

She traced his lips with her fingers. "I wouldn't let you."

Troy slept soundly on his back, his chest rising and falling slowly with each contented breath. Crys snored lightly, her head on his chest, one arm spread out across his body. With their legs intertwined, they lay tangled together after a blissful night of lovemaking, conversation, and room service. Crys had gotten answers, for better or worse, and had gone to sleep content in his arms. She thought she was dreaming when her cell phone began to vibrate on the bedside table. It took a while before the sound of it stirred her from her dream.

She looked at the caller ID. *Vanessa.* She looked over at Troy, alarmed. He was still asleep. Crystal looked at the time. It was 8:41 A.M.

She slipped out of bed, and ducked into the bathroom. She locked the door, and climbed into the empty bathtub, pulling the shower door shut as if doing so created a soundproof barrier of some sort. The last thing she wanted was for Troy to wake up.

"Hello?" she whispered.

"Crystal?" Vanessa sounded like she was crying.

She answered in the same hushed whisper. "Yeah," she said. "I'm sorry, I'm in a meeting. Is everything okay?"

Vanessa was definitely crying. Crystal could hear her sniffling.

"Troy is cheating on me. I know he is."

Crystal shut her eyes, and chided herself for answering.

"Calm down, Vanessa. What happened?"

"He stayed out last night. Now he's not answering my calls."

"Listen, it could be anything. Don't jump to conclusions."

Crystal leaned her head against the bathroom wall. She heard Troy moving around in the suite. She climbed out of the shower, still whispering. "You think he's hurt?"

"I don't know," Vanessa whined.

Crystal squeezed her eyes shut. "Let me call you back after my meeting. Okay?"

"I'm sorry to bother you," Vanessa said. "I just don't have anybody else I can talk to."

Crystal felt lower than before. "It's no problem," she lied. "I'll call you back as soon as I can."

She hung up the phone, and cursed under her breath.

When she emerged, Troy was sitting on the edge of the bed.

He greeted her with a smile on his face so wide that it made her smile, too. She walked over and he pulled her close.

"I wish I could stay right here with you all day."

She lay beside him propped up on one elbow. "Why can't you? My schedule is clear for once."

He pouted. "Dru is forcing me to meet with those same investors I introduced you to at his party. Today's the day they cut the big checks. I can't get out of it."

"Congratulations. What time is your meeting?"

"Three o'clock at my office. I should be finished by four thirty. I can come to Brooklyn after that." He was anxious to get back in her arms again.

She thought about it. Maybe this was all going too far.

Troy seemed to read her thoughts. "I'm not in love with Vanessa."

She looked at him.

"Running for office is my father's chance to get his own identity. For years, he's been tied to my uncle." Troy thought about how he felt when he learned that his uncle's drug money had financed his father's businesses. That the seed money to start the family business had come from Uncle Don's illegal dealings. Stuart Mitchell had started as a front for Uncle Don's money. Money that had financed their rise from low-level street hustlers to power brokers, both in the entertainment industry and in the streets.

"My father needs me to play this game. To string her along for a while so he can stay close to her father." He shook his head. "That's all it is. I don't love her. The only woman who has my attention right now is you."

Crystal hated herself for believing him.

He left just after 10:00 A.M., and she didn't wash his scent off right away. She lay in the bed until late checkout time, then rode home on the subway, still smelling him with every step she took.

She opened the door to her brownstone and knew right away that something wasn't right. The house felt different, the energy somehow off. She walked into the kitchen and noticed that the toaster was positioned at an odd angle. She was compulsive about things like that and knew she would never have left it that way. The hairs on the back of her neck stood at attention and she grabbed a knife off the butcher block. Slowly, she stepped through her kitchen and into the adjoining dining room. Her heart pounded in her chest as two figures came into focus. One of them large and looming, his face set in a menacing scowl. The relief of recognition washed over her. *Tyson*. Her eyes darted to the man standing behind him, smiling.

She dropped everything.

"Daddy?"

Quincy smiled at his daughter. "Hey, Sydney."

Vanessa stood by the door with her bags packed. Tears streamed down her face and Troy was pretending that he wanted her to stay.

"It's too much," she was saying. "It's bad enough that things are shaky between us. But this whole thing with your brother. Now you're staying out all night. We should just take a break for a while."

"I told you what happened. I was drunk. Dru took me home, and let me crash on his couch. You can ask his wife." Dru and his wife often lied for Troy, providing him with alibis for times like this.

"I know, but—"

"Listen." Troy pulled her toward him. Reluctantly, she melted into his arms. "I've been distracted lately. You're right. Work has my mind going in a million different directions at once. Wes is another headache. But I'm dealing with him." He squeezed her tighter. "None of that has anything to do with how I feel about you. You're my baby. We're getting married. I fucked up last night. I shouldn't have stayed out all night. But I was at Dru's house. On his couch." He kissed her forehead. "You've been thinking too much again. You know how you get." He tickled her until she giggled. Once he saw her dimples, he knew he was back in.

He gave her his credit card and let her buy some new shoes. Then he hit her with the next swindle.

"I'm going out of town for a few days. I'll be back on Sunday."

She didn't argue. That was the Vanessa he was used to. The one who didn't challenge him, didn't ask too many questions. Lately, that was changing. The engagement itself had come after Vanessa and her mother had applied the full-court press on him like they were basketball wives on steroids.

He packed a bag, kissed her good-bye, and headed for Brooklyn.

She dabbed at her eyes, overcome with emotion at the sight of her father. Free, unshackled, in his own clothes, and without the watchful gaze of guards. He was home. She hadn't stopped smiling since she saw him.

"I still can't believe you lied to me about your release date."

He shook his head. "I didn't lie. I just didn't tell the whole truth." He looked at his nephew Tyson. "I wanted to ride home with my nephew here and drop in unannounced."

Tyson grunted. A large, looming presence, her cousin was a sight to behold. To say that he was the muscle of the family was putting it mildly. He was a man of few words. But he loved his favorite uncle Quincy.

"I listened to everything you told me while I was away. About your big brownstone in Brooklyn, and your fancy car, and all that. But I wanted to see how you're really living." He looked around. "I'm impressed, baby girl."

She stared at him. "What happened, Daddy?" Her voice was small, like the little girl who wished she was brave enough to ask it years ago. "The whole story, I mean. The truth. What happened with the diamonds?"

Quincy looked at her and realized he had never been able to tell her. His phone calls, letters, and visits were closely monitored and recorded. For the first time, it truly hit him that he was free. He resisted the urge to cry and lit a cigarette instead.

He cleared his throat.

"You know I was hustling back then. I used to get money with this nigga and his crew uptown. Long story short, Don was doing his thing. He had the connect, and his boys were ruthless. They were into everything. Drugs, guns, breaking and entering, scams, you name it. Money!" He clapped his hands together for emphasis and flicked the ash from his cigarette into the plastic ashtray on the table.

"I used to fuck with them—" He looked at his daughter apologetically. "Pardon my language, baby girl. You know I been away a long time. That's the way niggas talk in there." His smile melted her heart.

She shook her head at him, laughing. "Please! You must not remember that I grew up with Aunt Pat."

Quincy laughed. He remembered that his sister-in-law cursed like a drunken sailor. He couldn't wait to see her again and catch up on all that he had missed.

"So, you used to fuck with this crew from uptown," she reminded him.

Quincy chuckled, hearing her curse. She would always be his baby girl, even though she was turning twenty-nine this year.

"We was tight. Or so I thought. We used to party together, travel. Him and his wife, me and your mother. Anyway, one day, he came and told me about a hookup he had in Midtown. Some jewelry store. We could run up in there, get a couple of pieces, and be out. He had a guy who worked there. He was gonna buzz us in and he knew the owner would be there that day. The owner was the only one with the safe combination. That was where the good shit was. So, we mapped it out, made sure the guy on the inside was ready, and we did it. Just me and him. We got in there and we tell him what time it is . . . this is a robbery and all that. This muthafucka . . . the owner? He gonna tell the nigga to kiss his ass. He's not opening the safe. The inside guy is trying to act like he don't know us, because the plan was never for anybody to get hurt. At least not on my part."

He paused and took a long drag of his cigarette. He had repeated these events in his mind so many times. Still, it was painful to say it all out loud.

"I'm watching the guy the whole time, telling him to do it or he's gonna get hurt. I got my gun on him. The situation was under control." He shook his head. "The nigga hits the guy in the face with his gun. Busts his face wide open. The guy is leaking all over the place. Now he's scared. He's sorry. He's gonna give up the combination. He gives it up and I walk over to the safe, open it up, start pulling shit out. Next thing I know I hear a shot."

She felt like she was there. She tried to imagine how her father must have felt in those moments.

"Don shot the guy in the head. The guy was squirming, struggling to like . . . live." Quincy shook his head. "Don shot him again. The guy on the inside—fucking Shu from uptown. Snitch nigga. Anyway, he started bugging out, spazzing. 'Yo, what the fuck?' Don is cool as a cucumber. He looked at me and was like, 'Q, you got the shit?' I nodded, and we got the fuck out of there." He took one last drag on his cigarette and stomped it out in the ashtray.

"We got in the car and he was dead silent. I didn't have nothing to say to him. Far as I was concerned, he was crazy. He didn't have to kill that man. At the same time, I was there with him so there was only so much I could say. I knew I shouldn't have been there. All day I kept feeling like I shouldn't go." He shook his head in regret over the one decision he wished he could go back and change. "Something in my gut was just like . . . it wasn't right. I went anyway and now there was a fucking manhunt for the killers of an Orthodox Jew store owner in the Diamond District. Shit was hot. He dropped me off in Brooklyn and I thought he would come in and we would split it all up like usual. But when we got there, he was like, 'You hold it, Q. I gotta go back to Manhattan. It's gonna be hot. Just hold it. I'll come get mine.' And he left. That was the last time I seen Don."

She stared at her father, anxious for him to continue. He sipped his Heineken before continuing.

"I couldn't sleep that night. I stayed up, thinking. I felt like something wasn't right. Don had fucked up, killed this man. Both of us were wanted for robbery. I woke your mother up early the next morning. I told her to pack as much of her shit in a little overnight bag as possible. I gave her a bunch of money and told her to go stay with your aunt and your grandmother in Staten Island until I came to get her."

He recalled the look on Georgi's face that morning. She looked afraid, but was doing her best to put on a brave face. She had taken the kids, the money, and the diamonds and gone into hiding.

"I told her not to contact me no matter what. And I waited. I wanted to see if Don was gonna get greedy when he came for the diamonds. Cuz we had a lot. Ten loose stones. Clear babies! A bunch of other shit. We had over a million dollars in jewelry. But we couldn't move it. Too risky at the time. Then Shu's dumb ass let the cops get inside his head. Next thing I know, Don is locked up. The cops are questioning him. I should have ran then." He lit another cigarette.

"Why didn't you?" she asked. It was the logical thing to do.

He smiled. "Georgi loved New York. And I didn't want to leave my family behind. So, I waited." He exhaled the smoke. "I figured the cops couldn't prove shit if they couldn't find shit. Sure enough, they came. They called themselves raiding our little house in Brooklyn early one morning. I was ready for them, though. They didn't find shit. Then they searched my car."

He looked at her then. "They found a gun in my car that wasn't mine. I didn't put it there. Never used it. In fact, there were no fingerprints on it at all. Like somebody cleaned it. But it was the murder weapon. I knew right then that Don had set me up."

Quincy's jaw tensed. "They still didn't have the jewels, though. Your mother had them. But they didn't need them. Don got out and I went to jail for murder."

Her heart broke all over again for her dad. He had not been innocent. By his own admission, he had set out to rob the jewelry store, but he hadn't gone to jail for that. Instead, he went away for a crime that his so-called friend had committed and framed him for.

"So now it's your turn," Quincy said. He tapped his cigarette over the ashtray and smirked. "What happened with this guy you met at college? How did he find you?"

She frowned a bit at the way he had phrased the question. He seemed to be implying that Troy had set out after her like a hunter. She shook her head. "We met at college. He was in my math class and I was struggling. He tutored me and we fell in love." She didn't look at her father, afraid that she might see skepticism on his face. She couldn't handle that. At this point, she needed to believe that it had been real.

"When we came home for the holidays, he invited me to meet his family."

"Where was your mother?" Quincy had wondered for years why Georgi would ever allow their daughter to go to such an occasion without her.

She didn't want to acknowledge the fact that her mother had been out gallivanting with her flavor of the week. "I can't remember," she lied. "It was the holidays. She might have gone out shopping or something. Anyway, Destiny went with me. They lived in Harlem, but on the richer side of it."

Quincy nodded. He had been to Fox's home many times for social gatherings. Don's brother tried to pretend that he was above the street life. But Quincy knew that there had been plenty of times when Fox called on his little brother to fix his problems. Fox wasn't getting his hands dirty directly, but he was in on it, too. The big house uptown had been one of the ways Don came through for him. He got the permits and building inspections done under the table, and Fox was able to conduct an expensive renovation with practically no red tape.

"I met his uncle at that party." She could scarcely say the man's name now. It was synonymous with so much pain, both emotional and physical for her family. "He seemed nice. But when I looked back on it later, he was baiting me. Questioning me." She shook her head. She had been so eager to impress Troy's family and friends. What a fool she felt like now. "I never thought he would know you. What were the chances of that?" She laughed at the absurdity even now. "I listened to you earlier when you spoke about your days as a hustler. But I was too little to remember any of that. My earliest memories are of Staten Island, living with Mommy and Malik, eating over at Aunt Pat's and Grandma's house. It was a much smaller world than the one you described today."

Quincy nodded again.

"I knew you as Daddy and not as this gangsta. So I'm sitting there running my mouth about you, about Mommy." She shook her head at herself. "Later at the hospital when we were waiting for Malik to come out of the coma, Destiny remembered something. She said that Troy's uncle looked at his brother funny when I said Mommy's name. Then, when I said your name, she thought she saw the uncle smile a little. She shrugged it off at the time. When we left, Troy's uncle had his driver take us home. I guess that's how they found out where we lived."

Quincy shot a look at his daughter. It was unsettling to her. For a brief moment, he seemed almost angry.

"You're bugging." He shook his head, dismayed, and swigged the last of his beer. "They found out where we lived the first time your boyfriend came to pick you up."

Crys felt dread wash over her. She shook her head.

"He was in on it the whole time," Quincy said. "You telling

me that all this time you thought this nigga Troy was innocent?" He wanted to laugh at her. If she had been one of the dudes in jail, he would have roasted her mercilessly. But she was his daughter, so he went easy on her. He wished more than ever that he had been around when she was growing up. He would have never raised a daughter this naïve. "The whole thing was a setup, and he was in on it." He said it with finality, as if believing otherwise made her a total fool.

She swallowed. She felt an incredible tug-of-war in her heart between the love she had for her father and the love she had never stopped feeling for Troy.

"Daddy," she said softly. "He didn't know anything about you when we were at Howard."

"He had to," Quincy said defiantly. "You said yourself that you weren't raised in the streets. He was. He had to be if he was Don's nephew."

She still looked doubtful and it pissed him off.

"So you're telling me his brother was in the streets enough to beat your brother to death, but this nigga Troy was spotless?"

"I'm saying—"

"He done sold you on that same shit Fox is selling." Quincy altered his voice and posture mockingly. "Oh, no. I'm not like my brother. My brother is the bad guy. I'm the businessman." He laughed, although the situation didn't amuse him much. "That nigga played you, baby girl."

She felt like crying. She hated that her father was so convinced. It was causing her to doubt her own convictions.

"You're probably right," she said. She shrugged.

He got up and took another beer out of the fridge. He was enjoying his newfound freedom. But he hadn't forgotten how it felt to have it taken from him.

"You do a lot of thinking when you're locked up. I did mine

while I was in solitary for three months when they sent me up north." He cracked his beer open. "I ain't no saint, you know what I'm saying? I was wrong. I was getting money the fast way. I chose to go in there and rob that man. I could have dealt with it better if I went away for robbery. I did that. But I didn't kill that man. I didn't shoot him twice at point-blank range. It was nineteen ninety-one the last time I got to walk around like this and get my own beer whenever I felt like it. Nineteen ninety-one! Think about that. All for something I didn't do. And the man that did do it . . . the nigga who put his hands on my wife and killed my only son, and played mind games with my daughter"— he shook his head at the weight of it all—"he gonna walk away with no time served?" Quincy smiled sinisterly and shook his head. "Nah."

He swigged his beer, set it down on the table, and looked at his daughter.

She sighed and the tears came back again.

Quincy watched her closely. He had spoken to his wife and was well aware that their daughter had gone quite far in her quest for revenge. He could see that it had taken its toll on her. Tears poured from her eyes faster than her tissues could keep up. He knew that the weight of it all had finally begun to crush her.

"Malik would be proud of you." He saw her back straighten and her tears slow as the words sank in. "He would look at everything you've done and he would be proud. He would tell you it's not your fault."

She choked back a sob and squeezed her eyes shut.

"It's not your fault, Sydney. That's what he would tell you. You didn't know. There was no way you could know." Quincy stood up and walked over to where his daughter sat. He squatted beside her so that they were eye to eye.

Tyson stood watching silently in the corner.

"You came this far. You don't have to go any further. I'll take it from here, baby girl." Quincy wiped her tears.

She sniffled and shook her head. "No. I want to finish what I started. But the plan has changed a little bit. I think we can take the whole family down."

She got her dad settled in at his new place and picked up take-out from her favorite place on the way home. She took a much-needed shower and got ready for Troy's arrival. She felt safer on her home turf now that her father was home and still her hands shook slightly from nervousness.

Troy arrived right on time. She peeked out between the blinds and watched him approach her door. His walk had always turned her on. Tonight was no exception. He rang the doorbell and she greeted him, smiling.

"Hello." She held the door wide.

He stepped into her foyer and took off his coat. She hung it up in the hall closet and then turned to face him again. She drank him all in. His toned chest bulged against the black T-shirt he wore. His biceps peeked out from beneath its sleeves. His ebony skin shone against the dark denim jeans he wore. He kicked off his construction Timbs at the door. He looked delectable.

He stepped into the living room. "I can tell you decorated this place yourself. It's feminine and masculine at the same time. Just like you."

Crystal scoffed at that. "I am not!"

Troy nodded. "You are. All tough and fragile at the same time."

She shrugged. She wasn't sure that she agreed, but she chose not to argue now. "Okay."

She offered no protest when he came near. She didn't pretend not to want it just as badly as he did. She kissed him, throwing all of her caution and concern to the wind. She led him by the hand down the hall to her bedroom. As they climbed into her bed, she felt all the doubt and uncertainty fall away. She told herself that this was all part of the plan.

REDEMPTION

He opened the door and ushered Crystal inside. She looked around, smiling.

"So, this is where the magic happens, huh?" They were in his office at Stuart Mitchell's main location in Harlem. He was showing her the place during off-hours on Friday night. Dru had called and asked him to pick up a client file and drop it off to him. Troy agreed, figuring it was the least he could do for him. Dru was covering for him yet again. For the past two days, Troy had been living a double life, holed up in Crystal's house while Vanessa thought he was out of town. When Crystal had gone to work earlier in the day, Troy had spent the day there, under the guise of being the head man in charge. He pretended to focus on figures and statistics when all he was really focused on was Crystal and the way her eyes lit up when she smiled.

"This is it." He motioned toward a set of plush leather chairs, then shut his office door halfway. The place was empty, all the staff having gone home hours ago.

Crystal sat on top of his desk while he searched through his drawer for the file. She noticed an expensive pen set, a calendar, and a black-and-white photo of a beautiful, Lena Horne-esque woman.

"Your mother?" she asked, gesturing toward the picture.

Troy nodded and smiled proudly at the portrait. "Yeah."

"She was beautiful."

"Thank you." He leaned forward and kissed her softly. "So are you."

She gripped his face in her hands and kissed him deeper. He groaned and pulled her closer to him, upsetting some of the papers on his desk.

She grinded back at him, encouraging him. Troy leaned into her and gripped her tightly around her waist. With his lips at her neck, he tugged at her leggings until they came down. He freed one leg and placed it on his shoulder, grinding into her wetness. Crystal slowly winded her hips, trying hard to take in more of him.

Vanessa stood watching them through the partially opened door with tears streaming steadily down her face.

Caught up in the ecstasy of how Troy was making her feel, Crystal was abruptly rocked by a powerful force from behind. She was suddenly aware that someone was screaming and it dawned on her that Vanessa was there, raining down blows on her head. Vanessa swung wildly, connecting with Crystal's jaw and the side of her head. Gone was the harmless and naïve arm candy Troy had been parading around town. In her place was a scorned, raving madwoman. And she was out for blood. She charged at Crystal as she and Troy scrambled off the desk. He managed to grab Vanessa just as she grabbed a stapler off his desk and hurled it at Crystal's head, narrowly missing her.

"You fucking *bitch*! I trusted you." Vanessa's chest heaved with fury. "You sent me fucking cupcakes!" She tried to charge at Crystal.

"Calm down!" Troy yelled over and over.

"Get the fuck off of me!" Vanessa sobbed. She kicked at Crystal, but Troy had grabbed her in a bear hug from behind. She could only scream as Crystal scrambled back into her clothes. Vanessa watched through the tears pouring from her eyes.

"Listen!" Troy was saying. "It's not what you think!"

"I saw you!" she hissed. "I watched you fucking her just now."

He couldn't argue with that.

Crystal managed to get herself together. She looked at Vanessa and felt sorry for the girl. There was no way to tell her now that she was just a pawn in all of their games.

"I'm sorry," Crystal offered sincerely.

"Let me go!" Vanessa wriggled free at last.

Crystal grabbed her boot and held it up like a weapon. She was ready for battle.

Vanessa looked at Troy. "Wow. You made me look like a fool." She hocked back and spit in his face, the action occurring before she knew it. She wanted to fight him, to tear at him, and hurt him the way that his rejection over so many years had hurt her.

He stood frozen, aware that he could really hurt her at that moment. Slowly, he wiped the slob off of his face.

"What, am I not good enough? I'm not nice enough? Who do you think you are?" She shook her head, enraged at him. "You think you're a god, walking around playing chess with people's lives. All for your own gain. You take from everybody, and you never concern yourself with what's left afterwards."

Troy was disgusted. Even now as he stood listening to her tirade, he wanted to punch her in her face.

"Everybody told me your family was trash. They were right."

He called her name as she stormed out, even though he knew there was nothing else to say. He looked at Crystal helplessly.

She held her head where Vanessa had pummeled her from behind. She locked eyes with Troy.

"Now what?"

Fox was furious. Crystal and Troy sat with him in the living room of his Harlem mansion. Neither of them had the guts to look at him. He paced the floor anxiously, his attorney and staff secretary watching in silence.

Troy stared at the headline in the *New York Times*.

WILLIAM "FOX" MITCHELL MONEY LAUNDERING PROBE

Troy was distraught. Two weeks had passed since Vanessa had busted him and Crystal together in his office. She had sent movers to collect her things, changed her number, and cut off all ties with Troy. Crystal had gone back to work, anxious each day over whether or not she would be asked to step down as editor in chief. She didn't think they'd be stupid enough to ask for that and she was right. The days went by with no mention of any shake-up at the magazine.

That didn't stop the whispers around the office from the staff and her other colleagues. Although Crystal and Troy had been careful not to be seen together in any compromising positions since their discovery, and they had not confirmed any relationship between them, it was the worst-kept secret around the offices of *Hipster* and Stuart Mitchell. Everyone was buzzing about it. Oscar had been the only one bold enough to voice his suspicions, cornering Crystal in her office one Friday afternoon.

"If you're trying to keep it a secret, you might as well give up. All it takes is for someone to watch the way he looks at you. It's obvious that he's smitten." Oscar had been smiling when he said it, since he found the whole thing incredibly romantic and deliciously taboo. Crystal, however, was not amused. One part of her plan was going terribly awry. She was desperately trying to keep her emotions in check. She refused to admit that she had already started falling in love with Troy.

Fox's fall from grace had been public and shameful. Now he had his name splashed across the paper with the words "money laundering" right beside it. He was embarrassed. This time by the good son from whom he least expected it.

Fox looked at Crystal. He should have known she was too attractive for his son to resist. Foolishly, he had hoped Vanessa would be enough for him. He realized now—too late—that it had been too much to ask from Troy. To love the woman *he* chose, and to be content with what was a good life. Just not the life he had chosen for himself. He thought about the sacrifice Troy had made years ago, when he was forced to leave Howard and return to New York. He had been in love then, too. That time, Fox had asked his son to do the unthinkable. To choose family over love; to turn a blind eye to the savage destruction of a girl who had meant everything to him. Fox shook his head in self-pity. He deserved this. It was some kind of divine retribution for the pain he had allowed his son to suffer years ago.

Still, this was bad. It was hard to be philosophical when his shame and embarrassment were still so raw. His political aspirations were over. And worst of all, he knew that somewhere Don was having the last laugh.

He sat down at last, his head in his hands. Troy watched his father, wracked with guilt over the part he had played in this. "I'm sorry," he said. "I really am."

Crystal hated that she had been summoned here. Like Vanessa, Fox's pain was collateral damage for a much bigger war than the one he was fighting. She hated seeing him broken this way, his dreams dashed and his reputation in tatters. Worst of all, Fox hadn't said a word to her since they got there. It was like he had called her there just to make her see what her lust had done to ruin him. She was anxious to get this all over with.

They spent another hour in the purgatory that Fox's home had become. A thick sense of sadness loomed over the place as the man and his staff made peace with the fact that his political prospects were over.

Crystal and Troy walked into her brownstone afterward, feeling dejected. Troy, especially, looked like he had lost his best friend.

"Are you okay?" she asked gently. She sat beside him on the sofa.

He offered a weak smile. "Yeah," he said. He looked at her. "You know what I feel the worst about?"

She shook her head. She had no idea which part of it all was eating at his conscience the most.

"It's the relief I feel." He saw the surprised expression on her face, just as he had anticipated. "I know. That's terrible, right? My father's career is in the toilet and I feel relieved."

Crystal frowned. "Why?"

He tucked a strand of her hair behind her ear and touched her cheek tenderly. "Because I don't have to hide how I feel about you."

He pulled her close to him. With their noses inches apart, he stared into her eyes.

"I love you."

She felt too choked up with emotion to respond.

He stared at her, searching her eyes deeply. "I'm happier with you than I've ever been in my life."

Troy kissed her. His kisses traveled south until he tasted her sweet spot. She closed her eyes, fighting away the guilt and pain that tugged at her. She quieted her mind and did her best to bring herself back to what she was feeling, how it felt with him between her legs this way. She fought the urge to cum, reluctant to allow herself the satisfaction. She didn't deserve this. Didn't deserve the way he drove her body to heights she'd never known with any other man but him. Sensing her hesitation, he stopped abruptly. Crystal's breath caught audibly in her throat.

He kissed her, sliding himself inside her as he did so. She clung to him so desperately that he looked at her, wanting to lock in the memory of her face this way. Crystal's expression was somewhere between helplessness and pure pleasure.

He slowed his pace. Despite the physical desire he felt for her, this moment was more than just a physical thing. He connected with Crystal on a level he hadn't with any woman before or since. With his body, he forced her legs wide and sank himself deeper inside of her, forcing her to moan in pleasure. She grinded her hips on him with such intensity that his eyes widened in the darkness of the room.

Crystal pushed him back hard and he slid out of her. She pounced on him unexpectedly, mounting him and sliding her slick pussy up and down around his rock-hard warrior until she accommodated more of him than she ever had before. Troy groaned in pleasure as he felt her tighten around his girth, grinding mercilessly on him. Her nails dug into his chocolate skin and he felt them piercing, tearing at him. He kissed her and she bit his lip. Troy growled in response. It was on now.

He smiled in the dark, though he wasn't sure if she saw it. It didn't matter. She had awakened a monster in him that he hadn't unleashed on her before. She slapped him hard across the face, winding her hips on him erotically. He grabbed her neck, squeezing it firmly while she clawed at him and rode him like a stallion.

"You love me?" His eyes bore into hers. He had said those all-important words to her and she had yet to say them in return.

Crystal's eyes welled with tears. She did. She loved him so much. But admitting that wouldn't solve a thing. All it did was further complicate a situation that seemed more impossible by the moment. She pushed her hands toward his face, wanting to hurt him the way that she was hurting.

Troy grabbed her hands and flipped her onto her back, pinning her down. This time, there was no use fighting back. He had her glued to the couch, his dick grinding deep until he came in violent shudders inside of her.

He held her face in his hand firmly, forcing her to meet his gaze. "Do you love me, Crystal?"

She shook her head, shaking the tears free that had been waiting for the chance to fall.

He loosened his grip, wiped her tears, and kissed her softly.

She exhaled deeply, nodded, and answered breathlessly, "Yes." She hated herself because it was true. She did love him, despite all the warnings in her head that she shouldn't. She *couldn't*.

His smile seemed to illuminate the whole room. "I love you, too."

They lay together afterward in bed with their legs intertwined. She rested her head on his chest, rising and falling as the pace of his breath slowly steadied. He held on to her tightly, his fingers in her hair.

Darkness enfolded them as they lay together on that final night. Crystal couldn't sleep. She lay awake restlessly, consumed by thoughts of what lay ahead for them over the next twenty-four hours. She watched Troy as he slept, aware that it was for the last time. She chided herself for it. She knew it was torture, memorizing his face this way, his body. Inhaling his scent. Watching the rise and fall of his chest. She would recall all of it later, she knew. Later, when she would be alone with her thoughts, trying desperately not to let them linger on the euphoria of the past few weeks.

Troy woke up the next morning and reached for her. She smiled as he smothered her neck and chest in feathery kisses.

"I want you to come with me to meet my father today."

She saw the range of emotions he experienced. First surprise, then happiness as it occurred to him that this was a major step. He realized that Crystal seldom spoke about her family. As immersed as she was in the drama unfolding in the Mitchell clan, he couldn't recall a single instance of her mentioning her own family. He was honored that she wanted to take that step.

He nodded.

"Okay. Let's do it."

For the next hour, Crystal felt like she was in a fog. She showered, dressed, and did her hair in silence. Troy, on the other hand, was like a new man. He whistled along to the songs on the radio as they prepared to go. He was on top of the world. Meanwhile, Crystal had never felt so detached from reality in her life.

As they left her home, she shut the door slowly, aware that when she returned she would still feel his presence there. That those four walls were no longer her own. That the home had become *theirs*.

She climbed behind the wheel of her Audi and smiled at him. "Ready?"

He smiled back. "I think so. Never been in a car with you driving before. I think I might be nervous."

Crystal laughed. "You should be."

During the drive, Troy asked questions about her dad.

"What's his name?"

"Quincy." She glanced at him, looking for a spark of recognition. But Troy simply nodded.

"Quincy Taylor," she said, turning onto Pitkin Avenue.

Troy wasn't paying attention. Otherwise the name of Crystal's father might have rung an alarm bell. Instead he was focused on the neighborhood they had driven into. Crystal's part of Brooklyn was on the rise. *This* was not Crystal's part of Brooklyn. Abandoned homes and buildings dotted the street. Homeless people pushed shopping carts full of bottles and cans down the middle of the street. They passed bodegas with clusters of men in ill-fitting clothes holding court outside. Troy knew they weren't in Kansas anymore. He tried his best not to show his discomfort. He didn't want Crystal to feel embarrassed by the conditions her father was living in. He wondered if this was why she seldom mentioned her family. If they were struggling economically, she might be ashamed. He squeezed her hand reassuringly as they pulled up in front of an old run-down brick house. Troy looked at the tattered blinds hanging in the window and the thick overgrowth in the patches of grass at the front of the house. He forced a smile.

"This is it?"

Crystal could sense his discomfort, though he was doing his best to hide it. "Yup," she said. "This is it." She got out of the car and slammed the door shut. Troy could sense her tension and wondered about the state of Crystal's relationship with her father. He had felt her anxiety ever since she had announced that they were going to see her father that day.

They walked up the stairs and rang the bell. Crystal avoided looking at him. Troy reached for her hand. Reluctantly, she gave it to him, and he squeezed it comfortingly.

"You alright?"

She nodded. "Yeah," she lied.

The door swung open and Quincy stood before them. He smiled at the sight of his daughter and pulled her into a warm hug. Stroking her back reassuringly, he greeted her.

"There's my girl. Come on in."

She stepped across the foyer and turned back to hold the door ajar for Troy. He followed her in and stood face-to-face with her father. Troy extended his hand.

"Nice to meet you, sir. I'm Troy."

Quincy nodded. "Troy," he repeated. "Okay. Nice to finally meet you." He gestured toward the living room and they all stepped inside.

Troy pretended not to notice the peeling paint on the walls, the ratty, worn sofa with the stuffing poking out, and the dirty carpeting. He took a seat and smiled at Crystal's father like nothing was out of sorts.

She watched him, knowing what he must be thinking. His noble avoidance of the poor conditions only made her heart break more for him. He had no idea what he had just walked into. She sat beside him and prayed that it would all be over quickly.

Quincy sat across from them.

"So you're the infamous Troy Mitchell." Quincy sized him up. "My daughter has told me a lot about you."

Troy was visibly surprised by that. He smiled at her, happy that she had spoken of him.

She tried to force a smile in return, but she couldn't. Troy noticed and his own smile faded. "You okay?" he asked.

She nodded, though it wasn't true.

Quincy got his attention again. "You work together, is that right?"

Troy nodded. "Crystal works for one of the magazines my family owns."

Quincy's smile widened. "The Mitchell family."

Troy got a sinking feeling in the pit of his stomach. He looked at Crystal. Something about this didn't feel right all of a sudden.

"I'm very familiar with your family, Troy. You all have been very successful."

Troy shrugged. He thanked Quincy, but hoped they wouldn't stay on the subject long. It seemed distasteful to speak of his family's success while sitting in what looked like an abandoned home in a run-down neighborhood.

"I was actually friends with your uncle years ago." Quincy watched for Troy's reaction.

Troy's eyes widened. "Really?" he asked. "Uncle Don?"

Quincy nodded. "Yeah. Good ole Don." He smiled. "We used to get money together back in the day."

Troy frowned. He looked at Crystal. "Did you know that?"

She glanced at her father and nodded, avoiding eye contact with Troy.

Quincy was grinning like a Cheshire cat.

"Sure, she knew." He laughed. "Ole Don and I go way back. Matter of fact"—he stood up—"come downstairs and let me show you something real quick. This will blow your mind."

Crystal exhaled slowly. Suddenly, she felt light-headed. Her pulse raced and the room felt like it had begun to spin.

Troy stood up, completely unaware of what was going on. He followed her father toward the stairs. Quincy began walking down and Troy was right behind him. Crystal willed herself to stand up. On wobbly legs, she followed them downstairs.

The basement was wall-to-wall cement with an odor that suggested no windows had been opened down there in quite some time. Cobwebs hung loosely in the corners as Troy ducked under the construction beams. Quincy led them down the length of it, then moved around a bend.

As they rounded the corner, a pair of men came into view.

Troy spotted a large man standing against the wall. The man was glaring at him menacingly, a gun clutched tightly in his right hand pointing toward the floor. Another man sat facing them in a chair. Troy stopped in his tracks and started to turn. But two more men were behind him now, shoving him forward. He got closer and realized that the bloody and badly beaten man slumped in the chair was his brother, Wes.

His head whipped around in Quincy's direction. "What the fuck?" He turned back to face her. "What's going on, Crystal?"

Quincy smiled. He gestured toward Wes and let out a laugh. "First of all, that's not her muthafuckin' name." He shook his head. Without another word, he drew back and punched Troy dead in his face, sending him reeling backward.

Instinctively, Troy came back at him, puffed up and ready for a fight. But Tyson stepped forward, looming large over Troy, forcing him to back down. He pointed the gun at his head.

"You should sit down." Tyson's tone suggested that it wasn't a request.

Troy slowly sat in a chair beside his brother. Wes was bruised and bloody. His lip was swollen and one of his eyes was practically shut. He glared at Troy in silence.

Troy looked at Crystal. "You want to tell me what's going on here, Crystal?"

Tyson frowned and looked at his uncle. "Why the fuck does he keep calling her that?"

Quincy laughed. "Because that's who he thinks she is," he explained. He looked at his daughter, then at Troy. "All this time, I can't believe you never figured it out. I think it shows how little you thought of her. Really, it's insulting that you didn't recognize her. Even after all the pain your family caused." He looked at his daughter, his eyes narrowed. "I wonder if he even remembers what he did to you, Sydney."

Troy stared at her. He squinted his eyes, trying to see it. She watched the pieces slowly come together in his mind. The realization spread across his face like a virus. She watched his mind wander back ten years to several months ago, and then to the moments before they had arrived here today.

Wes, too, groaned, aware now of why they were here. He had been ambushed as he stepped out of his apartment complex the day before. Heading toward his car in the underground parking garage, he had been knocked unconscious from behind. He had woken up here and suffered a brutal beating for hours at the hands of these strangers he had never seen before. He had thought it was some gunrunners from Yonkers who had been giving his uncle some heat. But now it all made sense. He remembered Sydney and how Troy had been heartbroken afterward, crying and distraught over losing her. The aftermath of that day had torn a hole in the brothers' relationship that was irreparable. Wes remembered how savagely he had beaten Malik that day. He struggled against the restraints that held him in the chair, more desperate than ever to get out of there. He knew that he would never walk out of here alive.

Troy's heart galloped in his chest. His mouth went dry. He looked at Crystal and saw hatred in her eyes as she stared at him.

Troy was still staring at her, dumbfounded. "I still don't understand," he said.

Crystal sat down on a wooden stool that had been abandoned in the corner. She took a deep breath. "Okay," she said. "Let me explain."

I USED TO LOVE HIM

Fall 2006

Sydney tucked her anthropology book further beneath her arm as she headed across the Yard toward her dorm room on campus. It was Howard University's infamous homecoming weekend. Everyone had caught the fever. The Phi Beta Kappas and Alpha Kappa Alphas chanted, stomped, and stepped, practicing their routines. Students milled about like a multihued wave of black excellence splashed across the canvas of Washington, D.C. Howard homecoming was a can't-miss event for anyone in the DMV (D.C., Maryland, and Virginia) area between the ages of eighteen and twenty-five. Sydney, though, wasn't sure what all the hype was about.

She clutched her books as she pushed stubbornly against the throng, anxious to get back to her dorm room. Boasting a 3.90 GPA, she was one of the top students in her freshman class. Sydney easily excelled at writing and public speaking and wanted to become a journalist. Math had been giving her a hard time, though. So she had posted on the bulletin board that she was in need of a tutor. Checking for a response would be out of the question, though, as she saw the density of the crowd that had gathered. She just wanted to get back to her room.

Going to the homecoming festivities wasn't on her agenda. Sydney didn't like the big crowds of intoxicated people that accompanied most college parties. She reached Drew Hall and pressed her way through the mob of students that spilled into the hallway from the stairwell that led to her room. As she inched her way closer, she could hear a voice above the fray.

"Dress to impress! This is gonna be the party of the year. If you ain't there, you ain't nowhere!"

A girl Sydney recognized from one of her classes forced a flyer into her hand and was gone as quickly as she had appeared. She spotted the girl a moment later, already further in the press. Others like her had fanned out and were passing out what looked like the same flyer. The party was going down that very night, according to the guy addressing the crowd with the booming voice as he stood atop one of the tables in the lounge. Sydney glanced at the flyer.

Bison Pride! HU Homecoming Weekend kicks off with Yardfest with headliner Ludacris. Battle of the Dynasties Greek Stepshow will be Saturday night at 7 P.M. Fur party to follow at Look Lounge with performances by Lil Jon, Chamillionaire, Dem Franchize Boyz, and Bubba Sparkxxx.

"You see me every day in class. And you know I'm the best student. So why didn't you just tell me that you need a tutor?" a voice behind her demanded.

Sydney turned, frowning, and laid eyes on a cute and familiar face from her math class. Troy. She couldn't stand him.

"Your name is Sydney, right?"

She knew that some of the girls in her class would be flattered that he had taken the time to learn their name. She reminded herself then that she had posted a notice on the bulletin board with her name. So he didn't deserve too much credit. This guy was too self-absorbed to learn anyone's name. She cleared her throat.

"Yeah," she answered.

He smiled at her. "Why didn't you just come over to me in class and tell me you needed help?"

She hated hearing that. She wanted to dismiss him and say that she didn't need help, even though she desperately did. Troy was an asshole. One of those students who was a prodigy and wanted everybody to know it. Every day in class, he boisterously called out the answers with ease while Sydney struggled on the first step of an equation. Their classmates seemed enamored by him. Even the professor laughed at his antics and encouraged the rest of the class to express as much enthusiasm as Troy did. Sydney was competitive and in her other classes she excelled. But math was her Achilles' heel. And this smug asshole reminded her by answering every question correctly every Tuesday and Thursday when their math class met.

"I think I can find somebody who's . . . maybe a little—" Sydney struggled to find a word that wouldn't insult Troy.

"Cheaper?" he offered. "I won't charge you." He knew that most of the other students weren't as fortunate as him. "I know your money's probably tight. No biggie."

Sydney was offended now. Sensitive about the fact that her father was in jail, she took pride in the fact that her mother had managed to hold the family down single-handedly in his absence. How dare this nigga assume that she was in need of his philanthropy? "I'm not broke." She said it harder than she meant to.

Troy's smile faded. "I never said you were."

She scowled at him, the expression on her face rich with distaste. "I need somebody who's patient," she said. "You're too . . . I don't know if I can stand your personality honestly. And if you—"

"You want me to tutor you or not?" Troy interrupted. Now he *was* offended. The smile he had been wearing was long gone now.

She sucked her teeth. "Watch how you talk to me," she warned him. "Don't get slapped."

Troy laughed at the thought of that. "You know better," he said. His smile broadened as he stroked his face conceitedly. "Why would you want to slap a face like this?"

She glared at him, but reluctantly admitted to herself that he *was* cute even though she still didn't like him. Thick eyebrows accented his deep brown eyes, his blemish-free skin was like smooth chocolate pudding, and he was clean-shaven with a perfectly lined-up fade. She fought the smile that threatened to burst forth, forcing her face into a scowl instead.

He continued. "I'm here minding my business over by the bulletin board on my way back to my room and I see your cry for help. I come over here offering my services, free of charge. Answering *your* bulletin. And you insult me?"

She tried not to laugh. What a pompous prick. "I'm not insulting you. Just stating the obvious. You think your shit don't stink. Just admit it."

A slow smile crept across his face. He loved a challenge. "My shit stinks a lot, actually. But I get your point."

She couldn't battle her smile anymore.

"Okay," Troy said. "Maybe I joke around a lot."

Sydney nodded.

"But you'll pass the class." He adjusted his backpack. "Guaranteed."

She needed to pass. Her financial aid depended on it. Despite her mother's incredible ability to finance a comfortable lifestyle for them, she knew that Howard was expensive. Tuition without grants and financial aid could cripple a family. She wanted to achieve this degree on her own merit and that meant maintaining an excellent GPA to keep the cash rolling in.

"Why do you want to help me for free? We've never even had a conversation." She knew his type. He was handsome and he knew it. He took full advantage of his role as the freshman Casanova. She had taken note of his preference for the Beyoncé look-alikes around Howard. The girls with lighter skin, exotic eyes, and long hair. The ones who put makeup on and spent hours on their hair. Girls like her mother. Sydney was nothing like that. And until today, she'd doubted that Troy had ever even noticed her.

"You're Keisha's friend, right?" Troy asked.

Of course! That explains it, Sydney thought. Keisha was her roommate with a body like a Coke bottle. She was certainly Troy's presumed type. "Yes," she said, smiling triumphantly. She'd been right about him all along. Certainly he wanted to tutor her to get close to Keisha.

Troy nodded, too. "She's going out with my boy Daryl."

Sydney frowned. "D-Bo?" That was the only name Sydney ever heard nowadays. Keisha talked about him all the time. Sydney had met the guy a few times. But she wasn't at all impressed by what she saw. He was a jokester, a clown. Her disapproval of him was obvious and he spent little time in their room. Instead, these days Keisha was in D-Bo's room more often than she was in class.

"Yeah," Troy said. "That's what they call him. Anyway, he's my roommate. Keisha's in our room all the time, chilling. She said you been stressed out about some class and it's all you ever talk about. I never thought it was math because you never say too much in class. When I see you, you're always by yourself with your nose in a book. Then I saw your note and I remembered what Keisha said. I put two and two together and now I'm offering to help. Consider it a favor for my boy D. Maybe now Keisha will be nicer to him if I can help you pass."

He winked at her. What Sydney didn't know was that Troy had watched her for weeks. Not in a scary stalker way. But with a genuine interest and perhaps even a bit of reverence at how she carried herself, how intelligent she was, how organized and focused. Class after class, he quietly observed her from the back of the room. She seemed like the type of girl who had it all together. Her need for help was the perfect way for him to spark a conversation.

Sydney nodded slowly. She would have to check Keisha for speaking her business to other people. But Sydney was glad that Troy's motives were nobler than she had first thought.

She sighed. "Math is the one class I'm struggling in." Her frustration was obvious. "It's not my best subject. I'm an English major."

He smiled again. Nice teeth, she noted.

"Okay. Well, I'm your guy. I can help you pass. And I'll try not to interrupt your precious little sentences, Miss English Major."

Sydney stared back at him silently for a moment. "You're in *this* dorm building?" she asked incredulously. Now she was beginning to question whether or not she was blind. She had moved into Drew Hall upon her arrival at Howard back in August and she was sure that she would have noticed Troy among her housemates. She always assumed that he lived in one of the other dorm buildings.

"Yeah," Troy said, "just transferred here. I was living off-campus before."

"Oh. Does your family live near here?" she asked.

Troy shook his head, glancing at some other students passing by. "Nah."

Sydney waited for him to say more, but he didn't. "Oh, okay," she said. She smelled a story there. She wondered what it was. "Welcome to Drew Hall."

"Thanks." He smiled as he tucked his flyer into the back pocket of his jeans. "You going to the party tonight?"

She shrugged. "I don't know. Maybe."

Troy nodded. "Not the partying type?"

Sydney shook her head. "Not really. I want to stay focused on the real reason I'm here." She gestured at the books in her hands.

"No doubt." Troy got jostled a little by the crowd around them. "I'm in room one-oh-four. Let me know when you want to get started." He waved at her and then waded into the crowd.

Sydney watched him go, smiling still. "Jesus," she whispered under her breath. Despite her reservations about the guy, it was hard to ignore the fact that he was fine.

When she got back to her room, her roommate Keisha was standing at the foot of her bed, staring at numerous outfits laid out across it.

"Hey, girl," Keisha greeted Sydney. "Help me decide what to wear to the party tonight. I have to look good!"

Sydney tossed her books on her bed. "Why were you talking to D-Bo and his roommate about me the other night?" She plopped down on her bed and glared at her friend.

Keisha looked guilty. She hadn't expected the guys to rat her out. She had only been venting about Sydney's whining and how it was getting on her nerves. "Sorry, girl. I was just worried about you."

Sydney sucked her teeth. "Worried for what? You make it sound like I was gonna slit my wrists or something."

Keisha laughed. "Well, shit, you sounded like you might! You were practically in tears about the possibility of losing your financial aid. You couldn't talk about nothing else!"

Sydney shook her head, though she knew it was true. She had been obsessing over the issue for days. "Do me a favor, please? Don't talk about me to D-Bo or any of his nosy friends from now on."

Keisha nodded. "I won't. Don't be mad." She made a mental note to slap the shit out of D-Bo and Troy when she saw them later.

Sydney stared at her, letting her squirm a little. "I'm not mad," she admitted at last. "Not this time."

Keisha smiled and headed for her closet.

"Don't you think Troy is cute?" she asked over her shoulder.

Sydney pictured him in her mind—the way his lips moved when he spoke; his smooth chocolate skin. "He's cute."

"He's arrogant, though," Keisha said. "I kinda like it."

Sydney frowned slightly. "Sounds like you like him as much as you like D-Bo."

Keisha turned around. "Maybe I do." She shrugged. "I met D-Bo first. We hit it off and I really do like him. But then I met Troy and I was like . . ." Keisha's eyes widened in mock surprise. "If I would have met him first, I wouldn't even have looked twice at D-Bo."

Sydney watched Keisha frantically searching the floor of her closet on her hands and knees for the match to the black boot in her left hand. Keisha had a body like an hourglass with a pretty face and dimpled smile to match. She turned heads wherever she went. Sydney wondered whether Troy wanted to tutor her as a favor to D-Bo after all. Maybe it was actually a way for him to get closer to Keisha.

"Are you going to the homecoming party tonight?" Keisha called out, her voice muffled by the contents of the closet. Finally exasperated by her fruitless search, Keisha sat back on her heels and narrowed her eyes at Sydney. "Girl, you better start enjoying the fact that we are in the best years of our lives!"

Sydney rolled her eyes and lay back on her bed. She knew that Keisha was about to launch into one of her tirades about being free, independent, and away from home.

"No parents, no curfews, no stumbling in late and trying not to wake anyone. We are *free,* Sydney! Miles away from home with a gang of rappers descending on our little college town in search of a good time." Keisha practically glowed at the thought of it all. "We've been here for almost three months and you never go to any of the parties. All you do is sit in this room with your nose in a book. There's a whole lot of fun to be had out there, Z. You're missing all of it."

Sydney stared at the ceiling. It was true. She preferred the solitude of her dorm room whenever Keisha was out having fun. She didn't consider herself a loner. But unlike Keisha, Sydney didn't need crowds, music, or alcohol to have a good time. Still, as she thought about the cutie Troy from math class, she thought she might make an exception just this once. She looked at Keisha. "Maybe you're right. I'll go with you tonight."

Keisha jumped up and down with excitement. "Yay! Now get up and figure out what you're wearing. If you're going with me, you have to look good!" She playfully tossed a pillow at Sydney, hitting her in the head.

Sydney tossed the pillow back at her, got up, and headed for her closet in search of the perfect look. She saw Keisha pick out a different pair of boots, and a pair of Guess jeans with a tight matching T-shirt. Sydney sorted through her clothes. She wanted to look nice, but she didn't have anything sexy to put on. Day to day, she opted more for comfort than sex appeal. Unlike many of her peers, Sydney's mind was more focused on her future career than on attracting the horny guys that littered the college campus.

Her mother, Grandma Bonnie, and Aunt Pat had been three matriarchs in a family void of male role models. Her grandfather had passed away from a heart attack when Sydney was an infant. Aunt Pat had never married and her daughter Destiny's father had never been in the picture. And Sydney's own father had been incarcerated since Sydney and her older brother, Malik, were three and eight years old. Against the backdrop of New York's gritty streets, Sydney, Destiny, and Malik grew into adulthood, shielded from dangers seen and unseen by the women who loved them. When their grandmother died the summer before Sydney entered college, it had been a devastating blow to the family. Grandma had been the glue that kept it all together. In her absence, a noticeable void had been left. Now Sydney felt a need to do her best academically in order to honor her grandmother's memory.

While Sydney sifted through her closet, Keisha watched her. She smiled, wondering what her mousy little roommate would wear now that she was finally going to take a stab at having a social life.

Sydney and Keisha took the Metro to the homecoming party and the train was packed with other young people en route. Sydney noticed that many of the girls were dressed provocatively. Lots of makeup, perfume, tight clothes, and sex appeal.

She had second thoughts about her outfit, but quickly shrugged it off. This was who she was. Aunt Pat, who often served as Sydney's own personal motivator and pep talker, had driven the message home clearly that she never needed to compete with anyone else.

Aunt Pat was confident, laid-back, and down-to-earth. The complete opposite of Sydney's mother, Georgi. As little girls, they had never been close. Sydney's mother was the beauty of the pair or at least the superficial definition of beauty that men seemed to gravitate toward. Sydney's mom had the winning combination of a big ass, long hair, and a tiny waist. Her face was also lovely. But with a closer look and a little conversation, most people quickly surmised that she was shallow, self-absorbed, and utterly neurotic about her looks. Already beautiful, she had spent thousands of dollars a month on beauty treatments alone. She always wanted diamonds and designer clothes. Georgi Scott used to get her hair and nails done every week and was always dressed to impress, stepping out of the newest whip on the arm of the newest hustler. At least, that had been the case in her heyday.

Aunt Pat, on the other hand, couldn't care less about what anyone thought. Of the sisters, Pat had been closer to their mother, Bonnie. While Georgi was out painting the town on the arm of Sydney's father, Pat was at home, gleaning wisdom from their mother. Learning that the silent one is usually the most powerful one. That she didn't always have to talk loud and act raunchy to stand out. Pat was far more popular in their social circle than her sister was. Everybody gravitated toward her because she was funny and her biting wit was often lost on the less intelligent among them. But the smart ones got the jokes and they loved her for it. Pat was the life of the party.

Aunt Pat often reminded Sydney that whatever she felt about herself on the inside would reflect outwardly to others. Sydney felt good about the way she looked tonight, even if she was the only female with most of her body covered. She held her head high as they neared the venue.

HOMECOMING

The club was packed. Music and laughter filled the space, as the DJ moved the crowd. The dance floor was full and the energy was high. Keisha was greeted constantly by people she knew. Smiling broadly, she was in her element as she mingled with her friends. Sydney wasn't surprised that only fifteen minutes after they arrived, Keisha had disappeared into the crowd. Sydney didn't mind. She stood near a wall on one side of the room and rocked to the beat of "Yo (Excuse Me Miss)" by Chris Brown.

"Hey," she heard a voice, but didn't see anyone familiar as she looked around those closest to her in the crowd. "Sydney," the voice came again. Then she spotted him. Troy sat comfortably on one of the few white leather seats lining the walls of the club. He had a white T-shirt on, black jeans, and Jordans. As simply as he was dressed, he still managed to look better than all of the other guys present. Sydney couldn't help but smile. She walked over to where he was and he moved over so that she could sit down beside him. The girl who had been seated beside him seemed annoyed that she was expected to move aside for Sydney.

But Troy leaned over to her and with a discreet yet sultry voice said, "Excuse me, please, sweetheart."

The girl looked at him and very reluctantly slid aside to let Sydney sit between them. Sydney tried hard not to laugh, but it wasn't easy. Troy grinned, too, as she squeezed in next to him.

"Hey," he said again. "You look nice."

Sydney smiled and wondered why her pulse was racing. "Thanks." She looked around at all the people. "It's packed in here tonight."

Troy nodded. "I just saw Daryl and Keisha at the bar. They're having a good time." He looked around at the partyers milling about. "You having a good time?"

Sydney nodded. "This is my first time at a party since I came here. I usually go to—"

"Yo, Will!" Troy called out to one of his friends across the room. Troy's friend hollered back and headed their way. Before she knew it, Will was standing there, holding an animated conversation with Troy as if Sydney was invisible.

Sydney caught the girl next to her chuckling at how Troy had cut her off. It made her angry. She slid off the banquette and walked off, calling out to Troy over her shoulder, "I'll see you later." She heard him say something as she melted into the crowd, but she didn't care. She chastised herself for being distracted by his good looks. Troy was clearly a jerk. She knew his type. One of those rare students who was both a cool kid and a geek, smart enough to excel academically and savvy enough to make it look enviable. Add arrogance and a brusque demeanor to the mix and you had Troy.

"Why'd you walk off like that?" he asked as he came up behind her.

Sydney rolled her eyes, dismayed that he had followed her. "Troy . . ."

"I cut you off again, right? I'm sorry." He was laughing. "I know, I get distracted."

"You're self-absorbed," Sydney corrected.

Troy stopped laughing. "Me? Self-absorbed? You're crazy."

Sydney shrugged and focused her gaze on a group dancing nearby.

"You think I'm self-absorbed?" Troy shook his head and sipped his drink. "Really?"

Sydney nodded with an apologetic look on her face.

Troy smiled. "Maybe a little."

The DJ switched to Sean Paul's "Temperature." A couple was dancing nearby and both Sydney and Troy were distracted by them. The girl was bent over with her butt grinding on the guy's crotch. She touched her ankles and shook her ass on him as he braced himself against a wall and thrust himself against her. Sydney looked away. But Troy seemed utterly amused. As he laughed, his beautiful teeth seemed to gleam in the dimly lit club. Sydney nudged him playfully and he looked at her, still smiling.

"What?" he asked. "Come on. You know you want to dance like that with me."

Sydney laughed.

"Come on," he teased. "Show me what you got, Sydney Taylor."

She laughed with him and then looked at him questioningly. He knew her last name, too?

Troy looked at the drink in his hand and seemed to catch himself. "I'm sorry. You want me to get you a drink?" he asked.

Sydney shook her head. "No, thanks." She gestured toward his cup. "What are you drinking?"

Troy grinned slightly. "Bacardi," he admitted. "I don't drink all the time. It's homecoming weekend."

Sydney shrugged. "Do your thing."

"So, where you from?" Troy asked.

"New York," she answered.

"Me, too," he said. "What part?"

"Staten Island. How about you?"

"I live uptown." He sipped his drink once more. "I never knew they had black people in Staten Island," he said.

Sydney chuckled. "Well, we're definitely out there. Lots of us, too."

"But Staten Island ain't really New York City. You know what I'm saying? It's more like Jersey, ain't it?"

"No." Sydney always marveled at how little people knew of the city's fifth borough. "It's not."

Troy shrugged. "I always pictured it like a bunch of houses with white picket fences and all that. You know, real suburban. So you must be rich, then," he said, smiling.

She laughed. "Please! The struggle is everywhere. Don't get it twisted."

Troy's eyes widened. "The struggle? What you know about that?"

Sydney sucked her teeth. Truthfully, she wasn't even sure how her mother did it, aside from the men she befriended over the years to keep her company and keep her shopping. But Sydney had practically grown up in Aunt Pat's home, where money wasn't always so readily available. She had seen plenty of struggle in her young lifetime.

"I know enough," she said simply.

"Is that right?" He never would have guessed it. Sydney was different than the other girls. After class, she usually gathered up her things and headed straight to the next one. She never seemed to be hanging around doing nothing and was never found among the clusters of girls who stood around in the hopes of attracting male attention. For that reason, he had watched her. Intrigued by the girl who didn't bother blending in. She wasn't in college scouting for a husband. Sydney stood out in all the right ways. He never would have guessed that she came from hard knocks.

The DJ called for everybody's attention as he introduced the first act. Everybody rushed the dance floor, which was directly in front of the elevated platform serving as the stage. People were pushing and shoving their way to the front. A few exchanged heated words as the pandemonium escalated. The DJ yelled for everybody to chill, and security moved in to calm the crowd. Troy and Sydney stood on top of a nearby platform to get a better view. Lil Jon took the stage wearing an eclectic outfit and hollering the lyrics to his hit song "Snap Yo Fingers." The crowd sang along in unison.

Sydney rapped along from where she stood atop the platform. Troy bobbed his head, too. But he was more interested in watching Sydney let loose. He was so used to seeing her serious academic side that it was entertaining to see her unwind. Without realizing it, he smiled as she passionately rapped along to the song. Sydney caught him smiling and stopped singing, embarrassed.

"You laughing at me?" she asked shyly. She had gotten swept up in the moment.

"Nah," he said, shaking his head. "I'm enjoying it. Keep going."

Sydney laughed and sang along with the next verse as Troy stood smiling and nodding his head to the beat. Suddenly someone was reaching for Troy's hand and pulling him down onto the dance floor. Sydney recognized that it was one of the girls she had seen on the Metro earlier. The girl was squeezed into a body-hugging black dress. She was tugging at Troy, pulling him closer. Lacing her arms around his neck, she danced with him provocatively. Sydney watched for a moment and then forced herself to turn her attention back to the performance onstage.

As the other partygoers reveled all around them, Troy danced with the girl for a few minutes. Then he gently peeled her arms off of him and politely shooed her away. Pissed, she stomped off to where her girlfriends stood waiting and frowning at Sydney and Troy. Their looks were so venomous that Sydney looked at Troy in dismay.

"You just made me four new enemies that fast. What did you say to her?" she asked.

Troy laughed. "I told her that I already pissed you off tonight and she was only making it worse."

Sydney frowned. "Did you really say that?"

Troy nodded, laughing. "It worked, didn't it?"

Sydney laughed and shook her head at Troy. Lil Jon moved on to a song that she didn't know all the words to and she climbed down from the platform and stood next to Troy. The crowd around them jostled Sydney so that she was pushed even closer to him. She could smell his cologne and it smelled divine.

"This is why I don't like parties," she yelled over the noisy crowd. "All these people . . . I hate it."

He leaned down closer so that she could hear him over the music and mayhem. "You want to leave?" he asked. "We can go if you want."

Sydney was surprised. *We?* She had been battling a nagging thought all night. What did Troy want from her? Guys like him never noticed girls like her. She wondered what his angle was. "We'll miss the rest of the show," she said.

Troy shrugged. "It's okay. I've seen all these people perform before. Nothing new." He set his cup down on a nearby table.

Together, they left the party. Once outside, the cool October air felt good on their faces. As they strolled leisurely toward the Metro station, Sydney let out a sigh of relief.

"Whew!" she said. "I hate crowds like that."

"Me, too," Troy said. "That's another thing we have in common. Both from New York, both don't like crowds." Smiling, he said playfully, "Both good at math."

Sydney laughed. "I wish." She flashed Troy a brilliant smile. "What's your major?"

"I'm majoring in business, minoring in finance," he answered. "I like working with numbers."

"Good," she said. "You can be my accountant someday."

Troy laughed. He was thinking way bigger than that. "Maybe I will," he humored her.

They walked in the direction of the train station. They talked about their classmates, about the upcoming midterms, and the differences between New York and D.C. Their conversation flowed freely and never felt forced. Sydney was impressed. Troy was smart, handsome, and very ambitious. He was still boisterous and overly energetic and a bit macho. But by the time they arrived back at their dorm, Sydney was smitten. Troy walked her to her door and bid her good night with nothing more than a wink and a smile. And it was enough to melt her heart completely.

Troy started tutoring Sydney the weekend after homecoming. Sydney was no quick study. She struggled with the complexities of their statistics class. Even with Troy's help, it took two sessions before she grasped even the basic concepts of the course. He did his best to be patient with her. But it was a struggle.

On the night of their third scheduled session, Troy and his boys were celebrating D-Bo's birthday. Somehow, the group got their hands on some bottles of Alizé, and before long all of them were twisted. Unaware that the fellas were out getting wasted, Sydney waited for Troy in the dorm lounge. When he stumbled in at close to ten, she could tell immediately that he was in no condition to study. Troy was even louder and more obnoxious than usual.

"Yo, sing that shit again!" he was yelling to one of his friends. "How that shit go?"

He spotted Sydney and his smile widened. He grabbed her by the waist, and began grinding on her, dancing to "U and Dat," which his friends were drunkenly singing. D-Bo and the rest of the guys started cheering him on loudly, laughing, whooping, and hollering. Sydney was embarrassed. She pulled away, finally shoving Troy into the couch. He lay there on his back, still laughing. Then coughing. Next he was vomiting all over the psychedelic lounge carpeting.

Troy's friends stopped laughing and began gasping and making noises of disgust and repulsion. They laughed and grimaced while he threw up all over the floor. Sydney ran to the nearby resident assistant's room and grabbed rolls of paper towels. Running back to the ugly scene, she sopped up the remnants of Troy's evening as best she could. Troy's body was wracked by spasms as it expelled the remaining contents of his stomach. It was his turn to be embarrassed as Sydney took charge and got his friends to help get him to his room. They managed to get him there, tossing him on his bed before leaving to laugh among themselves at their friend's drunken misfortune.

Troy lay splayed across the bed until he caught his breath. Throwing up had taken a lot out of him and he needed time to gather himself. Sydney looked around his room. D-Bo's side was messy and disheveled with rap posters lining the walls and clothing littering the top of his bed. But Troy's side was meticulously neat, almost compulsively so. Everything was in its place. A calendar and a picture of a dog were the only things on his side of the wall. Sydney marveled at how organized he was. Except now as he lay in stark contrast to all of that order, sprawled across his bed on his back with his arms outstretched over his head.

Troy groaned and rolled over on his side.

"I'm never gonna drink again, I swear." His words were slurred and he was drooling a little. But somehow, he still managed to be kind of cute.

Sydney caught herself grinning at him. Once aware of herself, she snapped out of it and grabbed a bottle of mouthwash from atop his dresser. She poured some into the cap and handed it to Troy.

"Sit up and swish this around in your mouth. I'm sure it tastes like garbage in there right now."

Troy lay there, willing himself to sit up. It was pointless.

"I can't."

He looked like a sick little boy all curled up on his side like that. Sydney shook her head. She pushed some of the debris on D-Bo's bed over and carved out a seat for herself. Sitting across from him with the mouthwash cap still in one hand, she wondered who Troy really was.

"You got a girlfriend, Troy?" Sydney watched girls flirt with Troy every day. Many of those girls were aggressive. He seemed to revel in it, eating the attention up. But she hadn't seen him showing any serious interest in any one of them. Sydney wondered if he had a girlfriend back in New York. She did her best to convince herself that she was only mildly curious.

He mumbled something incoherent into his pillow.

"What? I can't hear you." Sydney hadn't realized how badly she wanted the question answered until now.

Troy wiped his face on the pillow and took a deep breath, only to erupt in a loud hiccup. He threw his head back against the pillow in defeat.

"I said"—he hiccupped again loudly—"no. I don't have a . . . girlfriend. You want to be my . . . my girlfriend?"

Sydney shook her head in pity. "You're so drunk right now." She laughed. Later she would write in her diary about how relieved she was that Troy didn't have a girlfriend. She even added hearts at the end. It was so cliché.

"I like you, Sydney." Troy sat up at last, slowly. He made a weak attempt at reaching for the mouthwash. "Your name sounds like a . . . like a news anchorwoman. 'In Canarsie, this is Sydney Taylor, Eyewitness News!'" Troy punctuated his impression with a newsworthy smile, then burst into laughter at his own joke.

Sydney chuckled at him, stood up, and walked over to Troy's bed. She sat beside him and handed him the cap. He swigged some of the mouthwash and handed the cap back to her. Sydney set it on the dresser, aware that the opened bottle of Scope was the one thing askew among Troy's perfectly stacked belongings. His neatness was an unexpected surprise. She grabbed a plastic cup from an open pack and handed it to him. He spat out the mouthwash and Sydney was relieved. He still smelled like a distillery, but the stench of his vomit was lessened some.

It took a while before his words began to make any sense. Troy sobered up slowly. While doing so, he went on a tangent, chattering incoherently about high expectations and the black male experience. Sydney listened, piecing together what he was telling her like it was a complicated puzzle.

"It feels so good to be away from home. All that pressure and shit. They tell me to work hard, but for what? They already have their plans for me. What if I have my own plans?" Troy rambled.

"Who are they?" Sydney asked.

"My father." He hiccupped and shook his head. He lay back flat on his bed. "My uncle."

"They expect a lot out of you?"

Troy shrugged. "Yeah. But I got my own plans. I'm not about to waste my life being like them."

Sydney frowned. "What do you mean 'like them'?"

He hiccupped again. "When society looks at me, they think they got me all figured out. And if I left it up to my family, they'd let me feed right into that stereotype. But I'm not going out like that. That ain't my story."

Sydney stared at him, rapt. "What's your story?" she asked.

Troy shrugged again, held his breath against the hiccups. Finally, after several long moments, he spoke.

"My mother died when I was thirteen years old." His voice was low and melancholy. "I'm still not over it. I know that sounds crazy—"

"No, it doesn't." Sydney's heart went out to him. "Doesn't sound crazy at all."

Troy was grateful for her compassion. "I was always closer to her than I was to my father. My brother Wes was always Dad's right-hand man, while I spent the most time with my mother. She understood me completely. My pops . . . he's cut from a different cloth. All the men in my family are. But my moms could tell from early on that I wasn't built for the life my father and my uncle wanted me to live. She shielded me from it."

Sydney listened. She had never heard Troy sound so serious before, so honest. In fact, she realized, Troy had never spoken about his family at all until now. She wondered what he was alluding to as he described his family dynamic. But she dared not interrupt as he continued to pour his heart out.

"Nobody in my family wanted me to come to Howard. They all tried talking me out of it. But I kept hearing my mother's voice in my head. Telling me that I'm not like them. That I don't have to take the easy way out. So that's why I'm here. To prove her right and to prove them wrong."

"How did she die?" she asked gently.

"Breast cancer," he said. "It happened quickly. She was diagnosed and then she was gone." Troy sighed deeply. "Ever since then, my family's never been the same. My brother started getting in trouble more often. I felt like I was watching him self-destruct."

"Is he your younger brother?" Sydney asked.

"He's five years older than me. He's more like my uncle, Don. I'm like my dad."

Sydney smiled. "What are they like?"

Troy shrugged. "My father is smart. Keeps his hands clean. Uncle Don is . . . different." He seemed to hesitate a minute. "He's not like my dad." He looked at Sydney then, thinking that he had said more than he should have.

"I bet your mother would be proud of you," she said softly. "You're here doing what she always knew you were capable of."

He shrugged. "I miss her."

Sydney thought about her own mother and how devastating it would be to lose her. Hearing Troy speak so longingly of his mom, Sydney felt guilty for constantly complaining about her own.

"Sometimes, I picture her face in my mind." Troy had closed his eyes and seemed to be envisioning her. "I still hear her voice in my head sometimes. Every day she told me that I could do anything. She always told me that I think too small. She said I could be the first black president of the United States if I decided to do it. That all I had to do was stop dumbing myself down to make the people around me feel comfortable."

Tears spilled forth from the corners of his eyes and Sydney felt her heart break for him.

"I used to always try to downplay my . . . my intelligence, my talents, and all of that. I thought I was being humble so my friends wouldn't feel overshadowed by me. But she hated that. I never could fool her." He sniffed. "She was the only person in my life who ever really knew me." What broke him down even more was the realization that he would never be fully known, fully understood, and accepted in that way by another human being again. He pulled himself together and wiped his face on his nearby bath towel. He was embarrassed now that Sydney had seen him cry. That was the last thing in the world he wanted. As he wiped his face, it occurred to him that this was the first time he had allowed himself to cry in years.

"I'm sorry," he croaked.

"Don't be," Sydney said. "You needed to get that out. Keeping it all bottled up will make you crazy." She leaned forward and touched his forearm compassionately. "If you ever want to talk about her, I'm here. I'll listen. Your mother sounds like she was a great person."

He nodded. "Thanks."

"But don't make a habit of drinking like this. I know it's your friend's birthday. And I'm sure it felt good to drown out your troubles for a little while. But don't get used to this."

Troy nodded. A slight smile crept across his lips. His mother would like Sydney, he decided. She had already mastered the art of subtle nagging—a skill his mother was famous for. "You're right," he said. "Good advice." He sat up, a little woozy still, but better now that he had gotten so much out of his system. He cleared his throat. Changing the subject, he asked, "What's *your* story, Sydney?"

Sydney thought about it. "Well . . . I have a brother. Malik. He's older than me."

"Y'all close?" Troy asked.

Sydney shrugged, unsure. "I guess so. I'm closer to my cousin, Destiny. Probably just because we're both girls and it's easier to relate to her. We grew up practically side by side. Our mothers are sisters, but they're complete opposites. But my grandmother kept them together when she was alive. She was always the mediator. My mother traveled a lot and I spent a lot of time at my grandma's house. And my aunt Pat worked all the time. So Destiny would be there, too. I guess you could say growing up with her was like having a sister who didn't live with me all the time."

Troy nodded. "You and your cousin are close in age?"

Sydney nodded. "Two years apart," she said. "Destiny's older. She didn't go the college route, though. She's working as a medical assistant at the same hospital where my aunt Pat works. They're so close." Sydney smiled wistfully as she said it. "It's not like that with me and my mom." Her smile faded. She often envied her cousin Destiny for getting the "cool" one as her mom. Aunt Pat was funny, down-to-earth, and so easy to talk to. Sydney's mom, Georgina, was much more self-absorbed, much more concerned about image and reputation. "Not that my mother is mean or anything," Sydney clarified. "She's just not the warm and fuzzy type."

Troy nodded again. "How about your father?"

Sydney's expression changed and Troy noticed. She averted her gaze. "He's in jail." She looked down as she spoke, not wanting to see any sympathy in Troy's eyes. "But it's cool. My brother and I still have a relationship with him despite all that. And my mother somehow manages to make it all work out."

Troy could tell that she wasn't really cool with it at all. He tried to imagine Sydney as a young girl growing up in the hood while her mother struggled to make ends meet. "Your mom sounds like a strong lady."

Sydney smiled then. "She is. That's where I get it from."

Troy didn't doubt it. "Seriously. To raise an honor student, pretty much by herself . . . that's impressive."

Sydney was proud of her mother for that. "My grandmother helped, too. She died earlier this year, so I know how you must feel about your mom. Losing Gran was the hardest thing I've had to deal with so far." She sighed. "But at least she's not suffering anymore. I try to live my life so that she would be proud of me. I understand what you were saying earlier about wanting to prove society wrong and debunk the stereotype. I feel the same way. Drinking, getting high, having sex. That's not for me. I didn't want to be a statistic so I don't do those things. I've never wanted that type of lifestyle. That's why I came to Howard out of all the schools I was accepted to. I wanted to be around other black students like me, who want more for themselves and for our race. People who want to be part of the solution, rather than contributing to the problem."

Troy listened to Sydney speaking so passionately and felt his respect for her soar. But there was one piece of information that she had divulged that piqued his interest. "So, you're saying you're a virgin, Sydney?"

She felt instantly horrified. It hadn't been her intention to reveal that nugget. She replayed her own words in her head. "I never said that."

"You said you don't drink, get high, or have sex."

"I don't. But that doesn't mean that I never had a drink in my life. I just don't do it all the time." Sydney fought to keep her voice under control. She was mortified.

"You ever get high?" Troy was smiling at her.

Sydney shook her head. She never had. "Just forget it," she said, praying that he would let it go.

Troy sat up, grinning now that the conversation was getting good. "You ever had sex, Sydney?"

Sydney felt hot suddenly. "That's none of your business," she said, surprised herself at how embarrassed she was. She stood

up and began gathering her books. She felt silly now for waiting around for Troy to tutor her while he was out getting drunk
with his friends instead, for having a crush on this fool, and for
still being a virgin in a world where it seemed that everyone was
happily getting fucked except her. "It's late. I gotta go."

Troy stood up to try to convince her to stay. He was enjoying the time he spent with her. He wasn't sure what it was about
Sydney, but she had his full attention. She wasn't as exotic-
looking or as outgoing as some of the other girls, but it didn't
matter. There was something he found sexy, even comforting
about her presence, and he wanted to keep her there with him
for as long as he could. But he stood too quickly and the room
started spinning. As he looked at Sydney and prepared to mouth
the word "Wait," bile rose up in his throat. He squeezed his lips
shut to block the surge and his cheeks puffed up like a fish's. Troy's
eyes widened in horror and both he and Sydney scanned the
room frantically for somewhere he could let loose. Finally, Sydney grabbed a nearby trash can and thrust it in Troy's face just
in the nick of time. A flood of vomit surged forth while Sydney
held her breath and tried not to smell the foul stench. The whole
scene was disgusting and the grimace on her face illustrated it.
Troy finally expelled all that he could and fell back on his bed,
weak and breathless. He lay there in silence for a long time before
he found the strength to manage a conversation.

"You're trying to kill me just because I asked a question."

The statement was so absurd that Sydney cracked up laughing
and Troy joined in.

"What the hell did you drink tonight?" She held her nose
against the odor.

Troy groaned in agony. "Everything!"

D-Bo came back to the room then and, on entering, balked
at the stench and the sight of his clearly ill friend.

"Yo, you are really fucked up," D-Bo observed, eyes wide.

Troy let out a long, deep sigh. "I'm never gonna drink again."

Sydney scrunched up her lips in disbelief. "Yeah, right. That's what they all say. Until the next party." She looked at D-Bo and shook her head. "He's your responsibility now. You're the one who let him get like this."

D-Bo shook his head. "It ain't my fault. He has to have like three or four drinks before he can get his nerves up around females."

"Shut the fuck up, D-Bo!" Troy's voice was muffled with his face pressed against the mattress. But Sydney still detected the urgency there. She smiled. Was Troy Mitchell *shy*?

"Next time I see you with a drink, I'm gonna slap it out of your hand," she said.

Troy shook his head slowly with his eyes closed. "I feel like shit."

Sydney watched him and wished she could make it better. "Get some sleep. You'll feel better in the morning," she said. She gathered her things and walked over to his bed. Gingerly, she touched his arm. "I'll come and check on you when I wake up."

Troy watched her leave. He didn't want to see her go. But he watched as she turned back to him one last time. She flashed her prettiest smile before she shut the door, leaving him anxious for morning to hurry up and come.

After Troy's drunken episode, he and Sydney spent a lot more time together. He tutored her and she became so adept at statistics that she began to challenge him from time to time. It was an odd occurrence for Troy, being attracted to someone intellectually as opposed to physically. Not that he wasn't attracted to Sydney's natural beauty. But what piqued his interest most of all was the fact that she made him think. Few of the girls he came in contact with bothered to see past his good looks and notice that Troy possessed intelligence and a drive for success that was unusual for a young man his age. He and Sydney grabbed lunch together on the regular and would get lost in conversations about any and everything. She told him that she loved to paint, a hobby she had picked up during sleepaway camp one summer when she was a little girl. He offered to let her paint him in the nude and then couldn't stop laughing when she covered her face, hysterical at the thought.

Sydney challenged his way of looking at things. Yet she wasn't afraid to let him take the lead if he knew more about a particular subject. She wasn't just smart, she was creative and spoke in broad strokes and bold colors. She fascinated Troy. He admired her ambition and her brilliance, especially coming from such humble beginnings.

"I want to win a Pulitzer Prize someday," she told him once.

They had been in Troy's room and she had been helping him pack for the Christmas holiday. Their relationship had blossomed into a close friendship ripe with flirtation but no action. Neither of them had made a move toward taking their relationship a step further. Instead, they allowed the chemistry between them to grow to a fever pitch.

"I think you can do it," Troy said. He threw several pairs of balled-up socks into his suitcase.

"I know I can." Sydney folded his T-shirts neatly and imagined life as the recipient of worldwide acclaim.

Troy smiled. "You say it's me, but you're the cocky one."

Sydney pretended to be offended. "I'm not cocky. I just have high self-esteem."

Troy nodded. "You should. You got it going on."

Sydney felt her pulse quicken. She wanted Troy in the worst way. They hadn't even shared a kiss, despite the signals she thought she had been giving off that she was available. She was aware that she was falling for him, but she hadn't been bold enough to risk rejection by being the first to take things further. Until now.

Maybe it was the fact that they were going home for four weeks or that she just wanted to know what it was like to be a woman in the truest sense. There was certainly no mistaking the electricity between them. For the longest time Sydney had felt an unmistakable thrill whenever Troy was close to her. If their arms brushed accidentally, a spark shot through her body, hardening her nipples instantly. When their eyes locked, she detected a hunger in him that made her long to be devoured. As she stood folding his T-shirts, she looked at him and could no longer stand it.

"Troy . . ."

He was piling pairs of jeans on top of his dresser. He didn't stop, but answered, "What?"

Sydney cleared her throat. "Before we go home . . . I want to lose my virginity." The voice didn't sound like her own. It was bolder, more certain of it than she truly felt. Sydney couldn't believe she'd had the courage to utter the words.

Troy turned to her and stared. He swallowed and she watched his Adam's apple shift.

"You sure about that?" he asked at last.

She nodded, aware that she had never felt this vulnerable before.

Troy stared at her, taking her all in. She was nervous. He could tell by the way she gripped the T-shirt in her hands for dear life. Truthfully, he was afraid of what Sydney made him feel. It was unlike anything he'd ever felt for a female before. He wanted to protect her the way that a big brother would. He was able to talk to her like she was one of his boys, but at the same time, a part of him wanted to ravage her and to make her scream his name. He was confused by what was going on inside of him and didn't know how to respond.

He licked his lips. Several thoughts came to him at once. Sydney was definitely the unexpected object of his attraction. His flirtation with her had been harmless and innocent. Unlike Sydney, Troy was no virgin. He had gotten his share of panties from the "light, bright, and almost white" girls that he favored along with most of his peers. Sydney often chided him about his preference for girls who stimulated his dick but not his intellect. And, now here she was, giving him the green light. He wondered if she knew what she was in for.

Troy seemed to hesitate. "Why me?" he asked.

Sydney wasn't sure how to respond. She had been holding out for true love and she wasn't sure if that was what she felt for Troy. What she did know was that his presence, the sound of his voice, the feeling of his touch against her skin—those things made her stomach flip and caused her heart to race. If this wasn't love, it was the closest thing she had ever felt.

"I like you." Her words seemed insufficient. "I trust you." Her voice was soft, but she had never been surer about anything. Troy was the one she wanted to give herself to.

Troy stared at her silently for a few moments. Then he began to clear his bed, removing the suitcase he had been packing. He fluffed his pillows and dusted off his sheets before he faced her. He looked at her questioningly, though he said nothing. He walked over to the door and locked it, aware that a locked door was the unspoken signal between him and D-Bo that they were entertaining female company.

Sydney held her breath as he crossed the room to her. He palmed her face gently with one hand, looming over her for several tense moments. Finally, he leaned in and kissed her slowly at first. He seemed to hesitate again, stepping back a bit and looking down at her. He took her hand in his, a sexy smile teasing one corner of his mouth.

"I like you, too, Sydney." He licked his lips. "A lot."

He glided his thumb across her hand in one smooth stroke and it sent chills up her spine the likes of which she'd never felt before. With that one gesture, he left her feeling woozy. Suddenly he stepped in close and kissed her with so much passion that it left her breathless. She had never been kissed like this.

Troy scooped her up easily in his arms and set her down on his bed just inches away. His kisses intensified. He fisted her hair in his hands, not too roughly, but enough to let her know that he was in control. Sydney responded to him with intensity, her hands roaming his chest, his face, arms, his back . . . and then!

Sydney's eyes flew open in shock. She had felt the pressure against her thigh while he was kissing her and had convinced herself that she was imagining things. But there was no mistaking the length and considerable girth of the penis that she held in her delicate hand. Even without having much experience with dicks, she could tell that this was a very large one. She had jerked her boyfriend Jason off back in high school a time or two. But that felt like child's play now that she felt the weight of Troy's penis in her hand. She wanted to flee, but how could she? Troy was clearly too excited to turn back and his kisses were making her feel slick between her legs in ways that she never had before. Sydney felt like she was somehow floating outside of herself. She moaned softly, her body trembling in a mixture of fear and bliss.

Before she realized it, he was peeling her out of her shirt and standing back to admire her in her pale pink bra. The color against her brown skin made his dick jerk forward in excitement. Sydney gasped. Troy looked at her and for a fleeting moment she thought she saw pity in his gaze.

He stepped toward her and slowly unhooked her bra. He could feel her heart racing as he slid it off and stroked her breasts. His hands were firm, but his touch was gentle, as if they had all night. She closed her eyes and lost herself in his rhythm. After a few moments he stopped and stood back, admiring her body with an unrelenting gaze.

Subconsciously, she covered her breasts with her shirt. "I—"

"Let me see you," he interrupted. "Don't cover yourself." He caught the urgency in his voice and stilled it. "Please."

He watched her lower her arms shyly. He almost felt like he was dreaming. This was too good to be true. Who knew she was hiding a body like that under all those clothes? "Damn," he breathed. "You're beautiful, Sydney."

She relaxed a little.

His expression conveyed his reverence for her. In his eyes, Sydney was special, pure. And she was letting him touch her. The thought of being the first man she allowed inside her body felt like a privilege and he had never been as aroused as he was right now. Still, he willed himself to take his time.

He stroked her nipples with his thumbs and bit her lower lip, sucking it softly in his mouth.

Sydney sucked back and again gripped his dick in her hands in disbelief. She didn't know how she was going to handle this thing. But she figured, she might as well come to grips with it— literally. Troy seemed surprised by her boldness, but he didn't stop her. Instead, he let out an encouraging growl and climbed on top of her. They peeled each other out of their jeans in a tumble of belt buckles and zippers. Sliding their ankles free, they came together, raptured by the feeling of their bodies pressed together, skin against skin.

Sydney gripped his back and sucked on his neck. Troy pulled her panties to the side and slowly slid his middle finger inside of her. Sydney tensed a little, clinging to it, beckoning his finger further. She was so, so tight. He sank his finger a little deeper within her walls and felt her practically pulsating around it. Her pussy felt so warm and wet. He stroked at her clit, strumming her pain with his fingers. Sydney got lost in the feeling and closed her eyes. Troy handled her body like it was a work of art. He was fully in the moment with her and the realization touched her so deeply that she fought the urge to cry.

He took one nipple in his mouth and then the next, never losing his rhythm between her legs. Sydney pulled him toward her and kissed him deeply, hungrily. She wanted him so badly. Troy urged her legs apart and sat back, watching his own hands work her pussy expertly. Sydney watched, too, and she couldn't believe herself. What kind of magician was he?

Without warning, he bowed his head between her legs and bit the inside of her thigh. She gasped at the sensation. Somewhere between a tickle and a pinch. He kissed her inner thighs, gripping them tightly in his hands. Suddenly, he spread them wide and began to eat her hungrily. Sydney moaned, so gone. A million rapturous thoughts raced through her mind at once. She watched him eagerly devouring her, and he was so incredibly good at what he was doing. Troy's tongue danced inside and out of her. She gripped his head and spread her legs even wider. It only made him lick and suck her pussy harder, softer, then harder and again softer, in such a perfect way that the tears she'd kept at bay before plunged forward now. Sydney cried as she came in his mouth.

Troy had her right where he wanted her and he knew it. His dick was rock hard as he came up for air. He fumbled around in his things for a condom. Sydney watched him, spent. She wondered where he found condoms big enough to accommodate him and wondered if they came in sizes. If so, surely he was an XXL.

A mixture of fear and anticipation filled her. She was about to go through with it. She prayed that it wouldn't hurt too badly.

Finally he pulled a condom out and unwrapped it, rolling it over his girth. Then he climbed on top of her and looked into her eyes.

"Tell me if I hurt you, alright?"

Sydney swallowed hard and nodded. Another tear slid from her eye and she was embarrassed. Before she could wipe it, Troy kissed it away. Then he kissed her softly on her lips. "I'll stop when you tell me. Okay?"

Sydney nodded again and held him tighter. Troy kissed her deeply. He rubbed the head of his dick against her entrance, nudging it slowly within her walls. Sydney held on for dear life. She groaned against the pain and felt him draw back a little. She was grateful that he was being patient. She had never been more afraid in her life.

"Okay," she whispered to herself. She felt him resume his slow and methodic thrusting, urging himself slowly deeper and deeper inside her. He took his time, gently pressing himself further until they both felt the dam break. Sydney cried out softly and Troy growled deeply in animalistic pleasure as her creamy slickness surrounded him. His rhythm was perfect, slow and steady, pushing himself gently deeper with each stroke. Slowly, the pain was replaced by pleasure and she gripped him tighter. Troy let out a throaty growl again as Sydney began to rock with him. He couldn't believe how wonderful she felt. He had never experienced anything like this. It was something like magic. He came in long, glorious spasms of ecstasy, holding Sydney tightly in his arms.

Together they lay breathlessly for several moments. Troy couldn't believe the sensations his body was feeling. All of his sexual experiences thus far had been with women who were no strangers to it. Even the most seasoned among them had a hard time accepting all of his girth inside of them. He definitely hadn't managed to get all of himself inside of Sydney and still she had given him the most explosive orgasm of his life. He had never been with a virgin before. He felt himself getting aroused again and wondered what kind of voodoo she possessed inside of her. Reluctantly he slowly slid out of her and then kissed her softly. He looked at her speechlessly, then cleared his throat.

"Wow," he said. He looked at her, concerned. "You okay? Was it okay?"

Sydney smiled. "Okay" was an understatement. "Yeah," she answered. What she had just experienced surpassed every one of her expectations. She couldn't describe what she was feeling if she tried.

"I never . . ." Troy struggled to find the right words. "I see you every day, but I feel like I'm seeing you for the first time."

Sydney didn't quite understand. "What do you mean?"

He touched her hair, such a lovely mess on her head at the moment. "That was like . . . I don't know. That was special or whatever."

Sydney smiled shyly. "Special or whatever." She knew that for macho Troy that was quite a statement.

"How do you feel?" he asked her. He needed to know. Because right then he was feeling something so intense that he might have described it as true love if he didn't know better. In fact, part of him wondered if he indeed did know better. He felt vulnerable and it was an emotion he was incredibly unfamiliar with.

Sydney searched for the right words to answer his question. She wanted to say that she felt the closest thing to love she'd ever known. But she wasn't sure if it was the real thing. And she certainly didn't want to scare him off with the L word so soon after their relationship had taken such a serious turn. Still, she had no doubts about what they had just done. She wanted to tell him that she liked the way he made her body feel, but that he fucked her mentally every day. But she was too embarrassed to say those things out loud. Instead, she said, "I feel good."

"How long were you thinking about this?" The question had been lingering at the back of Troy's mind ever since Sydney had offered her virginity to him. He stared at her, her face still aglow from the way he had made her feel.

Sydney met his gaze. "It's like I said before. I like you. And I trust you." She hesitated. "Can I trust you?" she asked softly.

Troy smiled at her, the way that always seemed to melt her heart. "Yes, you can. Definitely." He licked his lips, eyeing her seductively. "I like you, too."

He kissed her, and Sydney held on to him for dear life. She got lost in the moment, the feeling of his skin against hers, the motion of his tongue in her mouth. A breathy moan escaped her as he pulled her on top of him and palmed her ass in his strong hands.

A sudden knock at his room door interrupted their romantic moment. Sydney's eyes widened in horror. The last thing she wanted was to be caught buck naked in a guy's room like so many other girls on campus. The gossip and whispers would be unrelenting if word got out that the Goody Two-shoes in Drew Hall was giving it up to cocky Troy Mitchell. She gripped the sheet and held it tightly against her body as she dismounted him.

Troy climbed out of the bed and watched as Sydney scrambled for her clothes. He smiled at the sight of her naked body, wiggling into her clothes nervously.

"Relax," he said. "It's probably just D-Bo."

Sydney continued dressing in a rush. She didn't want the whispers that would inevitably ensue if D-Bo or anyone else found out that she and Troy had crossed the line. She watched Troy pull on his sweatpants and head for the door. He slid his feet into his sneakers and hesitated, allowing her time to finish getting dressed before he opened it.

D-Bo stared at Troy with an expression of disbelief. "Yo, my dude! You been in here for like two hours! I ain't never seen this door locked for that long. You good?"

Troy fought the smirk that crept across his face. "Yeah. Can't you come back later?"

D-Bo balked at the suggestion. "Later? Nigga, we leaving tomorrow. I gotta pack my shit up, too."

Troy glanced back at Sydney. She slid her feet into her Reeboks and grabbed her belongings. With embarrassment etched on her face, she approached him.

"I'm gonna go," she said softly. "I need to pack, too." She peeked sheepishly at D-Bo and saw the shocked expression on his face. Clearly, he hadn't expected *her* to be the girl responsible for Troy's locked door.

A broad smile spread across D-Bo's face. "Sydney, wow! How you doing?" His tone was mischievous and she felt her face flush with embarrassment.

Troy noticed and tried to put her at ease. "You don't have to leave, Sydney."

She shook her head, more anxious than ever to get out of there. "I'm gonna go finish packing," she said again.

Troy sighed. "Alright then, I'll come by your room afterwards." He leaned down and kissed her gently on her lips. Unlike Sydney, he had no reservations about anyone finding out about their new relationship. He was feeling her, and at that moment he didn't care who knew it. He lingered with her there, smiling down at her, their faces merely inches apart, clearly reluctant to see her leave. D-Bo cleared his throat and snapped him out of it.

"I'll see you later," she said softly. She avoided making eye contact with D-Bo as she walked off toward her room. She realized that she needed to take a shower. Part of her was tempted to let the scent of Troy linger on her for hours longer. But the stickiness between her thighs was aching to be cleansed and she wanted to address that immediately.

Floating from the euphoria of what had just transpired in Troy's room, Sydney entered her own to find Keisha sleeping. Though it was early in the evening, Keisha was exhausted from the day's classes and her late nights spent grinding herself on top of D-Bo. Sydney crept slowly through the room, gathering her shower caddy and a change of clothes before slipping back out and heading for the bathroom. She picked her favorite shower stall and lathered up, her mind on repeat over what had happened only minutes ago. She wanted it to happen again and again.

As she washed, she noticed the trickle of blood that streamed down the drain with the sudsy water. She couldn't believe that she was a real woman now, no longer a virgin. She thought about what this meant for them. They hadn't discussed it. But the way he looked at her before, during, and after they made love was something new. She knew for sure that something had changed between them. She wondered how they would define their relationship from now on. Then she wondered if defining it was necessary at all. She imagined that they might just fall into a rhythm the way they had in bed. She wanted to feel his lips on her again, feel his stiffness deep inside of her where no one else had ever been. As she toweled off and slid into a pair of clean panties and her Howard sweats, she thought about the way he looked at her. It made her smile.

She entered her room to find Keisha wide awake now.

"Hey, Z." Keisha sat on her bed with her back against her pillows, her legs pulled up against her chest.

"What's up, sleepyhead?" Sydney put her things back in their place and tossed her dirty clothes into her hamper.

"Troy came looking for you," Keisha said.

Sydney's eyes darted in her friend's direction. "He did?"

Keisha nodded. "He said to tell you he couldn't wait for you to finish packing. He's waiting for you downstairs in the lounge."

Sydney couldn't fight the wide smile that snuck up on her. "Oh," she managed. She tried to act nonchalant, but her awkward body language gave her away.

Keisha beamed. "You did it with him, didn't you?"

Sydney's eyes widened in surprise. "What?"

"You heard me!" Keisha's eyes narrowed suspiciously.

"Did what?" Sydney fought the urge to laugh.

"Don't make me hurt you!" Keisha glared at her roommate mockingly.

Sydney pressed her lips together to keep from smiling any harder.

Keisha stared at Sydney unrelentingly. "Tell me!" she demanded. "Did you give it up to Troy or not?"

Sydney could no longer fight the broad smile that stretched across her face. She nodded. "Yeah," she admitted at last. She threw herself onto her bed and hugged her pillow tightly. "Keisha, seriously, I feel like I'm dreaming. I still can't believe it!"

Keisha scrambled to the edge of her own bed and squealed with delight. "Sydney! Tell me everything!" Truth be told, Keisha was a little envious. Sure, D-Bo was cute, and he thought the sun rose and set with Keisha. But there was no denying the fact that Troy was sexy as hell.

Sydney let out a wistful sigh, as she replayed the night's events in her mind. Still, she knew better than to divulge too much. Aunt Pat had often warned Sydney and Destiny to be careful not to tell other women too many details about their relationships. "A woman will hang on your every word, and the whole time she's plotting on taking your man. You better keep your cards close to your chest! Don't let them bitches know any more than they need to know!" Aunt Pat's words resonated in Sydney's mind like a distant echo.

She smiled at Keisha. "It was perfect," she said. "Romantic and sweet." She smiled dreamily. "Perfect."

Keisha's smile faded and the expression on her face turned skeptical. She hated to rain on her friend's parade. But she didn't want to see her get hurt.

"Be careful," Keisha said. "I'm not trying to blow your high or anything. But Troy might be kinda out of your league. He's a player. Don't forget that."

Sydney glanced at Keisha. Her heart sank at the suggestion that what had just transpired between them had been anything short of magic. The way he looked at her, the way he clung to her, the passion and intensity in his touch. Those things couldn't have been faked.

Seeing the crestfallen expression on Sydney's face, Keisha backpedaled a little.

"I'm not saying that you can't look out for yourself . . ."

Sydney sat up, swung her feet around to the other side of her bed, and nodded. "Good," she said. "Because I got this."

She grabbed her room key and headed for the door. "I'll be back later," she called over her shoulder.

Keisha watched her go and hoped that her instincts were wrong about trouble. Something told her poor little Sydney was in over her head.

By the time Sydney made it to the student lounge to meet Troy, he was dozing off in a corner while SportsCenter played on the overhead TV. Sydney walked over and gently touched his face. He looked even more handsome than usual. Troy stirred when he felt her touch. He smiled as his eyes opened and settled on her.

Sydney Taylor, he thought. Who would have known she had all that going on underneath her bookworm exterior?

"You running from me?" he asked. He glanced at the clock on the wall. An hour had passed since he had gone looking for her.

"No." She sat down beside him. "Not at all."

Troy sighed. He gestured toward his cell phone at his side. "My pops called me a little while ago. He's upset. My brother got himself into some trouble. It's no big deal, but my father's pretty pissed off. He's going to send somebody to pick me up first thing in the morning so I can get home and . . . you know, help them deal with it."

Sydney frowned without realizing it. Troy was vague with details of what sort of trouble his brother had found himself in.

"What can you do to help?" she asked. Smart as he was, Troy was just a college kid. She wondered what contribution he could make to whatever trouble his brother was in.

"The usual," he answered with his trademark smile in response to Sydney's gentle probing. Then he shrugged. "Keep them from killing each other."

Her eyes widened. She shifted in her seat eagerly. She loved a good story. Tucking her legs beneath her, she rested her chin on her hand as she leaned on the arm of the sofa. "What's the story with that?" she asked.

"My brother Wes is a real live wire," Troy explained. "He likes to push the boundaries." He touched Sydney's face tenderly. "Don't worry about it. When I get home, I'll help everybody sort things out. That's what I do."

Sydney smirked at the reemergence of Troy's cocky side.

What had once repulsed her was now a sexy side effect of his ability to disarm people with his intelligence and his charm.

They escaped to Troy's room, equipped with condoms, snacks, and a mixtape of slow jams he produced from out of nowhere. He had persuaded D-Bo to spend the night in Keisha's room. Troy was eager to steal every precious moment with Sydney before they headed home for the holidays. They made love in all the ways young lovers do. And Sydney was gone, falling in love with the man who would take her heart and shatter it in a thousand pieces.

ONE COLD WINTER

December 2006

The holiday break had been incredible so far. Christmas was fast approaching and Sydney had no idea what she could give Troy besides her heart, which he already owned. Each day, Troy seemed to find new ways to woo her. They caught a movie or two, though they spent most of the time kissing and touching each other in the darkened theater. Once they went to the American Museum of Natural History and walked amid the displays with their hands intertwined. He enchanted her with his deep conversation, attentive silence when she spoke to him, and gentle kisses in between. The cocky genius from her math class was just a front, she realized. Troy Mitchell was really a calm and thoughtful man who was loving her like she was the only woman in the world.

They slipped away every couple of days to Aunt Pat's apartment. Georgi's overbearing ways had sent her daughter fleeing to her aunt's house so often that Pat had given her a set of keys. When she grew weary of trying to live up to Georgi's high standards, Sydney went there. Aunt Pat was often at work, doing double shifts at the hospital to make extra money, and her cousin Destiny

would often be out with her friends. Sydney seized those opportunities to steal away with Troy, doing naughty things in her
aunt's apartment with him. They made memories together during that cold and snowy winter break. Once Troy surprised her,
renting a suite at the W for the weekend. She had little trouble
convincing her mother that she was going on some college retreat for extra credit. That weekend had been one for the record
books. He had made her come alive.

Sydney's mother had become distracted lately by a man she
was dating. He was vice president at a bank in Midtown and
he was occupying most of her time these days. Georgi was out
on the town with him several nights a week, relishing the feeling of being on the arm of a powerful man again, which was a
natural aphrodisiac for her. For once, she was so distracted that
she was giving her daughter a much-needed break from her constant scrutiny.

For Troy, it was more than just a physical thing. He was consumed by thoughts of her when they weren't together. She was
nothing like the other girls he knew. Most of the ones he'd encountered had been shallow, self-serving, always with some hustle, some angle. But there was none of that in Sydney. She wasn't
naïve. Not really. But she had an innocence that made him feel
protective of her. He wanted to show her the world. His world.
The one where he was the prince, groomed for greatness on a level
that his father and his uncle had only dreamed of. He could tell
that Sydney had fallen for him and he was feeling the same way.
He decided to invite her to his uncle Don's holiday party. It
would be the first time he ever brought a girl home to meet his
family.

Her cousin Destiny insisted on going with her to the dinner party. She hadn't met Troy face-to-face, but Sydney talked
about him constantly. Determined to have her cousin's back, she

made sure that Sydney RSVP'd with a plus one. Troy said it was fancy, so they should dress up. Sydney worried about what Destiny would wear, but didn't want to insult her by making suggestions. Destiny had a flamboyant style. Colorful, flashy, and loud were words one might use to describe both her fashion sense and her personality.

To Sydney's surprise, Destiny arrived at her place looking rather nice in a tight black dress and black heels. Destiny was a big girl with a beautiful face and curves that would make every man in the room do a double take. She couldn't help it. No matter what she wore, her hips, butt, and boobs entered the room like *boom*. Tonight, though, she had reined it in. Her braids were gathered together in a neat bun on top of her head. She looked pretty and unusually understated. Sydney knew instantly that Aunt Pat had helped her go shopping. Destiny was usually the type for big, bold earrings and bright colors. Tonight she wore basic black and her only accessories were a pair of pearl stud earrings. Sydney smiled.

Her own look was painstakingly perfect. She wore a winter white wrap dress with a pair of caramel suede stiletto booties. She had saved long and hard to buy those boots and was excited to wear them tonight. Destiny helped her get her hair together.

"So, where's Aunt Georgi?" Destiny asked. "Usually she's on you like white on rice. Why is she letting you spend so much time with this Troy guy and she never met him?"

Sydney looked at their reflection in the mirror as Destiny brushed her hair into a cute updo with bangs. "Mommy's dating again. You know how she gets."

Destiny glanced at her cousin sadly. She knew all too well. Sydney's mother fluctuated between two extremes. She was either completely obsessed with every aspect of her daughter's life when she was single or she was completely obsessed with whatever man was acting as her sponsor at the time. Through it all, Georgi had maintained her stunning looks. While her dad aged drastically during his prison stint, her mom kept it together.

"She tell you where she is this time?" Destiny asked the question gently. She put the finishing touches on her cousin's hair and sat down on the bed. Aunt Georgi would go to Europe, the Caribbean, or wherever her man took her at the drop of a dime. Often Sydney had no idea until she got a phone call from her mother after days of silence.

"Yeah. Connecticut. Some banquet. She'll be back late tonight. This one's kinda nerdy. She'll be bored soon, I can tell." Sydney laughed. She knew her mother like the back of her hand. Or so she thought. "But she's having fun for now and it's keeping her off my back. So, it works for me." She sighed. She couldn't wait to see Troy tonight. She was eager for Destiny to meet him, too. She valued her cousin's opinion a great deal.

Finally, when they were both satisfied with their looks, Troy arrived to pick them up for the party.

The first real clue that there was more to Troy Mitchell than Sydney was aware of came when he pulled up to get the girls. A black Mercedes pulled up, tinted windows shielding the occupants. The car gleamed against the bright lights of the streetlamps. Sydney watched as Troy slid out of the driver's side and another man rose from the passenger side. The guy with Troy was big, looming large like a bodyguard as he walked toward them alongside Troy.

Destiny cleared her throat. "What do you know about this guy?" Destiny asked. She was intrigued already. This wasn't the type of guy she expected her cousin to meet and fall in love with at college.

"I don't know," Sydney muttered. Her mind was reeling at

the sight of her man, the beauty of that car, and the question of who the hulk was walking with Troy.

Troy greeted Sydney with a light kiss on the cheek. He turned to Destiny, smiling. "Hi," he said. "I'm Troy." He extended his hand to her, all the while maintaining eye contact. Sydney knew that scored points with her cousin. Aunt Pat often reminded them that a real man always looks a person in the eyes.

Destiny was impressed. "Hello, Troy. I'm Destiny."

He squeezed her hand. "This is my brother, Wes." He gestured toward the smooth chocolate action figure at his side.

Sydney shook Wes's hand and peered up at him. He had an imposing presence and though he greeted her warmly, she noticed that he didn't smile much. He had dark, menacing features and his face seemed set in a perpetual frown. Though he was even more handsome than his brother, his facial expression and body language were certainly not as inviting as Troy's.

Destiny peered around them at the car parked nearby. "Whose car are you driving, Troy?"

Wes managed a tiny smirk then. "It's mine. You like it?"

Destiny beamed. "Yup."

Troy laughed. "Wes is letting me drive it for the first time. But he's acting like he's my father, telling me to slow down and all that."

Wes shook his head. "He got a lead foot, ladies. I'm gonna warn you now." Wes was trying to be nice to his brother. Since their mother's passing, the gulf between them had only grown wider. He was hoping that by having Troy around him more, he might rub off on him. He believed Troy needed some hair on his chest. Too much college and not enough conflict.

Troy assured them that they were in good hands, and suggested that they get going. "Uncle Don made us promise that we'd get right back. He takes this party seriously."

Wes was eyeing Destiny's curves in that dress as the group moved toward the car. "Destiny, you can sit in the back with me," he said. "Sydney, you sit up front with Troy."

Troy laughed at that. "Now you can be a backseat driver for real."

"Just don't get in an accident." Wes opened the car door for Destiny.

Troy did the same for Sydney. He squeezed her butt slyly as she slid in past him. Sydney smiled in delight. She was hoping to sneak away with Troy at some point tonight. She wished that Destiny and Wes would somehow disappear.

Troy got behind the wheel and headed for the bridge.

"How old are you, Wes?" Destiny was facing him in the backseat, her eyes searching him for clues. She had plenty of questions.

"Twenty-four." He looked at her and winked. "How about you?"

"Twenty," Destiny answered. "What do you do for a living?"

Troy interjected. "Our family runs a chain of businesses uptown. Barbershops, dry cleaners, tailors, that type of thing."

Sydney suspected that wasn't the whole truth. A couple of times, Troy had alluded to his father's disapproval of Wes's lifestyle. She supposed Wes wasn't as involved in the family business as Troy was trying to imply. She kept her mouth shut, though, eager to hear the next in Destiny's litany of questions.

"You cut hair?" Destiny asked.

Wes laughed. "Do I look like I cut hair?" His voice was gruff, but his expression revealed that he was tickled by Sydney's outspoken cousin and her interrogation.

"You look like an assassin," Destiny said flatly.

"Aye! That's not nice! What's wrong with you?" Sydney craned her neck to glare at her cousin sitting behind her.

Troy laughed loudly.

Destiny held her hands up in surrender. "No offense," she said to Wes.

He shook his head. "None taken, sweetheart." He shifted in his seat, his frame too large for the backseat of his own car. Destiny could tell that he was more accustomed to being in the driver's seat. "What's your story?" he asked.

Sydney smiled in the front seat. Troy had asked her the same question once. In the weeks since then, they had gotten to know each other quite intimately. Yet she sensed that there was still so much for her to learn. Troy took her hand in his, swept his thumb across hers, and she smiled at the familiar gesture. It had become the equivalent of a kiss when they were in a crowded room. His touch sent shivers through her every time.

"I'm just a girl from Staten Island. Well, Brooklyn, really. But my mother moved to Staten Island when I was a kid. My grandmother followed. Then Sydney and her family came after that."

Wes nodded. "One big happy family, huh?"

Destiny nodded. "You got a girlfriend?" she asked boldly.

Troy and Wes both laughed. Sydney looked at her cousin like she was crazy. Troy steered the car expertly through the traffic.

Wes finally composed himself enough to nod. "Yeah," he said. "I'm seeing somebody. But if I wasn't, you'd be just my type."

Destiny frowned a little. "What does that mean?"

Wes looked out the window as he spoke. "You seem like you don't have a problem speaking your mind," he said. "I like a girl with a strong opinion. I can be a lot to handle, so I like somebody who can withstand a challenge."

Sydney looked at Troy sidelong. "Sounds like somebody else I know."

Troy laughed. "I guess it runs in the family," he admitted. "Believe it or not, I'm the calm one. When it comes to keeping a level head, I'm usually the one who keeps the peace. Wes can be a hothead."

Destiny's mouth watered, but she caught herself. Wes was taken, she reminded herself. "Is your girlfriend coming to the party tonight?"

Wes shook his head. "She's out of town."

Sydney wanted to pinch her cousin, but she couldn't reach her. Eager to steer the conversation elsewhere, she cleared her throat.

"Who else is gonna be at this dinner?" she asked.

Troy smirked. "You might see a few familiar faces," he answered coyly. "But mostly just my family. My uncle, Don. My dad might come through."

Sydney's antennae went up. She had just assumed that when he mentioned his family dinner that his father would certainly be attending. She was beginning to wonder if she and Troy had more in common in the parenting department than she had previously known.

Troy regaled them with drunken tales about the mayhem that unfolded at previous holiday dinners with his family. Aunt So-and-So and Uncle Such-and-Such did this and that. Sydney didn't keep track of all the names. But she did notice the easy laughter the brothers shared as they reminisced. By the time they arrived at the big impressive home where the dinner was being held, they had all grown quite comfortable with one another. The energy between them was lively as they exited the car and walked down the long graveled driveway toward the house.

"This is a really nice house," Destiny said. She thought Sydney had it good, but whoever lived here had real money.

"Thank you," Troy said, smiling. "This is my father's house."

Destiny's eyes widened. Sydney, too, was impressed, though

she did her best not to make it too obvious. This was nothing like the Harlem she had imagined Troy growing up in.

Wes swung open the heavy doors, ushering them into a large and impressive foyer. Music blared and laughter and conversation could be heard from somewhere down the hall. Sydney looked around. Sparkling wood floors, gleaming white walls, and a large chandelier were the only décor. Still the space screamed opulence and the old house had plenty of charm and character. Sydney couldn't wait to see more.

A woman appeared. Her natural hair graced her head like a halo as she smiled. She reached for everyone's coats and Sydney had to resist the urge to hug her. The woman exuded love. "Everyone is having cocktails in the great room."

Sydney nodded, thanked the woman, and she and Destiny followed Troy and his brother toward the great room. Destiny linked her arm through Sydney's as they walked.

"What kind of life is this, Sydney?" Destiny gawked at the paintings on the wall. She was no art expert, but they sure looked expensive.

"I'm not really sure." Sydney's own eyes darted around the home as they walked. The sounds of voices and music filled the halls, and Destiny snapped her fingers to the beat of Chaka Khan's "Ain't Nobody." Sydney joined in. Having her cousin along made her feel more comfortable as they neared the great room.

GHOSTS

A couple of dozen people mingled, danced, and sipped drinks in fancy glasses. The cathedral ceilings were painted in a vibrant gilded gold. The floor-to-ceiling windows were framed in deep mahogany wood that looked as opulent as the house itself.

"Girl!" Destiny said it all in just one word. Men in tailored suits and women in fabulous looks and flawless makeup enjoyed themselves. Conversation and laughter filled the room.

"He's *handsome*," Destiny said, gesturing toward the opposite corner of the room where a full bar had been set up. An older man stood talking to a group of people, all seeming to hang on to his every word.

"Cut it out. He looks old enough to be your father," Sydney muttered under her breath.

Destiny frowned. "I just said he was handsome. Get *your* mind out the gutter." She looked at him again. "I should hook him up with Mama."

Sydney laughed. "Stop trying to hook us all up with Troy's family. I heard you in the car." She finally got the chance to pinch her cousin and she did so. Destiny squirmed. "Cut it out," Sydney warned.

Destiny smiled guiltily. "I was just fishing for information. You hardly know this guy. Clearly." She looked around them. "All this money came from barbershops and dry cleaners?"

Troy rejoined them after speaking with a few people nearby. He was wearing all black tonight, his suit seemingly custom-made for him.

"Thanks again for inviting us," Sydney said. "This is a really beautiful home."

"Thank you." Troy nodded graciously.

"You grew up in this house?" Destiny asked, looking around in awe.

Troy nodded. "Yup. But, we didn't get to hang out in here much. When we were kids, this room, the study, my parents' bedroom—those were places kids weren't allowed. You know how it is, right?"

Sydney nodded. She knew all too well. Georgi Scott had very clearly drawn the line, enforcing the rule that the living room and Georgi's own bedroom were off-limits. If Sydney had company, she had to entertain them in her own room, the kitchen, or the yard. Destiny, though, had a different experience. Pat was much more liberal than her sister. Destiny slept in her mother's bed even now.

They listened, intrigued, as Troy continued. "Me and Wes spent most of our time away from home. My mother had an apartment on the Upper East Side that she pretty much raised us in. This house was my father's." He looked at Sydney, almost apologetically. He knew that growing up without her own father she hadn't been afforded the same luxuries. "I know it sounds crazy." He shrugged. "My parents weren't like a traditional couple. They lived apart most of the time. This house was more or less where they entertained. Or where my pops came when my mother was mad at him. We all spent weekends here when family was in town. But my mother was a simple woman. She preferred the smaller space, the closer feeling she got in that apartment." He thought back on those days when his mother had reigned over the household like the queen that she was.

"My pops likes the limelight. The wow factor. When we were here, this room was where my father and his cronies would hang out. My mother and her friends would have parties here sometimes. Now that I'm grown, it still feels like I'm a little kid, sneaking downstairs to see who would drink too much, who would fight."

They all laughed. Sydney and Destiny both glanced around, trying to imagine who it might be tonight. It was hard to picture any of these poised and polished people getting twisted.

Moreover, Sydney was amazed at the opulent life that Troy was living. She couldn't believe that the cocky guy she had fallen for was connected to a very wealthy, successful, and powerful family. The possibility that Troy might be rich had never occurred to her.

"Is your father here?" Sydney asked.

Troy nodded. He gestured toward the older gentleman Destiny had noticed when they walked in. "That's him."

Sydney and Destiny both gasped. It seemed that each of the Mitchell men was finer than the last.

"What's his name?" Sydney stared at the man she now allowed herself to admit was quite handsome. He stood now, speaking closely with a beautiful woman, who looked vaguely familiar. Sydney tried to recall where she had seen her before.

"William Mitchell. His friends call him—"

"Troy, there you are. Have you been hiding from me?"

He turned to find a lovely familiar face smiling up at him.

She hugged him around his waist and he pulled her close, smiling at Sydney.

"This is my little cousin, Zoe. And this is my girl, Sydney, and her cousin Destiny."

Sydney felt her heart race at his introduction of her. *His girl.*

"Your girl? What?" She stared at Sydney in wide-eyed amazement.

Sydney smiled at Zoe, trying hard to steady her racing heartbeat. "Nice to meet you, Zoe."

"Nice to meet you, Sydney!" Zoe was beaming.

Sydney liked her already. She could see the resemblance between the cousins.

Troy smiled at her proudly. "Zoe's my favorite member of this family to be honest. She's a big brat, but she won't admit it."

The girl pouted in a mock tantrum, her arms folded across her chest in protest.

Sydney laughed.

"Whatever!" Zoe said. "How long have you had a girlfriend? And why am I just hearing about it?" She stared at him accusingly.

Troy's father now joined their group.

"What's up, Dad?" Wes grinned, but didn't appear to Sydney to be especially excited to see the man.

"Wes." Fox's smile seemed more like a sneer.

Sydney watched them closely, wondering what the story was with these two. She recalled Troy mentioning that his father and brother shared a contentious relationship. Clearly that was true, judging by the unspoken tension between the two of them now.

Troy stepped forward. "Dad, this is Sydney. And this is her cousin, Destiny."

Both ladies smiled at the handsome man and his eyes widened as he took them in.

"Sydney!" His smile was wide and sincere now. "Troy has told me all about you."

Sydney's heart raced. Troy had spoken about her! She wondered what he had said, how he had described her.

Troy had spoken of her, although he wasn't pleased to hear his dad mention it now. Sydney was a name he uttered often lately. He really seemed to like this girl, which got his father's attention. His father was eager to learn more about her.

"It's very nice to meet you, Mr. Mitchell."

He shook his head. "Call me Fox. 'Mr. Mitchell' makes me sound like an old man."

Sydney smiled, nodding.

Fox looked at his son and winked. "She's prettier than you described."

Troy smiled, happy that Sydney had his dad's approval.

Another man approached the group, and Sydney couldn't help noticing how handsome he was. The man was tall like Troy and appeared to be in his midfifties with an unmistakable swagger. He had a deep ebony complexion and jet-black hair, his sideburns thick and perfectly lined, and his goatee full and beautiful. His eyes were deep-set, piercing, and thick eyebrows hooded them. He wore a dark suit with a charcoal gray shirt unbuttoned at the collar and no tie. To Sydney, he looked like a work of art.

Destiny's mouth fell open at the sight of him and Sydney nudged her to snap her out of it. Destiny corrected herself quickly. But it was clear that both women were intrigued by the beautiful stranger in their midst.

Troy noticed their reactions and laughed.

"Ladies, this is my uncle, Don." He gestured toward the women. "Uncle, this is my girlfriend Sydney Taylor and her cousin, Destiny."

Don nodded in greeting. "Very nice to meet you, ladies." His voice was deep like Barry White's and Sydney got goosebumps.

"Don is my younger brother. But he still tries to boss me around." Fox smiled as he said it, but Sydney knew some of their history. She was aware that, at least in Troy's opinion, Don was the head of the family. Birth order did nothing to change that.

Don shrugged. "I'm just the voice of reason."

"With that voice, you could reason with me anytime." Destiny muttered it under her breath and looked Don up and down like a hawk.

Sydney smiled and discreetly pinched the shit out of her cousin.

"Oww!" Destiny said, squirming.

"Uncle Don, Sydney's from Staten Island. Didn't you say you used to date a girl from there back in the day?" Troy smiled at his uncle, recalling the stories he told him and Wes growing up.

Don nodded. "I did." He looked at Sydney and winked, sending shivers up her spine. "Italian girl from New Dorp. She used to let me drive her car all the time." He smiled, revealing a perfect set of teeth. "Red Camaro. I loved that car!"

Fox shook his head, laughing. "Don had them white girls going wild back then."

Sydney and Destiny laughed. They both tried imagining how fine Uncle Don must have been in those days. Sydney noticed that, like his nephew Wes, Don didn't smile much. But when he did, it made his handsome face absolutely irresistible.

A woman took the mic and announced that dinner was being served in the dining room down the hall. She urged the guests to make their way over.

Troy whispered in Sydney's ear. "After dinner, I want you to come upstairs with me."

She glanced at him with her eyes narrowed. "For what?" She

wasn't about to risk doing anything frisky and getting caught during her visit to Troy's family home.

"I want to show you something," he said, taking her by the hand. He led her toward the dining room, where guests were heading to dinner. She tried to imagine what he had up his sleeve. Along the way, Zoe caught up to them and whispered to Troy. Unable to hear their exchange, Sydney wondered what had Troy's cousin so fired up.

Destiny was at her side again.

"Oh, my God, Sydney. All these men are so fine!" Destiny didn't know which of the Mitchell men was the sexiest. "Damn! Did you see Uncle Don?"

Sydney laughed. She was glad that Destiny was here with her tonight. "I saw him," she said, nodding. "Fox, too! I'm starting to feel like we should have brought both of our mothers here tonight. There's a Mitchell man for all of us!"

Destiny laughed. She caught sight of Troy and his younger cousin whispering conspiratorially on the side. "You think she's talking about you?"

Sydney shrugged. "Who knows? But, I'm not worried about it." She smiled triumphantly. "I know Troy cares about me. I'm not too concerned about what anybody else thinks."

Destiny nodded. "You're right."

They followed the stream of guests flowing into the formal dining room. As they made their way to their seats, Troy introduced Sydney to a few people whose names she tried to remember. Family, neighbors, and friends all found their places in the large room. The same floor-to-ceiling windows that dotted the rest of the home were present here as well. Two large chandeliers hung from the center of the ceiling. Directly beneath them was a long, grand Art Deco dining table. The head table had ten chairs on either side of it with one seat at each end of the table.

The setting was exquisite. Tall candlesticks flickered from two extravagant candelabras in the center. Fox took a seat at one end of the table. Uncle Don sat at the other.

Sydney took note of where Troy and Wes opted to sit. Troy sat nearest to his father, while Wes took the seat closest to their uncle, Don. Sydney took a seat next to Troy and Destiny sat across from her.

"Mr. Mitchell, you have a beautiful home," Destiny said.

Troy's father smiled graciously. "Thank you." A member of the staff whispered to him discreetly about wine choices.

Destiny spread her napkin in her lap like her mama taught her. She sipped her water and watched everyone at the table closely.

She saw Troy and Sydney whispering and laughing together. Zoe watched them, smiling. Destiny could tell that Zoe was like a little sister to Troy. Watching her smile at the young couple in love, she could see that the young lady meant Sydney no harm.

Uncle Don, meanwhile, sat back in his seat, looming large like the lord of the manor. Like Destiny, he surveyed the table, eyeing everyone and watching how they interacted. The two of them locked eyes and he offered her a weak smile. Destiny swooned and looked away shyly.

The guests began to indulge in the soup and salad that was served. It offered Destiny a welcome distraction from the penetrating gaze of Troy's uncle. Looking into his eyes had shaken her. He had a gaze as if he could see right through you. As if he could read your whole life just by staring at you.

And then there was that voice! She trembled now as he addressed the room.

"Thank all of you for being here tonight. My brother doesn't really see the need for us to throw this party year after year. But it's important. To me, at least."

He looked around at each guest at his table. His gaze settled on Sydney, then Destiny. She shifted in her seat, uncomfortable under the weight of his stare. Sydney seemed not to notice. She was too preoccupied with Troy's stolen glances, his tickles, and whispers. The two of them could scarcely keep their hands off of each other.

Don continued. "Family is the most important thing in life. Good friends are, too. Most of you have been a part of the Mitchell family for many years. We trust one another. We look out for one another. We break bread together, prosper together."

"I know that's right!" some lady called out. Several of the guests laughed and cosigned the sentiment.

Don grinned. "My brother and I get a lot of the credit for the success this family has enjoyed over the years. But, truthfully, everyone in this room helps make it possible." He raised his glass. "But this party every year is our tribute to all of you. There's gifts for everyone, of course." He smiled and several of the guests voiced their approval.

An immediate wave of alarm washed over Sydney. It had never occurred to her that she should bring a gift. It was a silly oversight. She had been so focused on looking good that she had come to the party empty-handed. Her head snapped in Troy's direction, eyes wide.

"You didn't tell me—"

"Don't worry about it." Troy smiled at her knowingly. "You didn't need to bring anything. At the end of the night, after everybody leaves, my uncle gives us all the stuff they gave to him. It's like a grab bag."

Sydney relaxed then, but marveled at the same time. "What kind of things do they give him?" She wondered what kind of gift you would give a man like that.

Troy smiled while he chewed. It was an odd expression that

he somehow still made sexy. "Cases of wine. Watches. Season tickets sometimes. He has everything he wants and then some." He shrugged. "He doesn't need their gifts."

"What does he do again?" she asked.

Uncle Don's voice interrupted them.

"Here's a toast to all of you. You're family whether you're blood or not. And we appreciate you all for what you add to the mix."

Everybody toasted. A few clinked glasses. Then they all took a drink. Sydney and Destiny indulged, too, smiling at each other giddily over the rims of their wineglasses.

Uncle Don looked at his brother. "Fox, you want to say something?"

Fox shrugged. A slow smile emerged on his handsome face. "Everybody knows I'm not the social one. I leave that up to Don. But I'm glad to see you all."

A few people chuckled at Fox's lukewarm greeting.

"Most of you are no strangers to this house. But for those of you who are"—he looked at Sydney and Destiny—"welcome. Make yourselves at home. *Mi casa es su casa.*"

The girls both thanked him for his hospitality. Sydney's cheeks were sore from smiling.

"Troy, how long have you and Sydney been dating?" Zoe asked.

Sydney shifted in her seat, uncomfortable now that everyone's gaze had shifted toward them. She focused her own eyes on Troy, wondering how he would respond to the question and to everyone's scrutiny.

"Not long," he said coyly. He looked at Sydney and smiled. "We met at school."

A couple of "aah's" and smiles fluttered around the table.

More bread came out and Destiny's eyes darted around the

room at all the servants scuttling about. One man in a black suit stood quietly observing. Destiny watched him make eye contact with Uncle Don. Watching closely, she saw Uncle Don give the very slightest nod of his head and the man in the suit gestured toward a member of the staff. Immediately, the wine came forth, the waitstaff refilling every glass.

Destiny was intrigued, but also slightly afraid of Troy's uncle. She watched him closely, but was careful to avoid making direct eye contact with him. When he looked her way, she took another sip of her wine and pretended she liked it.

Uncle Don's voice filled the big room again. "Sydney, this your first time in Harlem?"

All eyes turned toward her again. She dabbed at her mouth with her napkin before answering.

"No, of course not." She scoffed a little. She sensed the condescension in his tone. "I'm not originally from Staten Island," she said. Suddenly, the truth didn't sound fancy enough. She wasn't in the mood to defend her borough again. In this grand house, in the company of this grand family, she felt that her humble upbringing needed a little embellishing.

"I was born in Brooklyn," she pointed out. "My family moved to Staten Island a few years ago."

Destiny stopped chewing and looked at her cousin like she was crazy. The whole family had moved to Staten Island when Sydney and Destiny were in preschool.

"Is that right?" Uncle Don took a sip and sat back. "What part of Brooklyn?"

"East Flatbush." She sipped her wine. She liked the taste of it.

"So, your family is from the grain." Uncle Don smirked. "I had some friends out in East Flatbush back in the day."

Sydney nodded. "Small world." She smiled. "I've been to
Harlem before. But I've never seen Harlem like *this*!" She looked
around at the art, the opulence, and the beauty of the room and
its occupants. More food was served. "You have a beautiful house,
Mr. Mitchell, I mean, Fox."

He winked at her. "Thank you. But if you like this house,
you should see my brother's place. Don has an apartment over-
looking the whole city."

Sydney glanced at Troy's uncle, who shrugged his shoulders
modestly, and continued to chew his food. "It's aight."

People laughed at that, including Wes. She noticed that, like
his uncle, Wes seldom smiled.

"Uncle Don is being modest. He has the kind of life I want
to have someday." Wes looked at the man admiringly.

Destiny noticed the expression on his dad's face, hearing his
son say that. Fox seemed wounded by it.

"Your parents still together?" Uncle Don asked. He looked
at Sydney, a smile in his eyes, but not on his lips. They were set
in a line instead.

Destiny glanced at her cousin.

Sydney was feeling a buzz from her perpetually full glass of
wine. She shook her head. "No."

"You live with your mom?" Zoe butted in.

Sydney chided herself for not realizing sooner that Uncle Don
was Zoe's father. She could see the resemblance now as clear as
day. She nodded.

"You have brothers and sisters?" Zoe was pushing it now and
she knew it. She could sense Troy's glare as his eyes bore into
her. She did her best to avoid looking his way. She knew he
wouldn't appreciate her prying, but she was curious about the
new chick he was calling his girlfriend.

"I have a brother. Malik. He's older than me." Sydney shoved some chicken in her mouth, hoping that eating would place a barrier between her and Zoe's questions. It wasn't that she had anything to hide. She just didn't like having all eyes on her. She glanced at Troy, hoping he would throw her a lifeline.

He noticed. "Let her eat," he said. He smiled at her reassuringly. This type of shit was why he never brought girls home. His family was close and their circle of friends wasn't very wide. Anytime someone new was introduced to the group, their approach was often relentless.

He looked at Zoe. "Why don't we talk about your boyfriend? What's his name?"

Zoe's eyes widened. She looked at her father defensively. "I'm not—I don't have a boyfriend." She had said something to him earlier about a boy she was hoping would ask her to prom. She damn sure hadn't expected him to bring it up now in front of her father. She glared at Troy now as he smiled, chewing his food.

Troy was happy that his ploy to divert attention had worked. For the moment, at least.

Uncle Don didn't take the hint.

"What's your mama's name?" he asked Sydney.

"Georgina." She cleared her throat.

Uncle Don glanced at his brother. Fox locked eyes with him for a fleeting second. It was a small detail that happened quickly. But Destiny noticed.

"What's she do for a living?" His curiosity had been piqued.

Sydney shrugged. "She does secretarial work sometimes. But for most of my life she was a stay-at-home mom."

"Howard's an expensive school," Uncle Don said. "How can she afford to send you there?" He ate a little.

Sydney smiled, proud of her mother for the way she managed to hold things together in her father's absence. "Honestly,

I'm not sure how she does it. But she always seems to find a way to take care of me and my brother." Sydney knew that her mother had a penchant for staying on top. She was always the one with the latest bag, shoe, or car. And she made sure that Sydney and Malik stayed dressed to impress. They had always attended the top private schools, participated in after-school activities, and had gone on family vacations several times over the years. Georgi never kept a job for long. But she had what Sydney believed was a considerable savings account. They had never wanted for much.

Uncle Don nodded. "And your father. What's his name?"

Troy gave Uncle Don the side-eye. Don pretended not to notice.

Sydney thanked the woman who refilled her wineglass. "Quincy."

A longer glance passed between Uncle Don and Fox then. Destiny caught it and wondered what that was about. Somewhere in the back of her mind, an alarm bell sounded. But a platter of mac and cheese arrived, distracting her easily.

"He live in Staten Island, too?" Fox asked.

Troy sucked his teeth. He knew the subject of Sydney's father was a sore one. "Yo! What's with all the questions?"

Sydney touched Troy's arm. "It's cool." She smiled reassuringly and looked at his dad. "My father is upstate. He's incarcerated." She waited for the shocked reaction she usually got when she said that. Instead, she was met by the sympathetic expressions of people all too familiar with the life she was describing. "He's doing twenty-five years," she added for good measure.

Uncle Don stared at her blankly, one hand gripping his glass. "Quincy Taylor, huh?"

She nodded.

"What's he in for?"

Sydney looked at her cousin. Destiny was torn. She wanted

her cousin to deflect the question somehow. At the same time, she hoped Sydney wouldn't feel any shame over her father's mis- · fortune. After all, for better or worse, he was her father. Uncle Quincy loved his family. There was no doubt about it.

Sydney looked at Troy. He shook his head.

"You don't have to answer if you don't want to, Sydney." His tone was low. But in the silence of the room, everybody heard it.

Sydney shrugged. Fuck it, she thought. "Robbery and murder."

Zoe's eyes grew wide again, though she had certainly heard that story before. She had seen a lot at her young age. Still, hearing that Troy's new college girlfriend from Staten Island by way of Brooklyn had a little grit surprised her.

"Is that right?" Uncle Don said again. He sat back in his seat. This time he smiled the old-fashioned way. "It's all good. Happens to the best of us sometimes." He licked his lips, seemingly deep in thought. "Must have been tough on you, though. You must have been a little girl when he went away."

Sydney nodded. "I was three years old. My brother was eight. But over the years we got to know him through visits, letters, phone calls. That kind of thing." She took a sip of her wine, feeling a little more relaxed speaking on the subject now.

"How far up north is he?" Uncle Don gently prodded.

"Clinton Correctional. It's up in—"

"Up by Canada," Uncle Don finished for her. "I got a few friends up there. I'm familiar with the place."

Sydney nodded, a bit relieved by that.

Troy glanced at his uncle, wondering why he had so many questions tonight. Usually, Uncle Don was laid-back, quiet. Tonight, he was uncharacteristically chatty. Troy wondered why. He glanced at his father. The expression on his face was unusual, too. He looked like a man who had suddenly lost his appetite.

Fox stared down at his plate, pushing his food around, thinking. He dared not look at his brother again. This was too good to be true.

"Well, this is heavy dinner conversation, Daddy." Zoe looked at him with disapproval etched on her face. She caught herself and glanced at Sydney apologetically. "I'm sorry, Sydney. No offense. But I thought this was a holiday party."

Fox nodded. "You're right. Let's all have dessert and open our gifts from Don. Maybe he'll be feeling extra jolly this year. Santa's been good to us."

Uncle Don grinned. "Indeed."

DIAMONDS ARE FOREVER

The rest of the dinner conversation was light, focusing mostly on Zoe's upcoming travel plans. Sydney understood now that her insistence on shifting the topic of conversation was entirely selfish. Zoe hardly cared about Sydney's squirming in her seat, what really bothered her was that no one was paying attention to her. She'd bought thousands of dollars' worth of clothes in preparation for her trip to St. Barts and she would be sailing and tanning while everyone else was shivering in New York, she bragged. Accustomed as she was to the spotlight, when she wasn't in it Zoe was texting, looking bored, or adjusting her cleavage in her dress. Although Sydney remembered Troy saying that Zoe was his favorite cousin, she agreed with him that she was also a brat.

Dessert was served and at the same time a couple of servers wheeled out two carts full of beautifully wrapped gifts. Destiny grabbed a slice of German chocolate cake, ignoring the presents. She assumed that none of them were for her. She was, after all, just Sydney's guest. But, to her surprise, just as she prepared to shovel a forkful of chocolatey goodness into her mouth, she heard someone call her name.

The lovely lady with the natural hair who had greeted them earlier was back. She now held up a box and called out Destiny's name, searching for her among the guests. Destiny raised her hand and the woman smiled, passing her the present. Destiny glanced at Uncle Don. He stared back at her as if expecting her shocked reaction.

"Merry Christmas," he said. He knew she was wondering how he'd known to include her. What she didn't know was that Uncle Don was a very important man in Harlem. Everyone who entered his circle was vetted beforehand. He had gotten the names and ages of Sydney and her guest ahead of time. Troy had provided them, along with Sydney's address, days ago. It was all part of Uncle Don's process. He had sent Wes along with Troy to Staten Island to pick up the ladies. All part of his insistence on ensuring that no one who got close to the inner circle meant them any harm.

Sydney and Destiny both eyed their gifts, wondering what was inside. Destiny's was a red-and-white-striped box and Sydney's a smaller white box wrapped in shiny green ribbon. Finally, they opened them, and Destiny gasped in surprise. Inside were a pair of fur earmuffs and a set of matching gloves. She loved them and slid her hands inside the luxe leather gloves lined with the same fur that covered the earmuffs. They were the softest things she'd ever felt. She wondered what kind of fur it was, but dared not ask and expose her ignorance.

"Thank you, Uncle Don," she said breathlessly. "These are beautiful."

Sydney opened her box to reveal a pair of pearl and diamond earrings. They were beautiful, the diamonds twinkling in the candlelight. She smiled and thanked Troy's uncle. Many of the other guests joined the chorus, grateful as they were for the generous gifts the man had bestowed upon each of them. Sydney wondered how much it cost him to lavish his guests this way each year. Certainly, this was the party they all longed to be invited to when the holidays rolled around.

The conversation got livelier now. The food, the liquor, and the gifts had them all feeling festive and giddy. Laughter filled the air and voices grew louder in an effort to be heard amid the chatter coming from all sides. Sydney and Troy touched hands a few times, even stole a kiss or two amid the party's backdrop. Destiny and Zoe even struck up a conversation about music and fashion, both of them discovering that they had similar interests.

The hostess was back, smiling at all of them. "Ladies and gentlemen, let's begin to make our way back into the great room for cocktails and music."

The guests began to file out, ready to drink, dance, and celebrate. Destiny excused herself to use the ladies' room. Troy took the chance to steal Sydney away for a moment.

"Come with me." He took her hand and led her out of the dining room.

They walked down a long hall full of beautiful paintings and sculptures before arriving at a wide spiral staircase, which they climbed to the top. At the landing, they entered what felt like a completely different home. Her heels sank into lush, thick carpeting that ran the length of the hallway. Clearly, this upper level was where Fox unwound and relaxed when his travels and hectic schedule died down. They passed several closed doors and Sydney had to battle the request to see each one.

"Are all of these bedrooms?" she asked.

He thought about it, counting them in his head. "Five of them are." He pointed to a door they passed as they walked. "That's one of the bathrooms."

"How many of those?" Her curiosity was piqued.

"Four."

Sydney tried to imagine growing up in a place this grand. She wondered what advantages she might have had in life, what experiences she might have enjoyed. Not that she hadn't had a cozy life herself. But it had certainly not been on this level. Her tiny bedroom back at her mother's house had felt perfectly acceptable until now.

"I told you I didn't spend most of my time here," Troy said, as if reading her thoughts. "My mother's place feels more like home to me."

Sydney nodded. "Still," she said. "Your family must be doing big business to afford a life like this."

"My father bought this house in the late eighties. I was probably one or two years old. Drugs were taking over Harlem and this place was really run-down. The woman who owned it had no way to maintain it. She was old, sick, and her kids and grandkids were losers. She sold it to my father dirt cheap. And he fixed it up and made it what it is." He led her to a door at the far corner of the hall. "Before that, we lived in the Bronx. So did Uncle Don. And life was a lot less glamorous."

He opened the door and she followed him into a room so large that she drew in a breath in shock. "Oh, my!" She laughed then, thinking she sounded like Dorothy in the Land of Oz.

"This is my room." He smiled.

She took a look around. The room was mostly empty, except for a queen-sized bed with a large headboard that extended halfway up the wall. Two more floor-to-ceiling windows graced this room, something she had marveled at throughout her time in the sprawling home. A dresser, desk, and a recliner lined the wall. There were no posters, no photos or mementos whatsoever to reflect the childhood he must have enjoyed in this space.

She turned to him. "How many girls have you brought in here over the years?" A smile teased her lips as she asked the question.

Troy laughed. "Cut it out. I don't want no other girl. I only want you."

Sydney shrugged, a bit unconvinced.

"I know seeing how I live is a little bit of a surprise," Troy said. "I didn't tell you too much about my family on purpose. Most people I meet have a hidden agenda. They want to get close to me and my brother so they can ask for a favor from my dad or Uncle Don. People see the cars, the homes, the wealth, and they want to take it. But when I met you for the first time I met somebody who was unimpressed by me."

She laughed at that. She had been turned off by the cocky Troy she first encountered. But now she understood his arrogance a little better. It would be hard not to have a chip on your shoulder when you grew up like Richie Rich.

"In school . . . as far back as I can remember really, people wanted to be my friend because of who I was. But you didn't know me. You got to know me and you're one of the few people in my life who truly cares about me. I love you for that."

Her eyes darted toward him. She held her breath.

He stared back at her. "You heard me. I love you, Sydney. I trust you. So I brought you here tonight to show you all of who I really am. When I went away to Howard, I lived off campus at first. I was that dude around campus because I had a fancy apartment not far from school. D-Bo and all of them used to hang out there and it got pretty wild. It was the first time I really got a taste of what it was like to live on my own. Of course, I got in trouble, and Dad threatened to bring me back home. Instead, the school convinced him to put me in one of the dorms so I would have some type of supervision. Then I met you." He smiled at her. "I feel like it was fate or something. I know I was supposed to meet you, to be with you. I feel connected to you."

She felt the same way. Her heart was racing.

"Wow," she said.

Troy came close and kissed her. "I love you," he said.

She looked up into his eyes. "I love you, too." She had never meant anything so much in her life. "I'm just letting it all sink in," she said honestly. "Your family has a lot of money." She looked at him, unsure. "Is all of it legal?"

Troy took a step back. "It depends on what you mean by 'all of it.'"

Sydney looked confused. Rightfully so.

"My father owns legitimate businesses. They're very successful. My uncle makes his money in the streets. I can't tell you too much about that, because I don't get involved in that. For a long time, I had no idea what my uncle did to make money. I just knew that if Dad's businesses were in trouble, Uncle Don came through and saved the day."

Sydney nodded. "In exchange for what? Just on the strength of them being brothers?"

Troy looked at her strangely. For a moment, he was tempted to lie in defense of his father. But so far there had never been any lies between him and Sydney. He didn't want to start now.

"Dad always told us that the streets are a dirty business and we should steer clear. For a long time, Wes and I went along with that. But the older we got, Wes started asking questions. He started listening harder, hearing things. He's the one who told me that my father does plenty of so-called 'dirty business' behind closed doors. Now, he thinks my father's a hypocrite." Troy shrugged. "Maybe he is. I'm not sure. I'm just getting my education, keeping my hands clean so I can be the son my mother wanted me to be." He looked at her, aware that what he was saying might sound too good to be true. "Seriously."

She nodded. She believed him.

"Regardless of what my father is or isn't . . . regardless of who my uncle is, I'm just Troy. Without all this." He gestured around the big room.

She nodded again. "I know." She thought about how lucky she was as he kissed her again. She had a feeling this was the beginning of a relationship that would change her life.

He led her back downstairs, where they rejoined the party. Destiny had struck up a conversation with Zoe over in a corner. Sydney and Troy joined them.

"You two lovebirds finished being nasty?" Zoe asked, her eyes sparkling in the light of the room.

Troy laughed. "Mind your business, little one. I'm still mad at you for that stunt you pulled at the dinner table."

Zoe feigned innocence. "What stunt?"

Uncle Don interrupted before Troy could respond.

"You guys enjoy yourselves. Troy, when the ladies are ready to go, I'll have Butch bring them back to Staten Island. You can ride with them if you want. Just let him know when you're ready."

Troy nodded and they all thanked Uncle Don for his generosity. They partied the night away, never realizing they were pawns in a very dangerous game they were completely unaware of.

Sydney awoke the next morning feeling giddy. She sprung out of bed, showered, and dressed with a song on her lips as she thought about last night. Meeting Troy's family, feeling his lips against hers, hearing him tell her that he loved her had her floating on a cloud as she came downstairs for breakfast.

Her mother stood in the kitchen preparing breakfast. She was in a wonderful mood of her own. Having spent the past couple of days with her new beau, she was feeling sexy and alive. She smiled brightly at her daughter as she entered the kitchen.

"Good morning," Georgi said. "I made French toast and some eggs and sausage." She took a sniff of the bouquet of roses that sat atop the island in the center of the kitchen. Her guy Adam had sent them over this morning.

"Thanks," Sydney said. She noticed the extra pep in her mother's step as she glided across the kitchen setting the syrup on the table. "Where's Malik?"

"He went to that basketball clinic at the college." Georgi tried not to worry about Malik. Although he was twenty-three years old, he was far less focused than Sydney. Malik worked odd jobs, but was much more preoccupied with having fun. Like most of the boys his age, he spent his free time drinking, partying, and making everybody laugh. These days when Georgi looked at her son, she saw shadows of his dad, echoes of the free-spirited young man Quincy had once been.

Sydney nodded. She recalled her brother mentioning the basketball clinic he was running on Saturday mornings. Good for him, she thought. She dug into her breakfast.

"What are you doing today?" Sydney asked. "Going to the gym?" Her mom was a big gym rat who went several times a week.

"No," her mother said. "Today I'm going to stay in the house for once. I have to do some work around here. I've been on the go so much that this place looks like a war zone. I'll do some cleaning and then later on I'll take my car for a wash." Georgi flitted about, placing things back in the cabinet, loading the dishwasher. She looked like a woman half her age in her T-shirt, leggings, and her hair piled high in a topknot.

"Why are you already dressed this early?" Georgi asked. "Where are you going?"

"I'm going to meet Troy in Times Square. He's looking for a new pair of sneakers that just came out and I promised to go shopping with him."

Georgi glanced at her daughter. "Who is this Troy?" she asked. "He's occupying an awful lot of your time these days." Georgi heard Sydney speak about her new college boyfriend quite often. She knew the young couple had hung out a few times since Sydney was home for the holidays. But she hadn't had the chance to meet the boy face-to-face.

Sydney smiled. "You'll like him. He's a good guy. Comes from a good family. I was going to ask you if I can invite him over for dinner."

Georgi nodded. "Yeah. Invite him. I want to meet him." She finished clearing off the counter and turned to face her daughter. "How was his family's holiday party last night?"

Sydney smiled. "It was fun. Me and Destiny had a nice time. I really like him, Ma." She stopped short of telling her that they were already in love. She hadn't even told Destiny yet. She knew that if she uttered the L word, she would likely be met with skepticism. What she and Troy had was something so special, so pure that she didn't want to share it with anyone else. "I can't wait for you to meet him," she said.

Georgi smiled and Sydney was struck by how lovely her mother was. Later, when she reflected on that morning, she would be reminded of her mother's beauty at that moment. She looked happy, at peace, light and free. Like a dainty fairy with her hair piled up on top of her head and an oversized T-shirt on. Sydney's mother had always been a stunning woman, but on this morning it wasn't all about the makeup, Botox, and expensive hair extensions. Georgi's beauty was natural and real and it made Sydney smile. She finished her breakfast and went upstairs.

An hour later, Sydney was on the Staten Island Ferry bound for Manhattan. Troy was meeting her there. She was excited to see him again, alone this time and not in the company of family and friends. She mentally rewound the details of the ride home from the party. Troy and Uncle Don's driver, Butch, had dropped Sydney and Destiny off at her house just after 1:00 A.M. Destiny had spent half the night laying in Sydney's bed recapping the party. To Sydney's delight, Destiny loved Troy. She was impressed by his family, too. Not only were they clearly successful, but they seemed so down-to-earth and real. By the end of the night, the girls had participated in a *Soul Train* line in the middle of the great room, and watched Zoe and Wes have a dance-off to old-school hip-hop. Sydney laughed now, just thinking about it.

Destiny had left early that morning, eager to get home to shower and change before work. But before leaving, she woke her cousin up and whispered something to her. "You're gonna marry him someday, Sydney. I can feel it."

Sydney smiled, her eyes still hooded by sleep.

Destiny's eyes danced as she spoke. "I like him. And I can tell that he cares about you." She hugged her cousin before she left.

Sydney smiled about it now, as she disembarked from the ferry and found Troy easily standing out amid the sea of people in Whitehall Terminal. He gave her a sweet kiss in greeting, then together they headed for the uptown 1 train. Sydney noticed Troy texting.

"Who's that?" she asked, gesturing at his phone.

"Uncle Don. He asked me to let him know when we're on our way."

She frowned a little. "Are we seeing him today?" She had hoped to have Troy to herself the whole afternoon.

He shook his head. "Nah. He's letting us use his empty apartment up on Sixty-first Street."

She breathed a sigh of relief, grateful it would be just the two of them today.

"Uncle Don moved out of this spot a year ago," Troy continued. "Now he's in a bigger place uptown, but he didn't sell his old one yet."

She nodded. "How did you convince him to let us go there?"

He shrugged. "Uncle Don understands. He can tell that I'm feeling you. Last night, after I dropped you off, he sat up talking to me till, like, three o'clock in the morning."

Sydney looked at him. "Talking about what?"

He smiled. "You."

She smiled so hard, it made him laugh.

"Don't get hype. We didn't *just* talk about you. He asked about school. We talked about the party."

"What about me?" She pouted a little.

He grinned at her. "He asked how we met and how your grades are."

She drew back, a bit surprised by that. "My *grades*? Why does he care about how *I'm* doing in school?"

"He wants to make sure that you're smart enough to keep up with me."

Sydney laughed.

"Anyway, I asked him to suggest a place I could take you to spend some time alone with you."

Her heart warmed.

"He offered me his place, just like that. He said to text him when we're on our way so he can let his doorman know."

Sydney couldn't contain her excitement. She squealed in delight and snuggled into him as they rode the train together to Midtown. When they emerged on Fifty-ninth Street, they held hands as they walked to Uncle Don's apartment. Sydney felt like the world was all their own. She felt mature, euphoric, and so blessed to be in this relationship. Everything in her young life was going exactly as planned. It didn't occur to her until later how unreal it all was.

The apartment was empty except for some staging furniture the realtor had brought in to help sell the place. Although it was unfamiliar to her, Sydney pretended that this apartment was theirs, and imagined a life with Troy in a space like this. She wanted to cook meals for him, to shower with him, and wake up beside him each morning. She wanted to shop for groceries with him, and do all of the things grown-ups in love enjoy. Troy, too, was grateful for their time alone. She had stolen his heart, there was no question. Christmas was two days away. He had something special in store for her.

He pulled her close and kissed her sweetly. She melted into him, eager for the way he made her body come alive. He did just that, stroking her long and deep, kissing her everywhere, coaxing her with erotic whispers. That winter afternoon would be etched in both their memories for the rest of their lives.

Georgi finished cleaning up downstairs after Sydney left for Manhattan. It was nice having the house to herself for once. For the past couple of days she had been in a lavish hotel with her boo. But there was nothing like returning home to her own bed. She had come upstairs and cleaned the bathroom and had tidied up her bedroom as well while watching *The Best Man* for the umpteenth time. Now her home was looking good, smelling good, and the scent of her favorite holiday candles wafted through the house. She sighed and had a rare moment of contentment. She hadn't been truly happy since Quincy went away. The years since then she'd been making every attempt to replicate the joy that bubbled within her before her husband was stolen from her. A lot of time had passed and these days she was beginning to wonder if she might find love again. She wasn't there yet. But she was in love with that feeling couples experience in the early days of their romance. Malik and Sydney were doing all right. Life was good. Now all she wanted to do was get in the shower and take a much-needed nap.

She walked toward her dresser and slid open her underwear drawer. Sorting through them, she reached for a pair of black Victoria's Secret panties. Her hand grazed the lacy fabric and she was suddenly jolted by the throbbing bass of thumping rap music. The shock of the sudden sound caused her to nearly jump out of her skin. She hadn't heard Malik come home. But she assumed he was the source of the radio blasting from her sound system downstairs.

In a rage, she dropped the panties. She hadn't expected him to come back so soon. And she sure wasn't about to have her peace disturbed by this shit. She flew out of the door and headed toward the stairs, calling his name.

"*Malik!*" she called out to her son loudly, hoping to be heard over the music. She was pissed. Was this what he did when she wasn't home?

Georgi rushed toward the stairs. Suddenly, it occurred to her that the music was unusually loud. What if it wasn't Malik? She was filled with a strong sense of impending dread. The music pulsated in her ears. She thought about her gun in her bedroom. She turned, on her way to retrieve it, and saw a figure barreling down on her. Her body recoiled in fright, but the man was on her. He grabbed her by her T-shirt and yanked her roughly toward the stairs. He covered her mouth—her whole face, really—with one big, heavy hand. His other arm encircled her small frame in some kind of reverse bear hug. Georgi screamed against his hand, but was drowned out by the blaring music. He dragged her down the stairs roughly, her feet and ankles banging against the stairs. The bastard seemed familiar with the layout. He dragged her through the shortcut, walking her through the kitchen the back way and into the living room.

Two men stood staring at her, their faces twisted into angry sneers. The one she *didn't* recognize was tall with a scar that ran the length of the left side of his face. He held a large bat in his hand. She had never seen him before. The other was a clean-cut, but equally menacing figure she recognized instantly. Even before their eyes locked in a cold stare-down, she knew it was him. The moment that cold, rough hand covered her mouth, she knew.

Don—*Uncle* Don to his nephew Wes, who was restraining her now—smiled at Georgi. Smiling was something that he seldom did and as he stood there now, it looked strange on him. She looked away, her eyes darting to the man beside him. She prayed for some humanity in his eyes, some compassion. She found instead the cold glare of a killer, taught long ago not to ask questions. Just get the job done. Don had made today's agenda quite clear. Get the money and get out. Or kill everybody.

The guy with the scar turned the volume down a little on the sound system. It was still loud, but not earsplitting like it had been.

"Well, well, well," Don said. "Look who it is." He stepped closer to her. "I ain't seen you in years, Georgi." He spoke with the casual ease of someone who runs into an old acquaintance on the street.

She laughed, though the brute had her face twisted at an odd angle. His hand still covered her mouth, but less tightly now. She forced her words out through the gap between her lips and his palm. "Not since you set Quincy up." She struggled in vain against the beast holding her tightly. She wanted to spit on Don. She had respected him once. He had disappointed her by the depths he'd sunken to in the name of self-preservation.

Don stood inches away from Georgi. He sized her up. The years had been kind to her. "So, this is where you been hiding. Right in plain sight."

She kicked at him, her foot nearly connecting with his balls, too. Don jumped back, pissed now that she wasn't instantly remorseful as he had hoped she might be.

"Calm down!" He glared at her, his patience thin. "You know I'm not the one to play with." He stared her down, the music drowning out their voices. Georgi knew that was intentional. Everything Don ever did was calculated and planned. "Let's handle business and I'll leave," he said. "We can keep this short and sweet. Where's my shit?"

Georgi panted, breathless after giving her all to that kick. "What are you talking about?" she asked, frowning. The goon holding her tightened his grip even more. She winced a little, well aware of what Don was capable of. He and Quincy had shared war stories plenty of times while sitting around her dining-room table back in the day. Liquor- and weed-fueled tales of men they had tortured, money had extorted, people who had gone missing. She wished Quincy was here now to see Don leering at her this way, his cruel, hate-filled stare making her knees quake.

Don shook his head. "Georgi, I don't want to have to hurt you. But I didn't come here to play games. Let's get this over with before Sydney gets hurt."

Her eyes flew open then. "Sydney? What the hell do you know about my daughter?"

Don laughed. He sat down on the edge of her sofa. "How you think I found you after all this time?".

Her breath caught in her throat. She swallowed hard. A million wild thoughts ran through her mind at once. At the forefront was her fear for Sydney's safety.

"Right now, she's okay. But that could change. It all depends on you."

Georgi screamed and fought with all her might against the man holding on to her. He covered her mouth again and tussled with her a little, but easily subdued her before backhanding her hard across the face for good measure. She lay pinned beneath him on the floor, stunned now and slightly dazed. Wes loomed over her, staring down at her with an expression that dared her to scream again. His large hands were balled into fists. She could see the imprint of a gun at his waist. She considered grabbing for it, but he had her arms pinned beneath his knees.

Don pulled out his own gun now and set it beside him on the sofa.

Georgi began to cry at the sight of it. She wasn't ready to die. And if he did kill her, what would happen to her children? She had no idea what Don might do to them. Her kids were innocent in all of this. But she knew that she couldn't say the same for herself. Fear weakened her guts. "Please," she pleaded between sobs.

"Shut up!" He cocked his gun. "I could have killed you already if that's what I came here for. So calm down and listen."

Georgi fought to catch her breath.

He glared down at her. "All I have to do is say the word and your daughter is dead. It's that simple. And your son could be coming in that door any second. What's his name again? Malik?" Don was grinning now. He saw her eyes go wide when he said it. "Yeah, that's it."

She began to cry again. Not just out of fear for her children, but by the fact that Don knew so much about her family. She wondered what else he knew.

"Listen, I'm gonna ask you again. Where's my shit?"

Georgi tried to keep her voice steady as she spoke. "What *shit*, Don? I don't know what you're talking about." She shook her head, dismayed.

He stared at her, unmoved. "Georgi." He shook his head. "You gotta stop playing with me."

"I'm not," she said, her voice anxious and high-pitched. "I never got involved in you and Quincy's business. You know that. I don't know what you're talking about."

Don gave her a look of disbelief. "You were always right in the middle of Quincy's business. What, you think I forgot? Always at the parties, always helping him stash the drugs, move the guns, hide the money."

Georgi sucked her teeth. "That was before the kids were born, Don. You know that. I wasn't on the scene like that all the time."

He smirked a little at the memory of her back then. He had always liked Georgi. Over the years, she became like a little sister to him. Her man, Quincy, had been Don's right-hand man. And Quincy loved his lady. Georgi had been fly with the perfect blend of sweetness and streetness. Quincy had always kept her close. He knew she was bad and never wanted to give another hustler the chance to offer her a better deal. Quincy had loved showing her off until they got married and started a family. Then he stopped bringing his wife around as much, encouraging her instead to make friends in their Brooklyn neighborhood rather than hanging in Harlem. Don realized now that he should have seen it coming then. The way Q strategically started drawing a wider line between his work life and his personal one. Q's Brooklyn became his alternate universe, his hideaway after he had done his dirt uptown with Don and his crew.

"I guess you want to do this the hard way," he said. He stared at her, waiting for her to respond.

She quivered under his menacing glare. "You talking about that thing in the Diamond District?"

Don grinned. "Yeah. That *thing*. The reason your husband is doing twenty-five years in Clinton right now. That two-million-dollar diamond heist that went wrong. A man got killed. Some diamonds came up missing. That thing."

Georgi couldn't look at him anymore. She knew exactly what Don was talking about. Quincy had accompanied him on that heist. They had an inside man who worked for a jeweler in Manhattan's Diamond District. He buzzed Don and Quincy into the building dressed as delivery men. The robbery should have taken a couple of minutes, but the jeweler put up a fight. Quincy said that he tried to calm Don down, tried to quell his rage. But Don had shot the jeweler anyway, twice in the head.

It had seemed to Quincy that the whole thing was more about Don's pride than anything else. He couldn't accept the fact that the man had the balls to defy him. Don was a man accustomed to having his way. Like most Harlem natives, he liked to put on a show. Any sign of disrespect, especially in front of his protégés. When Don ordered the man to empty the safe, the man twice boldly told him no to his face. Q had seen the look in Don's eyes. He told Georgi about it afterward. Despite Quincy's pleas, Don shot the jeweler. They managed to snare several precious stones and a handful of assorted pieces before escaping.

It hadn't taken the authorities long to hone in on the inside man. It had happened quickly. Under tremendous pressure from the cops, he had given Don up in exchange for a sentence of five years. Don was arrested, though the jewels had never been found.

Mysteriously, in the days after Don's arrest, the authorities raided Quincy's home in Brooklyn, arresting him after discovering a gun that matched the murder weapon in his car. From the start, Q knew it was a setup. After the robbery, Don had taken the gun with him, seemingly anxious to get rid of it. How it wound up in Quincy's car was a mystery he found easy to solve. The authorities raided Quincy's home, but found nothing. All it took was for the forensics team to confirm that the gun in the car was indeed the murder weapon. He was locked up for the better part of his life.

"Don, you got a lot of nerve coming in here like this," Georgi said boldly. "*Fifteen years* Quincy's been away. For something he didn't do."

Don leaned toward her. "You don't know what Quincy did or didn't do. You weren't there. All you know is what he told you." He sat back again. "Quincy took something that belongs to me. We're not talking about something small. Couple hundred, a few thousand. Maybe even a couple *hundred* thousand, I might look the other way. Q was my boy. But it's more than a little bit." His expression was serious. "I want that money. I want it today, Georgi." He looked around the room. "I see you got some expensive taste. Got this big home theater system. This is a nice neighborhood you're in, too. You been having your fun. Spending my money. Now it's time to pay up."

She shook her head. "I don't have nothing that belongs to you, Don." Her voice shook as she spoke and it pissed her off. She didn't want him to know how scared she was. "If anything, you should be here to give Quincy some money for taking the fall for you."

Don looked at her smugly. "The cops locked Quincy up. Not me."

"You set him up."

"Where's the diamonds?"

"Fuck you, Don."

Wes slapped her so hard that the sound of it resonated in the room against the beat of the blaring radio.

He stared down at her.

She was dazed, but she twisted her face into what she hoped was a sneer. It was a source of pride for her that Quincy had managed to outsmart Don the way he did. But, behind her bold front, she was scared to death.

"What did Q do with the diamonds? Just tell me. Who has them? That shit was so hot, there was no way he moved it before he got locked up. He could have never done it that fast. So what did he do? Leave it with you? It wasn't at your house in Brooklyn, 'cause we went there, searched everything. You left a house full of furniture, clothes, shoes, everything. You left there like you were coming right back. But you disappeared, just you and his kids. His mama stayed. She was at his little trial every day. But not you. You never came to court once. You and Q were like Whitney and Bobby, but you were missing. Y'all must think I'm retarded or something. I knew he set you up, sent you off somewhere with the dough. I looked for your black ass everywhere." Don shook his head. "Where's my shit?"

Wes pulled her up to a kneeling position. She wondered if this was it. She began to pray out loud.

Don was seething. He laughed at the irony that she was hiding in plain sight the whole time. Right there in Staten Island, probably mocking him every time she spent his money.

Wes pulled his gun out and held it by his side.

Georgi was crying more softly now, praying silently. The cold steel of the gun against her face sent shock waves through her body. The gun was heavy, the force of the blow rocking her. The next one caught her on the arm as she attempted to block the blows raining down on her. She felt the pain of the pistol-whipping against her face, arms, and head. Balled up on the floor, she attempted to shield herself beneath the coffee table. She felt like she might pass out at any moment. Throbbing pain seared through her body. Wes stomped at her legs now, his heavy winter boots grating against her fragile frame. Her leggings offered little barrier between her skin and his Timbs. She prayed even louder, her voice drowned out by the music. She wasn't sure if the volume had been turned up or if something had shifted in her brain during this beating. She prayed that it would stop. And then, just like that, it did.

The blows ceased and she felt the looming presence of Don's merciless goon recede. She dared to peek out of the one eye she could still see through and she saw what looked like a struggle. Feet moved around the room as if a bunch of people were doing some awkward dance. She heard a steady ringing in her ears and tried her best to ignore it. She focused instead on the feet in the room, all dancing around. She thought about her own feet, counted them in her mind. She tried to wiggle them while she counted. One foot. Two feet. She felt encouraged. She could at least move her feet. At least she wasn't paralyzed. The ringing in her ear was nonstop, but at least her feet worked. She watched the dancing feet again, all circling one another in some unrehearsed routine. Slowly, her mind wandered back to life. She realized the men were fighting, not dancing.

She forced herself up on her elbow, every nerve in her body aching from the beating she had just endured. Still foggy, she narrowed her eyes, and the scene before her suddenly came into focus.

Malik!

Malik had come home from his basketball clinic and could hear the music from outside of the house, and immediately sensed that something was off. His mother never listened to music that loudly. Especially not *new* music. Georgi loved everything old-school. She would never be blasting "Throw Some D's." He stood there with his keys in his hand, contemplating. He moved to unlock the door. The key turned in the lock. But before he could push the door open, it swung abruptly on its own. He flew forward from the force of it and was snatched quickly by a man he didn't recognize. He saw a large scar on the man's face and knew immediately that his whole family was in trouble.

The man pulled him into the house and bolted the door. He dragged Malik through the foyer where he saw his worst nightmares come to life. His mother was crumpled in a ball, crawling pitifully toward the coffee table in a failed attempt to crawl beneath it. A big man was beating her with a large gun. A third man stood like a conductor directing a twisted symphony.

Malik was dragged into the room and shoved forward. He tried to assess the situation in a desperate attempt to get them out of this. The conductor, dressed in a leather jacket, moved to turn down the volume on the stereo. Malik made his move. He charged toward the man beating his mother. The man with the scar intercepted him, though. He swung a baseball bat directly at Malik's chest, sending him reeling backward.

Wes stopped his assault on Georgi and joined them. They fought to wrestle Malik to the ground. Don was telling them to get him on his knees and put their guns to his head. His best bargaining chip had just arrived. But Malik would not go down without a fight. He charged forward again. Don was yelling at Wes, ordering him to "fuck that nigga up." This time, Wes swung his gun on Malik and the cold steel connected with the young man's skull, buckling Malik momentarily.

Georgi cried out, but the words came out jumbled. Unaware that her jaw was broken, she sobbed, watching Wes continue pistol-whipping her son. Malik recoiled, dazed and in pain from the force of the blows. Georgi cried out louder. The music drowned out the sound.

"*Okay!*" she yelled. "Okay! *Please! I'll tell you!*"

But Don had that look in his eyes that Quincy once described. The look of a man possessed. He fixated on the sight of the men beating Malik, who no longer even had the strength to fight.

"*Fuck him up, Wes! Kill that muthafucka!*" Don bellowed.

Wes delivered a brutal and merciless beating until Malik stopped putting up a fight. Malik stood, attempting to raise his hands in surrender. But Wes smashed his gun into Malik's head so hard that the crack was audible despite the noise around them. Malik fell helplessly in a bloody heap. For good measure, Wes kicked him so hard in the face that Georgi watched her son's teeth spill out onto the floor. She closed her eyes and cried from the depth of her soul. From where she lay, Malik looked dead. Don's two goons stood over his unmoving body. She felt like her heart might burst in her chest. Her worst fears had been realized.

Don walked toward her, satisfied now that he had made his point. He meant business. Quincy owed him something. He wasn't leaving without it.

He pulled Georgi up by her hair, now tousled, caked with blood, and wild around her face. She winced at the pain of him pulling against the follicles in her already pounding head. The ringing in her ears was deafening now. The music sounded like a record playing backward.

Don pointed his gun at her face. Then, with a twisted grin

on his face, shoved it roughly in her mouth. The metal tasted foreign in her mouth, death tickling at her tonsils. He looked deep into Georgi's eyes, an unspoken conversation already under way. Finally, he asked her, "You gonna tell me where it is or not?"

Slowly, she nodded.

THE LONG KISS GOOD NIGHT

Sprawled out on top of blankets on the floor of Uncle Don's apartment, Troy kissed Sydney deeply. His hardness pressed against her. Light-headed from his kiss and from the liquor they'd been drinking, Sydney felt like she was dreaming. His arms were wrapped around her, his hands roamed her body. She wore only a cotton tank top and panties. His hands were up under her top, teasing her. A moan escaped her lips and then Troy was on his knees, his lips pressed against her stomach, her hips, and thighs. Slowly, he slipped her panties down her legs. Then he was on top of her, kissing her again. Sydney came alive.

She tugged at his shirt, her hands eager to touch his skin. He wiggled out of it, and she gripped his arms and his back desperately. He unbuckled his pants and pulled them down, his hand on his most powerful weapon. His heart thundered in his chest.

"Mmm," he growled, spreading her legs apart, and pushed himself inside her wetness.

Sydney gasped, pleasure searing through every vein. His lips were on her throat, his tongue against her skin as he moved inside of her. Sydney felt so tight around his thickness, her moans excited him even more. She grinded back against him and with each stroke he dove deeper inside of her. The hardness of the floor against her back left her no escape from the power and intensity of his massive dick. He slid his hands underneath her, scooping her ass into his hands. Sydney held on for dear life, her breathing heavier now. She wrapped her legs around him tightly and matched his rhythm as best she could despite the power of his penis. Her legs began to quiver and her voice climbed several octaves. The orgasm rocked her, great waves rippling inside of her. The force of it sent Troy over the edge as well. He came in volcanic spasms that left him breathless.

They lay together afterward on the floor of Uncle Don's vacant apartment, staring up at the ceiling, still winded from their lovemaking.

She broke the silence. "I don't want to leave here. I wish we could stay just like this."

He smiled. "What would we eat?" He looked at her skeptically. "Can you even cook?" He had a playful gleam in his eye as he imagined a naked Sydney cooking for him. The very thought made his dick start to grow hard again.

Sydney laughed. "I can cook. Aunt Pat taught me. She says a woman who can't cook is like a man who doesn't have a job." Sydney shrugged. "My mother can cook just enough to get by, but Aunt Pat takes cooking seriously. She taught me well."

He nodded. "Good to know." He thought about them living together. "Uncle Don would let us have this place, too. If we wanted it." He imagined it for a moment. "But we belong at Howard. This is not our world. This is somebody else's. We'll create our own."

She propped herself up on one elbow and looked at him. "What's our world gonna look like?"

He squeezed his eyes shut. She giggled at the sight of him like that. He looked childlike, innocent.

"We're gonna make our own money," he said. "We'll have a lot of it." He kept his eyes closed, but pulled her closer. "You'll win your Pulitzer Prize. I'll run a big corporation in my mama's name."

She smiled, pleased that his vision was so in line with her own. "Why did you decide to do the right thing instead of being drawn into your uncle's business like Wes?" Every time they were together, Troy spoke of his determination to emulate his father. He wanted to play the role of the straight man. The one who never got his hands dirty. Or so he thought.

Troy stared at the ceiling in silence for a moment. The truth was he hadn't figured out the answer to that question, either.

"My mother tried to shield us from the truth about my family's businesses at first. She made us think Uncle Don was some kind of legit businessman. But then my dad lost a whole bunch of money in a bad investment. Uncle Don bailed him out and Wes started asking questions. He wanted to know how Uncle Don could afford to do that. Meanwhile, we had never seen the man go to work. His kids had cars at, like, fourteen years old. Money was pouring in. When Wes found out the truth, he put it right in my father's face. Basically, taking drug money is the same as making drug money in my brother's opinion. He feels like my father's a hypocrite. And to him, Uncle Don is the man. He makes the money, gets the respect and all that." Troy shrugged.

Sydney watched him. "What do *you* think?"

"I think my father tries his best to be a good man. And I think in his own way my uncle does, too. They go about it in different ways. For me, neither one of them is the bad guy." He looked at her and gently moved a strand of her hair away from her pretty face. "I guess you could say I'm somewhere in the middle."

Sydney thought about that. The sun had begun to set, the fading light pouring in through the parted curtains in Uncle Don's apartment. She snuggled in next to him and decided that she was willing to see what "the middle" was like with Troy. This feeling was one she never wanted to end.

His cell phone buzzed and he reached for it. Glancing at the screen, he was surprised to see a text from his uncle.

Text me when you're ready to take Sydney home. I'll send Butch to pick you up.

Troy's eyebrows raised a little. Uncle Don was being awfully generous. He set his phone back down and pulled Sydney close again. It was a Saturday night and Sydney had no curfew. Now they didn't have to rush for the last ferry departing for Staten Island at a decent hour.

Sydney gestured toward his phone. She had seen the way his expression had changed when he looked at it. "Everything alright?"

He nodded. "Everything is perfect."

Pat read the text message again for the thousandth time. It was from Georgi.

Bring the box to my house. It's an emergency.

The box. That box told a story so scandalous that the sisters had never really discussed it. That box represented many unvoiced truths that they had chosen to sweep under the rug in

favor of a see-no-evil, hear-no-evil mentality. Despite that phi-
losophy, Pat knew the moment she read that text message that
Georgi's dirty deeds had finally caught up with her.

Pat grabbed her car keys and headed out the door. She called
over her shoulder to Destiny. "I'm going out real quick, Destiny.
I'll be right back." The door swung shut behind her.

Destiny lay on the couch watching TV, completely unaware
that the dinner party she and her cousin had gone to last night
had resulted in a wild chain of events that would rock her family
to its core.

It didn't take long for Pat to realize that her sister was in trouble.
Every time she called her, the call was sent to voice mail. The
text had been brief and ominous. The reference to "the box" made
her nervous. Georgi had never asked for it before.

One morning in 1991, Georgi had come running to her
mother's house with the kids in tow. Years before, their mother
had moved to Staten Island at a senior living complex there. Pat
applied for a job at a hospital nearby and followed her there soon
after. Life in the "forgotten borough" was much quieter, slower,
more family oriented. The community was more closely knit and
Pat found friends there. She met a man, became pregnant, and
suffered the heartbreak of abandonment when he left her after
Destiny was born. Her mother had been by her side through all
of it. Georgi, on the other hand, had been nowhere around until
that morning.

Mama had gotten the children settled in her spare bedroom
while Pat peppered her sister with questions. Where was Quincy?
What had happened? Why had she left Brooklyn with only the
clothes on her back? Georgi had leveled with her. She feared
for her very life and wanted to come clean in case it all caught up
with her somehow.

Quincy's intuition had kicked in the night of the robbery. He spent a sleepless night thinking about all the diamonds and the jewels in his house. Something in his gut told him something wasn't right. By the time the morning came, Quincy was nervous as hell. He gave Georgi a lockbox tucked inside a small suitcase. He didn't tell her what was inside at first. Didn't give her the key. He just instructed her to leave as if she were taking the kids to school, but instead head to Staten Island and stay at her mother's until further notice. She was to contact no one and keep a low profile until he told her otherwise.

Georgi had never seen her husband so shaken. He wasn't himself. That alone gave her reason to be nervous when she arrived at her mother's apartment in Staten Island. Georgi and Pat sat up drinking and talking far into the night. The robbery was the top story on the local news. The manhunt was intense and it didn't take long for the sisters to surmise that the contents of that box had to be what was stolen. Once word came that Quincy had been arrested, Georgi became even more paranoid. She rarely even went outside. So afraid of being recognized or spotted by Don or one of his cronies, she remained holed up in her mother's apartment or at Pat's. The sisters grew closer then. And their children forged a bond as they grew up so close in age.

Georgi survived at first by living off of the cash she had managed to grab from the safe before her exit. That money kept her afloat for the first year. She communicated with Quincy through his mother. Although the letters bore her name and address they were written by Georgi and packed with coded language. In their own version of Morse code, they talked about the progress of his case, about the kids, their living situation, her need for more money. Then Quincy was sentenced and all hope for his release was lost. It was time to move the diamonds.

Through his mother, Quincy got the key to the lockbox to

Georgi. She opened it one afternoon with Pat by her side. The black pouch with the gems inside seemed so harmless in the palm of her hand. But the weight of what it had cost them was heavy— Quincy was in jail and Georgi was in hiding with two kids. She was afraid, but now she had moves to make.

She gave two of the stones to a man she and Quincy met years ago. His name was Paz. He was Brazilian and his name meant "peace." Quincy had moved some stolen gems through Paz's hands years ago behind Don's back. Paz worked for a man who worked with Don. While the two big men did business, the two protégés exchanged information. Weeks later, Paz helped Quincy move a few emerald rings and two diamond necklaces. The deal had earned them both a pretty penny. In the weeks afterward, neither of their bosses got wind of it and their alliance was cemented. Now locked up and helpless, Quincy sent Georgi to meet with Paz and prayed that he could still trust him.

Paz could have given him up. Instead, he took the diamonds, valued at close to a million dollars, and gave Georgi seven hundred and fifty grand in cash. Paz would move the jewels on the black market and make nearly twice what he paid. But Georgi didn't care. She was in a bind and there was no one else she trusted to help her. All of the jewelry from that heist was hot. In the wrong hands, those diamonds could put them all in jail. Paz did his thing and did it quietly. Georgi couldn't have been happier when it was all over. Quincy, too, was pleased with the deal. It gave his wife enough money to set herself up with the kids in a comfortable and quiet life in Staten Island. Money to bury Quincy's mother when she died two years later. Georgi hadn't been able to attend the funeral. Still afraid that Don might be lurking somewhere, she grieved for her mother-in-law alone at home while the services took place. Quincy attended his mother's funeral in shackles, flanked by two federal police officers. His children attended the service, accompanied by his sister, Shana. After the service was over, Quincy went back to jail and the kids went back home to their mother into obscurity. Until now.

Since then, Georgi had rarely come back to that box. Paz got locked up for theft in an unrelated case. His sentence of eight to ten years made it harder for Georgi to make moves. Quincy wanted her to be patient. He didn't want to see his wife and kids placed in any type of jeopardy. He said to hold on for a while until he could figure out a way for her to move the jewels without Paz and minimize the risk of her freedom at the same time. Still loyal to Quincy, even after so much time had passed, Georgi tightened her purse strings. She hated it. No more trips to the salon, no mani-pedis. She began to feel like a caged lioness, anxious to get out of her cage and get back to being the life of the party. She longed to get dressed up and go out. But Quincy said it was time to save money.

In essence, it's what tore them apart. Georgi woke up one day and realized that she had turned into a ghetto version of a soccer mom. Her kids were in school all day, while she perused the mall on a budget, watched corny daytime TV shows, or sat around the kitchen table getting fat with her mama and Pat. Georgi grew bored. In the absence of all the spending she'd become accustomed to, she began to feel less attractive. She became depressed. It began to feel like she was being forced to make a choice between the man she loved and the love she had for herself. While incarcerated, Quincy communicated with Georgi through his sister, Shana. She was the one who had to deliver the news that Georgi had moved on. She did ten years as a prisoner's wife before calling it quits in the hopes of finding love again. Quincy didn't take it too hard. He didn't put up much of a fight. Instead, he told himself that Georgi deserved to be happy. He had several pictures of her taped to the wall of his jail cell.

In every one of them, she was smiling. Seeing her smile had made him feel like he could conquer the world. Her joy was contagious when she was at her best. He wanted her to smile again, even if he couldn't be the man to make it possible.

In the time he'd been away, Georgi had moved about half of what Quincy had given her. With the proceeds of those sales, she had bought her house, financed Sydney and Malik's education, invested a portion in the financial market, kept Quincy's commissary stocked, and financed quite a comfortable life for herself and for Quincy's family as well.

Pat had never asked for a dime. She didn't want it, didn't believe in a life of robbing, stealing, and killing to get ahead. She liked her brother-in-law Quincy. Liked him a lot, in fact. She believed he was the only man who could truly handle Georgi. Quincy was a go-getter. There was no laziness in him. But the danger that went along with the life he lived always repelled Pat. It had repelled her mother, too. That was one of the reasons Georgi had stayed away all those years while she and Quincy were living the high life. Georgi's family would rather live a calm and mediocre life than a flashy and opulent one plagued by fear and the threat of danger at every turn.

And now here Pat was parked outside her sister's house with the box in her lap. She had no idea what awaited her on the other side of the door. But she had to find out. She prayed that Quincy's sins hadn't come back to bite Georgi where it hurt.

Knees trembling, she approached the house. She noted the drawn blinds, but otherwise the house looked normal. There was no noise, no outward sign of trouble. She rang the bell.

The man who opened the door looked vaguely familiar. He was handsome, kinda tall, brown-skinned with piercing eyes. He smiled at her.

"Come in, Pat. Georgi's in the living room." He gestured in that direction.

Pat took a nervous step forward, looking around. She saw no immediate signs of trouble as she stepped into the foyer and Don shut the door behind her, bolting the locks securely. Pat swallowed and walked toward the living room. She saw a man with a large scar standing near the sofa. Then she spotted a crumpled mass at his feet. Someone had been beaten bloody, unrecognizable. Pat froze. She couldn't make out the man lying on the floor, his shirt drenched in his own blood, part of his face smashed into a bloody pulp. Her breath came in spasms and it slowly occurred to her that she could hear her sister sobbing. She spun around and saw her then. A large man stood looming beside her, a grimace on his face. Georgi had been badly beaten, too. Lumps on her head, sections of her hair yanked out, blood dripping from cuts on her face and on the side of her head. Her eyes were swollen and black. Her mouth hung open in an odd and gruesome way. She was crying, the sound so heart-wrenching that Pat began to cry instantly.

"Malik!" Georgi was trying to say. "It's Malik!"

Pat gasped. Her head snapped back in the direction of the crumpled man on the floor. Her nephew? She wondered where Sydney was. Pat cried harder, her eyes darted toward all three of the men in the room. She prayed they didn't plan to beat her, too.

"Is that Malik?" She was nearly breathless.

Don nodded. "Yeah. Unfortunately, he hurt himself trying to convince his mother to give me back something that belongs to me. Now I think Georgi is convinced that she should return it all to me. She said we should contact you and you would set things straight. Did you bring it with you?" He glanced at her empty hands. The man with the scar moved in a little closer to her.

Gripped with fright, Pat could barely stand. "I have it. It's in my car." Raised in the streets of Brooklyn, this wasn't Pat's first time in a situation like this. She knew that if she came in empty-handed, they would at least give her a chance to speak; a chance to convince her sister's captors to let her go.

Don frowned a little. Wes glanced out the front window, parting the curtain slightly and peering out. He saw the blue Civic parked at the curb. He glared at Pat.

"Give me your keys."

Pat quickly handed them over.

The man with the gun pointed his gun at Pat. She began to plead for her life.

"Be quiet," Don said. His point had been made. He believed that the condition of her family members should serve as a sufficient warning of what he was capable of if Pat chose not to cooperate. He glared at her. "If he goes out there and this is a setup, I'm killing you, your sister, and then I'm gonna finish off your little nephew here. You understand?"

Pat nodded. Her whole body quaked.

Wes walked outside, while Georgi continued to wail. Malik lay lifelessly on the floor and Don stood idly by. Pat prayed silently. Even though she knew there was no ambush, no cops lying in wait, she couldn't help wondering whether these men would kill them all once they got what they wanted. She didn't know that Don had already emptied out Georgi's bank account. He had forced her to write down her pin number, had gotten her bank cards, and siphoned the little money she had in her accounts. He had transferred the money into dummy accounts he set up for situations like this. Now it was time for the big payback.

After several long, tense moments, Wes returned with the box that had been sitting in full view on Pat's front seat. He wondered if this woman knew the value of what was inside. If she did, she had taken an incredible risk leaving it there. He entered the apartment frowning. He handed the box to Don, suspicion gnawing at him. Then Wes moved toward Georgi and she recoiled in fright.

"Is all of it in there?"

Georgi didn't answer.

"I asked you a question." Wes loomed over her.

Georgi nodded her head. "Everything I have is in there."

Her words were barely understandable, her speech jumbled, her jaw slack. Wes stared down at her.

Don watched the exchange. He set the box down on the table and sat down on the sofa.

"Where's the key?"

Georgi looked up at him, her eyes pleading. She held her hands up in surrender, quite a feat since every muscle in her body ached. She tried to get up from the floor, but the agony was too intense. Finally, Wes pulled her up on her feet. A searing pain tore through her, causing her to cry out. Still, she forced herself to move toward the fireplace. A heart-shaped box sat between family photos of the Taylor family on vacation in happier times. Pictures of Sydney and Malik at school. She retrieved the key from the heart-shaped box nestled there amid photos of a life that box had financed.

With a trembling hand, she gave it to Wes. He tossed her aside, sending her falling onto her chaise, her broken ribs sore and aching.

Wes handed the key to his uncle and Don anxiously opened the box and examined its contents. He recognized a few things immediately. Two Rolex President Series watches, three diamond rings, a pair of diamond and emerald earrings. He held up a small black velvet pouch and poured out sparkling diamonds into his palm. He looked at Georgi.

"There were ten of these."

She stared back at him without responding.

He shook his head. "Where's all the cash that Quincy had? Two hundred thousand in cash." He shuffled the small bundle of hundred-dollar bills at the bottom of the box and looked at her, unsatisfied. "So, I handed your husband close to two million dollars in jewelry and two hundred thousand in cash. And you're giving me back . . . this?" He held up the box. "There's about a thousand dollars here, Georgi. Some of the diamonds are missing. I know what was in that box when I gave it to Quincy."

Georgi was glad that her mouth wasn't functioning properly. She might have told Don that he knew the contents of the box so well because he had been the one to fill it up after pumping two bullets into an innocent man's head. Now she feared that he might do the same to her, to Malik, and to her poor sister, who had always been innocent in the whole thing.

Don nodded, as if digesting the fact that he had taken a loss at Quincy's hand. Still, he was happy to have recouped some of his losses. He returned the contents to the box, locked it, and stuck the key in his jacket's inside pocket. He turned his attention to Pat.

"You got the rest of my money?"

She shook her head vigorously. "No! I never touched your money. I never wanted what was inside that box." She looked at her sister, hoping that all the years of their mama's lectures were ringing in her ears now. "I value my life. I would never put it in jeopardy over some drugs, guns, money . . . none of that shit is worth my life." Tears rolled down her pretty brown face.

"Please . . . you got your stuff. That's all she has. My nephew is laying there . . . please just let us get him to a hospital."

Don stared back at her, unmoved. He didn't say anything for a while. Finally, he took two steps toward Pat. He looked her in the eyes. "What happened to your sister and your nephew? What you gonna tell them when the ambulance gets here?"

Pat shook her head. "Somebody robbed them."

He smiled. "What did they take?"

She played along. "Nothing really. She didn't have much."

Don liked that answer. He smiled, then turned to his nephew and his boy Black and gestured toward the door. He picked up the box and walked over to Georgi. He squatted down so that they were eye level.

"Tell your husband that he still owes me. When he gets out, I'll be looking for him." He winked at her. "It was nice seeing you again. I hope your boy feels better."

He stood up and turned, walking out with the box tucked under his arm. The two goons backed out after him, their guns trained on the victims in their wake just in case one of them tried to be a hero. Finally, they were gone.

Pat dialed 911 with trembling fingers.

Sydney was a bit tipsy now. She and Troy had polished off what was left of a bottle of Grey Goose from Uncle Don's cabinet. Their time together today had been the sweetest thing. Fresh out of the shower now, she began to get dressed. Troy stepped into the room and smiled.

"You're sexy."

She felt a little exposed as he stared at her. But she liked it. She wiggled into her jeans.

"So are you."

He had one arm tucked behind his back. He brought it around now, revealing a long box in his hand. She froze, her eyes wide. "What is this?"

He smiled. "It's your Christmas gift. I can't wait anymore. I saw it and I thought about you. I want to see it on you." He handed it to her, realizing that he was oddly nervous. He had never been more eager to please anyone. Sydney had his heart.

She opened the box. A beautiful diamond necklace glistened in the light. She drew in her breath, truly aghast. She had never seen such an exquisite piece of jewelry. She shook her head. "This is too much!"

He laughed. "It's not enough." He stepped forward and kissed her. "You must not know how I feel about you."

She held on to him, shaken by the magnitude of his gift. "Wow," she said. "Troy, I don't know what to say." She shook her head again. "Thank you."

He took it from her and hooked it around her neck, clasping it securely in the back. "You're welcome."

Sydney looked in the mirror and watched the diamonds sparkle and dance against the light. Her own gift for Troy—a Rocawear varsity jacket—paled terribly in comparison. "I didn't think . . . I got you something simple," she explained.

He turned her face toward him. "It's not a competition. You don't have to give me anything. Just let me do my thing. This is how I show my affection. I don't expect nothing in return."

Sydney stared at him, feeling an odd sense that this relationship with Troy was too good to be true. She looked at her reflection again. Her fingertips gingerly touched the necklace and she smiled. "It's gorgeous, Troy."

He smiled. "You like it?"

She nodded. "I love it."

His cell phone vibrated. He glanced at it. "Butch is downstairs. Let's go."

Sydney finished getting dressed, gathering her things. Her cell phone battery had died and she silently chastised herself for not bringing her charger. It was near midnight and she wondered whether her mother would worry about her. She was, after all, just supposed to be out for a day of "shopping" with Troy. She shrugged off her guilt, though. Since Butch was bringing her home, she'd get there far quicker than if she had to take public transportation.

She found Troy in the living room, having an angry whispered conversation on his cell phone.

"Why can't you tell me over the phone?" he demanded. "Explain what that means."

Uncle Don was on the other end, telling Troy that he was not to get into Butch's car. "You can't go to Staten Island right now. I need you here."

"For what?" Troy asked again. "Did something happen?"

Don worried that Sydney might be standing beside his nephew while they spoke. "I need to talk to you face-to-face, Troy. I'm telling you to send Sydney home with Butch. He's downstairs waiting. After she leaves, I'll come get you and bring you uptown. I'll tell you everything when I get there. Just trust me."

Trust him. Those were words that resonated with Troy. He did trust his uncle. He had been looking forward to riding back to Staten Island with his girlfriend, though. Now apparently another family emergency required his attention more. "Okay."

Troy hung up the phone. He turned and found Sydney standing behind him. "I have some kind of family emergency. My uncle won't go into it over the phone. He said I should send you back with Butch—"

"It's okay." Sydney saw the apologetic expression on Troy's face and shook her head. "You go see about your family. I've hogged enough of your time for one day." She kissed him, touching his face tenderly. Afterward, she looked at him, drinking in his handsome features. "I love you." Her eyes twinkled with joy. "And I love this necklace." She touched it again.

He kissed her. "I love you, too." He walked her downstairs, greeted Butch curbside, and thanked him for bringing Sydney home.

"Get her there safely."

Butch smiled. "You know I will."

Sydney gave Troy a long kiss good night. The wind blew fiercely, a cold New York winter swirling around them. They didn't feel a thing. Wrapped in each other's arms, they were in their own world.

Reluctantly, he held the car door open and Sydney climbed into the back of the Bentley.

"Take care," he said. He shut the door, not realizing that the door was shutting on their love as well.

They were both certain they would see each other again. Oblivious to the fact that their warring families had clashed in a way that would tear them apart.

UNFINISHED BUSINESS

Sydney's ride home with Butch had been smooth and uneventful. They talked about the upcoming holiday and his plans to surprise his kids with new computers. She touched her necklace several times during that ride, still amazed that Troy loved her enough to spend so much money on their first holiday as a couple. She knew that monetary gifts were superficial. Still, she couldn't wait to show her mother what her boyfriend had given her. She knew that even Malik, who was usually full of jokes and sarcasm, would marvel at the clarity and brilliance of her gift.

She showed it to Butch while they were at a red light on the West Side Highway. He stared at it wide-eyed.

"Beautiful!" he said. "My wife would love a necklace like that."

She smiled, her fingers rubbing the stones gently. "How long have you been married?" she asked.

"Twenty-two marvelous years," Butch said. "Her name is Nancy."

Sydney noticed how happy he seemed when he said her name.

She hoped that someday, when they were married as Destiny had predicted, Troy would say her name with that same sparkle in his smile.

They pulled up to her block and saw sirens the moment they turned the corner. Sydney's eyes widened. She wondered who had gotten hurt. She craned her neck toward the window as they slowly approached her house. Then she saw the crime-scene tape draped across her own yard. She gasped.

"Please stop!" she yelled at Butch. He did, unaware of the situation his boss had sent him into. Sydney climbed out without bothering to shut the car door behind her. She ran toward her house.

A cop stopped her as she approached.

"I live here!" she explained.

"Sydney?" the officer asked.

She nodded. "Yes."

"Okay. We've been looking for you." He looked relieved.

She was panting breathlessly. "What happened?"

"This is an active crime scene. Your family is at the hospital. You should come with me."

Sydney felt tears stinging her eyes. Blindly, she followed the cop toward a squad car parked at the curb. She glanced back over her shoulder, looking for Butch. But he was already gone. She frowned, wondering why he had disappeared so quickly. She turned back and focused on what the cop was telling her.

"There was a robbery. Your mother was at home when the break-in happened. Then your brother walked in on it. He's fighting for his life. But the doctors are doing everything they can. Your mother is in stable condition."

She cried, cursing herself again for allowing her phone to die. She needed to call someone, needed some words of comfort from a familiar voice. Instead she was forced to cry on the officer's shoulder, wondering what had happened to her family, wishing it were all just some terrible bad dream.

The siren blared as they raced through the streets of Staten Island. Sydney wished Troy had come with her. She needed him now. She had never been more afraid or felt more helpless.

Finally they arrived at the hospital. The cops escorted her to the ER where her mother lay stiffly on a gurney. Her body was wrapped in bandages. Her jaw had been wired shut. She looked terrible. Her eyes had turned a ghastly purple and her face was swollen. Her wrist was broken and bandaged. Her hair had bald patches caked with dried blood. Sydney began to cry.

Destiny came to her cousin and embraced her. "It's gonna be okay," she consoled her. "Aunt Georgi is tough. She's gonna be fine."

Sydney choked back a sob. "Where's Malik?"

Destiny looked at her mother. Aunt Pat sat near her sister's bedside. She looked at Sydney, her eyes scanning her for signs of trauma. "Malik is in a coma, Sydney. He's got swelling and bleeding on the brain. They beat him up pretty bad."

Sydney's heart sank. "Where is he?"

The officer that brought her in stood near the doorway. "I can bring you to him."

"I'll come with you," Destiny said.

The officer led the way and Destiny took her cousin by the hand, aware that what she was about to see would be difficult for her. When the cop was out of earshot, she whispered, "Sydney, are you okay? Did they hurt you?"

Sydney frowned. "They who? I was with Troy."

They arrived at Malik's room and nothing could have prepared Sydney for what she saw. Malik was lying in a hospital bed bandaged seemingly from head to toe. A doctor was explaining that they had inserted some type of metal plate in his head to help him heal somehow. He had endured blunt force trauma to his head, a brutal beating that left him breathing with the aid of a machine. Sydney wept into her cousin's shoulder. Malik lay with his mouth wide open, a ventilator inserted there. He looked like he was already gone.

She looked at Destiny. "What happened to him?"

Destiny was aware that the cop was all ears. Her mother had filled her in on what she knew. Still, she chose her words carefully as she replied. "Some strangers came in and they were robbing your mom. Malik walked in on it. Maybe he tried to save her. They beat him, took what they could, and left. Aunt Georgi is hurt pretty bad, too. Good thing my mom stopped by after work. She found them like that and called the police." It wasn't all a lie, Destiny reasoned.

The officer closed in on Sydney again. "Where were you this afternoon?"

Sydney looked at him. "I was with my boyfriend on Sixtyfirst Street."

"Did your mother or brother call you at all today?"

She shook her head. "My battery died. I didn't get any calls for most of the day." She would never make that mistake again.

Destiny led her cousin back to Aunt Georgi's room. Sydney, still shaken from the sight of her brother, wept at her mother's feet.

A detective stood in the doorway and greeted everyone. Aunt Pat stood up as he approached her.

"I just wanted to give you my card," the man said. He spoke softly to Aunt Pat, aware that she had been traumatized upon finding her loved ones this way. "If you remember anything else, you give me a call."

Aunt Pat took the card and thanked him. He left and she tucked it into her purse. Destiny rose and shut the door behind the detective. As an awkward silence descended, Sydney felt like she might self-destruct.

"Why isn't anybody saying anything?" she asked. She became aware, for the first time, that her mother, aunt, and cousin were all looking at her oddly.

Georgi mumbled something and Aunt Pat scrambled for a notepad at the bedside. She gave it to her sister. Georgi began to write. Finally done, she handed it to her sister.

Pat passed the pad from Georgi to Sydney.

She read her mother's handwriting. *Where you been all day?*

Sydney was filled with guilt. She had been wrapped in Troy's arms all day, making love with reckless abandon while her family was terrorized. "I was with Troy."

"Where?" Aunt Pat repeated. "And how did you meet this Troy?"

Sydney felt anxious suddenly. What kind of questions were these?

"We were at his uncle's apartment." Her voice shook. She wondered why she felt so ashamed. All of them stared at her, their eyes accusing. "And I met him at school like I said." She looked at Destiny for clues. "What's going on?"

Aunt Pat sighed. "Troy's uncle, Don . . ." She didn't know where to begin. Destiny had filled her in on the party Troy brought them to the night before. Now the pieces were starting to come together. Though the women had told the police nothing, they were aware of how a crazy twist of fate brought Troy and Sydney together and led Don right back to Georgi's doorstep.

Sydney's heart raced. She wondered what the hell Troy's uncle had to do with any of this.

"Troy might have been in on this from the start." Destiny hated to think the worst. But the irony of it all was too hard to ignore.

Sydney frowned. "In on what?" She stared at them all in disbelief. *"This?"*

"Uncle Don knew your father," Destiny explained.

"Years ago," Aunt Pat added. "They parted ways on bad terms." She lowered her voice, paranoid that someone might be listening. "Don's the one who did this."

Sydney gasped. Tears flooded her eyes. She shook her head, refusing to believe this was even possible. She thought about Troy, about the uncle she met at his holiday party. She thought about the family emergency Troy had been called away on just as she was leaving. She tried to recall his demeanor all day. Had he been in on it all along? She couldn't believe it. She wouldn't.

"No," she cried. She shook her head as if doing so might make it all go away.

Aunt Pat looked at her sympathetically. "I was there, baby. I saw the man." She felt anxious just at the thought of him. Destiny had described the man she and Sydney met at the party last night. Destiny had described Don to a tee. "I will never forget the look in his eyes." Aunt Pat shook her head.

Destiny's heart broke watching her cousin standing there processing the information she was hearing. She knew that Sydney was in love with Troy. She had believed that he felt the same way. Now she wasn't so sure. "Sydney, I think Wes was there, too." Her voice was low as she spoke. She took no enjoyment out of telling her this. "Aunt Georgi knows Uncle Don and recognized him from before. But she didn't know the other two guys he was with. The way she described the big one . . . the one who beat Malik . . . it sounds like it was Wes."

Sydney closed her eyes, the world feeling like it was crashing down around her.

"Who is Wes?" Aunt Pat asked.

Sydney opened her eyes again and her gaze locked with her

mother's. Behind the clear signs of battery evident on her face and the contraption keeping her jaw in line, Georgi's expression was angry. There was no doubt about it, she was pissed. Sydney realized that her mother thought this was all her fault.

"He's Troy's brother," she said, her voice barely above a whisper.

Aunt Pat hung her head, dismayed that apparently they had all walked right into a trap.

Georgi signaled for the notepad back. With her left hand, she wrote on it as legibly as she could. She raised the pad back in Sydney's direction.

Where did you get that necklace?

Sydney touched it. She had forgotten it was there.

"Troy," she whispered. The tears poured forth again.

Her mother stared at her for a while. Then she reached forward and snatched it roughly from Sydney's neck. She clasped the broken necklace tightly in her fist and looked away while her daughter cried.

The sobs wracked Sydney's body as the reality of it all sunk in at last. She knew that she would never see Troy again. Worse, she wasn't sure whether her brother would survive. And if he did, whether he'd ever be the same again. No matter how hard she tried, even though no one voiced the sentiment out loud, she believed that it was all her fault. It would take years before she learned the whole truth. In the meantime, all she had were a million unanswered questions and the burden of a broken heart.

DOWNFALL

Down in the basement of the abandoned house on Pitkin Avenue, Crystal stared at Troy now as it all sunk in for him. He sat with his eyes closed as he processed the reality that Crystal Scott was really Sydney Taylor.

He opened his eyes and looked at her.

"At first, I was offended that you didn't recognize me," she said. "But it's not completely your fault. I changed everything about myself. Made a new life. Sydney was a plain Jane. But Crystal is a vixen."

She sounded crazy to him now, speaking of herself in these terms as if she weren't both women. She stared down at him, her gaze filled with a combination of love and loathing. For the past ten years, she had been consumed by the thought of revenge. Troy had done her and her family dirty. Malik was dead. Her mother had never been the same. Her father had spent the past twenty-five years locked up in jail. They had lost everything. The pain her family experienced had been unbearable.

She reflected on all she had been through. All the years she spent obsessing over reports about the Mitchell family in the press. None of her peers had understood her fascination with the publishing giant or her decision to leave a promising career at *Sable* behind to join the ranks of *Hipster*. She had slyly woven herself into the fabric of the family business, earning Fox's confidence, and landing the top position at the magazine. She got into Troy's bed, earned his trust, and studied his movements. She had gone through his phone, perused his e-mails, his files, his accounts, his everything. All in a quest to bring him and the entire Mitchell family down. What she hadn't counted on was falling in love with him. To her dismay, the passion between them had been as undeniable as her bloodlust.

Several times, she had been tempted to call the whole thing off. She was in love with him, no matter how hard she tried not to be. Troy had stolen her heart again. But then she would see her brother's face in her mind. Different variations of him. The young, vibrant, smiling Malik and the beaten, swollen, disfigured one. She would witness her mother walking through life afraid of her own shadow. She would talk to her father while he served a sentence for a crime he hadn't done. And those reminders were all the fuel that she needed to press forward.

Troy spoke up at last, his voice hoarse with emotion. "I always thought about what it would be like if I ever saw you again. Now I'm here and I don't know what to say."

He was being honest. A million times, he had rehearsed it in his mind. How he would explain, apologize, confess. But all of that seemed pointless now.

His voice betraying the unexpected emotions that consumed him, he said, "I didn't know what they were going to do."

Wes sucked his teeth and looked at his brother sidelong. "You knew!" he insisted. "Don't lie." His expression was menacing, but she could see the fear in his eyes that he was doing his best to camouflage.

Quincy looked at his daughter. "See?"

"Shut the fuck up!" Troy yelled. He looked at Crystal . . . Sydney . . . he wasn't even sure who he was seeing anymore.

"I swear I didn't know what they were going to do." He looked her in her eyes sincerely as he said it. "I really loved you. That was no game." He shook his head. "I didn't know they were gonna do that."

She glared at Troy, angry at him and at herself. She should have known that he was too good to be true.

"So, I'm supposed to believe that meeting you at Howard was a coincidence. And our families having beef was a coincidence, too?" She looked at him like he had lost his mind.

He spoke anxiously, aware that time was running out. "I swear! When I met you, I had no idea that our families knew each other. You had no idea who I was and I had no idea who you were. We fell in love. And then I brought you home to meet my family." He thought back to that night. "During the whole party, I kept wondering why my uncle was so interested in you. He kept asking you questions. But you didn't seem to mind. I didn't realize then that he was connecting the dots. It was some shit that had nothing to do with us."

Crystal watched him, analyzing his facial expressions and body language as he spoke. Looking for signs that he was lying.

"After we brought you home that night, I went back to my father's house. Uncle Don sat up talking to me. He told me that he knew your mother. He didn't tell me the details. He just said that he knew your mother and he was gonna stop by and see her. He wanted me to keep you out of the house for the day. He told me we could use his empty apartment to hang out until he called me. I didn't think anything of it."

Crystal looked skeptical. "So, you didn't know what was really going on?"

He shook his head.

Wes laughed. "Uncle Don told you he was gonna rob her mother."

"*Shut up, Wes!*" Troy shouted over him.

"Nah, nigga, you shut up. Stupid muthafucka." He looked at Crystal, sneering. "Uncle Don told me the whole story. I knew exactly why we were going to Staten Island that day. But he told Tinker Bell here that he was gonna rob y'all while nobody was home, so Troy was supposed to keep you out of the house until the coast was clear."

She looked at Troy. He was staring at the floor, trying desperately not to cry.

When he spoke, his voice was barely audible. "I never thought anybody was gonna get hurt."

"You knew. And you didn't tell me." She thought about Malik, walking into an ambush. She imagined the fear he must have felt. The pain.

"My uncle came and got me that day after you left the apartment. When I got in the car, I could see that he wasn't his usual self. He wasn't making eye contact with me. He seemed a little more animated than usual. More talkative. But he wasn't giving me any information about this emergency that was so important. We got to his apartment and Wes was there." Troy looked at him now angrily. "His clothes were full of blood and he had cuts on his hands. I could tell that something went wrong that day."

Crystal remembered the condition she had found her brother in when she arrived at the hospital. Malik had been beaten so badly that the doctors had given him only a fifty-fifty chance of survival. She swallowed hard now, hearing Troy basically confirm that Wes had been personally responsible.

"A couple of my uncle's other boys were there. They all sat

me down. I knew right away that it was bad." He looked Crystal in the eye. "He told me that your father was an old friend of his." Troy glanced at Quincy tentatively.

Crystal felt her body tense. She shifted uneasily on the stool.

He kept looking at Quincy. "He told me that your father stole something from him. Something very valuable. And my uncle had been looking for it for years. Even though your father was locked up, he had stashed something that meant a lot to my uncle. Stashed it with your mother."

Crystal's heart was pounding in her chest.

"When you showed up at the holiday party and mentioned your parents' names, my uncle realized who your family was. He planned the whole thing without either one of us knowing it." Troy's expression was sincere. "I swear to God, Crystal. By the time I knew what happened, the damage was done." He shook his head. He wasn't looking at her now. "For years, I was in denial about who my uncle was. But after that night, I learned. I never forgave him for it." Troy shook his head. "I'm so sorry for what happened to Malik."

Wes was sick of this shit. He laughed maniacally, his eyes fixed on Troy. "You know how you sound right now? Like a fuckin bitch, nigga. As usual. Just like you were afterwards." He looked at Sydney . . . Crystal . . . whoever she was. "This nigga cried for days like a fuckin' girl! Got so depressed over you that he couldn't handle it." He looked at Troy now, disgusted by him. As far as he was concerned, he had never had any heart. "All over some pussy. Weak muthafucka! You gonna sit here and beg, and apologize to this bitch—"

Tyson hit Wes so hard that the whole chair went flying across the room. Wes, still tied to it, lay on his side groaning. Tyson untied him and stood back, waiting for Wes to get on his feet. The other goons who had been lurking in the shadows stepped forward.

Troy watched, his eyes wide with fear. Quincy pulled out his gun.

Troy began stammering an apology. "I can't make excuses for the terrible shit my family did. But I'm so sorry. I'm sorry for the part I played in it. I'm sorry, Crystal . . . Sydney."

She thought about what Wes had said. That Troy knew his uncle planned to rob her family. "Did you give me that diamond necklace to make up for what you thought your uncle would take from me?"

Troy stared at her. There was no right answer.

She touched her collarbone absentmindedly now, remembering the feeling of it dangling there for those few brief hours.

She met his gaze. "My mother hated me after that night. She never said it. But I could see the hate. I could feel it when she looked at me. Malik died in that cold, miserable hospital. He was already brain-dead by the time they got him to the hospital. We had to sneak out of there in the middle of the night. Out of fear of your family and what your uncle might do to us. We never even got to bury my brother. No funeral. No closure. All we have is a jar full of his ashes." She looked over at Wes. "You still have your brother, but I don't have mine."

Wes finally got up on his feet. He stood in front of Tyson, shaking from the effort.

Troy pleaded with Tyson, his hands high in the air. "Please! Please, don't do this."

Tyson was mocking Wes, coaxing him to fight. "What happened to all that mouth you had last night? Huh?"

Wes could barely stand. Even through the haziness, he was aware that they were about to take him out. But he wasn't going down without a fight. He charged at Tyson, trying to flip him over in a wrestling type of move. Tyson tussled with him for only a moment before hitting him in the face with the butt of his gun. Wes went down hard.

Quincy punched Troy in the face. Before Troy could recover, the two thugs pounced on him, stomping, kicking, punching him as well as Wes. Tyson joined in and savagely all of the men beat both brothers. Crystal stepped back, staring at the melee.

Tyson pulled Troy up on his knees. Wounded and beaten, bleeding from his mouth, Troy looked at Crystal and said, "Please, don't do this. I'm so sorry for everything that happened. I would bring your brother back if I could." He saw the cold glare she directed his way.

Tyson held Troy in place, forcing him to watch while they beat Wes viciously. Quincy cracked Wes across the bridge of his nose with the cold steel of his gun. Wes seemed to be leaking blood from everywhere.

"Stop!" Troy screamed at the top of his lungs. Wes was broken already. As ruthless as he was, no one deserved to be beaten this way. *"Stop! That's enough!"*

Quincy turned on Troy, his eyes full of the blind rage he had been harboring for years.

"Who yelled 'stop' for Malik?" His booming voice echoed off the walls in the basement. "Huh?" he bellowed. "Who the *fuck* cried out for *my son*?"

Quincy walked back over to Wes and kept swinging. He thought about the last time he saw Malik. It was during a visit to the jail where he had served more than two decades for the Mitchell family. As he swung, landing blow after powerful blow, Quincy thought about Malik, crying out the way that Troy cried out now. He imagined him scared, helpless, powerless against this monster. Quincy thought about Malik until he beat Troy's brother to death.

Troy watched with bloodstained tears cascading down his cheeks. Although Wes was a murderer, he was still his brother. Troy looked over at Crystal. She stood with tears pooling in her eyes. She quickly wiped them away and glared at Troy. "Now you see how it feels. A brother for a brother."

Tyson dropped Troy and he fell to the floor, weak from the beating he had suffered. He looked at his brother lying a few feet away and knew that Wes was dead. He wondered if they were going to kill him, too. He couldn't imagine a scenario that would have him walking out of here.

Gingerly, he twisted his neck in Crystal's direction. "What can I do? Please? Anything, Crystal. I'm sorry. Let me make this right."

Quincy charged over and kicked him in the face. Troy writhed in pain.

"An eye for an eye. That's what you can do. I spent twenty-five years in jail. Twenty-five years." Quincy shook his head and let that marinate. "Your uncle is gonna pay me back for every second."

Troy trembled from both fear and the cold floor in the basement.

"I need some type of compensation for the time I lost, the shit he stole from me, and my family's pain and suffering. That's what the fuck I came for. And I ain't leaving without it." Quincy cocked his gun and pointed it right between Troy's eyes.

As far as Quincy was concerned, he had died in prison the day they came and told him that his wife and son had been attacked. He hadn't lived since the moment Malik breathed his last; when Georgi went on with her life without him; when Crystal graduated high school and then college without him being there to witness it; when his own mother passed away and he couldn't be there to hold her hand as she took her last breath. Those things had killed him slowly over the past twenty-five years.

But his daughter had set things right again. She had devised a plan to tear the walls down from the inside. He looked at her now like the proud father that he was and nodded.

"You can go now, baby girl," Quincy said. "Me and Tyson got it from here."

Crystal hesitated. She looked at her father, unsure. He nodded again and gestured toward the stairs with his chin. She looked at Troy and saw the look of panic on his face.

"Please," he begged her. "Please! I didn't know. I swear to God!"

She hated herself for loving him. For ever getting involved with him in the first place. Troy and his family had turned her soul dark. Now they had reached the point of no return. There was no going back. She turned and walked slowly toward the stairs, her heart breaking more with each step.

Troy was pleading now. "I'll give you whatever you want. Money, whatever. Please!"

She cringed at the despair and urgency in his words and felt her conscience tugging at her. She reminded herself that Malik had probably cried out just as loudly and she kept right on walking.

She heard a shot when she reached the top of the stairs.

Tears streamed down her face as she opened the front door, climbed into her car, and got the fuck away from this part of Brooklyn.

EPILOGUE

April 2017

It took weeks for her to summon the courage to return to work. Weeks spent grieving the loss of more than just Troy and what they shared. She was grieving the loss of her desire to truly live. Despite all the years of plotting and planning, and the fact that she had successfully pulled off her ambitious scheme, she felt no satisfaction.

She had expected to feel some sense of relief after everything was over. It had all gone perfectly. Ruining Troy's relationship with Vanessa. Crippling Fox's bid for public office and humiliating him in the process after a probe had been launched into the suspicious funding that had financed his company in the early years. The Mitchell family name was in tatters. But the most gratifying of all had been watching Uncle Don go to jail for the murder of his nephew.

Quincy had fired one round into Wes's head, although he was already dead. Tyson and his goons had discarded Wes's body at the site of one of Quincy's old haunts. It was an abandoned building in the Bronx that Don still owned after all these years. Back in the day, Quincy had helped his former friend end the lives of many of his enemies there. Now he planted Wes's body there and stashed the gun in the bushes nearby. An anonymous caller had phoned in a tip. And it didn't take long before the trail led back to Don. He was languishing on Rikers Island, awaiting trial. Quincy planned to be in the courtroom every day.

Despite all of that, she wanted nothing more than just to crawl up in a ball and cry. She did just that for many days after leaving that run-down house in Brooklyn. Her father had spared Troy's life, just as she had made him promise that he would. It was the one condition she had for her involvement. She would deliver Troy to Brooklyn, but she made her father promise not to kill him. Instead, Quincy had forced Troy to sign over two million dollars from the Stuart Mitchell accounts. Tyson beat him even more for good measure, then they had left him there in that old house on Pitkin Avenue with the promise that they would surely kill him and his father if he went to the authorities.

But Troy hadn't gone to the police. Instead, he had let her win. Only it didn't feel like winning. She didn't feel any victory whatsoever. The loss of him was so palpable that she felt a very real ache in her soul. She had broken his heart, crushed his pride, and left him in financial tatters. Still, none of the spoils of war were enough to compensate for the complete sense of loss she felt inside. The fact that Wes was dead and that Don was in jail gave her little solace. Troy was gone and so were her hopes for true love in this lifetime.

She stared proudly now at the latest issue of *Boss* magazine. She had resigned as editor in chief at *Hipster* in the weeks following Wes's death. Stuart Mitchell had given her a generous bonus "for all her years of service." But she knew that it was just more hush money. She never saw Troy again. He and his father were scrambling to maintain control of the family businesses. But Stuart Mitchell eventually crumbled under the burden of govern-

ment asset seizures and legal fees. *Hipster* was sold to Time, Inc.
And once more, Crystal had reinvented herself. She and Oscar
joined forces again and had created *Boss*, a magazine for millen-
nials on the rise. The publication was still in its infancy. But
Crystal was confident that she and Oscar would make it a success. She had already proven with *Hipster* that she had what it
took to win.

Quincy moved down to Maryland and rekindled what remained of his life and his romance with Georgi. The pair had
lots to catch up on and many years of distance to make up for.
Quincy and Crystal were still rebuilding their relationship. It was
easier now that their obsession with revenge had been tragically
satisfied. Crystal remained in New York, content with the life she
had forged for herself there. Her mother worried about her even
more these days. Now that she had conquered an evil giant, she
worried that Don or his cronies might hurt her. Crystal left her
Brooklyn brownstone. There were too many memories of Troy
there. She lived in Murray Hill now. Tyson kept a close eye on
her, aware that danger could still be lurking. These days, she was
constantly looking over her shoulder. The Mitchell family had
been known to hold grudges.

She sat now at a sidewalk café in her neighborhood. Spring
was beginning to take form and she peered from behind her sunglasses at the blooming flowers around her. The winter had been
brutal. The temperature matching the icy finality of things.

Crystal knew she was forever changed. Gone was the woman
with a sunny disposition. In her place was a serious and no-
nonsense one. Her staff tiptoed around her, desperate to avoid
being the recipient of one of her blank and cold stares. She had
laughed to herself at the irony the other day. She was now as
feared and lamented as her old boss Angela Richmond had been
back at *Sable* magazine in the early days. Crystal had abhorred

working for that woman, who seldom smiled and always gave a clipped response to anyone who dared to bother her with a question. She feared that she was becoming the same person. She wondered what Angela's story was. Perhaps she, too, had loved and lost in such a devastating fashion. Crystal mused that she might invite the bitch to lunch one day. They might have more in common than she once thought.

Crystal knew that she would move on someday. Eventually, she would regain the fervor she had lost last fall. She had plenty left to live for, after all. She was young, single, successful, and wiser than she had ever been before. Whether she ever experienced it again, she counted herself blessed that she had known what it was like to be in love. Even if it had cost her everything. Few could say they had really experienced that.

She left a generous tip on the table, tucked her copy of *Boss* magazine under her arm, and glided down the block in her Gucci slingbacks, headed for home. She would spend the afternoon holed up in her apartment preparing herself for an upcoming "Women in Media" conference. She had been invited to be the keynote speaker, an honor that she was very proud of.

Troy watched her as she sauntered ahead of him. He was often there, unbeknownst to her, watching her from a distance. He had become a man obsessed. He had created fake social media accounts just to follow her and see where she was going, what she was doing. He read everything she published. Every article. Every blog. He adjusted his Ray-Bans and watched her walk into her apartment building.

Surely she knew he wasn't going to let her get away that easily.